TRACEY JANE JACKSON

BOUND BY BLOOD

Book #1 in The Cauld Ane Series

Bound by Blood is a work of fiction. Names, characters, places, and incidents are the products of the author's imagination and are used fictitiously. Any resemblance to actual events, locales, or persons, living or dead, is entirely coincidental.

Castle Photo by DAVID ILIFF
(Wiki Commons – License: CC-BY-SA 3)

Cover Art
Jackson Jackson

Cover Models
istockphoto image

Published in the United States

Other books by Tracey Jane Jackson

The Bride Price
Civil War Brides Series, Book #1

The Bride Found
Civil War Brides Series, Book #2

The Bride Spy
Civil War Brides Series, Book #3

The Bride Ransom
Civil War Brides Series, Book #4

The Rebel Bride
Civil War Brides Series, Book #5

The Bride Star
Civil War Brides Series, Book #6

The Bride Pursued
Civil War Brides Series, Book #7

The Bride Accused
Civil War Brides Series, Book #8

Acknowledgments

A big shout out to Leah Banicki, who assisted me with the title of this book and was so kind to do a beta read. A HUGE thanks to Ellen Tarver who has always done such an amazing job with editing and this time was no different. Kristen Lakin was instrumental in naming my karaoke saloon and is always a constant cheerleader.

Samantha is a character based closely on my best friend, Christy. She has been my best friend for almost twenty years and is responsible for introducing me to my husband. If for some reason, she suddenly turned into a nasty troll, I'd still be forever grateful for that introduction alone. Christy is funny, beautiful, loyal and as quiet as a church mouse. It really is a miracle we became friends at all, as quiet people scare the crap out of me, but she persevered in talking to me and we have been closer than sisters ever since.

Christy and her family lived with us for a year before they set out for the mission field in Pohnpei, Micronesia. When her husband took a short term mission trip alone, leaving her here with their three kids, she dubbed herself my wifey for lifey. A term that has stuck.

I almost didn't write this dedication, as I'm still quite peeved that she left me. Particularly to a place I will *never* visit. That's okay. I get her back in the end...you'll have to read the book to find out why.

A huge kiss to my husband is in order. He is my muse for every hero and lives up to my fantasies in more ways than one.

For Christy "Wifey" Jung
You have gone by several nicknames over the years...
but you are, and always will be, the sister of my heart.

CHAPTER ONE

SAMANTHA MOORE STOOD in the middle of her childhood bedroom and surveyed the damage as she tried to fit her life into two large suitcases. She'd moved out of the apartment she shared with her best friend and back home with her parents six weeks ago in order to take care of her "affairs" so she could start her life in Scotland with no unfinished business.

"Sam?" her mother called.

"In here, Mom."

Her mother pushed open the door and sighed. "Oh, honey, you're going to need to purge some of your stuff."

"You don't think I can get all of this on the plane?" Samantha raised an eyebrow. "Oh, ye of little faith."

Her mother laughed. "I'm more concerned that if you continue stuffing those suitcases, the plane won't be able to take off and land safely."

Samantha groaned. "I know. I've already filled six storage bins with stuff I want to keep and nine bags with stuff that can be donated."

"Well done."

"I just don't know what to take with me. I know nothing about Scotland, but I can't seem to part with what I've packed so far."

"You'll figure it out." Her mother smiled gently. "You're smarter than anyone I know."

"Book smarts isn't going to help me with this."

In all her twenty-five years, Samantha had never been anywhere outside of Georgia. Her focus had been on graduating first in her class from Mercer University and being the youngest research scientist in the world. Her specialty was hematology, and it was why she'd been offered a position with a large pharmaceutical research company in Edinburgh. But the thought of moving from her small town just outside Savannah to Scotland was overwhelming, particularly since she was painfully shy.

Samantha checked her watch. "Pepper was supposed to call me a while ago. She promised to help."

"She's probably running late at work."

"More than likely."

Pepper Brooks was Samantha's best friend and a self-confessed hippie. Well, sort of. Her mother certainly was, hence the name "Pepper," but Samantha was convinced there was an uptight snob buried deep within her friend somewhere.

Pepper had moved from California to Savannah in second grade and had attached herself to Samantha immediately. Which was fine by Sam—she needed someone to be her voice. Even at seven, Sam figured out that Pepper was a protector. She was happy to let Pepper fight her battles for her...even if she didn't always agree with Pepper's methods. They had been inseparable ever since.

Admittedly, Sam was much less shy than she had been as a child, but she still had difficulty speaking her mind to strangers. Her family and Pepper were a different story. Most days, she gave as good as she got.

"I swear, Mom, I don't know how she can go to school, work full time, take care of her horse, and then find time for a sanity break."

"I have a feeling her horse *is* her sanity break." Her mother wrapped an arm around Sam's shoulders and gave her a gentle squeeze. "But she is pretty amazing."

"No doubt," Sam agreed. "What time's Dalton going to be here?"

"Six."

Sam frowned. "Why so late? New lady?"

"Who knows?" her mother grumbled. "I've given up trying to figure out what your brother's doing with his personal life."

Dalton had been a high school football star and was now the most eligible bachelor in their small community. He owned a chain of high-end car dealerships around Savannah, and with access to any car on the lot, his playboy status was unbreakable.

"Sammi!" The unmistakable voice of Pepper could be heard from the foyer.

"Speak of the devil," Samantha said as she stepped to the hallway railing. "Up here."

Pepper glanced up at Samantha. Her hair was scooped into a messy bun on the top of her head and shone in the foyer light. She was the polar opposite in looks and personality of most of Samantha's friends, and Samantha adored her. Pepper made friends easily and could talk to anyone about anything. Petite and blonde, she was the epitome of a southern belle, without a southern bone in her body. She'd wrapped a bandana around her head and, with her overalls, she looked like a forties pinup girl.

"You look like you're dressed for World War Two."

"You like?" Pepper rested a hand on her hip and chuckled. "It's laundry day."

"Very cute."

2

Samantha's mother leaned over the railing. "Come on up, honey, and I'll check on dinner. Will you join us?"

"Yes, please! Thanks, Mrs. Moore." Pepper waved a piece of paper in the air as she jogged up the stairs, two at a time. "You're never going to guess what's happened!"

Samantha laughed. "You won the lottery and are going to join me in Scotland."

Pepper bobbed her head. "Yes."

Samantha snorted as she made her way back into the bedroom. "You're hilarious."

"No, seriously. Not the lottery, per se, but I got into MGA."

"What?"

Pepper handed her the notice. "I auditioned for MGA. In Edinburgh. They accepted me. I've committed to their one-year advanced course."

"MGA?" Samantha skimmed the letter. "Performing arts? Seriously? Pepper, this is a lot of money. How are you going to pay for this?"

"I have almost eight-thousand saved."

"To train Jonesy for the trials!"

Pepper waved her hand dismissively. "Trials, shmials."

"I thought winning the Olympics was the most important thing in your life. Or at the very least, getting away from your mother while you're training him. He's the reason you haven't dated or done anything outside of school or work for three years."

"Priorities change, I guess." She shrugged. "And, technically, I will be getting away from her...all the way across the ocean."

"What about Jonesy? You were essentially the midwife to his mother. You've raised that horse since birth."

Pepper's composure slipped, but she pulled it back...a little *too* quickly. "It's just a year. I'll have no problem finding a nice young girl to look after him for me. And Mom can look after Rover."

Sam recalled the discussion of what to name Pepper's rescue pup. It came down to either Rover or Fido.

"Pepper." Samantha handed her back the letter. "What's really going on? You've always said that acting and singing was for fun and would never take priority over becoming a vet. I'm still not clear on how you'd be able to finish veterinary school and train for the Olympics at the same time...but then again, you're the dreamer."

"You make that sound like it's a bad thing."

Samantha shook her head. "Not at all. I envy it and you know it. Spill."

"I can't just want to join my best friend for an adventure in a land full of sexy men?"

Samantha smirked. "You assume all Scottish men look like Ewan McGregor."

3

"And you assume they all look like Gobber the Belch."

Samantha giggled. "Is it weird we went to see *How to Train your Dragon* and we don't even have kids?"

"No, because we took Chelsea's kid as a cover…she got a free afternoon, and Chase got to see a movie with his favorite spice."

"Okay, you have me there, but still, what's really going on?"

"Nothing. Really. My mom's just driving me crazy."

"You've been home for less than a month," Sam pointed out.

"I know. At least she passes out drunk more nights than most, but still, I probably should have stayed at our place."

"Sorry."

Pepper waved her hand dismissively. "I'm the one who can't stand the thought of living alone. It's not your fault. But I do need to make a change."

Samantha sighed. "Yeah, you should get out of there, but don't you think this is a bit drastic?"

"Nope, not at all. I just want to go somewhere where there's no drama."

Samantha couldn't stop the laugh. "So you're going to *drama* school."

"How about we halt this fascinating conversation and I'll help you finish packing?"

"Okay, okay. You're off the hook for now. Just give me some notice before you arrive. I'm assuming I'll have to find a two-bed-room place to rent, huh?"

"I'll take the couch," Pepper said. "I'm not picky."

Samantha choked in response. "Says the woman with champagne taste on a beer budget."

"Oh, I at least have enough to spring for the sparkling wine."

"Nice. Let's get to work." Samantha went back to the first bag she'd packed, thinking she could leave some of the clothes behind, but reluctant to part with any of her shoes.

* * *

Dr. Kade Gunnach sat behind his large mahogany desk and stared at the data in front of him. It wasn't promising. A knock on his office door elicited a frown, but he knew the inevitable couldn't be avoided. "Come in."

His brothers Brodie and Connall pushed inside and sat in the chairs across from his desk.

Brodie leaned forward and settled his arms on his knees. "So?"

Kade rubbed his forehead. "Nothing."

"At all?" Connall asked.

Kade shook his head.

"Shite!" Brodie stood and made his way to the bank of windows facing the university.

Connall dropped his face into his hands. "Have you told Fi?"

Fiona Gunnach was their only sister and the baby of the family.

"No," Kade said. "I thought Brodie could do that."

"Hell no." Brodie turned from the window, his hands in his pockets, an indication he was trying not hit something or someone. "Con should. He's the only one she won't kill...well...and Angus."

"What's the next step?" Connall asked.

"I've already hired someone...at a significant cost, but she's the best in the world," Kade said.

"Who?" Connall asked.

"Her name is Dr. Samantha Moore. She was top of her class and the youngest graduate of her university in a hundred years."

"Where'd you find her?" Brodie asked.

"I didn't. Duncan did."

"Obviously. But from where?"

"The States."

"Is she one of us?" Connall asked.

Kade shook his head.

"An outsider, Kade?" Connall snorted. "What about Angus?"

Angus McFadden was their sister's fiancé and one of the most talented doctors on staff.

"Angus did what he could, but he's not the best, Con. *She* is."

Brodie narrowed his eyes. "How do you know that?"

"Because Duncan spent six months trying to get her."

Brodie swore. "You can't be serious."

"I gave Angus a year, Brod. He's one of us and has a vested interest in finding a cure for Fiona's sake."

"So she probably knows, then," Connall said hopefully.

Before Kade could answer, the buzz of his intercom sounded and he pressed the button. "Yes, Anna."

"Your sister's here, Dr. Gunnach."

Kade glanced at his watch. "She's early. Go ahead and send her in."

Before he'd hung up with his assistant, Fiona sailed into the office. "Och, it's bloody hot in this building." She wore a sleeveless blouse and he noticed her skin was pink and blotchy.

Kade glanced at the thermostat in his office. Fifteen degrees Celsius...well below the danger threshold.

Fiona's dark, shoulder-length hair swung across her flushed cheeks as she dropped her purse on Kade's couch. She clapped her hands and then settled them on her hips. "All right, brothers, Angus said you had news."

"Well, hello to you too." Kade rose to his feet and made his way from behind his desk. "Where is your fiancé?"

"He's in the lab. Where else would he be?"

Kade was about to deliver a retort when his sister's eyes widened and she took three quick breaths. He stepped toward her, but Connall was faster and caught her just as she collapsed.

"Brodie, ice—now!" Kade snapped as he moved Fiona's purse so that Connall could lay her on the sofa.

Brodie waved his hand and the freezer door flew open. With another flick of his wrist, icepacks began to hurl themselves at Kade.

"What the hell happened, Kade?" Brodie snapped.

Kade shot him a look of annoyance, even though he knew Brodie's question was somewhat rhetorical. He and Connall packed the ice around Fiona.

Kade felt Fiona's forehead as he took her pulse. Grabbing his stethoscope, he laid it over her chest. She was warm and her heart was racing, but as the ice began to cool her down, her heart rate slowed to normal. He waited for her to take a deep breath and then get through the inevitable coughing fit, indicating she was going to be okay, before helping her to sit up. "You all right?"

Fiona groaned and nodded.

Kade's office door flew open and Fiona's very frazzled fiancé rushed into the room. "Fi?"

Fiona rubbed her forehead. "I'm all right, Angus."

Angus sat beside her on the sofa and wrapped an arm around her shoulders. Turning accusing eyes on the brothers, he asked, "What happened?"

Kade held a hand out to Brodie, who looked about ready to kill his sister's significant other. "We don't know, Angus. She was only here a few seconds before she collapsed."

Fiona took a deep breath and squeezed Angus's knee. "I'm all right, sweetheart. I just overheated."

"How could you possibly overheat in this weather?" Angus laid his hand on her forehead. "It's barely seventeen degrees outside and even cooler in here."

She pushed his hand away and rose to her feet. "I don't know."

Kade closed the door and advanced on his sister. "Fiona, where were you?"

She stared down at her engagement ring.

"Damn it!" Angus snapped.

"What?" Kade asked.

"Angus," Fiona admonished. "We'll talk about it when we're alone."

Connall grasped his sister's arm. "No, you'll talk about it now. What the hell were you doing before you came here?"

"You were at the library, weren't you?" Angus accused.

Kade swore. "Fi, I thought we'd been over this."

She scowled at her brother. "No, *you* went over it."

6

Without comment, Brodie retrieved a power bar from Kade's stash in his desk and handed it to his sister. She thanked him and opened the package.

"How long has this been going on?" Connall asked.

"Six months," Angus answered, and then turned to Fiona. "You promised you'd stop. It's not safe."

She frowned. "When did I ever say I'd stop? I promised I'd be careful, but I never said I'd *stop*."

"Fiona, the library isn't temperature controlled and the tunnels are worse," Brodie pointed out. "What the hell were you thinking?"

The private rooms below the city were known to very few people and housed many of the secrets and historical information passed down from generation to generation of Scots. The only way in and out was through hidden passages and tunnels that were often a good ten to twenty degrees warmer than the outside temperatures.

Fiona jabbed a finger toward him. "Don't you dare speak to me as though I'm an idiot, Brodie Gunnach. I know exactly what I'm doing and you have no say in it."

Angus sighed. "But I do. You are not to go there again."

Kade shook his head. No one told his sister what to do and lived to tell about it.

Fiona's eyes narrowed and she took a quick breath through her teeth. "We are not bound, Angus McFadden. You have no dominion over me."

"Fiona, I'm sure Angus wasn't—" Connall started.

"Don't!" she snapped. "Ganging up on me right now will not go well for you."

Connall raised his hands in surrender and took a step back.

"Fiona, you need to eat." Kade leaned against his desk and crossed his arms.

She waved the power bar. "I *am!*"

He raised an eyebrow and then turned to his brothers. "Con, why don't you and Brodie head on back to your offices. I'd like to talk to Fiona and Angus alone."

"You're playing chieftain now?" Fiona snapped, but took another bite of the power bar.

"*Verið varkár*," Angus warned.

"She doesn't need to be careful, Angus." Kade waved his hand dismissively. "She's in no danger."

Connall and Brodie left the office, and Kade spent the next thirty minutes attempting to stop Fiona from her dangerous pursuit, but at the same time, impressed by what she'd found out.

CHAPTER TWO

SAM ARRIVED AT Hilton Head Airport with her mother, father, brother, and best friend in tow. She was happy for the support. She couldn't believe her work had brought her this far. She'd always believed that with her personality she'd be holed up in a lab somewhere close to home and living quietly, perhaps with cats.

Okay, no. Not cats, I hate cats, but perhaps a few dogs and maybe a turtle.

"Sam?" her mom interrupted her thoughts.

"Yes?"

"The line's moving, honey."

"Oh, right." Sam pushed her bags forward.

Pepper smiled reassuringly. "You okay?"

"No, I'm petrified," Sam whispered.

"You're gonna be fine…and I'll be there in a few weeks to make everything better."

Sam smiled. "That does make me feel a little better."

"Do you have your happy pills?"

"I've already taken one…not that it's making much difference."

"You don't take off for two hours, Sammi, you'll waste them."

Sam shook her head. "I don't care. I don't think I could have gotten in the car if I hadn't taken one."

"How many did the doctor give you?"

"Four."

Pepper snorted. "What happens if you take them all before you even get on the plane?"

"That's what red wine is for."

Pepper giggled.

"Ma'am? I'm open over here," called a ticketing agent.

Sam walked with her small group to the agent. "Hi. Here's my passport and ticket number. I tried to check-in online, but I was told I needed to come to the counter."

The woman smiled and Sam was sure the thick layer of makeup would crack with the action. "Let me have a look." Her fingers flew over

8

the keyboard as she checked Samantha's ticket. "Hmm. Well, the reason you weren't able to check in online is because your ticket was reclassed."

"What do you mean?"

The agent took her bags then handed her a boarding pass and other paperwork. "You are now flying first class."

"Oh, wow. Thank you."

"You'll find the first-class lounge just past security. You can wait there until boarding."

Sam smiled and turned to her group.

"Shall we have dinner before you board the plane?" her father suggested.

"Are you sure you want to drag this out?"

He chuckled. "I'd like to keep my little girl here in Savannah until my death, but apparently, there's a big world out there she insists on seeing."

Sam sighed. "You waited three whole hours to lay on the guilt trip. Well done, Daddy."

"Impertinent child."

Her mother laughed. "You have no idea what impertinent means, dear heart."

"Perhaps you're right." He grinned. "All right, everyone, let's eat. I'm in the mood for seafood."

"Shocker!" Dalton retorted.

Sam grinned at her brother. She was surprised he was there, to be honest. He usually avoided the forced family get-togethers, and for some unknown reason, he was avoiding Pepper even more these days. They had said their good-byes the day before, so Sam hadn't expected him to see her off.

"Dalt, can I bug you for a minute?" she asked.

He shrugged. "Sure."

Sam pulled her brother aside and made sure the rest were out of earshot. "Do you know what's going on with Pepper?"

"What do you mean?"

"She's lost weight and she looks exhausted."

"She works a hundred hours a week, Sam. She probably *is* exhaustted."

"Well, can you at least keep an eye on her? Just check on her once in a while. You know what her mom's like. I hate that she's living back at home."

"I'm sure she's fine, Sam. She's a big girl."

Sam huffed. "Just do this for me, okay? I'm worried."

"Fine, sis. Whatever." He frowned. "I'd hoped you'd grow out of the bossiness."

"And I hoped you'd grow up. If wishes were horses…"

He mimicked her in a sing-song voice, but was interrupted by their father calling them back to the group. Her father took her mother's hand and the couple moved toward the restaurant, while Dalton followed.

Sam hung back and linked her arm with Pepper's. "Hey, are you really okay?"

Pepper smiled brightly. "Um, other than the fact you're leaving me? Perfect."

"Not long, right?"

"Yeah, yeah."

"I have something for you," Sam said as she rummaged in her purse.

"You do?"

"A going away gift." Sam handed her a wrapped package.

"You never got the whole concept of a going away gift, did you?"

"Go with it, Pepper. You'll love it."

Pepper ripped open the gift and laughed. A mini-book on fifty ways to cook with pomegranates lay in the palm of her hand.

Pepper squinted at the pages. "Is it for pixies?"

"I know, right? I couldn't believe it was real. I thought we could set up one of my microscopes and you could read out a recipe to me and we could experiment."

Pepper laughed. "Oh, my funny, funny friend. Don't go," she joked as they caught up with the rest of the family.

"What happens when you arrive, button?" her father asked.

"I'm being met by their recruiter, Duncan MacKenzie, or his assistant, Payton. One of them is going to take me to the hotel and then pick me up on Monday to take me to the lab."

Her father frowned. "I don't know about you being alone with a man you don't know in a strange city."

Sam agreed...on the inside. "He's very professional, Daddy. I'm sure he'll make sure I'm safe. It'll probably be Payton picking me up, anyway. Don't worry so much. My cell phone will be with me at all times and you have all the contact numbers to the lab."

Her mother squeezed her hand. "I'm so proud of you, sweetie. You're stepping out of your comfort zone and doing something very brave."

Sam smiled. "Thanks, Mom."

Dinner continued and before Sam knew it, it was time to leave her family and head to security. With tear-filled good-byes taking up a good ten minutes, she had to make a run for the gate, but luckily, she made it with just enough time to spare.

* * *

The first leg of the trip was over. Samantha made it to Dallas and would be heading to Heathrow and finally Edinburgh from there. She walked to her gate and took a seat in the first-class lounge. The waiting area wasn't entirely full, but she figured not many people could afford to fly first class to Europe. She accepted a soda from the helpful airline worker and took a seat by the window.

"Is this seat taken?"

Sam glanced up. A man, probably in his thirties, smiled down at her. Dark hair cut short, almost military style, framed a strong jaw, and chocolate-brown eyes widened as he waited for her reply. He was attracttive, in a quarterback kind of way. Her heart raced as she pondered why he'd want to sit next to her when the room was nearly empty.

"No." She bit her lip. "Feel free."

He took his seat and dropped his carry-on. "Are you flying to London?"

Sam shook her head. "Edinburgh."

His grinned. "Me too."

She forced a smile. "Great."

"Have you ever been to Scotland?"

"No."

"I go several times a year. It's a great place."

"Good to know," she said quietly and pulled out her iPod. She hadn't planned on Chatty Charlie sitting next to her.

"What are you listening to?" he asked.

"Nothing right now," she said, irritation giving her courage.

He chuckled. "Sorry. I'm a talker. I'll leave you to your music."

He pulled out his laptop and powered it up and Sam slipped her headphones on.

Finally, the doors to the gate opened and it was time to board. Sam gathered her things and made her way down the gangplank. The flight attendant showed her to her seat and Sam settled in for a long flight.

"Hello again," someone said.

She glanced up to see Chatty Charlie standing in front of her. "Hi," she said in suspicion.

"It would appear we're seatmates."

Of course we are.

He sat next to her and secured his seatbelt. As the flight attendant walked by, Sam flagged her down. "Excuse me, could I get some water please?"

"Of course, Dr. Moore."

The woman returned quickly with a bottle of water. Sam located her valium and popped a pill.

"Dramamine?" the guy asked.

She shook her head. "Stronger."

"Ah. You don't fly well?"

"That's an understatement."

"This leg of the flight's a breeze. I've done it a few times, and believe me, in first class you won't even know you're in the air."

"Let's hope so."

He held out his hand. "Cole Drake."

Of course it is. Would that be a soap opera name or a porn name? No, if you were a porn star, you'd be Randy Steel or something like that.

She tried not to giggle as she shook his hand. "Samantha Moore."

"Nice to meet you." He smiled. "I heard the flight attendant call you "doctor." What's your specialty?"

"Research."

"Are you on your way to the UK for business or pleasure?" he asked.

Nosy much?

"Sorry. Force of habit. I used to be a cop." He opened a magazine and smiled. "I'll sit here and keep my questions to myself."

Before the valium kicked in, Samantha read and reread the Gunnach Pharmaceutical dossier cover-to-cover twice. She just couldn't get a handle on exactly why she was needed. The company had invented some ground-breaking medications and devices that had saved a lot of people, but none of it was related to blood. She was beginning to wonder if her decision to throw caution to the wind might have been a mistake.

She blinked, her eyes feeling heavy as her body started to calm.

Her last coherent thought before she faded off to sleep was how nice Cole Drake's smile was.

* * *

"Ladies and gentleman, we'll be collecting any rubbish you might have as we prepare for landing. Please let us know if you need help with your customs forms as we come around."

Sam yawned, even though she'd managed several hours of sleep. Her soap star neighbor had, in fact, kept his questions to himself for the most part. When they'd both been awake at the same time, he'd struck up light conversations, and Sam found him funny and sweet, not to mention interesting. He'd spent several years as a cop before being recruited into private security and now, as an expert in his field, Edinburgh University had hired him as a guest lecturer. She was surprised to find out they were staying in the same hotel in Edinburgh.

"Dr. Moore? Do you have any rubbish?"

Sam glanced up at the flight attendant and smiled. "No. I'm all set, thank you."

"Excellent. Please don't hesitate to let me know if you need anything."

Sam nodded and settled further into her seat. She glanced over at Cole. His quiet snore indicated flying didn't bother him one bit.

"Flight attendants, prepare for landing."

Sam's heart raced. This was it. No turning back now…not that she could have, midair, but still, this seemed final somehow. As the pilot gave everyone instructions and the crew took their seats, Sam gripped the armrests and waited for the plane to crash.

Stupidly, she'd thought she could do without a valium for landing.

She felt a warm hand cover her wrist and she glanced at Cole with what she suspected was a grimace. "You're awake," she said, then under her breath, "Thank God."

He gave her arm a gentle squeeze. "I hope you don't mind. I know I'm a virtual stranger, but you looked like you might need a little support."

She bit her lip. "No, it's okay. I'm too scared to object. Take advantage of it while you can."

He laughed and the sound put Sam at ease. "You're doing great."

She squeezed her eyes shut and was genuinely surprised when the plane landed and came to a stop without incident.

"See? We're alive and the plane is intact."

Samantha smiled. "We're alive, yes. Plane intact? Can't be proven until we disembark."

"Don't you mean deplane?"

"Who are you? Tattoo?" she retorted.

"Off you go, then." Cole nodded toward the doors. "Enjoy your stay on Fantasy Island."

Samantha giggled and gathered up her carry-on bag and purse, heading down the gangway once the all-clear was given. Cole followed. Even though the day was crisp, Sam wrapped her hoodie around her waist and headed for baggage claim. She slowed her pace and was glad Cole took the hint and caught up with her. He was cute and seemed like a good guy. It might be nice to know someone on this new adventure she was on.

"Would you like to share a cab?" he asked.

"Thanks, but someone's actually picking me up."

"Oh. No biggie. Maybe we can meet for a drink at the hotel bar sometime."

She smiled. "Maybe."

"I'll leave a message for you at the front desk and we can plan something."

Sam took a deep breath. "Um…okay."

Arriving in the busy carousel area, she noticed a tall man holding a sign with her name on it. She approached him and hoped her smile didn't look like a frightened grimace. "I'm Samantha Moore."

"Welcome, Dr. Moore. I'm Duncan MacKenzie."

He was tall, close to six feet, and had dark red hair, blue eyes, and looked…well…very Scottish. She stared up at him, wishing Pepper were there. Pepper would have said something witty and smart, and charmed the pants right off him.

Okay, he'd keep his pants on, but still, she would have talked to him.

Which Sam wasn't doing.

She was standing there...staring.

Like an idiot.

"Shall I help you with your bags?" he asked.

"Oh, yes. Thank you," she said and led him to the carousel.

"It's quite brisk outside at the moment, you may want your jumper," Duncan suggested.

Jumper? What the heck is a jumper? Sam stared at him.

He pointed to the hoodie around her waist. "Your sweatshirt."

"Oh, no, I'm okay."

Duncan shrugged. "Suit yourself."

Sam let out a quiet sigh of relief when she saw her bags nestled together and making their way toward them. She hoped the drive wasn't long to the hotel...the thought of small talk turned her stomach.

"There they are," Sam said.

Duncan reached out and pulled them off the turn table as though they weighed as much as a toy poodle and set them on the ground. "Anything else coming?"

Sam shook her head.

"Right. The driver's waiting at the curb." He smiled. "Follow me." He wheeled her bags toward the exit and she followed...like a lamb to the slaughter.

The driver, another remarkably Scottish-looking man, dropped her bags in the trunk without a word and climbed into the driver's seat while Duncan assisted Sam into the car. This man, however, looked closer to her assessment of Scotsmen than Pepper's.

As they drove away from the airport, Duncan handed Sam a folder. "Payton booked your room for a little longer than expected. She is having minor repairs done to the executive apartments, which means you cannot move in right away. It'll be closer to a fortnight. I apologize for that."

"That's okay," Sam said as she skimmed the information swimming before her.

"All of our contact numbers are inside. Also, here is a cell phone for your business use. Payton has preprogrammed our phone numbers. If you need anything, give one of us a ring."

Sam nodded, although, he spoke so fast, she wasn't sure she was catching everything.

They arrived at the hotel and Sam had a difficult time concentrating on anything other than the architecture. The hotel was stunning, like something out of a medieval landscape, and she tried to take it all in as Duncan led her inside.

Duncan made sure the front desk had the corporate credit card on file for any incidentals, secured her room key for her, and waited for the bell-hop to arrive before taking his leave. "Right, Dr. Moore, I'll leave you here, unless you need anything further?"

"No, I'm fine. Thank you."

"Should you need anything, please let me know."

Sam smiled and nodded. Duncan left and she followed the bell-hop to her room. After walking inside, she turned to tip him, but he refused the money and backed out. Sam's heart began to race and her stomach felt a little queasy as she made her way to the windows at the back of the suite.

Something's wrong.

She grabbed her cell phone, scrolled to Pepper's number, and dialed it.

"Sammi?" Pepper answered, her voice rough from obviously being awakened. "Did you arrive all right?"

"Yes, I'm fine, but are you okay?"

"Just trying to get a nap in, but I'm fine. Why? What time is it?"

"Oh, sorry. It's about nine o'clock here. I have a really weird feeling. Are you sure you're okay?"

"Perfectly. The door's locked and the chair's metaphorically under the doorknob. What's wrong? You're scaring me."

Sam took a deep breath. "I'm fine. I'm probably just tired."

"Did you sleep on the plane?"

"A little."

She heard Pepper yawn and then, "Sorry. Okay. You're probably overwrought and you need to go to sleep. You know you're useless when you're tired...wait, no, that's me. You can live off one hour of sleep a week." Another yawn. "Sorry."

"It's okay." Sam chuckled. "Let's Skype tomorrow. You need to go back to sleep and I need to wash the airplane off me. I'll tell you all about the cute guy I met on the plane."

"What?" Pepper seemed much more alert now. "Seriously?"

Sam chuckled. "Yep. We're staying at the same hotel, and I even agreed to maybe meet him for a drink."

"Who are you and what have to done with my best friend?"

"I'm evolving. Aren't you proud?"

"So, so proud." Yawn.

"Go back to sleep."

"You're sure you're okay?"

"Totally," Sam said.

"Night."

Click.

Sam smiled and dropped her phone on the table next to the couch. She was being ridiculous. She needed to sleep. This was her first time away from home, and she was nervous. That was it. She took some time to put away her clothes and then headed to the shower.

She let the hot water cover her and sighed as she felt the travel wash away. But without warning, her heart started to race again. Something was definitely wrong, and the trouble seemed close. In pure Bible-belt fashion, she started to pray. The fear was replaced with calm, and Sam let out a sigh of relief.

Without wasting any more time worrying about it, she dried off and got ready for bed.

CHAPTER THREE

Kade let himself into his flat and dropped his keys on the foyer table. Almost nine o'clock. Today had been a long day, filled with revelations. Ones he wished had stayed hidden. Loosening his tie, he made his way to the bank of windows overlooking the university. The weight of leadership was heavy today and he felt isolated.

His brothers were of no help, and now his only sister was adding to the burden. He wanted to rail at her and drive home her stupidity for putting herself in danger, but he had to admit, she was doing something that might help her cause. If they could find out what happened several hundred years ago, maybe they could find out why she was in danger.

His phone rang, interrupting his brooding. "Hello."

"Kade, it's Duncan."

"How'd it go with the new doctor?"

"Outside of the fact that the woman is afraid of her own shadow and doesn't speak?"

"She doesn't need to speak, Duncan. She just needs to find a cure."

"True." Duncan sighed. "She *is* quite pretty, in an American way. What do they call it? Girl next door?"

Kade chuckled. "As long as she does her job, she can be the female equivalent of Rowan Atkinson."

Duncan laughed. "Well, she's safely stowed at the Balmoral and my job is done. Payton's picking her up on Monday and will bring her to your office. You can show her the lab and try to force a conversation out of her."

"I've given that responsibility to Anna."

Duncan laughed. "Coward."

Kade chuckled. "Maybe. Could also be that I don't have time to baby-sit and make small talk."

"Don't blame ye."

"Thanks for your help."

"I'll see you next week."

Kade hung up just as his doorbell pealed. *Great. Fiona.*

Pulling open the door, he stepped back with a quiet sigh. "Darling sister. To what do I owe the pleasure?"

"I hated the way we left things." Fiona brushed past him, followed by Angus.

Kade closed the door. "You could have called."

Fiona gave Angus some kind of silent request and Kade rolled his eyes.

"I'll just grab meself something to drink." Angus started toward the kitchen.

Kade raised an eyebrow. "Should I sit down?"

She smiled. "It might be a good idea."

He sat in his favorite chair and waited for his sister to sit on the sofa. "Will I need a hanky?"

Fiona shrugged. "I have a couple if you need one."

"Are we going to discuss any further visits to the library?"

"No. We're going to discuss you."

"Bloody hell," Kade grumbled.

"We need to discuss Shannon."

Kade pushed to his feet. "I'm not doing this with you, Fiona."

"She's in love with you."

He ran his hands through his hair. "No, she's not. She's jockeying for position, and I'll not be a part of it."

Fiona burst into tears and Kade sighed and sat down again, leaning over to give her hand a gentle squeeze. "Och, love, don't cry."

"You need to bind someone, Kade. I don't want to wait anymore."

"Fi, I can't bind someone if she's not my true mate."

She pulled her hand away and stood. "But you could still marry!"

He noticed Angus hovering in the corner, his hands fisted at his sides. Kade knew that if he wasn't chieftain, Angus would more than likely lay him flat on the floor. Males didn't take kindly to their mates being upset.

"Fiona," Kade whispered. "You're upsetting your fiancé."

Fiona stomped her foot and let out a series of creative swear words. "My goal in this bloody futile exercise is to upset *you*! I can't be bound until you are settled, and you seem hell-bent on shoving every eligible female to the curb."

"So, if I'm hearing you correctly—"

"Kade!" Angus warned.

"I thought you were getting a drink," Kade pointed out.

Angus crossed his arms.

"Forget it." Fiona rubbed her forehead and flopped back onto the sofa. "This is important to me, but if you're going to stand there and tease me, then I won't waste my breath."

Kade took a deep breath and his emotions calmed suddenly.

Odd.

He shook off the phenomenon and focused on his sister again. "I'm sorry, Fi. I know this is difficult for you, but I won't marry someone who, at the very least, doesn't have our best interests at heart. And I haven't found my true mate, so binding's not an option. Shannon is not the right woman, and I think you know that."

Angus made his way to Fiona and sat next to her. "He's right, sweetheart."

Fiona groaned. "Then you should bind me anyway. Screw the covenant."

Angus hissed and Kade watched his sister fold.

"I'm sorry. I didn't mean it," she backpedaled.

Angus lifted her chin. "That's treason, Fiona, and I'll not be party to it, no matter how much I love you. Hear me on this now. Yes?"

Tears slipped down her face as she nodded.

Angus wrapped an arm around her and pulled her close. "If anyone else had heard that, you know what could happen."

"I know. I'm just frustrated."

Kade settled his ankle over his knee and watched her. "I'm thinking in less than five minutes, we're going to have some company, so I'd suggest you calm yourself, sister."

The familial bond meant that they could feel extreme distress or happiness, and this certainly fell under distress for Fiona.

She nodded. "I'm sorry."

"I know this is difficult, but I plan to keep my promise to you," Kade said.

"I just don't understand why you keep finding something wrong with every woman you meet," Fiona complained. "It's not like you don't have choices! Just pick one already."

The door opened and Connall came in, looking haggard and concerned.

"Come on in, Con…no, really, no need to knock," Kade said as Connall settled himself on the sofa.

"What's wrong?" Connall asked Fiona.

Kade didn't hear Fiona's response as he studied his phone. He was sure Brodie would call any second, with Fiona's frustration radiating amongst the brothers.

His own frustration was starting to get the better of him when the call came.

"Hi, Brodie."

"What's wrong?"

Kade sighed. "We're simply having a difference of opinion, but all will be well."

"Who are you arguing with?"

"Fi." Kade frowned. Why didn't Brodie know that? Maybe he really was as distracted as Fiona accused. "Where are you?"

"Nowhere," Brodie said, his voice clipped.

"Blonde or brunette?" Kade asked.

"Neither."

"Ah, so it's Heather."

Brodie evaded his comment. "If you don't need me, I'll talk to you tomorrow."

Kade chuckled. "I don't need you. And wait a little while to call Fi. We have a few things to discuss."

"Be nice, brother."

"I'm always nice," Kade said, and hung up. He lowered himself into his favorite chair and smiled. He loved his family, even if they drove him crazy. Connall's ability to calm Fiona was something he appreciated. She was now leaning back against Angus, laughing at something Connall had just said, the tears quickly drying as she talked to her favorite brother.

"Better?" Connall asked.

Fiona nodded.

"Good," he said and then faced Kade. "So, not Shannon?"

Kade laughed and Fiona smacked Con's leg.

"Definitely *not* Shannon," Kade said.

"Excellent. She's a vulture."

"*Connall*, she is not," Fiona said.

"Of course she is," he pressed. "She doesn't care about Kade. She simply wants the highest place in the clan. You must be able to see that, Fi. If you can't, you're blind."

Fiona sighed. "I guess I can see it. I just think vulture's a little harsh. She's so nice."

"To *you*," Connall said. "She's nasty to anyone she doesn't think can get her closer to Kade."

"Have you seen this?" Kade asked him.

Connall shrugged. "Once or twice…certainly not on purpose. She's on her best behavior in front of me, but I've walked in on a few tense situations when she's speaking with others, and she's obviously had to backtrack. She's got everyone so on edge, no one will speak against her."

"I didn't realize it was that bad."

"It's probably worse."

Kade considered this information. Connall was sensitive and perceptive. An empath. He could read people quickly and accurately, and Kade always brought him in on meetings with new people. Connall could weed out the ones who could potentially harm the clan or the business. Shannon Fraser, however, was not one he could easily weed out. She was the daughter of one of the oldest and most respected families within their clan, not to mention the sister of someone Kade considered an ally. She could, however, be watched.

"Before you ask," Angus piped in, "Hamish knows what his sister's like, but you know he'll never speak ill about her."

Kade nodded. *As it should be.*

"Fi?" Kade leaned forward. "I promise that if I meet someone who is a good fit for me and the clan, I won't wait, all right? Even if she's not my mate."

Connall frowned at his sister.

Fiona grimaced. "I can't ask you to make that promise, Kade."

"No, you can't," Connall said, and faced Kade. "And you shouldn't be making a promise like that."

"The promise *is* mine to make, Con."

"Aye," Connall agreed. "Just don't sell yourself short."

Angus rose to his feet and pulled Fiona with him. "I think I should get your sister home. She needs to sleep."

Fiona gathered her purse and coat. Kade walked them to the door, hugging his sister, even though he knew she was still mad at him. She wanted to be settled with Angus. He understood that. But his job was not to please her, not this time. He had to do what was best for his people.

He closed the door and made his way back to the living room. Connall was on the couch, holding a couple of beers he'd retrieved while Kade said his good-byes.

"You read my mind," Kade said as he took the one Connall offered.

"I do that."

Kade chuckled. "You don't need to hang around if you've got somewhere to be."

Connall shrugged. "Here works."

Kade grinned and took a swig of his beer. He liked that answer.

* * *

Samantha collected her messages from the front desk and found a message from Cole. She called his room and agreed to join him for dinner Sunday night…reluctantly. He pointed out that she needed to eat anyway, and since she'd already bowed out of drinks the night before, she didn't feel she could blow him off again, especially since he'd saved her sanity on the flight.

They decided on Hadrian's, which was the Balmoral's casual restaurant of choice. Sam took care with her appearance, dressing a little nicer than she may have needed to, but her mother always told her it was better to be overdressed than under. Plus, Cole was cute. Even if he didn't make her heart race, he made her feel comfortable, and that was a big deal in her book.

She arrived at the restaurant a few minutes early, to find Cole waiting for her. He wore dark jeans, a black shirt, sleeves rolled to the elbow, and a vest. He looked more like a rock star than a cop. She smiled, and he made his way over to her, leaning down to give her a chaste kiss on the cheek. "Hi," he said. "You look beautiful."

"Thanks. You look nice as well."

"Our table is ready if you are."

Samantha nodded. "Definitely. I'm starving."

They followed the hostess to their table and Cole held Sam's chair while she made herself comfortable. He sat down and picked up the wine list.

Within seconds, he laid it down and patted the top of the leather menu. "I don't know why I'm looking at this. I don't know anything about what goes with what. Give me a beer list any day. Beer goes with everything."

"Do you even like wine?" she asked.

"Sometimes."

"I'll just plan on ordering a glass of something with the meal then," she said.

"Are you a wine connoisseur?"

She smiled. "Kind of."

"In that case perhaps a bottle might be better." Cole leaned his arms on the table. "Can I trust you *not* to order the four-thousand-dollar 1865 merlot?"

Sam gasped. "There's an 1865 Merlot? Do you know how rare that is?"

"I guessed...based on the price tag."

"Right." Sam felt her cheeks heat and she stared back down at the wine list, fighting the urge to run.

Cole laid his hand over hers and she glanced up at him. "I'd appreciate it if you'd order a bottle. If I don't like it, you can drink it all."

Sam pulled her hand from his and slipped it into her lap. "Plying me with wine so soon?"

He chuckled. "Am I that transparent?"

Sam had never been good at flirting, but she'd promised herself she'd try to make some changes. She supposed this was as good a time as any.

The waiter arrived and took their drink orders. Cole decided on a local ale and Sam went with water in order to save herself for the wine. After discussing options, she decided on a relatively new Pinot Noir their server suggested, hoping she wouldn't be disappointed. She hated bad wine even more than bad food.

When the server arrived with Cole's pint, Sam wished she'd ordered one. Cole pointed to the glass and smiled. "Want to try?"

Sam shook her head. "I have a rule never to mix alcohol. I'd have a wicked headache tomorrow, and that's just not a good idea, especially starting a new job."

"Better to be safe than sorry." He grinned as he took a sip. "It is good, though."

Sam groaned. "Thanks for rubbing it in."

"Next time, we'll stick to beer."

"Next time, huh?"

He smiled. "Well, I suppose it depends."

"On?"

"The answer to my next question."

Sam grinned. "Ask away."

"We've determined you know your early '80s television, but do you like football?"

"I *love* football."

"Good answer. If tonight goes well, football and beer's on me."

Sam wrinkled her nose. "What if it doesn't go well?"

"You're on your own, sister."

"Great. Now I'll be dreaming about pizza, beer, and the 49ers," she grumbled.

Cole choked on his drink. "49ers? I was not expecting that! How did a southern girl become a fan of a California team?"

"My best friend. She's a football fanatic…and from California. She kind of rubbed off on me. Of course, she threatened me with bodily harm if I continued to root for the Cowboys."

"Why were you rooting for the Cowboys?" he asked.

"Don't laugh."

He raised an eyebrow. "I'll try not to."

"My second favorite color is blue, and I thought red and gold was a weird color combo."

"What's your first favorite color?"

"Green."

"So why not root for the Packers?"

Sam snorted. "Ew. Ugly Green and puke yellow is way worse together."

Cole laughed, albeit quietly.

She jabbed a finger toward him. "Hey, I was twelve and making an attempt to like something she liked. In the end, I didn't really care, so I switched to the 'niners. Now, they're a habit."

"Well, that's a great reason to root for a team."

"Okay, mister expert, are you going to tell me you like the Patriots or Steelers, or something even more impressive?"

Cole tapped his fingers on the table. "I'm a diehard Lions fan."

"*Detroit* Lions?"

"Hell, yeah."

"What are you? The patron saint of lost causes?"

Cole grinned. "You're funny."

The server arrived with their meal and, once Sam approved of the wine, poured them each a glass. He left them and Sam felt compelled to find out more about Cole Drake.

"So, tell me, why the Lions?"

"Born and raised in Detroit," he said.

"Detroit, Detroit, or the outskirts?"

Cole chuckled. "Detroit, Detroit."

"Wow. I can honestly say I've never actually met anyone from Detroit. I thought once the car factories dried up, everyone got out."

"That's true to an extent. But my lineage isn't an auto one...it's law enforcement. We were lucky."

"It can't have been easy to watch friends suffer, though." A shadow crossed Cole's face and Sam figured she'd probably pushed a button with that comment. She was also a little surprised she'd made such a personal observation. "How do you like the wine?" she asked, in an effort to change the subject.

"It's very good. I'll be sure to defer to you in the future for all my wine choices."

"You can tell your friends you have your very own sommelier on speed dial."

"In my crew, that'll make me somewhat unpopular. But it can be our secret."

Sam smiled. "So, does the university typically fly their guest lecturers first class?"

Cole's eyes widened and then he smiled. "No. They waited too long to book my flight and only had first class available."

Sam hummed. "Lucky you."

The rest of dinner was much the same. Easy and comfortable conversation. Sam was pleasantly surprised by how much she connected with Cole. When the check arrived, he insisted on paying, even after her strenuous argument. He was gallant to the end, walking her to the elevator and kissing her cheek again. She'd felt comfortable enough to exchange phone numbers with him, but was glad he didn't ask to walk her to her room. She wanted to keep a few boundaries with him and ho-nor her father's request to keep her wits about her, which he'd followed with several instructions on staying safe.

She headed back to her room and checked to see if Pepper was online. She wasn't, so Samantha got ready for bed and proceeded to not sleep.

* * *

The next morning, Samantha's new cell phone rang and she answered it to Payton McFadden, Duncan's assistant, letting her know she awaited her in the lobby.

"I'll be right down," Sam said.

After checking her appearance in the mirror, Sam grabbed her satchel and purse and headed to the elevators. Stepping into the lobby, she was surprised by how busy it was.

"Dr. Moore?"

Sam turned to the pretty, young woman and smiled. "Yes, I'm Samantha Moore."

"I'm Payton."

"Hello. It's nice to meet you."

Sam shook Payton's hand and took in her appearance. She had dark red hair that she'd pulled into a tight bun at the base of her neck and she wore thick-rimmed glasses. She didn't wear a stitch of make-up, and looked a bit like a stern teacher, but her light blue eyes crinkled at the corners, softening her appearance. When she smiled, Sam felt like she was with an old friend.

"It's nice to meet you as well. I have a car waiting for us out front. Dr. Gunnach is expecting us, so we should go. Have you had breakfast?"

"No. I don't usually eat until lunchtime."

Payton tsked. "That will never do. Dr. Gunnach is quite the stickler on eating at regular hours. We'll grab something on the way to the office."

"Okay."

Sam tried to keep the irritation from her voice. She'd become an expert at hiding her opinion about overbearing men; however, she'd been subject to many of Pepper's tirades on the subject.

They found the car waiting for them. Gobber the Belch nodded as Sam slid into the backseat.

"Dr. Moore needs to eat, Alasdair, so if we could stop somewhere quick, that would be great."

"We better," Alasdair said. "The boss doesn't like people skipping meals."

Sam had a vision of Genghis Khan sitting at a large desk, waving pastries in the air as he ran Gunnach Pharmaceutical.

"There's a Starbucks close by," Payton said.

"Please don't go to any trouble," she argued.

"In that case, Alasdair, we'll just stop at the café in the building," Payton instructed. "Will that work, Dr. Moore?"

"Sounds great," Sam said.

Alasdair pulled away from the curb. Before Sam could get her bearings, he brought the car to a stop.

"We're here?" Sam asked.

"Close, eh?" Payton said.

Sam nodded. "We could have walked."

Payton groaned. "Not me. I don't walk anywhere I don't have to. I prefer to be driven."

Sam couldn't stop a laugh. "You sound like my best friend."

Payton slid out of the car and Sam followed. "Dr. Gunnach will meet with you for a few minutes, and then his assistant, Anna, will show you to your office and give you a tour of the lab."

Payton led Sam to the café on the bottom floor of the building, and she chose a small muffin and a large coffee. Her heart started to race again as she took the last bite, and she took a minute to attempt to calm herself. She'd been having these minor panic attacks since she'd arrived. Friday night's had been the worst, but this one had the potential to be just as bad.

What the heck is going on?

CHAPTER FOUR

"Angus, you can't push her like that," Kade warned.

Angus had stopped in at Kade's office before heading to the lab, in an attempt to force Fiona's obedience on the library issue.

"She needs to yield, Kade."

"Using words like 'yield' is going to get you nowhere with my sister. You've known her long enough to know that. And you saw her Friday night, she was overwrought. If I can't get her to 'yield,' I don't know how you'll be able to. She obviously needs a distraction. And she's right. You're not bound, so you can't actually force her into doing anything she's not willing to do."

"Which is something you could fix," Angus pointed out.

"Don't start."

"The bottom line is that you're chieftain, Kade. You have to stop this."

"I may be chieftain, Angus, but I'll not force her." Kade tried to stamp down his rising irritation. "What would you do if this were Payton?"

"My sister would bloody well do as she's told."

"Well, Fiona's not Payton. Besides, she's your mate. You have more sway over her than I do. Weren't you the one going on and on about the importance of being able to control your woman?"

"You're a bloody bastard, Kade."

"You'll watch your tongue, Angus." Kade fisted his hands on his desk and leaned forward. "The new researcher is arriving in ten minutes. I don't have time to spar with you this morning. Anna will introduce her to you later."

Angus bowed his head, his reluctant indication of submission, and stormed out of Kade's office.

* * *

Sam cleared away her breakfast and threw away her trash. Her emotions were calm again, so she shook off her confusion and followed Payton through the lobby and to the bank of elevators, popping a mint in her mouth as they stepped inside.

"The executive offices are on the top floor, but the lab is below us, so you're going for a bit of a ride, I'm afraid."

"I don't mind," Sam said.

So long as it's not a plane.

"How were the accommodations, Dr. Moore?" Payton pressed the top button. "Do you like the Balmoral?"

"Oh, please call me Samantha. 'Doctor' makes me feel much more important than I am."

Payton nodded. "Samantha. Thank you."

"In answer to your question, the accommodations are incredible. I feel very spoiled."

"Only the best for our researchers."

Sam grinned. "In that case, will there be caviar and champagne later? It's my lunch of choice."

Payton chuckled. "Most certainly."

The elevator doors opened and Payton led Sam to a large, ornate marble desk.

"Mornin' Anna," Payton said.

"Well, hullo, Payton." Dr. Gunnach's assistant, a portly woman in her fifties, smiled at Sam and rose to her feet. "You must be Dr. Moore."

Sam couldn't help but feel at ease. Anna's warmth seemed to pour out of her as she stepped from behind her desk to shake her hand. "He's expectin' ye, but I'll just give him a ring and let him know you're here."

"Thanks," Payton said.

"You go on back and he'll bring ye to me when it's time for your tour."

"Thank you," Sam said.

A slim hallway led to a large mahogany door that Sam likened to something from a medieval castle.

Payton knocked and the door opened seconds later. Sam thought her heart might stop…her breathing certainly did. Standing before her was the best-looking man she'd ever seen. Not a hint of Genghis Khan anywhere to be seen. Dark blond hair, longer than the norm, framed a chiseled jaw and potentially perfectly symmetrical face. He had a day's growth of beard, a little heavier than a five-o-clock shadow. His deep blue eyes sparkled and full lips smiled, revealing even, white teeth. She had to stop herself from placing her hand over her stomach.

Her heart was racing again, but she wasn't convinced it was just because of her attraction to him. As his hand covered hers, a strange language popped into her head and her heart calmed. She pulled her hand away in an effort to break contact, realizing that in that moment she may have gone certifiably insane.

Kade's morning had started well enough, he supposed. He'd gotten out of bed, which was a positive. His unsettled feeling continued, however. His conversation with his sister had produced nothing different than the argument on Friday, other than to elicit the silent treatment and occasional look of both anger and disappointment during Sunday dinner. He hated fighting with Fiona. She could deliver a guilt trip like no one he'd ever known.

The argument with Angus had only managed to irritate him and make him want to hand the mantle of chieftain off to someone else. He hated his lineage sometimes.

His phone rang. "Yes, Anna?"

"Payton and Dr. Moore are here."

"Thank you. Send them in." He took a minute to put his suit jacket on as he made his way to the door. The knock came and he pulled open the door.

His heart stuttered. She was magnificent. Long dark hair that she'd swept away from her face with a headband fell in waves over her shoulders, and light hazel eyes like the color of a reflection of trees on the water, met his and then dropped to the floor as her cheeks pinked. She wore dark grey trousers with a cream turtleneck, and what his sister would refer to as "sensible black shoes." He shook her hand and her eyes met his again with a perplexed expression.

He smiled as the ancient words swirled in his head.

Að eilífu maki minn. (Forever mate.)

She looked surprised, and he wondered if she'd heard them too. No, not possible. He took a deep breath, drawing in her scent. Clean, with a hint of vanilla. She pulled her hand back and slipped it into the pocket of her trousers.

"Dr. Kade Gunnach," Payton said. "This is Dr. Samantha Moore."

"It's lovely to meet you. Please come in." Kade stepped back and waited for the ladies to step inside. "Have a seat."

"Duncan needs me to run a few things across town. Do you mind if I do that now?" Payton asked.

Kade shook his head. "Not at all."

Payton handed Dr. Moore a lanyard with "Gunnach Pharmaceutical" written on the dark blue fabric. "Here's your keycard for the building, office, and lab."

"Thanks."

Payton squeezed Dr. Moore's arm. "I'm leaving you in good hands, Samantha. I'll swing by later today and see if you need anything."

"Thank you," Dr. Moore said.

Payton left and Kade indicated the chairs by the large windows. Dr. Moore made her way toward them. "What an amazing view."

"Yes." Kade had a few precious seconds to study her before she took a seat. He figured she was at least as tall as his sister, maybe a little taller. She was slender, and she carried herself with modesty. He could tell immediately she was shy, but exuded quiet grace.

"How was your weekend, Dr. Moore?" he asked.

"It was nice." She smiled.

"Did you explore the city at all?"

She shook her head. "Ah, no. I didn't get a chance. I was reading... and sleeping."

"Did you sleep on the plane?"

"Sort of."

He frowned. "I gave instructions for you to be booked in first class."

"Oh, I was, Dr. Gunnach. I just didn't sleep much." She blushed. "Excitement and all."

Kade got the impression she was holding something back, but didn't press. "I trust Duncan provided you the information about the position and our expectations?" he managed.

"Yes. I went through everything."

"Do you have any questions?"

She shook her head. "Not yet."

"Would you like to see the lab now?"

"Yes, please."

Kade rose to his feet and followed her down the hall and out to Anna's desk.

"Shall I show Dr. Moore her office?" Anna asked.

Kade shook his head. "No, thank you, Anna. I'll take care of that."

Anna covered her shock well, but perhaps not as quickly as he would have liked.

Kade had told her that he wanted to spend no more than five minutes speaking with the new researcher and then she was to come and rescue him. He'd told her he wanted her to show the new doctor to her office and to introduce her to someone who could give her a tour of the lab.

Someone who wasn't him. However, the moment he saw Samantha, that plan had gone out the window.

* * *

As Dr. Gunnach escorted her through the lab, Sam felt her body and mind react in a way she'd never expected. Gone was the nervousness she usually felt with strangers, replaced with an easy banter that had only ever been possible with her family and Pepper. This was the second man in less than a week that she'd felt at ease with.

No, that wasn't entirely true. She wasn't completely at ease with Cole. But with Dr. Gunnach, she was.

She wasn't sure if that was a good thing or not.

Maybe it's Scotland.

After touring the lab, Dr. Gunnach led Sam down a long hallway, pushing open another ornate mahogany door. Her name was printed on a plaque on the wall next to it. He stepped back so that she could precede him inside.

Sam took in the large room that would be her office. It was surprisingly bright; not at all what she'd imagined would be more like a medieval dungeon. Rectangular windows ran the length of one wall, butting against the ceiling, letting in an abundance of natural light. A large mahogany desk, similar to the one in Dr. Gunnach's office, sat in the center of the room, facing the door. Two overstuffed chairs were settled in the corner with a round table in between them. Bookshelves took up the wall behind the chairs and were already partially filled with medical journals. Overall, the office was cozy and welcoming while still retaining its professional air.

"I hope your office is to your liking," Dr. Gunnach said as he waved his hand toward her desk.

She set her purse and coat on one of the chairs. "It's beautiful."

"Our IT department will familiarize you with your laptop tomorrow morning, if that's acceptable. I thought you'd want a day to organize your equipment and make yourself comfortable."

Sam smiled. "Thank you, Dr. Gunnach."

"Kade, please."

"I don't think so."

"Why not? We are not so formal here."

Before she could respond, her office phone rang. "Work starts immediately, it would seem." She picked up the phone. "Samantha Moore."

"Dr. Moore, it's Anna. Is Dr. Gunnach still with you?"

"Yes, Anna, he is. Just a minute, please."

Samantha handed Dr. Gunnach the phone. She explored her office further, but when she noticed Dr. Gunnach had lowered his voice, she stepped outside to afford him some privacy. She made her way to the lab, using her new keycard to enter. There were other technicians in the room next to her, separated only by glass. With a staff of six, she'd have her hands full. She slipped her lab coat on—her name was already embroidered across the pocket—and began to go through the file cabinets.

"You're the new doctor, eh?"

Sam turned to the sound of the new voice and her nervousness came again in droves.

Nope, Scotland is of no help.

A large man, stocky and built like a wrestler, stood in the doorway. His dark red hair was trimmed short and he leaned against the threshold, his lab coat opened to reveal dark trousers and a green ribbed sweater. He was handsome, but he also scared her a bit. He was formidable in his gaze, and Sam slid her hands into her lab coat pockets, lest he see them shaking.

She forced a smile. "Yes. I'm Samantha Moore."

"I'm Angus McFadden."

"McFadden? Are you related to Payton?"

"Aye. She's me sister." He pushed away from the doorway and came toward her. "Ye've your work cut out for ye."

"So I've been told. Do you work in the lab as well?"

"I'm the one ye replaced, lass."

Sam swallowed. "Oh. Sorry."

He smiled. "Don't be."

"Angus?" Sam's eyes shot to Kade, who gave Angus a warning glare as he made his way to her. "Did you need something?"

Angus grinned. "No. I was just introducing myself to the new researcher."

Kade positioned himself in front of Sam. "I thought we'd agreed on an introduction at lunch."

"Aye," Angus said. "But I'm here now."

Standing behind Kade, Sam couldn't see what was going on, so she stepped to her right. By the expression on Angus's face, whatever was transpiring between the two men didn't look positive. Her heart started to race again.

"I'd like you to give Dr. Moore some time to acclimate to the lab, Angus. You can speak to her at lunchtime," Kade instructed. "Or tomorrow."

"I don't mind, Dr. Gunnach." Sam forced herself out from behind Kade and held her hand out to Angus. "It's nice to meet you...I'm sorry, what should I call you?"

He grasped her hand and smiled. "Call me Angus. We'll be working closely together, after all."

Kade's body shifted. "'Dr. McFadden' will suffice, I think."

Sam let out a snort...in her head. She'd never disrespect an employer out loud. She couldn't understand why Kade insisted on a formality he had just said his employees didn't observe, but as her heartbeat returned to normal and Angus left the lab, she decided to choose her battles. Arguing with Dr. Gunnach would not be a good start to her new job.

"I apologize for Dr. McFadden, Samantha. He can be overbearing and rude," Kade explained.

"He was fine." She glanced up at him. "I didn't realize I was replacing someone."

"Aye. Sort of. Dr. McFadden had asked to have a go at finding a solution to our problem, but he's not a researcher, and his specialty certainly isn't blood. He's engaged to my sister. I'm sorry, does he worry you?"

"Not at all," she lied. "I just wanted clarification."

"He won't be a problem. Don't give it another thought."

Sam smiled. "Where would you like me to start?"

Kade led her to the bank of refrigeration units and explained the contents to her—blood samples, along with tried and failed test medications.

"What am I looking for?" she asked.

"That's why you're here. We're not entirely sure. We know there's something blood-related, but not certain what."

"Ah. Okay." Sam pulled her hair into a lab net and slid her hands into latex gloves.

Kade watched her.

"I generally like to work alone," she said. "Fewer distractions."

He smiled. "I'll leave you to it, then."

She nodded and waited for him to leave. It took a minute, but he finally strode out of the lab. Sam forced herself to focus on the work at hand and not the man whose presence made her feel safe.

* * *

Kade kept his rage tempered until he stormed past Anna's desk and slammed his office door. Picking up the phone, he punched in Angus's number.

"Angus here."

"Get your bloody arse to my office! Now!"

Angus chuckled. "I knew it."

"Don't. You're on my last nerve, Angus."

"Aye. Shall I walk in, or would you like me to knock?"

Kade slammed the phone back on the cradle and yanked his office door open. "What the hell were you thinking scaring her like that?"

Angus stepped inside. "Scare her? What do you mean, scare her? I didn't mean to scare her. I just wanted to see what all the fuss was about."

"Did Duncan say something?" Kade snapped. "I'm going to kill him."

"Of course not." Angus held his hands up in surrender. "Fiona said you'd spent an exorbitant amount to get her here. I honestly thought she'd be some matronly woman with thick glasses and an overbite."

Kade swore and tried his best not to hit his soon-to-be brother-in-law. Most of the time, Angus's digging didn't bother him. They'd be friends even if Angus wasn't to be bound to his sister, but today, Kade's emotions were in a tailspin.

"Relax, Kade."

"You're to keep your distance, Angus."

Angus laughed, which only made Kade angrier.

"How am I supposed to assist her if I keep my distance?"

Kade's emotions calmed again just as his phone rang. He picked it up, grateful for the interruption. "Kade Gunnach."

"Hi. It's Sam...um...Dr. Moore. I'm sorry to interrupt."

"How can I help you?"

"I've found something and I'm wondering—"

"I'll be right down." Kade hung up and glared at Angus. "She's found something."

"Already?"

"Aye. We'll pick this conversation up later. After I remind my sister about keeping her mouth shut."

Angus scowled. "Watch your tone, Kade. You may be my chieftain, but you'll not insult my woman...even if she is your sister."

Kade shrugged, his earlier anger gone.

"Would you like me to come with you?" Angus asked.

Kade shot him a look that spoke volumes.

Angus grinned. "Right. You need to approach your mate carefully."

"Ye'll keep your thoughts to yerself, Angus McFadden. And ye'll not repeat any of this conversation to my sister. *Or* my brothers." Kade's brogue deepened when he was upset, and there was no doubt he was on his way again.

"They're gonna know as soon as they see you with her," Angus said. "I won't have to say a word. They'll feel it."

Kade's phone rang again and he sighed as he picked it up. "Kade Gunnach."

"Hi again," Sam said, her sweet voice soothing the rest of his dissipating irritation.

"I was just leaving."

"No, that's why I'm calling," she said, her voice shaky. "You don't need to come down here. I've been looking through the blood samples in the cooling unit, and I was just wondering if you might have access to fresh samples. I want to compare."

"I can get them."

"That would be great. I can't do much more in the lab right now, so IT has agreed to get me hooked up today."

"Excellent," he said, somewhat distracted by Angus grinning like an idiot.

"Thanks," she said. "Okay...bye."

The phone disconnected and Kade hung up.

Angus laughed. "You're done, brother."

Kade ignored him. "Where's Fiona?"

"She's with your mother."

"Damn it."

"Why?" Angus asked.

"I need a blood sample." He picked up his phone. "Anna? Find Payton for me, please."

"Would you like her in your office?"

"Aye," he said and hung up.

"What do you need Payton for?" Angus asked, his eyes narrowing.

"I told you. I need a blood sample."

"So you're going to use my sister as a bloody pin cushion? You know how she feels about needles."

Kade set his blood-drawing equipment on the table by the window. "Without Fiona close, I need another female, Angus. It's either my sister or yours."

"You have over a hundred of our people employed in this building alone."

Kade crossed his arms. "Are you questioning my judgment?"

Angus dropped his head. "No sir."

A knock at the door produced Payton McFadden. She didn't hide her surprise at the sight of her brother and Kade together. "How are the bulls today?"

"Payton," Angus warned.

"That good, eh? I can feel your irritation from the other side of the building, Angus. What did you do this time?"

Angus glared at her.

"Payton, I'm hoping I can take your blood," Kade interrupted.

"Don't you have quite a bit of it downstairs?" she asked.

"Aye, but Dr. Moore has asked for a fresh sample, and since Fiona's not close by, it falls to you, I'm afraid."

"Will she know it's mine?"

Kade shook his head patiently. "No. It'll be strictly confidential."

She bit her lip. "Okay."

Kade smiled. "I'll be gentle, lass. I promise."

"I'll just give Duncan a quick ring and let him know I'll be here for a bit."

"Anna already did," Kade said.

"Of course she did. All right." She took a seat and rolled up her sleeve.

"Did you eat?" Angus asked.

Payton rolled her eyes. "I know the rules, Angus. Of course I ate."

"You say that like you're a prisoner being forced to do something you don't want to," Kade accused.

Payton lowered her head in contrition. "Fyrirgefðu, höfðingi."

Kade lifted her chin. "No apology needed, Payton. You're not in trouble. I just hope you know the rules are in place to protect you."

"Aye," she whispered.

Kade washed his hands, slipped on gloves, and went about preparing Payton's arm for the needle. "Do you want to lie down?"

She shook her head. "No. I'm fine."

Kade took three vials. Angus hovered, but that was to be expected. He and Angus were more similar than Kade would like to admit. Over-protective to a fault.

Payton was a little woozy, so Kade insisted she eat something and rest until she felt better. He slid the vials into his pocket. "I have a change to Dr. Moore's living arrangements."

Payton blinked up at him. "Oh?"

"I'd like her moved to 3200."

Payton coughed and then swallowed quickly, her shock unmasked. "But that's the flat across from yours."

"Aye."

She glanced at her brother and then back at Kade before lowering her head and nodding. "I'll take care of it."

"Tomorrow at the latest."

"*Já, herra minn.*" (Yes, my lord.)

"Now, I'll let your brother take you to his office where you can recuperate."

She nodded and rose to her feet, a slight sway the only indication she felt additional effects from the blood donation. Angus wrapped his arm around her waist and assisted her from the office.

Kade locked his door and made his way downstairs, his mood improving with every floor closer to Samantha. He stepped out of the elevator and toward Sam's office. He was not prepared to see Alexander Baird leaning over Samantha, laughing at something she'd just said.

Hann mun ekki snerta þig. (He will not touch you.)

CHAPTER FIVE

Sam heard an angry voice in a foreign language push against her mind, and she started. She looked up to see Kade standing in her doorway and then glanced at Alex, who had literally jumped away from her.

"Dr. Gunnach? Is everything okay?" she asked.

"I have those samples for you," he said as he smiled at Alex.

Alex lowered his eyes and then his head. "Samantha…I mean, Dr. Moore's computer is all set up and fully accessible."

"Excellent, Alex," Kade said. "Is that everything?"

"Yes."

"Right. I'll come by and visit with you later."

Alex's body stiffened. "Aye. Thank you."

Sam frowned. She'd just been joking with Alex—something she found hard to do—but he'd put her at ease immediately, and now he stood like a reprimanded child and wouldn't even look at her. He slunk out the door and Sam stared up at Kade. "What was that all about?"

"Hmm?"

"You scared the poor man half to death," she accused.

Kade smiled, his face softening, and Sam's insides seemed to melt. "I didn't mean to scare him. I'll be sure to apologize." He held up three vials. "I have that sample for you."

"Excellent." She took them from him and headed to the lab.

Kade followed.

"You don't have to come with me, Dr. Gunnach. I'll call you if I find anything."

"Kade."

"I'm sorry?"

"I told you to call me Kade."

"I don't think that would be appropriate." Sam smiled at him over her shoulder. "Dr. Gunnach."

He raised an eyebrow. "It's almost time for lunch."

She checked her watch. "In thirty minutes." She waved the vials. "I need to look at these now or they'll be useless."

He nodded, but his expression was one of confusion. "I'll see you shortly, then."

"One more question," she said. "Are these from a patient I already have a sample from?"

"Aye. The number is on the vials. You can match them with the refrigerated samples."

"Thanks."

Sam stepped into the lab and heard the door close behind her. She felt Kade watching her, which just drove home how insane she felt. How could she possibly *feel* him watching her? She shook off her thoughts and got to work.

* * *

Kade left Samantha in the lab and headed toward IT. The appearance of Samantha Moore had certainly turned his world upside down. Not just because she didn't seem to be intimidated by him, but because he'd given up any thought of finding his mate years ago. He knew Fiona was going to push this new development as far as it would go; he just hoped she wouldn't force something before Samantha was ready.

Kade entered the IT department and headed toward his destination. Several people appeared both surprised and a little nervous to see him. They stood and lowered their heads. Kade had only once stepped foot into their corner of the building, to physically escort someone off the property. But that was years ago, and long before he'd put Alasdair in charge of security.

As soon as Alex saw Kade, he stood and moved from behind his desk. His eyes and head lowered as he waited for his chieftain.

"I trust my thoughts are known," Kade said.

"Já, herra minn."

"Excellent. You're doing a great job. Keep it up."

"Þakka þér herra." (Thank you, sir.)

Kade smiled and left the department. He checked in on Payton and found that she was already back at her desk, sorting out Samantha's new apartment. Angus had provided her with blood-clotting medication, which worked faster than expected.

As he made his way to his office, he was intercepted by Shannon Fraser. Anyone looking on would have thought they met accidentally, but something in Kade had shifted, and he now saw her for exactly what she was. A manipulator.

"Shannon, how are you this fine morning?" he asked.

"I'm doing well, Kade," she purred. "Do you have a few minutes?"

"I'm just on my way to my office. I have a meeting shortly."

"Perfect. I'll come with you. It won't take long."

He kept his irritation buried and led her to his office, passing a grinning Anna on the way. How had he not noticed his assistant's eagerness before when it came to Shannon? She was her niece, after all. Kade sighed. He needed to make some changes.

"That's not a good sound," Shannon said as he pushed open his office door. "Is everything all right?"

"Yes, just a lot of things on my plate at the moment."

"Anything I can help with?"

"No. We have it under control."

"Well, you be sure to let me know if I can assist."

Kade forced a smile. "What did you need, Shannon?"

"It's more about what you might need."

"Oh?"

She ran a fingertip across his desk and sauntered to the windows before turning to face him. "I know you have the shareholders' dinner at the end of the quarter, and I also know you hate to attend alone, so I'm offering my services."

Kade leaned back against the desk and crossed his arms. "Your services?"

"Aye. We make a great team, Kade, and I could make you look good in front of the men who hold stake in the company."

"I don't need you to make me look good, Shannon."

"Everyone needs an edge, Kade. Even you."

"I appreciate your offer," Kade said as he pushed away from the desk. "However, I believe Con will be attending with me."

Her lip popped out in a mock pout. Some men might have found it sexy. Kade found it irritating.

"If you change your mind, you will let me know, won't you?"

"I won't change my mind." He motioned to the door. "Now, I must get to my lunch meeting."

"Oh, are you introducing the new researcher to everyone today?"

"Aye."

She closed the distance between them and reached out to squeeze his arm. "Is there room for one more? I'd love to meet her as well."

He disengaged from her grip. "For what purpose?"

Shannon chuckled. "You sound suspicious. I've worked here as long as anyone, and I'd be happy to show her around, or just help as questions come up."

He paused for a few seconds. She *had* worked for him for a long time. In fact, from the moment the company was started. She was a wealth of knowledge and experience and would be a good resource.

"All right, Shannon, you may join us for lunch."

"Excellent. I'll see you soon."

She left his office and Kade checked his watch. He grinned and called Anna to let her know he'd collect Samantha and meet everyone in the executive dining room.

Kade made his way to the elevators, passing Anna on the way, still chatting with Shannon. He waved his access card over the electronic pad and pressed the button for the basement. He and his brothers held special "keys" that meant they could bypass any stops on their way to whichever floor they chose.

When the lift arrived at the lab level, Kade checked Sam's office. Finding it empty, he looked in at the lab and saw Samantha's head bent over her microscope and her mouth pressed into a thin line in obvious concentration. Kade hated to interrupt her, but missing lunch wasn't an option here.

"Hi." She glanced at him and then back at the microscope. "Is it lunchtime already?"

"Aye. Did you do your comparison?"

She straightened and nodded. "Yes. But now I'm just more confused."

"How so?"

She sighed. "The blood doesn't match."

"What do you mean?" he asked, intrigued.

"Just a second." She pulled the slide from the microscope, and after notating something in a file, she placed the glass in a box. Once she finished, she pulled off her gloves and hair covering.

Kade fisted his hands behind his back in an effort not to run his fingers through the glorious tresses now cascading down her back.

She waved him over to the computer terminal in the corner of the lab. "Let me show you what I found." She tapped her fingers over the keyboard and then stepped back. A split screen showed two blood samples. "When I looked at the fresh sample, that's the one on the left, the platelets aren't doing what they're supposed to. So that would lead me to believe the patient's blood doesn't clot correctly."

"Right."

She pointed to the one on the right. "But the one that was refrigerated looks perfect. Except for the faint blue sheen."

"Blue sheen?"

"It's strange." She sighed. "I probably just need to recalibrate the microscope."

Kade stared at her and couldn't stop his smile. She was staring at the screen, her mouth puckering into an adorable "O" that made him want to kiss her until she couldn't breathe.

"But I do think we'll need a few more samples," she said. "I'm sorry."

"That won't be a problem. We can do that over the next week or two."

She nodded. "Good. I'd like to take the samples myself, if you don't object. I don't want the chance of anything going wrong."

That posed a potential problem. Until she knew and accepted the truth about him and his people, he wouldn't be able to trust she'd keep the differences in the blood secret, but Kade nodded anyway. He'd talk with his brothers and they'd come up with a solution.

"Are you ready for lunch?"

Sam wrinkled her nose. "I feel like I just ate, to be honest."

"We try to adhere to a strict meal schedule here. You'll get used to it."

Sam hung her lab coat on a hook. "At this rate, I'm going to need to run an extra six miles to work off the calories."

Kade thought she could stand to gain a few pounds, but didn't voice his opinion. He held the lab door open for her and followed her to her office.

"Do I need to bring anything with me?" she asked.

"No. We'll be eating in the executive dining room."

She chuckled. "You have an *executive* dining room?"

Before he could comment, her cell phone buzzed. "Excuse me." She pressed the answer button. "Pepper? Everything okay?"

What kind of a name is Pepper?

"It's good," Samantha continued. "I'm actually headed to lunch, can I call you later? I know I don't. Long story. Yep. Yep, exactly. Okay. Bye." She smiled up at Kade. "Sorry. That was my friend, Pepper. I don't usually take personal calls at work, but we've been having a difficult time connecting since I arrived."

"Pepper?" Kade raised an eyebrow. "That sounds like such an American name."

Samantha laughed, a musical sound that caused a physical reaction within Kade. "I know. Her real name is Persephone." She gasped and slapped her hand over her mouth.

"What's wrong?"

She shook her head and groaned. "I can't believe I just told you that. I have never ever told another soul, not even my brother."

Kade's heart stuttered and he took a deep breath. "It'll be our secret."

Sam grinned. "Thank you. You may have just saved my life."

He laughed.

"No, really. Pepper would *kill* me if she knew I told anyone!" she said.

"I'll keep that in mind."

* * *

After locking her office, Samantha followed Dr. Gunnach to the top floor. She wondered when the white coats would arrive to take her away. I mean, really. Aliens must have invaded her body, because she just didn't act like this! She didn't tell long-kept secrets to strange men, and she certainly didn't turn into a puddle of goo every time one of them smiled at her.

"Does your friend like pomegranates?" Kade asked.

Sam's eyes widened. "You know your ancient mythology, I see."

He smiled. "You could say that."

"She used to. But I've ruined that for her, I'm afraid."

"How?"

"Whenever I find anything pomegranate related, I buy it for her. We've been friends since second grade, so I've given her a lot of pomegranate candles, pictures, mugs, jewelry. You name it, I've given it to her. When people see her collection, they assume she must love them, and they buy her the fresh fruit when it's in season. She actually hates the taste."

"I suppose if she were to admit her distaste, people would ask her why in the world she collects them, and that would mean she'd have to tell them her real name, eh?"

"You're quite intuitive, Dr. Gunnach."

He sighed. "Kade, please."

She lowered her head. "I couldn't."

"Yes. You absolutely could." The gentlest touch on her arm caused a jolt of energy to run through her and she looked up at him. He smiled and she bit the inside of her cheek in an effort not to sigh like a star-struck teenager.

Sam wondered how she could possibly call the sexiest man she'd ever met by the sexiest name she'd ever heard and not be a blithering idiot whenever she said it out loud. "I'll tell you what. When there's no one around, I'll call you Kade, but since I haven't heard anyone else do it, I just don't feel comfortable doing that publicly."

"Several people call me Kade. My brothers work here on occasion, along with Angus, and a few others."

She rolled her eyes. "Well, obviously your family would, but so far, I haven't heard anyone else in the office call you anything other than Dr. Gunnach, so I won't either. As for me, you have free rein to call me Samantha or Sam…as does Angus…and anyone else in the office."

Samantha felt his response, and didn't need to look at his face to know what he would look like. It was as if a jungle cat were holding back the need to strike.

She glanced up at him and he smiled, so she smiled back. Maybe she was wrong. The elevator doors opened and she stepped into a lobby of sorts. She felt the soft touch of his hand on her lower back and the words "*ástin mín*" floated in her mind.

"Did you say something?"

Kade shook his head, but his expression was one of mild surprise as he dropped his hand and nodded toward a set of double doors. "This way."

Sam followed Kade to the large doors and he used his keycard to gain entry. He pulled open a door and waited for her to precede him inside. A small group of people mingled around the room, including Payton, who smiled and made her way toward her. "Hello, Saman—Dr. Moore, how has your first day been so far?"

"Quite good." Sam smiled. "Thank you for asking."

"Why don't I introduce you to everyone?" Kade suggested.

Payton lowered her eyes and stepped away from Sam. Sam couldn't help but reach out and give her arm a squeeze. Payton caught her eye, her expression one of shock. Sam smiled and waited for her to smile back before following Kade to the rest of the group.

Sam couldn't figure out why everyone was so afraid of Kade. As she took in the people in the room, they all had the same reaction to him. First they lowered their eyes and then they lowered their heads. It wasn't until Kade was speaking directly to them that they'd engage with him. They didn't have any issues interacting with each other, but there was something different about Kade.

Then Sam caught sight of one of the most stunning women she'd ever seen. Tall, with long blonde hair, she didn't seem at all intimidated by Kade. She wore an obscenely tight mini-skirt that showed off perfectly shaped legs, and four-inch heels that bordered on hooker shoes.

The woman smiled, her eyes lingering on Kade for several seconds, and then she focused on Samantha and stepped forward. "You must be our new researcher," she said. "Kade's told me a bit about you. Welcome. I'm Shannon Fraser. I understand you're American. I have always wanted to visit. It seems so…I don't know, what's the word? Unrefined? As though it's waiting to be discovered."

Sam tried not to smirk. "I believe Columbus beat you to it."

"I suppose he did." Shannon let out a forced laughed as she held her hand out to Samantha. "It's nice to meet you. That's what you Americans say, isn't it?"

Condescending much?

Sam shook her hand and tried to appear genuinely happy to meet her. Her nervousness came back in droves. "It's nice to meet you too."

Kade's hand fluttered across her lower back and Sam felt instantly at ease again.

"Dr. Moore, this is Brodie, Connall, and Fiona. Unfortunately, we're related," Kade said.

Brodie scoffed. "Only when we choose to acknowledge you."

Fiona wrinkled her nose. "Speak for yeself."

Connall laughed as he held his hand out. "Ignore them, Dr. Moore, they might go on all day."

This one must be the charmer of the family.

Connall's hair was lighter than Kade's and swept away from his face. He reminded her of Dalton. Tall and lanky, fit but not too buff. She figured he had no problem finding women. His smile was one of practiced ease. Samantha shook his hand. "It's nice to meet you. Please, call me Samantha."

Connall glanced at Kade and then smiled down at her. "Samantha."

The brothers were all similar in looks—blondish hair, blue eyes, and chiseled jaws, although Kade and Connall looked the most alike. And they all looked young. Much younger than any of the men she knew who ran successful companies.

Brodie, whose hair was short, military style, looked like someone who wouldn't back down from a fight. He also looked like he spent hours in the gym. His shoulders were so wide, she imagined he'd have to turn sideways to get through a door.

Okay, maybe that was a little over-exaggeration, but still, he was huge.

Once Connall and Brodie were finished with their greetings, Angus laid his hand on Fiona's back and guided her forward. "Fiona is my ma—"

Kade cleared his throat. "Please, excuse me."

Angus raised an eyebrow and then focused back on Samantha. "Fiona is my *fiancée*."

Sam smiled. "It's nice to meet you."

"It's nice to meet you too," Fiona said. She had dark hair and was close to Sam's height. She was stunning, with her light complexion and flawless skin.

"Don't be intimidated by the Gunnach clan," Shannon said. "Their bark's worse than their bite."

Sam nodded, feeling like she was being sized up by the competition. *Did Shannon have some kind of a relationship with Kade?*

Kade stayed glued to Sam most of the hour. And Sam made sure she stayed close to Payton, mostly because she felt comfortable with her. Also present were a few of the lab technicians she'd met earlier that morning, and Anna joined them, along with Duncan.

Overall the group was friendly, but she felt their reserve as well. Even Payton, whom she'd had easy conversation with earlier, seemed to hold back and watch what she said to Samantha. Sam noticed that the majority of the group was careful about what they said to her and it put her more on edge…if that was possible.

Lunch wrapped up at exactly one. The group moved out of the room en masse and Sam followed. Kade wasn't far behind her and asked that she meet with him in his office instead of going straight back to the lab.

As the group waited for the elevators, Sam shook everyone's hands again. "Thanks for making me feel so welcome. I look forward to working with all of you."

"Will you follow me, please?" Kade asked.

"Of course," Sam said.

Kade guided her to his office and Anna stood with her head bowed behind her desk until they had passed. Kade stepped aside and let Sam enter his office first before closing the door.

"May I ask you a personal question?" she asked.

Kade raised an eyebrow. "You can ask me anything you like."

"Are you some kind of royalty?"

"Excuse me?"

She shook her head. "Sorry. Stupid question. Just ignore me."

Kade smiled. "It's not a stupid question, Samantha. It just caught me by surprise."

Okay, if a heart could stop beating and a person could still live, Sam figured it would feel a bit like how she was feeling at the moment. His lips saying her name just about had her sinking to her knees in a puddle of...well...goo. Goo was the only way to explain it. She felt gooey.

Sam smiled, or tried to anyway. "Never mind, don't pay any attention."

"How about I promise to answer the question, but a little later? When we know each other better."

That held promise.

Sam nodded. "So what did you want to see me about?"

"Honestly?" He grinned. "I just thought you might like a little time to decompress after being bombarded by all those people."

She let out the breath she didn't realize she'd been holding. "Oh, thank you."

Kade removed his jacket and laid it over one of the chairs. "I also thought you might like to know where the best jogging trail in Edinburgh is."

Okay, now she was a bit disconcerted by how little he missed.

She grinned. "I'd love it. I think I may need to start as early as tomorrow morning at the rate I'm going."

He led her to the bank of windows and pointed to the west. "That block of buildings there is where your flat will be. Just past that purview, you should see a trail in between a group of trees."

As she watched Kade point out various parts of the university campus and outbuildings, Sam couldn't help but notice his muscles ripple beneath his crisp white shirt. She suddenly wondered if her ridiculousness knew no bounds. She was noticing the man's physique, obsessing over it, really. She waited for a break in his information and made her escape. She needed to remember she was there to do a job, not fawn over the hot doctor.

CHAPTER SIX

Sᴀᴍ ʜᴇᴀᴅᴇᴅ ʙᴀᴄᴋ to her office and hit Pepper's number as she closed the door.

"Sammi?"

Sam sighed in relief. "Thank God."

"What's wrong?"

"Pepper, I'm in trouble."

"Why, what happened?" she squeaked.

"I think I might be falling in lust," Sam admitted.

There was a brief pause and then the sound of guffawing laughter and the whinny of horses in the background.

Sam dropped her head back against the door. "Pepper?"

"You totally freaked me out! I thought you were really in trouble!"

"I'm sorry. I just don't know what to do. I've never ever felt this way before."

"I know you haven't." Pepper was still laughing. "Who are you lusting over?"

"My boss!"

"Not the hottie on the plane?"

"Who? Oh, no. He's cute, but nothing compared to my boss. Pepper, he looks like he stepped off the cover of a romance novel, and on top of that, he has this incredible voice. He's Scottish, but there's something else there. If Alexander Skarsgård and Craig Ferguson had a baby, he'd sound like him. He has long hair and his name's Kade, for freak's sake. Kade! Did his parents do that to ensure every woman on the planet would want to procreate with him?"

"Long hair ala Brad Pitt in Legends?" Pepper asked, a hopeful sound in her voice.

"Think Keith Urban."

"Ooh…even better," she said breathlessly. "Holy cow. I might need to push my flight up."

"I'm losing it, Pep. Seriously, I think this might have been a mistake." Sam pushed away from the door and sat down at her desk. "I think I should come home."

"Don't you dare!" Pepper snapped. "You might be shy, Samantha Christene Moore, but you are no coward. Plus, this is your dream job."

Sam sighed. "I know, I know. I just don't know what to do. You know my rule."

"No mixing business with pleasure, yeah, yeah," Pepper droned. "Maybe throw that rule in the air and shoot the hell out of it."

"That's not a good idea."

"How do you know? Take a chance for once, Sam. What's the worst that could happen?"

"I could lose my job."

"One you don't actually need, right now, anyway. You have money saved, so if you had to come home and look for another job, you could."

Sam sighed. "True. I just don't know if I feel that brave."

"Brave, schmave."

Sam snorted.

"Does this fall into the category of being hit by a bolt of lightning wrapped in a rainbow?"

Sam couldn't stop a giggle. "Oh, Pep. Yes. Really, you should have been an ad-man."

"Let me tell you what you're going to do. You're going to throw caution to the wind and embrace whatever comes your way. Especially, if it's some hot Scottish guy."

"Pepper, he's not interested in me."

"How do you know? He could be feeling the same thing you are."

Sam let out a snort of derision. "Ever the romantic, I see."

"Do me a favor."

"What?"

"Just go with it. If it's meant to happen, then let it happen. Fall in love if you can."

"No! Falling in love with your boss is about as useful as a screen door on a submarine."

"Well, shut my mouth," Pepper retorted in a mock southern accent. "I mean, even a blind squirrel bumps into an acorn now and then."

"Pepper, stop. I just need to know what to do until you get here."

Pepper chuckled. "I just told you."

"You're no help."

"Okay, how about this?" The clank of a gate latching sounded in the background. "Try to get a glimpse of him naked. Maybe he's a troll under his clothing."

Sam couldn't stop the giggle that burst forth. "Oh, Pepper. I miss you."

"Just about nine weeks now, my friend. I'm counting down the days."

"Me too."

"Okay, I just put Jonesy to bed in his stall and now I need a glass of wine and a long hot shower to wash the horse off me."

"In that order?"

"Maybe I'll start and end with the wine."

"Nice. Thanks for the pep talk…pun intended," Sam said. "I'll Skype you over the weekend unless I have another crisis."

"Sounds good. Love you."

"Love you too." Sam hung up, dropped her cell phone into her purse, and pulled open her door. She nearly ran into Payton.

"Oh, sorry," Payton squeaked.

"My fault, Payton." Sam stepped back. "Come in."

"Thank you. I wanted to let you know your flat's ready?"

"My flat?"

"Sorry, your apartment."

"Really?" Sam's eyes widened. "I thought it was going to take two weeks."

Payton shook her head. "Well, there was a slight change. Dr. Gunnach had me make a switch."

"What? Why?"

Payton hugged her portfolio to her chest. "I'll let you ask him that."

Samantha smiled. "Okay."

"He asked me to see if you'd like to go on over now and make sure it's acceptable."

"I'm sure it'll be fine, Payton. I don't want to interrupt your day."

"You're not, and Dr. Gunnach insisted."

Who is this guy?

"Okay. If he insisted."

Payton peered down at her open portfolio. "If you like it, we'll organize your things to be moved from the hotel. Dr Gunnach said he's available to take you to dinner tonight if you'd like."

"Did he insist on that as well?"

Payton turned nervous eyes on her. "Oh, he would never, Samantha. Did I make it seem as though he would? I'm so sorry. He just wants to make sure you're comfortable."

"I'm sure he does, Payton. Don't worry." Sam shut down her laptop and set it in her leather bag, then gathered her purse. "I'm ready."

"Great. Alasdair is waiting downstairs."

Sam followed her from the office and locked it. "Are you sure this isn't keeping you from something far more important?"

"Right now, Samantha, you are my priority."

There was a finality in her statement. Like Samantha would have no chance of arguing with her or trying to make Payton change tack. They made their way downstairs and slid into the ever-familiar car that Alasdair stood sentry over.

They drove around the block and pulled up in front of the building Kade had motioned to earlier. "Okay, seriously, Payton, we could have walked."

"Well, you're free to walk on your own time."

"I take it running with me in the morning wouldn't be in your wheelhouse."

Payton's face contorted in horror. "I don't run. Not even when being chased."

Sam giggled. "I'll keep that in mind."

Payton grinned. "I have to run errands this afternoon, so Ali's going to wait here for me." She climbed from the car.

Sam followed.

The lobby of the building was somewhat unassuming, but the doorman was friendly and grinned at the ladies as he held the elevator door for them.

"Alan, this is Dr. Moore. She'll be on thirty-two," Payton said.

"Aye, Miss McFadden. I'll watch after her." He turned to Sam. "Welcome."

Sam smiled. "Thank you."

Once they stepped off the elevator, Payton led Sam down a long hallway. She slid the key into the lock and pushed open the door. "Here you go. If there's anything you need, let me know and I'll make a note."

Sam walked into the apartment and her mouth gaped open. Old met new in the large room. Floor-to-ceiling windows faced the university and the jogging path Kade had shown her earlier. The apartment was tastefully furnished with slim-lined and classic furniture. There were two bedrooms and two bathrooms. Payton called one of the bathrooms an en suite...the one Sam would have referred to as the master...but either way, the place had plenty of room for her and Pepper.

"It's beautiful, Payton."

"So you approve, then."

"Of course I approve. I can't imagine who wouldn't."

Payton smiled. "Excellent. Is there anything you'd like changed?"

Sam shook her head. "Nothing. It's exquisite."

Payton's phone rang and she answered it. "Hello, Dr. Gunnach. Oh, yes, we're here now. Yes, she's very happy. Yes, she is happy with it. I'm uncertain. Shall I ask her?" She pulled the phone away. "Would you like to join Dr. Gunnach for dinner?"

"I actually thought I might unpack and then order in. Is there a pizza place close by that delivers?"

"Yes."

"Great. Then I think I'll order in and take a rain check on dinner."

Payton nodded and relayed the message to Kade before hanging up. "Let's head on over to the hotel so we can get you checked out."

* * *

Samantha loved her new place. After she'd checked out of the hotel, her bags were delivered to the apartment and she went about unpacking.

Payton had left her the number to the local pizza place and once she'd taken a shower and dressed in sweats and a tank top, she ordered a large combination. Gluttony, she knew, but she was surprisingly hungry and at least she'd have some left over for dinner tomorrow night.

The doorbell pealed and Sam grabbed her purse and made a run for the door, her stomach growling. She pulled the door open as she rifled through her wallet. "What do I owe you?"

"Nothing."

Her head whipped up and she found Kade holding a pizza box and a bottle of wine, grinning on the threshold. He was entirely too gorgeous to be legal.

"What are you doing here?"

"Pizza delivery guy isn't working for you, eh?"

She laughed. "I don't tip unless you're wearing the hat."

"Ah. I'll remember that next time."

Sam waved her hand. "Come in."

She stepped aside and Kade walked in. Sam noted his jeans and soft long-sleeve tee. Totally opposite of the buttoned up suit he was wearing today. He was even better looking, if that were possible.

She glanced down at her sweats. New though they were, they were still sweats. She wore no make-up, and her hair was pulled up into a scrunchy. She groaned.

"Um, how did you…"

"Know what kind of pizza you liked?" he finished.

She raised an eyebrow. "I was going to ask how you got hold of my order, but we can go with that."

He grinned. "They accidentally delivered to me."

"Oh? I'm sorry. I must have given them the wrong address." She rummaged in her purse. "I wrote it down. It's somewhere in here."

Kade chuckled. "No, Samantha. I live here too."

She let out a nervous squeak and then cleared her throat. "Excuse me?"

"Down the hall. We're on the same floor."

She let out a relieved breath. "Oh. Right. Sorry. I didn't know."

"No worries." Kade glanced back at her. "Do you drink wine?"

She nodded as she closed the door. "Religiously."

"I hope you like red. If not, I have white at my place."

"No, I love red."

Sam followed him to the kitchen and watched as he pulled cabinet doors open looking for glasses and plates. Then it dawned on her that he'd hijacked her evening.

* * *

Kade watched her surreptitiously, hoping she wouldn't object to him being there. When Payton delivered the message that Samantha had wanted a quiet night in, he'd been philosophical about her decision...for about an hour. Then he'd realized he had no idea how he'd get through the evening without seeing her.

Payton mentioned she'd given Samantha the number of the local pizza delivery place, and he'd called the store at least four times before her order was confirmed. Once it was, he changed the delivery address to his and put his plan in motion.

He was somewhat taken aback by how fast his heart raced as he waited for her to open the door. He felt like a teenage boy with his first crush all over again. She'd answered the door, and he'd nearly bound her right then and there. She was stunning in no make-up and her hair pulled away from her face.

Kade went through the kitchen looking for what he needed. She watched him, but not in suspicion. More like curiosity with a little confusion mixed in.

He set the corkscrew on the counter and glanced up at her. "I'm sorry, Samantha, have I pushed my way in? Would you like me to leave?"

She seemed to contemplate the question for a few seconds and then she leaned over the counter and hummed. "That depends. If you leave, do I get to keep the wine?"

He shook his head. "No. It's a package deal."

She wrinkled her nose. "In that case, please stay."

Kade laughed. "I see where I lay in your list of priorities."

"What can I say?" She grinned and opened the pizza box. "I'm ruled by food and drink."

He grinned and poured her a glass of wine. She grabbed serviettes and took two large slices of pizza, setting them on her plate. Carrying her wine and food to the sofa, she set everything on the coffee table. Kade followed.

She sat cross-legged on the couch, her back against the armrest, and smiled. "So, is there something new with the blood samples?"

"Hmm?"

"Why you're here. I thought maybe you needed to discuss work."

He shook his head as he sat facing her. "Honestly, I just thought we could get to know each other."

"Oh. Okay."

"Is that all right?"

Sam reached for her plate. "I guess that depends on what that means. I don't like to mix business with pleasure, so to speak."

This was going to be harder than he thought.

"Well, we'll keep it professional, then." He sipped his wine. "You had some questions that I thought I might be able to shed some light on."

"The royalty one?" Sam grimaced. "Just ignore that. I'm chalking it up to my ignorance of the Scottish monarchy."

"No, you're not entirely far off."

"Oh, *really*?"

"My lineage is long and complicated."

"What do you mean, long and complicated?"

"Well, from what I understand, it started in Iceland over a thousand years ago and brought our clan, our family, here."

"You have roots that far back?" she asked.

He refrained from telling her that his lineage went back a lot longer than that. He wanted to ease her in. "Yes. Fiona's doing some research, and that's what we've found so far."

"Wow. History fascinates me."

"Me too."

"I can trace my ancestors back to the Civil War, I think, but that's not nearly as impressive." She sipped her wine. "Tell me about yours."

"I'll tell you mine if you tell me yours."

Samantha chuckled. "I'll tell you what I know, but seriously, I don't think it'll have much of a wow factor."

Kade shifted in his seat. She was going to drive him mad before he could bind her, he was sure of it. "Let me be the judge of that," he said.

"Okay. Fire away."

"Iceland was under Norwegian rule until 1380. That's when we came under the control of the Danish Crown. We were forced to give everything to Denmark, including our autonomy. The Danes didn't see us as worth protecting, so they didn't try to stop pirates from attacking our coastlines. In 1420, my ancestor chose to take the clan away. We sailed here."

Sam smiled. "I thought I heard an accent other than Scottish. Do you still speak Icelandic?"

He nodded. "I do. I also speak Gaelic and French."

"So you're a genius, then?"

Kade chuckled. "No, I just had very strict parents."

Sam bit her lip, making Kade want to kiss her. She was stunning. "Do you live near your parents?"

"My father has passed on, but my mother's a few hours away."

"Were you born here?"

"No. My brothers and sister and I were born in Iceland, although we've been here for many years. In fact, we changed our name shortly after arriving here. We used to be Haarde, but took on Gunnach as we acclimated to Scotland."

"Haarde? As in Haarde Pharmaceuticals?"

He nodded. "One and the same."

"Wow." Samantha cradled her wine glass in her palms. "I've always wondered what it would be like to be raised in a different country. I was born in the same town I just left. This is the first time I've been outside the States."

"There's comfort in that, don't you think?"

She shrugged. "I suppose. I tend to think of it more as boring."

He squeezed her knee. Perhaps too intimate, but Kade couldn't stop himself from touching her. "I can't imagine there'd be anything boring about you."

"Thank you." She smiled. "How does the clan thing work? Do you have a name and a tartan and everything?"

He chuckled. "We do. Clan Gunnach."

"Well, I feel dumb now."

"Why?"

"Logic would suggest your clan name would be your last name."

"Perhaps, but there are many other names within our clan."

Her eyes widened. "Oh, so your family is the head of the clan, so to speak?"

He grinned. "You could say that."

"Which means you *are* royalty...at least in your own mind," she joked.

"Exactly." He tipped his glass toward her. "Your turn."

"Hmm." Samantha leaned back against the arm of the couch. "I have a feeling there's more to the story, but what I remember is that my an-cestors were spread out over several states. When they say in movies and books that the Civil War was fought brother against brother, they were probably talking about my family. My great-great-great-great—give or take a few greats—fought for the South, and his brother fought for the North. They never healed the breach, and even though I have family in Pennsylvania, we've never met. The divide goes deep."

"Have you ever tried to reach out to them?"

"No. Isn't that terrible?" She sighed. "That's not one of my strengths, to be honest. Strangers intimidate me."

He felt her nervousness and couldn't stop laying his hand on her knee again. She calmed instantly and didn't object to his touch, so he kept it right where it was.

"I personally think your story falls into the wow factor category."

She blushed. "Well, thank you."

He lifted a photo frame from the console against the sofa. A young woman stood with a black horse covered in blue ribbons, her blonde hair pulled away from her face. Her smile was radiant. He turned the picture toward Sam in question.

"That's Pepper. At that particular show, she won first in every event, including dressage, which is her worst discipline." Sam smiled. "She was so happy."

"She and Connall would have much in common, I think."

"Oh? Does he ride?"

"Yes. He's a large animal vet. We refer to him as the other doctor Gunnach."

Sam smiled. "I'm sure he enjoys that."

Kade nodded. "He also breeds and trains Thoroughbreds. Mostly race horses, but his philanthropic activities involve anything of the equine variety. He's helped develop several medications for horses."

"Wow. Very cool. We'll have to introduce them, but we won't tell Pepper about the Thoroughbreds. She's an Arabian fanatic all the way." Sam chuckled. "She drilled that into me from a very young age."

"Do you ride?"

"I do. Well, I used to." Sam shifted in her seat. "I haven't for a while. As kids, we used to ride all the time, but then we grew up and high school kept us busy and then I went off to college. I rode mainly because Pepper did, and I enjoyed it, but it's her passion. I think she'd die if she couldn't ride. She also wants to be a vet one day. As well as ride for the Olympics and attend drama school."

"Really?"

Sam giggled. "Yes. She's the eternal six-year-old. I'm half expecting her to say she wants to win a pageant and be a pretty-pretty princess with a tiara. Her ability to dream while working her fingers to the bone is one of the things I love the most about her. It's virtually impossible to discourage her."

Kade smiled. "Tell me about the rest of the pictures."

Sam picked up a frame and pointed out her family, appearing a little contemplative as she settled it back on the table.

"What are you thinking?" he asked.

She smiled at him over the rim of her glass. "I'm thinking that you're different than many of the people I meet."

"How so?" he asked.

She shrugged, her face a lovely shade of pink. "I'm going to confess something that I may regret as soon as I've done it."

"You're safe with me, Samantha. Confess away."

"I feel totally comfortable with you."

Kade chuckled. "And that worries you?"

"A little, I suppose. You're the third person I've met since I arrived here that I don't feel nervous around, and that makes me suspicious." She cocked her head. "That's weird, isn't it?"

"That depends."

"On?"

"Who the other two are."

"What if you don't know them?"

"Hmm, then it's probably weird."

Samantha laughed. "Thanks."

He smiled. "I hope the other two are my employees. I want you to feel welcome."

"Oh, I do," she said. "And, yes, Payton is one of them. She's wonderful."

"She is invaluable to our company. I often threaten I'm going to steal her away from Duncan."

Sam pursed her lips. "What does he say?"

"It can't be repeated in a lady's presence."

"He has good taste." Sam sipped her wine.

"Who's the other one?" Kade asked, nervous that it might be someone he'd need to pull rank on.

"Oh, he's no one you know. His name's Cole. I met him on the plane."

Kade pulled his hand away. He didn't want her to feel the full effect of the jealousy rising in him.

"Are you okay?" Sam set her wine on the coffee table.

Damn it. He needed to get control of himself.

"Of course. Why?"

"I just got an unsettled feeling. It's strange."

"Strange?"

"Yes, I've had these little flutters of panic over the past few days, and I thought it was because I'm in a new place, but…" Sam rose to her feet and rubbed her forehead.

"Samantha? What's wrong?"

"Nothing. Everything. I'm sorry."

He stood and took her hand. "Tell me."

"I'm telling you entirely too much as it is. This *isn't* me."

He waited until he felt her heart calm and then he smiled. "When did you first have the panicky feelings?"

"When I arrived at the hotel on Friday night and this morning when I got to the office."

Friday night he'd argued with his sister and this morning, he'd had the heated discussion with Angus.

"Then there was right before I called you about the samples," she continued.

The news stunned him. Holding Samantha's hand and doing what only he could as her mate, calming her, he realized he'd underestimated his sister's connection to Angus.

She took a few deep breaths and he squeezed her hand. "Better?"

"A lot better." She raised an eyebrow. "I don't know how you just did that, but you seem to have the same effect on me that Valium does."

"Maybe we're simply connected on a different level than other people."

"*Right.*" Sam pulled her hand from his and took her seat back on the sofa.

He sat down as well and studied her. The depth of his emotion for her was humbling. Both Angus and his sister had described how it felt when they reached the age of mating and discovered they were to be bound to one another, but Kade hadn't grasped the intensity of Fiona's emotion. He realized how wrong he'd been to downplay her desperation.

No wonder he'd been willing to marry someone who wasn't his mate. He had no idea what it felt like to have one. Now was another story. He could never settle for anyone other than Samantha. His challenge would be not to rush her. He couldn't remember a time a *Cauld Ane* had been bound with a human, at least, not since he'd been old enough to pay attention to such things.

Her gentle touch nearly had him bounding off the couch. "Kade?"

"Hmm?"

"Where did you go?" She removed her hand from his arm.

"Sorry. I just remembered something I forgot to do."

"I hate it when I do that." She smiled. "Do you need to go?"

"Yes, I'm afraid I do." He rose to his feet again. "But we'll have to do this again soon."

She seemed to hold back something and he waited for her to quash his suggestion, but then she surprised him with, "That would be fun."

"I'll see you tomorrow then?"

She nodded. "Yes. I look forward to it."

He followed her to the door and leaned down, the desire to kiss her overwhelming, but he kissed her cheek instead and whispered, "*Draumur um mig, fallegt.*" (Dream of me, beautiful.)

"I don't know what that means, but it sounds incredible."

He grinned. "One day I'll tell you."

"Maybe I'll study Icelandic and figure it out," she challenged.

"If you want to learn, I'd be more than happy to teach you."

"I may take you up on that." She pulled open the door. "See you tomorrow."

"'Bye." Kade stepped into the hallway and waited for her to close and lock her door before heading to his flat. As he slid the key into the lock, he dialed Connall.

"It's happened," Connall said when he answered. "Samantha's the one."

"Aye." Kade entered his flat and pushed his door closed. "I'm in a pile of shite, Con."

"Why? Because your mate's an empath like me?"

"You picked up on that I see," Kade said. "But, no, that's not why."

His brother laughed. "I thought life was euphoric when you found your mate."

"Maybe. But what happens when your mate doesn't know she's your mate?" Kade countered.

"Good point."

"Do we know anyone who's bound a human?"

"Not off-hand. You'll have to ask Mum."

Kade groaned. "I'm not there yet, Con."

"You know Fiona's probably already told her."

"I know." Kade sighed. "But until I confirm it, she'll hopefully chalk it up to Fiona's desperate need to be bound."

"Well, then ask Fiona. She's spent hours in the archives."

"I suppose that's one way to get her speaking to me again."

"Certainly a more effective way, anyway."

Kade dropped his keys on the console. "She's going to want me to go faster with Samantha than I should."

Connall sighed. "She might surprise you, brother. You still see her as the ten-year-old girl in pigtails. Give her a chance and you'll see she's a great ally and friend, even if she's still our annoying little sister."

"You're right. I just get the brunt of her frustration most of the time."

"That's because you're the only one who can help her." Connall chuckled. "She's going to have every reason to make sure you and Samantha bond quickly, so she's going to be on her best behavior."

Kade rubbed his forehead. "*I* hope Samantha and I bond quickly, because I had a difficult time keeping my hands off her tonight."

"I don't envy you right now, I have to admit."

"I don't much envy myself." Kade flopped onto the sofa. "Hey, can you have Ali look into some guy named Cole for me?"

"Cole who?"

"Don't know. He was on the plane with Samantha. He sat next to her, apparently. She said she feels comfortable around him…" He had to stop himself from swearing as the jealousy rose.

"And you want her to feel a little *less* comfortable, right?" Cole finished.

"Aye."

"We'll get on it."

"Thanks. I'm going to call Fiona now," Kade said.

"Talk to you tomorrow…unless, of course, you need more of my wise words."

"No. Thank you. But don't worry, I'll take advantage of the fact that I have you here for the week. Once you go back to the horses, I'll lose you again."

Connall laughed. "Too true."

"Night." Kade hung up and dialed his sister.

CHAPTER SEVEN

SAM WOKE THE next morning before the sun rose. She was surprisingly awake as she pulled on sweats and prepared for her run. She discovered she'd missed a call from Pepper during her evening with Kade, but she hadn't heard her phone ring…*hmm, must've been too wrapped up in everything Kade.* She felt like she was falling hard and fast, and didn't like it, but had no idea how to stop it.

She'd expected him to kiss her when he left, but instead, he'd smiled a devilishly sexy smile and kissed her cheek. Sam had to bite her lip to keep from pouting. She couldn't remember the words he'd whispered, or she would have tried to look them up. So much for her hard and fast rule about dating the boss. She'd jumped at the chance of spending more time with him and couldn't wait to see him at the office.

The sound of traffic brought her back to the present, and she walked across the road and headed toward the jogging path, finding a lovely little bench she could stretch on. Footsteps sounded to her right, and she glanced over to see Cole coming toward her. She straightened, and tried to keep a perplexed look off her face.

"Hey you," he said.

"Hi," she said. "I didn't know you're a runner."

"Six days a week, if I force myself." He smiled. "I like to run before classes, so the concierge recommended this place. I came yesterday as well. Is this is your first day?"

She nodded. "My boss recommended it."

"It's a great trail," he said as he stretched. "Hey, did you check out already?"

"Yesterday. How come?"

"I called your room last night to see if you wanted to join me this morning, and they said they couldn't connect me. I asked if you checked out, but they wouldn't say."

She frowned. "That's weird. Why wouldn't they just tell you?"

"Maybe they think you're an international spy."

"Maybe they do." Samantha laughed.

"Do you mind if I join you?" he asked.

"Do you think you can keep up?"

"That depends." Cole raised an eyebrow. "Will you take it easy on me?"

"Nope," she said, and took off. She heard him laugh as he caught up to her. "Took you long enough."

They bantered back and forth for close to a mile before Samantha realized she was finding it difficult to run and talk at the same time. "Man, I'm outta shape."

"Maybe you just ate too much the other night," Cole said.

"Maybe. Could be how much I ate yesterday as well, and the fact I haven't had a decent run in over two weeks."

"What was yesterday?"

"Just a sec." Sam held her finger up and took a few deep breaths. It took a few minutes, but she finally got her second wind and felt like she wouldn't pass out. "Yesterday was my first day of work."

"Right. The 'wine and dine week,' as I like to call it."

Sam laughed. "Yeah, but on steroids. Seriously, these people eat like every two hours. I just can't keep up. You should've seen one of the assistant's faces when she found out I didn't have afternoon tea. I found a muffin on my desk ten minutes later."

"Wow."

"I know. She even came back to make sure I'd eaten it."

"Did you?"

"No. I couldn't. I was still full from lunch. She made me promise not to skip any more meals." Sam giggled. "Must be a Scottish thing."

"Must be," Cole said.

Samantha's phone buzzed and she unzipped her pocket, checking the caller ID without skipping a beat. She stalled and slowed to a walk. "Sorry, it's work."

Cole paced her. "No worries."

"This is Samantha."

"Good morning, Samantha, it's Payton."

"Hi."

"Are you all right? You sound out of breath."

"Yes, I'm fine. I'm on a run."

"Oh, I'm sorry. Our staff meeting was changed to ten instead of eleven and I wanted to make sure you knew. Shannon said she sent the information out yesterday afternoon via email, but that she hasn't gotten a confirmation from you."

Sam checked her watch. Seven forty-five. "I don't recall getting the email, Payton, but it'll be fine. I don't have anything else on my calendar that I'm aware of."

"Excellent. I'll let her know."

"Thanks for looking out for me," Samantha said. "I appreciate it."

"My pleasure. I'll see you later."

Samantha hung up and frowned.

"What was that all about?" Cole asked.

"Nothing. Just a miscommunication." Samantha sighed. "I should probably go."

"I'll go back with you."

She smiled. "Thanks, but I'm okay. You finish your run."

"Are you sure?"

"Of course."

"Okay. But let's get together this week."

"Okay. Where?"

"I found a great little American sports bar not far from here. I'll take you out for some beer and football," he said

Samantha nodded. "Sounds great. Call me and we'll figure it out."

He waved and took off. Sam walked to the entrance of the path, contemplating the missed memo. She didn't trust this Shannon character as far as she could throw her, but she figured this might be a battle she'd have to let go of.

She walked back to her apartment and got ready for work.

* * *

With the large grey clouds forming overhead, Samantha figured she'd probably need to buy an umbrella sooner rather than later. She chided herself for not bringing one. Luckily, she'd packed decent winter weather gear. She pulled on her beanie and matching scarf and shrugged into her dark green wool coat. After locking the apartment door, she pulled on her gloves and started toward the elevator. She stepped into the lobby and her heart raced when she caught sight of Kade. He was speaking with the doorman.

He was magnificent.

He glanced her way, almost as though he knew she was there, and smiled. A slow, let's-take-our-clothes-off smile. She bit the inside of her cheek, grimacing as she bit the same spot she'd bitten yesterday. Still, it kept her from letting out a squeal of excitement.

Kade excused himself from his conversation and made his way over to her. "Good morning, Samantha."

"Hi. How are you?"

"Better, now that I've seen you."

Sam let out a quiet snort. "Charmer."

"Where's your umbrella?"

"I completely forgot to bring one from home and haven't bought one yet. How soon will it rain, do you think?" As if on cue, the heavens opened and the rain came down in sheets. Sam frowned. "Well, that's just *great*."

Kade chuckled. "Lucky for you, I have one big enough for two."

"You walk to work?"

"Unlike Payton, I like to walk."

Sam raised an eyebrow, surprised he'd know that about an assistant.

He grinned. "Everyone knows her aversion to walking."

"Oh."

Once he guided her through the lobby and out onto the street, he opened the umbrella and held his arm out to her. She slipped her hand into the crook of his elbow and he pulled her close. "We're going to have to make a bit of a run for it," he said. "Ready?"

She nodded. "Ready."

They took off toward the Gunnach high-rise, ending up under the awning of the café within just a few minutes. Kade shook out the umbrella and grinned. "We made it."

Samantha laughed. "Yes, we did. You're a pro."

He opened the door to the café and waited for her to precede him inside. "I don't know about that, but keeping the beautiful woman next to me dry is a good motivation."

"You're really going to make me break all my rules, aren't you?"

Kade leaned down and whispered, "That's the plan."

A shiver stole up her spine, and she had to hold back the desire to kiss him in the middle of the small restaurant.

"Have you had breakfast?" he asked.

"Not yet."

"Neither have I. Will you join me?"

She checked her watch. "What about the staff meeting?"

"We have plenty of time. They also won't start without me."

"True," Sam said. "Yes, I'd love to join you."

Kade bought her breakfast, and they chose a cozy table in the corner to sit and eat. Sam tried not to notice his lips as he sipped his coffee and then smiled at her. She removed her coat in an effort to distract her thoughts.

* * *

Kade watched her as they ate. She looked like someone in a magazine, advertising the perfect American winter scene. She'd removed her black beanie and gloves when they entered the café, and as much as he loved the sight of her silken hair, the beanie was just so bloody adorable, he wanted to find an excuse to go back outside.

When she took off her coat, he had a moment of shock to see she was wearing a skirt quite similar to his tartan. If that wasn't some kind of a sign, he didn't know what was. And if there was anything sexier than a woman in tall boots and a short skirt, he'd like proof.

Payton had informed him that Sam had been on a run that morning when she'd called her, and he wasn't happy that she'd gone out so early alone. His next call had been to Alasdair to get a protection detail on her. He could potentially be overreacting, but once the clan figured out she was his mate, other people would as well. He'd taken care to rule differently than his father before him, but he didn't want to become complacent. "Kade?"

"Hmm? Sorry."

"Did you forget something again?" she asked.

He grinned. "No. I was actually trying to figure out the best way to get you to have dinner with me tonight."

Samantha raised an eyebrow. "You could ask."

Kade cocked his head. "Ah. That easy, eh? Right. Will you have dinner with me tonight?"

"No."

"What?"

Samantha laughed. "I said you could ask. I didn't say I'd agree."

"So, I'm back to my scheming then."

"That sounds ominous."

He squeezed her hand. "Only to you."

"We don't want that." She blushed and pulled her hand away. "Yes, I'll have dinner with you."

"Would you like me to cook for you, or would you rather go out?"

"You can cook?" she asked in delighted surprise.

"I can." He rose to his feet and held her chair for her. "You just tell me what you do and don't like."

"I like everything." Samantha stood and gathered her purse and outerwear. "But if you need time to plan, we can do it another day."

"Tonight will be perfect. I'll walk you to your office and we can go on up to the meeting together." She stalled and Kade found himself closing the distance between them. "Samantha? Are you all right?"

* * *

Samantha bit her lip and pondered the question. *Other than the fact that you're making me fall in love with you and that scares the freakin' pants off me? Yes, I'm fine.*

"I just don't want to keep you from anything. You must need to prep for the meeting, right?"

He shook his head. "Anna has everything under control. I'm yours for the morning."

Samantha forced a smile and nodded. "If you're sure."

He laid his hand on her arm and gently squeezed. "You want to run, don't you?"

She blinked in surprise. "You have no idea."

"Your fear is pouring off of you. Just relax and trust me."

"But I don't know you," she countered even as her panic began to fade.

"You know me well enough, Samantha. If you listen to your heart, you know you can trust me. It's important you don't sabotage your own feelings."

"Why is it important?"

"We'll talk tonight, all right?"

She took a deep breath and gave him a reluctant nod.

Kade's eyes bore into her. "Your mind is fascinating."

She frowned. "You acting like you can read my mind isn't making me want to trust you."

He chuckled. "Sorry. I'll stop now." He rubbed the arm he still grasped. "Calmer?"

"Yes." *Which doesn't make sense.*

"I know this doesn't make sense right now..."

She pulled away from his touch. "Okay, now you're just freaking me out."

"Why?"

He stared at her with such sincerity, she wasn't sure if she was being fair. But he seemed two steps ahead of her, and when she could focus logically, she knew something out of the ordinary was going on. She also knew she didn't think she could handle whatever it was.

"Samantha?" he pressed.

"Never mind. Let's just go."

"Would you rather meet me in the conference room?"

She grimaced. "Would that be okay?"

"Of course. Don't worry about this, all right? I'll explain everything."

He led her to the elevator bay and pressed the down button, waiting for her to step onto the elevator before pressing the up button. Samantha watched him as the doors closed, and her heart felt both bereft and nervous as she rode down to her office.

CHAPTER EIGHT

KADE BERATED HIMSELF as he made his way to his floor. He'd pushed too fast.

"Good morning, Dr. Gunnach."

"Good morning, Anna. Will you find Connall for me, please?"

"Uh, he's actually in your office, my lord."

"Excellent," Kade said, and stormed into his office.

"What's happened?" Connall asked as Kade slammed the door.

"Yer idiot brother's what's happened."

Connall laughed. "What have you done?"

"Doing. It's constant. Puttin' my bleedin' foot in me mouth is what I'm doing!"

Connall sat at the table by the window and waved his hand toward the other chair. "Calm yourself or Samantha's going to feel what you're feeling."

Kade dragged his hands down his face and nodded. "Bloody hell, Con. I had no idea it was like this."

"Do you want a change of subject?"

Kade dropped into the chair and sighed. "Please."

Connall slid a file toward him. "I found Samantha's Cole."

Kade couldn't stop a glare toward his brother as he opened the file. "He works for Fox Securities and is currently lecturing at Edinburgh."

"Aye," Connall said.

"Colton Drake." Kade went back to the file. "Shite, Con, could his name be any more stereotypical."

Connall laughed. "I thought it might be fake, but it's not."

"He's thirty-two, from Detroit, Michigan, and used to be a cop," Kade read. "What else?"

"That's just it. There's nothing else."

"What do you mean, there's nothing else?" Kade laid his hand on the folder. "That's impossible."

"Exactly. Alasdair's digging into it further."

"This stinks, Con."

"Yeah, I know. Hence, the reason Ali's digging further into it." Connall tapped his fingertips on the table. "There's something else."

"What?"

"Samantha. The word's beginning to spread."

"I figured as soon as Shannon saw us together, she'd know. I should never have let her come to the introduction lunch." Kade sighed. "I need to talk to Hamish about his sister. She needs to be leashed."

Connall's eyes widened. "I've never heard you speak so brutally."

"I want Samantha safe, and if Shannon can't keep her gossip to herself, she has the potential to do harm." Kade stood and faced the windows. "I think I'm going to need to move Anna."

"Really?"

"Aye. If Ármann gets wind of me mating with a human, we could have a few issues."

"But Anna's always been loyal."

"Aye, but she's also Shannon's aunt, and I can't take any chances."

"Who'll replace her?" Connall asked.

Kade raised an eyebrow.

"Duncan's not going to like that."

"I know, but we need to close ranks. Payton will be family and even if she wasn't, she's more trustworthy than any of us."

Connall nodded.

"Don't worry," Kade continued. "I'm not going to make any changes until after the stockholders' meeting, and I'll make sure Duncan's happy. What's the update on security?"

"Alasdair's got men on Samantha at all times now, but until you two are official, the danger is greater."

"I know." Kade's desk phone rang and he made his way to it. "Yes, Anna."

"Dr. Moore is asking to see you, but she doesn't have an appointment."

"Send her in. And in the future, Dr. Moore never needs to have an appointment."

"Aye sir."

Kade hung up and slipped the file into his desk drawer.

"I'll see you at the meeting," Connall said, and made his way to the door.

"Thanks, brother."

Connall opened the door just as Samantha raised her hand to knock, smiling at her as he ushered her inside. "Good morning, Samantha."

"Hi. Am I interrupting?"

"Not at all. I was just leaving." Connall made his exit and pulled the door closed.

Kade leaned against his desk and smiled. "Everything all right?"

Samantha pressed her lips into a flat line. "You tell me. I have that unsettled feeling again."

"Och, Samantha, I'm sorry."

"Were you arguing with your brother?"

He shook his head and held his hand out to her. "Not arguing with, just discussing something intense."

Samantha stayed put. "Oh."

He waved her over. "Come here. I won't bite." She stepped toward him, her hand shaking as she took his. Kade linked his fingers with hers and stroked her palm with his thumb. "We have so much to talk about."

"Clearly." Her face showed confusion as she looked up at him. "I just don't want to hear that every time I'm feeling unsettled or panicked, I'm going to have to hold your hand in order for the feeling to go away."

He smiled. "It won't always be like this."

"*What* won't always be like this?"

"This. The uncertainty and confusion of our acquaintance. We'll get to know each other and things will be calm."

She grimaced. "Why doesn't that give me any kind of comfort?"

His phone rang again and he let out a frustrated groan. "Tonight, we can talk uninterrupted until you're feeling calm...*without* holding my hand. All right?"

She nodded and he picked up his phone.

"The team is ready, Dr. Gunnach," Anna said.

"We'll be right there."

* * *

The staff meeting wrapped up and Samantha escaped to her office. As was her habit when she was deep in thought, she chewed the soft end of a ballpoint pen, which would render it useless within a few days.

Payton, Anna, and Shannon had been on hand to take notes and assist, as Sam was sure they did every week, but she couldn't help notice the curious stares from Anna...and the irritated ones from Shannon. Kade barely glanced at Samantha during the meeting and she didn't really have anything to add, so she didn't say much. She thought about calling Pepper, but a knock at her door put that idea on hold.

"Come in," she called.

Payton pushed the door open and stepped inside. "Hi."

"Hi. How are you?"

"Good. You?"

"Just dandy," Sam grumbled. "What can I do for you?"

"I brought you lunch," Payton said, and dropped a paper bag on Sam's desk.

"That's so sweet. You didn't have to do that."

"I also thought you might need a friend."

Sam dropped her pen on the desk and sighed. "And why would you think that?"

66

Payton shut the door and sat down. "Maybe because of the glares Shannon was giving you at the meeting."

"So it wasn't just me, huh?"

"Ignore her, Samantha. She's been sniffing after Kade for years, and he's rebuffed her at every turn. She can tell he…uh…likes you, so it's driving her mad. She's a nasty piece of work, but she has no power over you."

"I don't know why she's upset, Payton. I don't have any exclusivity when it comes to Kade, so I don't know why she'd even be worried."

Payton's eyes widened. "But you want it, right? The exclusivity?"

Sam shrugged. "I have no idea."

Payton smiled. "What can I do to help?"

"I think this is something I have to figure out on my own."

"I understand, but my door is always open, as they say."

"Thanks."

"One more thing," Payton said as she stood. "Should you need to pick something up from the market, please let me or Alasdair know. We can show you where the best shops are."

"Ooh, yes, please. I'd like to pick up a bottle of wine, if you can point me in the right direction."

Payton nodded. "I'd be happy to pick up whatever you need."

Samantha rolled her eyes. "You're spoiling me, Payton."

Payton chuckled. "Can't be helped. What would you like me to get?"

Samantha wrote down her favorites in order of importance and handed Payton the list. "If they don't have these, if you could ask the sommelier to recommend a red and a white that will go with everything, I'd appreciate it."

Payton took the list and smiled. "No problem. I'll bring them by your flat later if that works."

"That's fine as long as it doesn't interfere with your plans. You can bring them here as well. I can carry them home."

"My plans are to bring you wine. I'll see you later." Payton left her office and pulled the door closed.

Sam ate in relative peace and then made her way to the lab. She decided since she wouldn't be able to concentrate, she might as well observe her staff. She found them to be efficient and thorough, which didn't surprise her. Gunnach Pharmaceuticals was at the forefront of drug research.

Sam was surprised when the staff started to pack up for the day. She headed back to her office and found a gift bag sitting on her desk. She peeked inside to find a dark green umbrella nestled at the bottom underneath piles of tissue paper, and a card that had her name scrawled across the top. She opened the envelope and smiled.

In case I'm unable to keep you dry, this will have to do. K.

"Are you for real?" she said as she pulled the umbrella out.

"Is who for real?"

Sam let out a startled squeal as she turned to find Shannon Fraser in her doorway.

"Sorry. I didn't mean to alarm you," Shannon said with a smile.

A smile that looked more shark-like than human.

Samantha slipped the card into her purse and shook her head. "No problem. I was just packing up for the day. What can I do for you?"

Shannon sauntered in and sat down. "It's more what I can do for you."

"Oh?"

"Yes. With you being so new, I thought I could help you. I've known the Gunnachs for years. Kade and I, particularly, are extremely close, so should you have any questions, I'd be happy to answer them for you."

Samantha sat in her chair and forced a smile. She didn't really care at this point if it looked sincere. "That's so generous, Shannon. I appreciate that."

"It's my pleasure. Is there anything you'd like to know?"

"Not yet. I haven't really been here long enough to have questions pop up." Samantha rose to her feet. "But I'll certainly let you know if there is."

Shannon nodded as she also stood. "Please feel free to use me as a resource. I'll tell you everything you need to know. Kade and I have been *close* friends for years."

So you said.

"Thanks."

"I think he might like you," she continued.

"Oh?" Sam hoped she sounded nonchalant.

"I saw it at the meeting. Next he'll be asking you to have breakfast with him, and then perhaps he'll offer to cook for you. Something like that. It's his M.O."

How did she know? Did Kade tell her?

Sam let out a nervous laugh. "Good to know. Thank you." She gathered her coat and purse and guided Shannon out of the office.

"Do you have big plans tonight?"

Ooh, you just don't give up! Like I'd ever tell you what I'm really doing.

Samantha shrugged. "If you consider a pizza and whatever's on TV big plans, then yes, I plan to paint the town red."

"Perhaps one of these weekends, I could show you around Edinburgh. Once you've settled in."

Samantha locked her door and pulled on her coat. "That would be nice."

"Great. You just let me know what works and I'll set it up."

"Sounds good." They walked to the elevators and Sam hit the up button. "Are you heading out now?"

Shannon shook her head. "No, I have to meet with Kade in a few minutes."

The elevator arrived and Sam pressed the lobby button while Shannon pressed the top floor. Once the doors opened, Samantha forced another smile and stepped out. "Okay. You have a nice evening."

"Good night." Shannon waved and the doors closed.

Samantha shook off her irritation and started toward home. The rain had stopped, so she shoved her new umbrella in her purse and used the brief moment of exercise to push aside her insecurity. She didn't know how she was going to get through this dinner. She didn't know if she even wanted to.

When she arrived at her building, Alan greeted her with his familiar smile and held the door for her. "Miss McFadden dropped off a few things for you, Dr. Moore. Shall I have Jon carry them up for you?"

"I think it's just a couple of bottles of wine, which I'm happy to take up."

"Actually, ma'am, it's more like a case of wine." He led her to the security desk.

Jon, the young security guard, stood and smiled. Payton had told Sam that he was Alan's son and working to save for college. "Hello, Dr. Moore."

"Hi, Jon. My word," Sam said as she went through the bottles. Payton had purchased two of everything on the list. "She's thorough."

Alan chuckled. "That's one way of describing her."

"Yes, please bring them up when you have time." She checked her watch. "It doesn't need to be right this minute."

"I'm available now, Dr. Moore," Jon said. "I'm happy to follow you up."

"Okay. Thank you."

Samantha led Jon to her apartment and found an envelope taped to her door. She pulled it off and unlocked the door. Jon set the wine in the kitchen and then left Sam alone. She opened the note and smiled.

I've missed you today. Looking forward to seeing you at six. K

"You're killing me, Smalls," Sam groaned, and fired up her computer. Pepper was online, so Sam requested a video call.

"Hey, long-lost friend," Pepper said as she answered and adjusted her video camera.

"Hi."

"How's it going with Mr. Hottie?"

"I'm dying, Pepper. Seriously, this guy cannot be for real!"

"Why? 'Cause he has good taste and is falling madly in love with you?"

Samantha snorted. "He's not falling in love with me, but there's definitely something going on."

"But Miss Smarty Pants can't put it into a neat little pile that fits into one of her many compartmentalized boxes, right?"

"You got me."

"Well, I'd like to see you be messy for once. Find out more about him. You have *nothing* to lose, Sam."

"Except my sanity."

"Oh, honey, that was gone the moment you chose me as your friend."

Samantha laughed. "Good point. Okay, well, you better be available for sobbing sessions when this thing goes south."

"Way to stay positive." Pepper grinned. "But, yes, I'll be here whenever you need me. Now, is that what you're wearing to dinner?"

Samantha glanced down at her skirt and cardigan. "No?"

"Correct answer." Pepper tsked. "You need to be sexy girl. Not work girl. Wear the blue shirt and your Tommy Hilfiger's."

"Which blue one? I have two now, thanks to you."

"I was getting sick of the green. It was like your wardrobe was varying shades of a lawn. I was beginning to wonder if I should help you with your fashion or mow you."

Samantha laughed. "You are so out of control, Pepper!"

"Thank you, Scotland. I'll be here all night. Now, back to the subject at hand." Pepper grinned. "Wear the blue one that enhances the boobies."

Sam groaned. "Thanks for the reminder that I'm lacking in that department."

"Hey, you got the legs that go to the moon, and I got the jugs. We can't have it all, and believe me, I'd rather have your problem."

Sam sighed. "Okay. Hair up or down?"

"Definitely down."

"Good. I don't think I have the energy to "do" something with my hair."

"Says the woman who can step out of the shower looking like a model."

"This is why we're best friends." Sam giggled. "Oh! I keep forgetting to ask how work is now that you've taken on more hours."

"Oh, it's fine. I've been getting these weird anonymous gifts, though. Probably some whack-job wanting a free meal."

"Make sure you tell your boss if it gets to the stalking level."

Pepper laughed. "Not that he'd care, but I'm sure it's nothing."

"Okay, I better go. I'll give you a full report when it's over."

"You better."

"Love you."

"Love you too," Pepper said, and the call disconnected.

Kade glanced at the clock for possibly the tenth time. Five fifty-two. His heart raced in anticipation of the knock on his door as he paced the floor, looking for anything he might have missed. His place was immaculate. He'd brought his housekeeper in for a third time that week to make sure, and he'd taken care with the table setting, but he was still nervous.

Payton had assisted in purchasing everything he needed for what he hoped would be an impressive meal, and he'd made sure his wine room was stocked with Samantha's favorites. Payton had gone the extra mile to share her list from Samantha, and Kade almost kissed her. She'd also given him some insight into Samantha. Just a few things that only Payton would know and Kade would normally be forced to figure out. Tonight had to be perfect.

When the knock came, Kade pulled open the door and his breath caught in his chest.

Stunning.

There was no other word for her. She wore dark, form-fitting jeans, with a blue floral top that appeared to have been styled in an era long past. The shirt was gathered below her bust and then continued to just below her hips, enhancing her perfect form more than he thought he could ignore. Her hair was free of any clips or bands and fell in waves.

"Hi." He smiled and kissed her cheek, breathing in her clean vanilla scent. "You are beautiful."

She blushed as she smiled. "Thank you."

"Come in," he said, and stepped back.

"I brought a bottle of wine. I hope you like it," Samantha said as she handed it to him.

He studied it for a few seconds and smiled. "It's one of my favorites."

"Really? Great."

He closed the door and followed her into the apartment.

"Your place is lovely," she said as she gazed about the room. She seemed drawn to a small table with an ornate vase sitting in the middle. "These flowers are gorgeous."

"Thank you. They're fresh and grown locally." He held the bottle up. "Shall I pour us a glass now?"

"Yes, please." She slipped her hands into her pockets. "Can I help with anything?"

"How do you feel about chopping veggies?" He started toward the kitchen. "The salad's the only thing I haven't finished."

Sam followed. "It just so happens I'm the best veggie chopper south of the Mason Dixon."

Kade chuckled. "Excellent."

Payton was right. Samantha needed to feel included. She wasn't one to be catered to, and would feel uncomfortable if she couldn't contribute.

He organized the lettuce and various other vegetables on the counter while Samantha washed her hands. He then located a large bowl for her to put everything into. Samantha got right to work and Kade checked on the pasta boiling in the pot.

"How was the rest of your day?" he asked.

"Good. I spent the day observing. The team is amazing."

"Duncan doesn't hire second best. It's why he's paid the big bucks." He grinned. "And it's also why you're here."

Samantha chuckled. "Is the charm in your genes or something you learned?"

"It must have been learned," he retorted. "Because Brodie has none of it."

She waved the knife at him. "Careful. I'll tell him you said that."

"It's nothing I haven't told him a hundred times before."

With a sexy flip of her hair, she sighed and asked, "Do you have a towel? I don't want strays in the salad."

He handed her a clean tea towel and she wiped her hands and reached in her pocket. Pulling out a black band, she secured her hair at the base of her neck and then went back to preparing the salad.

"How was your meeting with Shannon?"

Kade frowned. "What meeting?"

Samantha paused in her cutting and studied him. "Just before I left, she came by my office and said you two had a meeting."

"There was no meeting." He leaned against the counter and crossed his arms. "Did she say why she came by your office?"

"She wanted to offer me help and information should I ever need it."

He fisted his hands at his side. "Did she happen to mention what kind of information she'd impart to you?"

Sam went back to her cutting with entirely too much vigor.

"Samantha? What did Shannon say?"

She continued to chop for a few seconds and then she laid the knife down. "She gave me some insight on what you do when you're interested in someone."

"Excuse me?" he snapped.

Samantha went back to her vegetables.

He took a deep breath, willing his anger to cool. "What exactly did she say, lass?"

She paused again and looked up at with a forced expression of bravado. "She said that when you like someone, you take them to breakfast and then you offer to cook for them."

"Bloody hell." Kade's irritation started to take over his calm again.

"Sorry. I shouldn't have said anything."

"I'm glad you did," he assured her. "The best bit of advice I will ever give you is to ignore Shannon Fraser and never believe a word of anything that comes out of her mouth."

Her eyes widened. "Well, I already figured that one out on my own." She went back to the salad. "What's the history with you two?"

"Our families are connected. She's wanted a partnership with me for years, but it will never happen." He sighed. "Your arrival has put her on alert."

"My arrival?" she asked. "How so?"

He didn't quite know what to say at this point. He didn't know how much he *could* say. "She's figured out that you're someone I'd like to pursue a relationship with."

Samantha dropped the knife. "I'm sorry?"

CHAPTER NINE

Sᴀᴍᴀɴᴛʜᴀ's ʜᴇᴀʀᴛ sʟᴀᴍᴍᴇᴅ against her chest. She wiped her hands on her hips and tried not to dash toward the door.

Did he really just say that?

"Samantha?" Kade made his way to her and took her hand. "Don't run. I know you want to, but I'm asking you to trust me."

She nodded, her heart calming again. "I know you are. I'm just not sure what to make of it. I've known you for less than two days, and you're telling me you want to pursue a relationship with me. It's all a bit much."

"Perhaps, but you feel the same, don't you?"

"I feel *something*. I just haven't figured out what it is. I'm not sure if it's insanity or not."

"Well, if you're crazy, then so am I. Why don't we aim for the sanatorium together?" He smiled and kissed her palm. "Will you give us a chance?"

Of course I will. I'm already half in love with you as it is. How about we just get married tonight and I'll be happy to have your baby too?

She shrugged. "I guess."

Kade laughed and leaned down to kiss her cheek. "I plan to kiss you properly before our evening's over. Think about that while we eat…I know I won't be able to think of anything else."

Let's skip the wedding and just get to the baby-making.

Samantha shuddered. "You are impossible."

"We could always have dessert first."

She pulled her hand from his. "Kade, stop it. I can't think straight when you're doing that."

"Doing what?" he asked innocently.

She narrowed her eyes at him. "Being all sexy and…and…cute."

"Ah, so you think I'm sexy." He leaned down. "And cute."

His lips covered hers and she didn't quite know what hit her. He pulled her close and she felt the hair band loosen and fall away. Then his fingers were tangled in her hair, and she didn't think about anything after that.

She grasped his shirt to keep from falling and her hands seemed to move of their own accord. She slid them up his back; his muscles were like granite under his soft cotton shirt.

The irksome sound of beeping permeated Samantha's psyche and she groaned.

Kade broke the kiss but had the forethought of mind to keep her firmly in his arms. If he hadn't, she would have melted to the floor.

"That would be the pasta," he said as he stroked her cheek. "Can I let you go?"

She nodded. He released her and made his way to the stove.

Samantha stood watching him, momentarily stunned. The boy could kiss. She didn't know what she'd been expecting, but she'd never felt like that with any of her past boyfriends…not that there were many…but she'd thought they were pretty great. Sadly, her experience was obviously lacking, and now she knew she'd never settle for anything less than mind-blowing. Kade Gunnach had just ruined it for any other man she might ever think to date in the future.

"Samantha?" She blinked up at Kade. His eyes sparkled with mischief as he grinned at her. "Was it as good for you as it was for me?"

"It was okay, I guess," she joked. "You?"

He laughed. "I have never experienced anything like that, to be honest."

She bit her lip. "Me neither."

"Are you hungry?"

"Probably."

He took her hand and ran his finger over her knuckles. "Why don't we eat and then we can hash some of this confusion out?"

Unable to fully form a coherent sentence, she nodded and helped him carry plates to the table. If anyone had asked her how the food was, Samantha wouldn't have been able to tell them. What she did put on her plate only got pushed around, and she barely tasted anything she managed to eat.

"This isn't really working, is it?" Kade moved his plate away and rose to his feet.

Sam shook her head.

He held his hand out to her and she took it. He led her into the living room and pulled her onto the sofa next to him. "What's going through your mind, love?" he asked.

"Too much to explain."

Kade smiled. "There's no rush, Samantha. We'll go at your pace. I'm not going anywhere; I just ask that you don't either."

She assumed her favorite position, cross-legged with her back against the sofa arm, and sighed. "I can't go anywhere. I signed a contract, remember?"

"I'll tear the damn thing up if it will make it easier for you."

"You really would, wouldn't you?"

He laid his hand on her knee and turned to face her. "I'd do anything to make this easier for you."

She placed her hand over his. "I believe you, and I'm not going anywhere. You just need to know something."

"What's that?"

"If you break my heart, Pepper will hunt you down and do some permanent damage. Don't think she hasn't done it before."

Kade laughed and pulled her onto his lap. She was so shocked by the action she let out a quiet squeak.

"I have no intention of breaking your heart. I just hope you don't break mine," he said.

She reached up and smoothed the worry from his forehead. "I promise I won't."

He kissed her and Samantha looped her arm around his neck as he pulled her closer. She broke the kiss and dropped her head onto his shoulder. "You need to stop. I don't know if I can take much more."

"Aye," he said gruffly.

She scooted off his lap, but stayed close, and he kept an arm around her. He kissed her forehead and they spent the rest of the evening sharing things about their lives that had nothing to do with their instant bond and unusually deep emotions. When Sam could barely keep her eyes open, she put some distance between them.

"I really should go home and get to bed," she said. "I need to run tomorrow before work."

Kade raised an eyebrow. "Do you want me to run with you?"

"I'd love you to join me sometime, but I have a feeling I'm going to need to work some things out alone."

"If you change your mind, call me."

"Okay." Sam frowned. "I'm sorry about dinner."

Kade smiled. "Don't worry about it. I'll bring the leftovers to the office tomorrow and you can join me for lunch."

She grinned. "Oh, I can, can I?"

"If you're lucky."

She rose to her feet and stretched. "What about the wine?"

"It'll be here waiting for dinner tomorrow."

"We're having lunch *and* dinner tomorrow, huh?"

Kade stood and wrapped his arms around her, running his hand across her back. "And every day after that, I hope."

She pushed him away gently. "Again, you need to stop doing that or I'll never make it home."

He sighed. "Are you saying my evil plan is thwarted?"

"Yes...definitely."

"All right, I'll walk you to your door."

"All six feet of hallway," she joked.

"I have to make up for my lack of gentlemanly behavior earlier."

"When weren't you gentlemanly?"

"I should have collected you."

"Oh, right. Yes. You should have." Samantha chuckled. "Don't think you're getting off that easily."

"Wouldn't dream of it. Come on. If we don't go now, I won't be able to say goodnight."

Samantha nodded and led him from the apartment.

* * *

The next morning, spurred on by the desperate need for a distraction, Samantha headed out for her run. Granted, she didn't manage the full six miles she'd set for herself, but four miles nearly did her in, so she headed back to her apartment hoping a shower would wake her up.

Alan smiled as he held the door open for her. "Good morning, Dr. Moore."

"Hi, Alan. Hey, if I have a few things delivered here, will Jon have time to bring them up to my place today?"

His expression darkened, but he recovered quickly. "That won't be necessary. I'll be happy to deliver whatever you need."

"Thanks."

"Ma'am."

Sam continued to her apartment and got ready for work. She didn't run into Kade in the hallway or the lobby, which made her a little sad. As she entered the Gunnach building, her heart began to race and she felt anger, thick and heavy in the air. Instead of heading to the lab, she pressed the button to take her to Kade's office.

Stepping out of the elevator, Sam felt a little sick. She took a deep breath and headed toward Anna's desk. It was empty, so she walked down the hall and knocked on Kade's door, even though she doubted anyone could hear her with all the yelling going on in there. She pushed in and stood frozen. Kade and Brodie were engaged in some form of heated discussion. Payton sat at the table, and she looked as though she'd been crying. Connall stood sentry, appearing to be waiting to break something up.

"What's happening?" Sam pushed the door closed, having to raise her voice over Kade and Brodie.

"Shite!" Kade snapped and ran his hands through his hair. "I'm sorry, lass."

Sam frowned. "Why are you so mad? What's going on? And why is Payton upset?"

Brodie's face reddened, and he slammed his fist into the wall, then yanked the door open and stalked out of Kade's office. Payton's hands shook as she wrung the handkerchief in her hand.

"I'm so sorry, Sam," Payton said, tears streaming down her face.

"It's not your fault," Connall said.

"It *is* my fault."

"It's not!" Kade snapped, and Payton jumped.

Instinctively, Sam closed the distance between herself and Kade and laid a hand on his arm. His ire began to calm and he closed his eyes and took a deep breath. "Thank you."

"Will someone please tell me what's going on?" she pressed.

"It's taken care of," Kade said. "Nothing you need concern yourself with."

"Except that Payton is crying and Brodie's pissed and your heart is still racing," Sam pointed out. She sent a pleading look to Connall and asked, "Will you *please* fill me in?"

Connall looked at Kade, who gave him a slight nod. "We had to let Alan's son go."

"Jon?"

"Aye," Connall said. "He has been indiscreet."

Payton groaned. "I should be the one losing my job. It's my fault."

Sam let out a frustrated grunt. "What happened? Why did you let Jon go?"

"I had to drop a few things off yesterday, including your wine, and Jon was there to help me. We started chatting." Payton sniffed, tears starting again. "I guess he said something later to Shannon. But I shouldn't have said anything to him to begin with, and now that poor boy is jobless."

"That 'poor boy' got a bloody good severance and recommendation, Payton, and he knew better," Kade snapped.

Connall held his hand out to Payton. "I think we should let Kade and Sam talk. Let's go find Brodie, eh?"

She gave a reluctant nod and rose to her feet. "I'm really sorry, my… um…Dr. Gunnach."

"It's not your fault, lass." Kade's expression softened. "I'll come see you later this morning."

She nodded and followed Connall out of the office.

Kade laid his hand over Sam's. "I'm sorry you got caught in that."

"I still don't understand what happened," she said. "People should be allowed to have conversations, Kade. You can't fire them for sharing information."

He took a deep breath and led her to the table by the window. "Have a seat."

Sam sat down and he did the same.

"Jon wasn't fired for having a conversation, Samantha. He was fired because he gave someone he shouldn't have private information. There's a difference."

"That someone was Shannon."

"Aye. Outside of you and me, Payton was the only one who knew you and I were having dinner together, and only because I'd asked her to do a few things in order to prepare for the evening."

"Why ask Payton? Isn't Anna your assistant?"

"Aye. But she's also Shannon's aunt."

"Oh," Sam said and leaned back in the chair.

"I trust Payton implicitly. She's one of the few. Shannon knows this, so somehow she made a plan with Jon, probably offering something she shouldn't have, in order to get information about our plans. I figured that out when you told me about your conversation with Shannon. Jon is young and easily fooled by a bonny lass, and today he learned a valuable lesson."

"So Payton feels responsible because she told Jon what was happening."

Kade shook his head. "That's the thing. She didn't. She was quite vague, however, Shannon put two and two together and made an educated guess. She was trying to upset you yesterday." He reached over the table and took Sam's hand. "I may have taken a woman to breakfast, but I've never cooked dinner for one. You're the first. I don't have an M.O. as Shannon tried to make you believe, because I've never felt this way about anyone."

A shiver stole up Sam's spine. "Oh."

"I'll make sure Payton is all right. She's invaluable to me and not just as an employee. I'll fix it with her."

Sam nodded. "Thank you. I really like her."

He smiled. "I do too."

"What about Jon? Should he really lose his job over something like this? It seems extreme."

"It's not extreme." Kade stood and pulled her from the chair. "Honestly, love, he'll have another job in a day. Don't worry about him."

"I'll worry less if you let me know when he finds something."

He smiled and stroked her cheek. "Fair enough. I'll let you know."

"Thank you."

He leaned down and kissed her and Sam couldn't stop the quiet sigh as he intensified the kiss. Then he broke away and chuckled. "That would have been a good way to start my day. Much better than a fight with Brodie. He can be difficult."

Sam nodded toward the large hole in the wall. "And strong, apparently."

"Aye." Kade's phone buzzed and he sighed. "I have a meeting, love."

"Oh, sorry! I'll get out of your hair."

He laid his hand on her back and guided her to a side door. "Might be better if you go this way. Wait a couple of minutes and then just turn right and it will lead you to the lift."

She chose not to pry. "Okay. I'll see you at lunch?"

He smiled and kissed her again. "Wild horses couldn't keep me away."

Sam rolled her eyes. "Good to know."

She left the office and headed toward Payton's office instead of the lab.

* * *

Kade answered his door and stepped back to allow Hamish entry.

He stepped inside and bowed. "My lord."

"Hamish." Kade closed his door and indicated one of the chairs near the window. "We need to discuss your sister," he said as they each took a seat.

"Oh?"

"Aye. She'll be here shortly, however, I'm informing you as you are the head of the family. She'll be brought before the Council—"

"What? Why?" Hamish snapped.

Kade sighed and filled Hamish in on the events of the previous two days. From the conversation about the shareholders' dinner all the way to Shannon's interaction with Jon.

Hamish stood and paced the office. "Bloody hell!"

Kade's phone rang and he answered Anna's call, giving her permission to send Shannon in. Shannon arrived, her countenance much less smug than it had been in the last few weeks.

"My lord," she said, her head bowed.

Kade stepped back, willing his emotions to calm. The sudden desire to wring her skinny neck rose rather quickly to his mind.

CHAPTER TEN

A LITTLE OVER two weeks later, Samantha woke so tired she nearly skipped her run—again. She hadn't slept well—again. Her dreams had been filled with Kade—again. She laid her fingers on her lips. His kiss the night before had surpassed the rest and he'd captivated her heart. She was officially in love with him, to the point of no return.

Since their eye-opening dinner, the two had spent nearly every waking non-working moment together. Dinner at one of their apartments was a given every night, and Kade made sure he took snippets of time out of the day for a "quick snog."

Shannon had been fired and had apparently left the city. Sam chose not to grill Kade about what happened with her. She was just grateful she didn't have to deal with her anymore. Kade had also assured her that Jon had found another job, which was probably why Alan was happier these days.

A week ago, Cole had taken her to the American bar he'd told her about and they'd watched football and drunk beer, laughing at things only they would get. But none of it mattered, because even though she felt comfortable with Cole, she couldn't fully focus. Her mind was filled with all things Kade and she'd ended the night early, thrilled when she found Kade home from his meeting with Pfizer, and available to spend the rest of the evening with her.

After several Skype sessions with her parents, they'd given her their positive opinions of Kade. Of course, they reserved the right to change their opinions when they met him, which would be when, exactly? Samantha had laughed and promised it would happen as soon as humanly possible.

Sam forced herself out of her cozy bed, knowing that if she didn't run, she'd start to obsess over the illogical state of her heart and that never did anyone any good, especially Pepper, who ended up being the sounding board to Samantha's stress.

She arrived at the running path to find Cole already stretching. He gave her a smile and waited for her to reach him. "Good morning, stranger. How are you?"

"I'm good. How about you?"

"Great. Did you get my text last night?"

"Oh, yeah! Sorry. I've been so distracted lately. Yes, let's do something. I'll figure out my schedule and we can plan a night. Maybe more football?"

"Sounds good," Cole said. "Would you like to run together?"

She held up her iPod. "I really need to lose myself to music this morning. Rain check?"

"No problem. I'll see you later." He waved and started his run.

She took a few minutes to stretch and then slipped her ear buds in. In the mood for something high-energy, she found her favorite album by Rayne Green and set her iPod to shuffle. The singer had disappeared several years ago, never to be seen again, making her music even more popular.

She saw Cole in front of her and there were a few other people coming back the other way. She figured there'd be more starting their runs, as the day was sunny and remarkably warm.

As Sam hit her second mile, her pace became muscle memory and she allowed her body to take over so her mind could wander. The scenery was stunning, and she drew a breath deep into her lungs. The air was so clean, and she could tell it would snow soon. She must ask Kade what the trees were that lined the path. They were magnificent.

Without warning, a hand snaked around her waist and yanked her off the path. She screamed, but the sound was stopped when something was shoved in her mouth.

* * *

Panic slammed Kade hard. His head whipped up and he grabbed his cell phone. Samantha didn't pick up, so he dialed Alasdair. He paced his office as the fear made his heart race.

"Not a good time, Kade," Alasdair said.

"What the hell happened? Who's watching her?" he snapped.

"Shite!"

"Alasdair!" Kade rushed to the bank of windows in a misguided effort to see something…anything.

"I'll call you back," Alasdair said, and then the phone went dead.

Kade closed his eyes and took several deep breaths. His heart started to calm, but he still leaned against the glass in an effort to "see" Samantha. His phone buzzed. "Ali. What's going on?"

"Everything's all right, Kade. She's safe."

"But she was in danger?"

"Aye."

Kade swore. "Alasdair, you better start bloody talking, or—"

"Someone else stepped in. That American."

"Colton Drake?" Kade seethed.

"Aye. He's taking care of her, and we got the one who grabbed her."

"*Grabbed* her? What the hell is that supposed to mean?" Kade snapped. "I'm coming down."

* * *

Samantha gladly took the comfort Cole was offering as he helped her stand and laid his windbreaker over her shoulders. "Better?" he asked.

"I don't know," she answered.

He wrapped his arm around her shoulders and led her to one of the benches at the side of the path. "Here. You should probably sit down."

She nodded and sat down next to him. He kept his arm firmly around her and watched her intently. She glanced at the man who'd attacked her. He lay unconscious on the ground. Sam remembered bits and pieces of the attack, but felt as though she were in a strange dream. The man had thrown her to the ground and shoved a rag in her mouth. She tried to fight, but he was strong, and she was reeling from the blow she received when her head hit the ground.

She remembered the man being hauled off her, almost like a rag doll, then blackness. When she came to, Cole was there and lifting her from the ground.

She shivered, and Cole tightened his hold. "Sam?"

She shook her head. "I'm going to be sick."

"Come with me."

He walked her to the edge of the trail and held her while she emptied her stomach. A good thing she'd followed her normal routine of waiting to eat. Cole handed her a bottle of water and Sam took a few sips.

"You really should sit down," he said, and guided her back to the bench.

"I do feel a little dizzy. Probably a mild concussion." There were several people milling around, including one she recognized. "Alasdair? What are you doing here?"

"I was driving by when I saw the commotion."

The police and ambulance arrived, taking her focus from the evasive response by the driver. They began to ask questions, none of which Sam could answer. She didn't know who her attacker was, and hadn't seen him lurking anywhere. The EMTs were taking her pulse and making sure she wouldn't pass out while Cole chimed in with his own information for the police, sounding official and using words that Sam could have sworn were swimming in front of her.

Kind of like little birds in a cartoon.

"Sam?"

She blinked and then felt a gentle squeeze around her waist.

"Sam, stay awake," Cole demanded.

"Samantha?" another voice entered the chorus.

"Kade?" Samantha watched him as he approached. He bent down and lifted her off the bench.

84

"Hey!" Cole snapped as he stood and laid a hand on her arm. "What the hell are you doing?"

"It's okay, Cole. This is Kade. He's my...uh...boss." Sam looped her arms around Kade's neck and frowned.

"I'm a hell of a lot more than your boss," he whispered for her ears only.

Sam nodded. "Yeah, yeah."

"How are you, sweetheart?" he asked.

"I feel clumsy enough to trip over a cordless phone."

He raised an eyebrow. "So, you feel dizzy then?"

She grimaced. "I think I might have a very mild concussion."

"That's what I'm afraid of."

"I did say *mild*, right?"

Kade grilled the EMTs before focusing back on Samantha. "I'm going to ask you a few questions, all right?"

"Fire away," she said.

"What's your name?"

"Minnie Mouse."

"*Samantha*," he warned.

"Samantha Moore."

"And where are you?"

"Currently in your arms," she retorted. "Although, I'm not sure how that happened, or why you don't just set me down."

"Your sense of humor is intact." He smiled, although his smile didn't quite cover the worry in his eyes. "Did you lose consciousness?"

Sam looked at Cole who nodded.

"She was out for a couple of minutes," he provided.

Kade frowned. "Are you feeling nauseous?"

"Not anymore," Sam said.

Cole nodded to the edge of the path. "She threw up."

"How long ago?" Kade asked.

Cole set irritated eyes on Kade. "Just before you arrived."

Kade frowned down at Samantha. "I'm taking you to the hospital."

"We can take her, Dr. Gunnach," the female EMT offered, her appreciative gaze raking over him.

Sam leaned closer to Kade, her possessiveness rising. "Don't be ridiculous. I don't need a hospital. I need a shower and a nap."

"No sleeping," he demanded.

"Joking." She yawned. "Sort of. Put me down, Kade. Seriously. I got a bump on the head, I didn't break my legs."

He set her on the ground and she pulled her arms from around his neck and stepped away, dizziness engulfing her almost immediately. She fell into Cole, who stood close by. He caught her, but she reached for Kade's arm and held onto him as though he were a life raft. "I misjudged a bit, I think."

Kade nodded and scooped her back up once Cole released her.

"I have the car," Alasdair said. "Fiona is waiting at your flat."

"Are you sure you don't want us to take her?" the EMT asked.

"No, I'm fine," Samantha stressed. "I don't need to go to the hospital."

Kade sighed. "If you won't go to the hospital, then I'm taking you to my place so I can keep an eye on you."

"Fine," Samantha grumbled.

"And where is that, exactly?" Cole asked in suspicion.

Kade ignored him and gave some instructions to Alasdair.

"Hey, buddy, I asked you a question," Cole pressed. "Where exactly are you taking her?"

Sam felt Kade's body stiffen and strange words swirled in her mind. *Ég mun drepa þig.*

She didn't know what they meant, but with the anger pouring from Kade, she figured they probably weren't good. She reached out and squeezed Cole's shoulder. "Cole, it's okay. Really. Call me later and we'll figure out another time to run together. Okay?"

Kade didn't wait for Cole to answer her. He turned and followed Alasdair to the car waiting at the entrance of the path.

"You know, I feel fine now," she said.

Kade set her feet on the ground and helped her slide into the backseat. He slid in next to her and pulled the door closed.

"What are you doing here?" she asked as Alasdair drove away from the chaos.

Kade watched her closely. "Alasdair called me."

Sam rubbed her forehead. "Do you communicate telepathically?"

"Excuse me?"

She dropped her head on the back of the seat. "Y'all just got there so quickly." Her head was spinning and her nausea was returning rapidly.

"Don't try to think. We'll talk it out when you're feeling better." He reached over and squeezed her hand. "Tell me about the man."

"I told the police I'd never seen him before."

He shook his head. "Not the one who attacked you. The other one."

"Cole? He's the guy I told you about. The one on the plane."

Kade ran his thumb over her hand. "Right."

"Why?"

"How well do you know him?"

"Well enough. I've known him longer than I've known you."

"That didn't answer my question," he accused.

She frowned. "Why does this feel like an interrogation?"

"I'm sorry, Samantha, I just want to make sure you're not in danger. There are a lot of people who'd like to get their hands on information our company has access to, and I want to make sure you're protected."

She let out a quiet hiss. "If you're suggesting I'd reveal company secrets to anyone, let alone someone I just met, then I don't know why you bothered to hire me."

"That's not what I'm saying." Kade grimaced. "I'm sorry. I'll explain more when you're feeling better."

Alasdair pulled the car to the back of their building and set the brake.

Sam felt less dizzy than before, but as soon as Kade released her hand and slid from the car, her dizziness returned.

He helped her out and then reached inside for her jacket. She had to lean against the car in order not to fall over, but as soon as he wrapped an arm around her waist, her vertigo calmed. Kade walked her to the elevator and they rode to the thirty-second floor. They made their way to his apartment and he pushed open the door.

Fiona rushed to them, her face whiter than usual. "What happened? Are you all right? Come sit down."

"Fi. Slow down, love," Kade said.

"Sorry. Bring her to the sofa. I'm making tea."

"I'm fine, really," Sam insisted. "Bump on the head. So not a big deal."

Fiona waved toward the coffee table. A black leather satchel sat in the middle of it. "I got your bag."

Kade smiled. "Thank you."

He settled Sam on the couch and then sat facing her on the coffee table. Opening his medical bag, he pulled out a pen light. "I'm going to check you now, all right?"

Sam nodded.

He leaned in and examined her eyes, then wrapped his large hands around her head, gently pulling her scrunchy out and pressing on her scalp to check for tenderness. She whimpered when his fingers grazed a particularly sore spot. He separated her hair and looked closer before sitting back on the table. "You have quite the goose egg, but no bleeding. We'll get some ice on it and I think you'll live."

"I think I said something similar, didn't I?" Samantha yawned. "Sorry, I just want to sleep."

"*That* you can't do."

Sam nodded. "I know."

"In a couple of hours, we'll see how you're feeling, and then, *maybe,* you can sleep."

"Okay. I'll just go home and take a shower."

"You're not going anywhere," Kade said.

"Please. I'll be fine. I'll get dressed and meet you at the office."

"You're not going to the office, Samantha. You need to rest."

"I have a job to do. One that you're convinced I'm going to screw up."

Fiona gasped and glared at Kade. "What?"

Kade squeezed Sam's knee and frowned. "I said nothing of the sort."

"You implied it," Sam countered.

"Pain makes you grumpy I see."

She couldn't help but smile. "You ain't seen nothin' yet."

"I look forward to whatever you have to throw my way." Kade leaned over and kissed her cheek. "In the meantime, I'll get you some tea."

He put his instruments back in his bag and Sam took her chance to escape. "It's okay, Kade. I need to get to work." She felt nausea overwhelm her, and sat down again. "In a minute."

Fiona raised an eyebrow in her brother's general direction, but Sam had no idea what they were silently communicating.

"Anna has canceled my appointments for today, and you can work on the samples as soon as you're better," he said.

Sam laid her hand on his arm and the nausea stopped. "Kade, really, I'm a big girl. I'm fine. I'll shower, and if you insist on me staying home, I won't argue, but I can't ask you to throw your entire day away."

"What if you pass out while you're in the shower and no one's there to help?" he countered.

He had a point, but she still didn't want to impose. "I won't pass out in the shower."

"I can take her home and make sure she's safe," Fiona offered and turned to Sam. "If you don't mind."

"No I don't mind." Samantha pulled her hand away from Kade. Nausea hit her like a wall and she grasped his arm again. "Okay, I don't know what the heck is going on at the moment, but something's not right."

Kade laid his hand over hers. "Tell me."

"I feel great as long as I'm touching you, but if I take my hand away, I feel like I've been hit in the head." She wrinkled her nose. "Just ignore me. I'm a little rattled."

"Let's put the shower idea on hold," Kade said. "We're not going anywhere for the moment, so you should rest and have a cup of tea."

"I'm fine. Seriously, I feel much better." Kade dropped her hand and Sam was hit with dizziness. "What the—?"

He wrapped his hand around her wrist and her dizziness dissipated almost as quickly as it came.

"I'll make that tea, eh?" Fiona said and escaped to the kitchen.

"What are you doing to me, Kade?" Sam asked as she sat back on the couch. "This goes way beyond the ability to calm me down when I'm upset."

Before he could respond, Sam's cell phone rang and she pulled it from her pocket. Cole's name popped up on the screen. "Hi, Cole."

"Hey. How are you?"

"I'm doing much better." Sam shifted in her seat. "Did they find out anything about the man who attacked me?"

"Nothing that they'd tell me. I have some contacts, so I'm looking into it."

Samantha bit her lip. "He was probably just some crazy guy."

"Maybe," Cole said. "Are you home?"

"No. I'm at Kade's."

"Are you comfortable with that? If you're not, I'll come get you."

"Bless your heart." Sam smiled. "I'm fine. I'm going home in a bit. He's just making sure I won't pass out without anyone around."

Cole hummed in agreement. "Probably a good idea. What about dinner tonight? I could swing by with a pizza."

Kade shifted beside her and Sam glanced at him. His eyes were strange—the outside rims of his irises were red. She couldn't stop a quiet intake of breath.

"Sam? Are you okay?" Cole asked.

She focused on the phone again. "Hmm? Yes. Fine. Sorry. Um, to-night—"

Kade stood, breaking contact with her, and Sam groaned. "Cole, I'm going to be sick. I'll call you back."

She hung up just as Fiona returned with the tea. "Kade!" she hissed. "Stop it."

"Stop what?" Samantha asked, her head pounding again.

Kade sat next to Sam again and laid his hand on her knee. The pain and nausea slipped away. Sam glared at him. "You *are* doing something!

What are you doing to me?" She pushed his hand away, regretting it immediately. "Ow! My head." He took her hand, but she slipped from his hold and tried to stand up. "Don't touch me."

"Samantha." Fiona reached for her. "Don't try to move." She took her arm and pushed her back onto the sofa. "Kade! *Calm sjálfur.*"

Samantha started to panic. "I need to go home."

"No, Sam." Fiona took her hand. "You need to stay until you're steady."

Tears streamed down Sam's face. "I'm going to be sick."

Kade said something Sam didn't understand, but by the look on Fiona's face, it wasn't something she approved of. He sat down next to Sam again and took her hand. "I am so sorry, Samantha. I shouldn't have done that. Let me help you."

The pain and nausea were once again gone, and as much as Sam wanted to flee, she also wanted to be free of the pain, so she let him hold her hand. "What are you doing to me? Please don't tell me it's some kind of witchcraft or some weird cult thingy."

He shook his head as he ran his thumb over her palm. "No. I promise. My personal beliefs would be in direct opposition to anything like that."

"Then what are you doing? How are you doing it?"

"Angus can do the same for me," Fiona piped in.

Kade shook his head. "Fiona."

"Sorry."

None of the fascinating conversation going on around her actually answered any of Samantha's questions. Her head just filled with more. Kade sat with her for almost an hour, testing her pain level every fifteen minutes or so until she didn't feel any more pain or nausea.

After forcing her to eat more food that she ever had at one sitting, he gave her the green light to go home and shower, but he insisted that she return once she was finished. She left his apartment, torn between confusion and feeling adored when he stood in the hallway and waited for her to let herself into her apartment.

Samantha closed the door and leaned against it, taking several deep breaths. Something strange was going on. She waffled between wanting to find out what it was and the desire to ignore it and hope it would go away. She was almost at the point of packing it in and going home. But she wasn't a quitter, even if sometimes she wished she were.

She dropped her keys on the console and sat down at her computer. She needed to talk to Pepper, but she must have left her cell at Kade's, and Pepper's Skype status was offline.

It would have to wait. For now, she'd focus on getting comfortable and then she'd deal with the strangeness surrounding Kade.

* * *

Kade closed his door and turned to find his sister scowling at him, her hands on her hips and her face rising in color. "Leave it, Fi."

"I will *not* leave it! You scared that poor girl half to death, after you purposely allowed her to feel pain because of what? Jealousy? You're a bloody spiteful bastard sometimes, Kade."

He slammed his hand against the wall. "I know it, damn it! I'm not proud of what I did, Fiona. But please, dear sister, continue to shove my pettiness down my throat."

Fiona's cell phone rang and she made her way to her purse. "This is not over." She answered the call. "I'm fine, sweetheart. Just giving my brother a verbal hiding. No, Kade." She glared at him. "I'm aware of that. But right now he's my brother, not my chieftain....and he deserves it."

Kade paced the floor while he waited for his sister to finish her conversation. He berated himself for his treatment of Samantha. He was the worst mate in the history of the world.

"You are not," Fiona said.

He hadn't realized she was even off the phone.

Fiona pulled him to the sofa, tugging him down beside her. "You reacted to an emotion you've never felt before. Granted, you didn't react well, but you're not the worst mate in the world. You're just not used to this."

"She deserves better."

"Then apologize. You'll work it out, but I do think you need to tell her everything. She's confused, and if she truly believes you're some kind of a witch, you'll lose her. Her beliefs are as strong as yours, and that goes against everything we hold true."

"How am I supposed to tell the woman I met less than a month ago that we are to be mated for life because I'm a near-immortal Viking and it's written in our DNA? And that once I bind her, she'll be joined forever to the chieftain of a clan almost two thousand years old?"

Fiona chuckled. "Perhaps reword it a bit."

"She'll run, Fi."

"I don't think she will. I think you run a higher risk of losing her if you keep her in the dark. She's going to need to know who we are eventually; otherwise, she'll never find a cure. I trust her, Kade. She's the one."

He nodded. "I know."

"Then trust her too. If you don't start now, you'll never have the bond you seek."

He smiled. "When did you get so wise?"

"Years ago. Where have you been?"

The doorbell pealed and Kade made his way to the door. Samantha stood in the hallway, her damp hair loose and falling across her shoulders. She wore form-fitting yoga pants and a long-sleeved tee. Kade's heart beat a little faster in response to her being so close.

"I think I left my cell phone here," she said.

"Come in." He stepped aside and waited for her to enter.

"How do you feel, Samantha?" Fiona asked.

"Much better. Thank you."

"Good." Fiona stood and gathered her purse. "I'm going to take off. I need to meet Angus and take care of a few things." She patted Kade's chest. "I trust I'm leaving her in good hands, right?"

He rolled his eyes. "Aye. Now, out with you."

"I'll see you tomorrow, Samantha."

"Okay." Sam waved and Fiona left.

Samantha leaned against the sofa and he saw her hands shaking as she clasped them in front of her. "Och, Samantha, I've scared you. I'm so sorry."

"No. You haven't. Can I just get my cell phone and I'll give you your space?"

He stood in front of her and grasped her hands, pulling them to his chest. She pulled away with a sigh. "What are you doing?"

"I want you to feel my heart."

She laid her palm over his chest, but Kade pulled it away. "No. Feel it with *your* heart. Close your eyes." Her eyes widened and he knew she was leery of him. "Trust me. I know I haven't earned it, but I will. Now, close your eyes."

She did as he asked and he linked his fingers with hers and closed his eyes as well. As they stood toe-to-toe, he felt her fear begin to dissipate like a vapor into the air. He knew the moment she recognized his heartbeat. He released one of her hands and cupped her cheek, stroking it as he covered her mouth with his.

She responded just as she had the night before…still, the fact she didn't hold anything back even though she didn't understand what was happening was humbling. He lifted her onto the back of the sofa, giving him better access to her mouth, and slid his tongue across her lips.

Þú verður mín að eilífu. (You will be mine forever.)

He knew she heard the words and half expected her to break their connection, but she slipped her arms around his neck and wove her fingers through his hair. It didn't last as long as he would have liked, however.

He felt a gentle tug and then she broke the kiss with a groan. "What was *that*? That was way more intense than before!"

"I have several things I need to explain."

CHAPTER ELEVEN

SAMANTHA PUSHED KADE away and jumped from the back of the couch. She needed distance. If she didn't get it, she'd rip off her clothes then and there and given him anything he asked for. He started toward her, but she held her hands up and shook her head. "No way, buddy. Do not move another inch."

He stalled, but his smile indicated he wouldn't stay away long. "Can we talk now?"

She bit her lip. "Um, sure. But you stay there."

Kade chuckled and ignored her demand. He strode toward her and pulled her onto the loveseat with him. Sam shifted so her back was up against one of the arms.

He draped his arm around the back of the sofa and smiled. "Do you want to ask questions now or later?"

"I don't know." She wrapped her arms around her knees. "I don't know what to ask."

"How do you like information delivered?"

She studied him for several seconds as she processed that question. He seemed to know her better than herself, and for some unknown reason, that didn't scare her. Nothing about him scared her...when she was with him. "I think in this case, you should just talk and I'll ask questions as they come up."

"Fair enough."

"One thing first," she said.

He grinned. "You're a fine kisser, lass."

She nudged his thigh with her foot. "You're not funny. What exactly am I hearing in my head?"

He raised an eyebrow.

"Oh, stop," she retorted. "I can't tell if it's Icelandic or Gaelic."

"You're asking about the language...not the fact that you're hearing voices?"

"I'm compartmentalizing. Besides, it's *your* voice, not multiple ones."

He ran his hand across the sofa pillow. "It's Icelandic."

"Why…how…am I hearing it?"

Kade set his head in the palm of his hand, but didn't answer.

"Kade?" she pressed.

Before anymore could be said, the peal of her cell phone broke the silence. Kade rose to his feet and retrieved it for her. She noticed his scowl as he handed it to her.

She shook her head as she answered the call. "Hi, Cole."

"Hey you. How are you feeling?"

"Much better, thank you."

"I'd kind of like to see that for myself."

Sam grinned. "I could take a picture and send it to you, if you like."

"Not exactly what I had in mind."

A gentle but firm squeeze of her ankle had her glancing into Kade's scowling face. "What?" she whispered, but he just shook his head.

"Sam?" Cole said.

"Sorry. I'm here with my boss and he was asking me a question." She gave Kade a challenging glare. "I'm all yours, Cole."

Kade stood and strode out of the room. Sam sighed. He was the most confusing human being she'd ever encountered.

"Can I swing by and see you?" Cole asked.

"Ugh. Not right now. I just want to veg in front of the boob tube and potentially sleep." Sam rubbed her forehead; a headache was fast approaching. "What about Thursday?"

"Thursday's good. Are you sure you're okay?"

She turned when she heard Kade returning. "Yes. I have a bit of a headache from the concussion. No biggie."

He had a glass of water and held his hand open. Two white tablets sat in the middle of his palm.

"For your head," he whispered.

Sam widened her eyes and then focused back on Cole.

"Okay. Well, call me if you need me," Cole said.

"I will. 'Bye." She hung up and stared up at Kade. "How did you know?"

"I can feel it." He handed her the glass of water and took her cell phone from her. "Take them."

"What do you mean, you can feel it?"

He narrowed his eyes. "Take the pills, Samantha."

"Why are you mad?"

He sighed. "I'm not mad, sweetheart. I just want you to take the pain-killers."

He sat next to her, forcing her body into the back of the sofa.

"And if I don't want to?"

He pulled the glass from her hand and leaned down, covering her mouth with his.

Gràdhach, take the pills.

She pushed him away. "Was that Icelandic too?"

He chuckled as he wrapped his arm around her knees. "No. That was Gaelic." He picked up the water and handed it to her. "Now, take the medicine."

"But my headache's gone." He broke contact with her and she gasped. "Ow…ow…ow!"

He laid his hand on her ankle and grimaced. "I'm sorry."

She popped the pills even though she no longer felt pain. "How are you doing that?"

"It's complicated, and something I'm not sure you're ready to hear just yet."

"You're not summoning something you shouldn't be, are you? I won't sit here and let you mess with the spiritual realm."

He shook his head. "No. There's nothing spiritual about this, and it's certainly not evil. It's physical, and it's just between you and me."

"Okay, even if I'm not ready to hear why, I'd still like you to tell me."

"I want to set up a ground rule first."

"Like?" she asked.

"Would you please stop referring to me as your boss?"

"But you are," she argued.

"That fact is irrelevant, Samantha."

Sam smiled. "What do you want me to refer to you as?"

"Fiancé?" he asked hopefully.

She snorted. "One, you haven't asked; two, I'm not there yet."

"Okay. Let's figure out my label after I fill you in on a few things."

"Start talkin' 'not boss.'" Kade leaned back and she grasped his arm. "But keep touching me. I like being pain-free."

He grinned. "Keep that in the forefront of your mind for me."

"I will. Now tell me."

"You and I will be bound."

Sam laughed. "With rope?" she asked. "'Cause I don't really do kinky."

He grinned. "No. We are meant to be together, forever."

Samantha let out a quiet snort. "Okay, crazy stalker dude, you are out of your ever-blessed mind."

He shrugged. "I said you weren't ready to hear it."

She pulled her leg away from his hand and stood. "We just *met!*" she argued. "You can't honestly expect me to believe that we're going to fall in love, marry, and live happily ever after just because you make some inane declaration that we're going to be tied together—"

"Bound."

"*Bound,* whatever!" Pain slammed against her temples and she tried to rub it away.

"Shhh...you need to calm yourself." Kade took her hand.

Sam let out a sigh of relief as her headache disappeared again. "What *is* this?"

"When we met, the connection began, but the moment I touched you, our *örlög*...fate, was sealed." He ran his thumb across her palm. "The reason our kiss today was different is because of the words spoken in the process."

"Which words?"

"Þú verður að vera minn að eilífu. They mean, you will be mine forever. They are some of the first words we speak to our mates."

"Mates?"

"Aye. Up till now, I've been attempting to take things slow. And when we make love, we will be bound."

Samantha pulled her hand away. "So this is a weird way to get me to sleep with you?"

"No. You misunderstand. We won't make love until I bind you...you have nothing to fear from me, Samantha."

"Until *you* bind *me?* You mean to tell me you hold control over my choice?"

"Sam, no. You have control over everything...you have all the power, in fact," he assured her.

Samantha was so confused, she couldn't think straight. The craziest part was that she knew he was telling her the truth. When she touched him, she saw his heart, felt his conviction, and knew that honor and integrity were things he valued.

Kade pulled her against himself. "I know this is a lot to process."

She tucked her feet under her bottom and nodded into his chest. The calm permeated her soul and she closed her eyes, allowing his strength to seep in. "I feel so...so..."

"I know. It's what happens between two mates. I can take your pain away. Whether it's physical or emotional. You can do the same for me."

"That sounds a lot like you're likening me to a chimpanzee or something."

Kade chuckled. "We can choose another word. It doesn't have to be 'mate.'"

She glanced up at him. "What was the word you said before? The Gaelic one?"

"Gràdhach?"

"Yes. What does it mean?"

"It means 'beloved.'"

"Why are the other words significant? Can you say them again, please?"

Kade gave her a gentle squeeze. "Þú verður að vera minn að eilífu."

"Wow." Her body tingled as he said the words slowly.

"They solidify the bond between us."

"This is all a little much. I will admit I'm attracted to you...I mean, who wouldn't be? But I don't know you well enough to know if I love you."

He kissed her cheek. "You're lying now, love."

She smacked his leg. "Could I get some semblance of privacy, please?"

"Probably not." He chuckled.

"At least you're being honest, I suppose."

"I just happen to know how *I* feel, so I'm hopeful you feel the same."

"Charming to the core, hmm?"

He stroked her cheek. "I love you, Samantha. Whether it defies logic or you don't feel the same way, it's the truth."

She sighed and grumbled. "Bolt of lightning wrapped in a rainbow."

"Hmm?"

"Pepper. She's got a knack for coming up with slogans, and she used to always say that love is like being hit by a bolt of lightning wrapped in a rainbow."

He kissed her, and Samantha's mind became a puddle of mush...no, goo. It was still goo. She broke the kiss. "I don't know what to say. I don't know if I can process this."

"There's no pressure. We'll get to know each other. You don't have to make any decisions right now."

"No, not that. Well, yes, that, but no...I don't know. I can't think straight right now. I can't function when you kiss me like that."

"I'll keep that in mind. Might help tilt the balance."

Sam couldn't help but smile. "You can find the humor in anything."

"I try."

She fiddled with a button on his dress shirt. "What did you mean by I have all the power?"

"Pretty much that I don't have any. Particularly when you're around."

"Oh." She wrinkled her nose. "I still don't understand how all of this is happening…physically or otherwise. You're not going to tell me you're a vampire or something weird like that, are you?"

Kade laughed. "Aren't they typically Transylvanian?"

"Depends on who you ask, I suppose."

"No, I'm not a vampire…at least, I don't think I am. My body doesn't sparkle in the sunlight, so I think I'm safe."

"Oh, funny."

"When you were first attacked, I felt your panic. That's why I arrived when I did. I knew where you were. My heart was able to find you…a bit like a GPS signal."

"Fiona said Angus did the same for her. Is he Icelandic as well?

"No. He's Scottish, but we're from the same clan," Kade explained. Sam shifted back to her favorite position, but this time when she backed up against the arm, he pulled her legs over his thighs, keeping them connected. "Why don't I start at the middle? It's really the beginning of my clan's story, so that might help."

"Okay."

"We arrived on Scottish soil and found unoccupied land in the Highlands. It's where we built our homes and incorporated the rest of the village."

"You say 'we.' You mean your ancestors, right?"

"That's an interesting question."

She frowned. He was right. Why would she ask something so rhetorical?

"Sam?"

She focused on him again and realized he was trying to get something across. She just couldn't grasp what. "Okay. What are you trying to say? The truth. All of it."

"When I say 'we,' I mean 'we.' Me included."

"You're what, thirty-something? Is there still unoccupied land in the Highlands of Scotland?"

"Not much of it anymore."

"And you couldn't just take it, right? You'd have to go through official channels and such."

Kade nodded. "Nowadays, aye."

Sam bit her lip. "So, did you buy land?"

"No, Samantha. We took it."

She jumped from the couch and nearly tripped over the coffee table.

"Careful," he warned and reached for her when she grasped her head.

She waved him away. "Are you a criminal?" she asked.

"No."

"Like you'd tell me if you were," she grumbled.

"You'd know if I were lying."

She let out a squeal of frustration and stomped her foot. "You're playing word games with me. Stop it. Just spit it out."

Kade leaned forward and settled his arms on his knees. "I arrived here with my family from Iceland in 1420."

"*Riiiiight.*"

He stood and made his way toward her. Samantha backed away.

"Sweetheart, listen to my heart rather than worry about the words. I'm going to tell you everything, but I need you not to run."

"I won't, but don't touch me. I need all of my emotions. Crazy or not."

He stalled and nodded.

"Are you trying to tell me you're close to six-hundred years old?"

"No."

"Okay, then what *are* you telling me?"

"I'm telling you I'm *over* six-hundred years old," he said. "I was born in 1410."

Sam started to pace. "No. No. No, no, no, no." She rubbed her head. "It's the head injury, isn't it? I'm hallucinating."

"I'm having a difficult time seeing you in distress, love. Will you let me help?" he asked.

"You won't try to do something to my mind, will you?"

Kade's eyes widened. "I can't, Sam. All I can do is ease your pain and worry. I don't have the power to manipulate you. And even if I did, I wouldn't."

She slipped into his arms and laid her head against his chest. Her pain and panic eased immediately and she took a deep breath as the calm covered her.

He ran his hands through her hair. "I think we should pause the information dump for a bit. I don't want you to overtax yourself."

"Let me decide what's overtaxing." She looked up at him. "Is this some kind of druid thing?"

"No. Iceland converted to Christianity in the tenth century. Our family and clan have been Christians for centuries, even before I was born, so when we arrived in Scotland, we continued to practice our faith. We are known as Cauld Ane."

"What does Cauld Ane mean?"

"Roughly translated, it means cold one."

"That doesn't sound pleasant."

He smiled. "We prefer the cold."

"So, is that another clan name?"

He shook his head. "No. It's more of our race."

"Race? What do you mean?"

"We are not entirely human," he said.

"Are you trying to tell me that God made you immortal?"

"No, we do die eventually, just not as quickly as humans."

"This doesn't make sense."

"I know it doesn't." He pulled her back onto the couch and wrapped an arm around her waist. "But I don't know who else would have made me this way."

"What about some kind of ancient curse?" she asked.

"Methuselah was nine hundred and sixty-nine when he died, so I think God has more say over our lifespan than anyone or anything."

She mulled the information over for a few minutes. "Do you have proof of all of this?"

Kade chuckled. "Ever the scientist, I see. Yes, I have proof. At home."

"What do you mean at home? You *are* home."

"No, this is where I live, but it's not my home. My home is in the Highlands."

Sam's eyes felt heavy and she couldn't stop a yawn. "How can you talk to me in my head?"

"It's because we are fated to be bound. I can talk to you when I'm touching you, sort of. Warnings mostly or our ancient mating words. At least until we're bound. Then we'll have more of a connection."

She shook her head. "That's not true. I heard you say something to Alex when he was helping with the computer. You sounded angry."

Shock covered his face. "Really?"

"Yes."

"I don't know how that's possible." His eyebrows puckered in confusion. "It doesn't make sense."

Sam snorted. "You question that, but not the fact you're pretty much immortal?"

"I've had six hundred years or so to get used to that."

"True." She yawned again.

"You need to rest."

"But I want to know everything."

"I know you do, and I promise I'll tell you everything in time," he said. "However, right now you're exhausted and should rest."

"You're probably right." She swung her legs over the side of the sofa. "I'll get out of your hair."

He rose to his feet and pulled her up. "You're not going anywhere. You'll nap here where I can keep an eye on you."

"I've kept you from work all morning, Kade. You must be slammed."

"The beauty of technology, sweetheart, is that I can work here while you sleep." He raised an eyebrow. "The question is, do you want to sleep on the couch or in the guest room?"

"Seriously, Kade." She picked up her cell phone. "Don't go to any trouble. I'll just go home and crash."

"Nice try." He shook his head. "You're going to sleep here. Come with me."

"Are all of you this bossy, or is it just you?" she grumbled.

"All of whom?"

"Your family."

He grinned at her over his shoulder. "According to my family, it's just me, although, Fiona's pretty good at it as well."

"Fine. I'll sleep here."

"Excellent choice."

Kade led her to a spacious guest room and pulled the covers back on the large bed. Samantha removed her shoes and slid into the soft sheets. The room was quite cool, so she pulled the covers to her neck and snuggled into the mattress.

"I'll be right back," Kade said.

He returned with a large woolen blanket and laid it over her. She ran her hands over the rough fabric. "Is this your tartan?"

"Aye."

Dark blues interwoven with greens incorporated all of her favorite colors. "It's beautiful."

"Thank you." He sat beside her and stroked her cheek. "Close your eyes."

"I don't want to."

He grinned. "I know you don't. Do it anyway."

"Kade?"

"Hmm?"

"I love you."

"I know." He leaned down and kissed her. "I love you too."

Sam closed her eyes as he whispered to her in either Icelandic or Gaelic…she wasn't sure, but she didn't care. It was beautiful.

Fara að sofa, elskan.

CHAPTER TWELVE

KADE LEFT THE door slightly open in case she needed him and then made his way to his office down the hall. He sat down at his laptop and pulled up his mail. As he scrolled through his messages, his cell phone buzzed. His mother's number popped up on the screen.

"Mother? Is everything all right?"

"I believe it's time you and I had an in-depth conversation," she said.

"What did Fiona tell you?"

"Och, Kadie, she didn't have to tell me anything. But on that note, you should have told me. It's been weeks."

"I didn't really know what to tell you."

"I know." He heard her sigh. "There are things that your father made me promise not to tell you until you'd found your mate, and now you have, haven't you?"

"Aye."

"Right. I'm sorry I've waited this long to speak with you, but I had no idea your mate would be human. As chieftain, you'll also need answers to a few questions."

"What questions?"

"Why don't you come up this weekend and we'll sit down and have a long chat?"

Kade sat up straighter. "I think that can be arranged."

"Excellent," she said. "I'll see you soon."

She hung up before Kade could say anything further, and he wondered what she could possibly tell him that had been a secret up until then. His cell phone buzzed again, and this time it was his head of security. "Alasdair? What did you find?"

"We found out who attacked Dr. Moore."

Kade sat back. "Who?"

"He was Cauld Ane. However, what's more disturbing is that there's some evidence that Shannon Fraser may have been involved."

"She should have been long gone by now."

"I know. We're looking into it."

Kade pinched the bridge of his nose. "Whoever was supposed to be watching Samantha this morning better be in my office first thing tomorrow morning."

"It was me."

"Excuse me?" Kade snapped.

"I was on deck to watch her."

"I told you to put someone else on her."

"I understand, but I chose to watch her and have Simon watch the area. She was my responsibility. But I was so caught up watching that Cole fellow, I missed the bigger threat. The attacker was trying to get to you."

"Bloody hell, Ali."

"I know, I'm sorry. It won't happen again."

"You're right. It won't. I'll talk to Hamish about his sister. We'll need to organize the Council earlier than I thought. You and Duncan get on hiring more men."

"All right. How many?"

"A hundred. I don't know." Kade sighed. "Enough to keep her safe."

"Kade?"

Kade turned to see Samantha standing in the doorway. "Ali, I'll call you back." He hung up and rose to his feet. "Are you all right?"

"I had a bad dream and then felt your stress."

"Come here, love." He reached out and wrapped his arms around her. "I'm sorry."

"Who do you need to keep safe?"

"You," he said as he stroked her hair.

"Me? Why?"

Kade took her hand and led her to the living room. "Have a seat. I'll get you some tea."

She lowered herself onto the sofa and frowned. "I don't want tea. I want you to answer my question."

He sat down next to her and took a deep breath. "The man who attacked you is someone who was trying to get to me."

"Why attack me, then?"

"Because *you* are the best way to get to me."

She pursed her lips. "Um, how?"

"As soon as my people saw us together, they knew you were my mate."

"How?"

"That's not something I can put into words. It's just something they knew."

Sam groaned and dropped her head in her hands. "I don't understand."

"I know. And I don't know that I can explain everything here."

"Why not?"

"Because I think you need to *see* everything. Me telling you something isn't going to convince you."

Sam cocked her head. "You think you're clever, don't you? Figuring me out so quickly."

Kade smiled. "If that's what you need to tell yourself to feel better, I won't argue."

"Okay, so then how are you going to "show" me the truth?"

"I'm going to take you home."

"What? When?"

"Tomorrow."

"Kade, I have plans with Cole tomorrow." She narrowed her eyes in suspicion. "Which you very well know."

He shrugged. "Cancel them."

"No." She felt his irritation and laid her hand on his leg, calming him. She grinned. "I kind of like this power."

"Doesn't change the fact you're going to cancel your date with Colton Drake, Samantha. If you want to simplify things and put it down to you and I dating exclusively, then do that. But you'll not spend time alone with another man."

"It's not a date. It's two friends getting together for a drink and to watch some foot—" Sam cut herself off. "Wait."

Kade stood and headed toward the kitchen.

"Kade?" Sam followed.

"Ready for that tea?"

"How did you know Cole's last name?"

Kade shrugged. "You told me."

"I did not." Sam glared at him. "What did you do?"

"What would you like for dinner?"

"Nice try." She laid her hand on his arm and closed her eyes, opening them again with a gasp. "You had him checked out. Is that how Alasdair got there so quickly?"

"What did you just do?"

"I got into your head, so to speak," she said. "You talk a lot."

Kade stared at her, confusion flooding his mind. He knew she was an empath, or she wouldn't be able to feel his emotions, but she shouldn't be able to read his mind so easily, at least, not until they were bound.

She raised an eyebrow. "But I can."

"Really?"

She nodded. "Yes. What does that mean?"

"Honestly, sweetheart, I have no idea. I think I need to call Fi."

"*After* you answer my question."

He smiled. "Which question was that? There were so many falling from your beautiful lips."

"Flattery will get you...well, nowhere today." She squeezed his arm again. "The fact you knew his name was Colton was more of a giveaway. F.Y.I., I didn't even know that little tidbit. Now, was Alasdair watching Cole?"

"No."

She narrowed her eyes in suspicion.

"He was supposed to be watching you," he admitted.

Sam gasped. "Why?"

"To keep you safe."

"That worked out well, didn't it?" she retorted. "In case you forgot to notice, it was Cole who came to my rescue."

He scowled. "I know."

She widened her eyes. "Ah, I get it. You're jealous."

"He's not who you think he is, Sam."

"I don't know him well enough to have formed that much of an opinion, Kade. We've been out twice—"

"When?" he interrupted.

"Once when I just arrived, and the night you and Connall met with the guy from Pfizer."

He dragged his hands over his scalp. "Why didn't you tell me that's what you were doing?"

"Um, gee, I don't know. Maybe 'cause it really wasn't any of your business."

"Sam," he admonished.

"Kade," she mimicked. "Look, what I do know is that he used to be a cop, but is now working for some security firm and lecturing at the university for a few weeks. He was extremely kind to me on the plane and kept me from panicking in the air. Granted, he doesn't have the same affect on me that you do, and I figured out that night over football and beer that I could only ever be friends with him, which is why I bowed out early and ended up at your place. But I do happen to like him, and I'm not going to *not* spend time with him just because you order me to."

"He's dangerous."

"*You're* dangerous," she snapped. "By your own admission, the simple fact you've decided we're supposed to be together forever has put me in harm's way. It was a good thing Cole was there this morning, or I may have something worse than a concussion."

"*Don't* say that." Kade grasped her arms. "I couldn't bear it."

"I'm sorry. I didn't mean to be cruel."

"I just want you safe."

"I know. I will be. Cole knows what he's doing...obviously." She settled her hands on his waist. "He's a friend, Kade. If you want me to agree to "date" you exclusively and make some grand statement about my faithfulness to you, I will, but I think you already know my opinion on that."

He studied her and then rolled his eyes and leaned down to kiss her. "You'll be home by ten."

"I'll be home when I darn well want to be home."

"Eleven."

Sam laughed. "No."

Kade rubbed her arms. "We'll leave Friday, so I want you rested."

"What about work?"

"Work can wait," he said.

"But you've just given me important information that I can use!"

"Like?"

"Um, like the fact we aren't the same," she pointed out. "I'd really like to draw my own blood and compare it to the samples you've given me. That blue sheen is fascinating. It must be there because of your preference to the cold. You have to be a little curious."

He shook his head. "Taking you home with me is more important."

"I must say, you're the easiest boss I've ever had in my life." Sam grinned. "You force me to rest, order me to ignore my "work," and now you're going to whisk me away to some exotic location for a vacation."

"It will be a working holiday."

"What about the lab?"

"I'll put Angus back in charge."

"Will he have a problem with that?"

"You let me worry about Angus," Kade said.

"What will the rest of the staff think about me being whisked away by the big Kahuna? This isn't going to endear me to anyone or foster respect."

"You'll be my wife; they'll respect you."

Samantha sighed. "You throw that around as though it's a done deal."

"I'm simply stating a fact. Whether it happens tomorrow or in ten years, we'll be bound and married."

"Kade," she said in exasperation.

"What?" he snapped. "I can't make you understand all of this in the course of an evening. I don't even know how to describe to you what this is like for me. I'm trying to go slowly, rather than giving in to my nature and binding you here and now. The truth is, I don't have to marry you in the way of your people to bind you."

"The way of my people?" His unease was rising and Samantha sighed. She laid her palm on his chest and waited for him to calm. "What do you mean you don't have to marry me to bind me?"

Kade groaned. "I shouldn't have said that. I don't want to scare you."

"Because saying that puts me at ease!" Sam's stomach roiled and she put distance between them. "Are you trying to tell me this binding process is going to scare me?"

"No, not at all." Kade frowned. "You're twisting my words."

"They're *your* words!"

He rubbed his forehead. "I'm bloody well mucking this up, aren't I?"

Sam took a few deep breaths. "Yes, you are."

"You don't candy-coat things, do you?"

"According to you, we don't have time for me to candy-coat things."

Kade chuckled without humor. "You're right. I'm a little on edge at the moment. That seems to be happening a lot lately. Come here."

"Not until you tell me about this binding thing."

He gave her a cocky smile. "I'd rather show you."

"I bet you would. Now, tell me."

"The binding will happen on our mating night. There are vows and then when we make love. That's what I meant when I said I don't have to marry you to bind you."

"Really? That's all you meant?"

"Essentially, yes."

"*Essentially?*" she squeaked.

"Sweetheart, there's nothing unpleasant about any of it. I promise. I'm not ready to tell you everything yet. Will you trust me?"

She bit her lip.

"Come here."

"I don't know if I trust you just yet."

"I know you don't." Kade closed the distance between them and pulled her into his arms. "Listen."

She closed her eyes. She knew he was telling her the truth, and although she wasn't fully convinced he was telling her the whole story, she wasn't afraid anymore. "You totally freaked me out."

"I know. I'm sorry." He lifted her chin and kissed her.

She pursed her lips. "So I guess we're going to the Highlands on Friday?"

"Excellent decision."

Sam snorted. "Like I had a choice."

He kissed her again. "I'll make it all worth your while."

"You really need to quit kissing me every time you want your way," she admonished.

"I kiss you because I can't stop myself." He gave her an evil grin. "Getting my way is a bonus."

* * *

Samantha woke Thursday morning and decided against a run. She still had a bit of a headache and was tired from getting to bed so late. She was just about ready to walk out the door when her cell phone rang. She knew it was Kade calling before she answered it.

"Good morning."

"*Góðan dag, fallegur*," Kade said.

"Which means?"

"Hello, beautiful."

"You haven't seen me yet, how would you know?"

Kade chuckled. "You're always beautiful."

"With that attitude, I think I'll keep you around."

"How did you sleep?" he asked. "I can feel your headache."

"I slept well, despite your attempts to keep me up all night. And yes, I have a bit of headache, but it'll pass."

He chuckled. "Open your door and I'll take it away for you."

She did as he asked and found herself pushed against the wall and kissed senseless. When he broke the kiss, it took a few seconds to catch her breath and realize she'd dropped her phone.

"Now how's your headache?" he asked as he retrieved her phone from the floor.

She grinned and slid the phone into her purse. "Gone of course, except you've made it difficult for me to concentrate on anything today."

"You're going to be with me most of it, so you don't have to."

"Don't you have meetings?"

"A few. But none that you have to be excluded from."

"Honey, please don't make me go to meetings if I don't have to be there. I hate them. I'd rather have my eyeballs plucked out by crows."

Kade laughed. "That's quite the visual."

"Well, it's true. If my headache isn't bad now, it will be if I'm forced to sit around a table and listen to people jabber about stuff I don't really care about. Just let me hide in the lab and get some work done."

He crossed his arms and leaned against the wall. "I don't know if that's a good idea."

"I can't imagine why not. I can wrap things up for our adventure and you can focus on what you need to do."

"And if I need you for some reason?"

She rolled her eyes. "You know that thing they invented *years* ago? The telephone?"

"All right."

"Thank you, oh, big and wise dictator." She pulled her coat on. "Now that I know a few of your secrets, does that mean you can tell me more about what you're looking for in the research?"

"I don't know what to tell you, honestly. I think a lot will be revealed this weekend...which reminds me." He veered off subject. "We have to push our trip to Saturday."

"How come?"

"The shareholders' dinner is on Friday night. In my eagerness to get you out of town, I completely forgot."

"That's okay. It'll give me an extra day to do some work...and a night off from you," she joked.

"Not if you don't want one."

"What do you mean?" She paused in gathering her keys and faced him.

He gave her his sexy smile...the one she could never say no to. "I was hoping you'd be my date."

"At a shareholders' meeting?"

"Well, it's more of a dinner than a meeting, but yes."

She frowned. "Is it a dinner with shareholders and their significant others?"

"Uh..." He shrugged. "Not specifically."

"Uh...then, no."

"What if I *make* it a dinner for shareholders and their significant others?"

Sam frowned. "You want me to come with you that bad?"

"I'm already having panic attacks about the fact I won't see you tonight, so yes, I want you to come with me that bad."

Sam laughed. "If you were truly that affected about me hanging out with Cole, I'd know it, but you're cute for saying it."

Kade pulled her keys from her hand and dropped them on the table. "Cute?"

"What are you doing?" she asked.

He covered her mouth with his and lifted her to his height.

Ég vil að þú manst þetta þegar þú ert með honum.

The words floated into her mind and then his thoughts, heavy with emotion, followed. Sam slid her hands into his hair and matched his passion to a dangerous level. The images flashing in her mind were lowering her guard. Snippets of what looked like individual frames to a movie flickered in her psyche. She and Kade were making love and her appearance was very different from what she saw in the mirror. She was beautiful.

Samantha quickly realized that if they didn't stop, they'd never make it to work.

It was Kade who finally broke the kiss and groaned as he lowered her back to the ground. "That was different."

"What *was* that?" Sam tried to catch her breath. "Is that how you see us? Me?"

"Aye. Does that scare you?"

"No. It's sexy as hell."

He laughed. "Well, you are. I don't understand why you don't believe me."

"Because I've always been the geeky girl who hid behind her gorgeous best friend. Pepper's the one who got the hot guys. Not me."

"Och, love. You're the most beautiful woman I've ever seen." He stroked her cheek. "Worlds apart from even Pepper."

"Charmer."

He kissed her nose. "I'm simply stating the truth."

"Thank you." She patted his chest. "Now, are you going to tell me what your little warning meant?"

"What warning?"

"Nice try. Your tone wasn't one of endearment."

"I just want you to be careful," he said. "That's all. We should probably get going. I have a meeting in less than an hour."

Sam let him escape…for now.

"What are you scheming?"

"Me?" she said innocently. "Nothing. I was just thinking I'd continue where I left off in the lab." She wrapped her scarf around her neck. "I noticed something strange in the samples yesterday."

"What do you mean, strange?" Kade asked.

Sam leaned against the back of the couch. "You know how you have the vials numbered?"

"Yes."

"The notes from Angus state that they're all from women within the same race, but not family, correct?"

"Aye."

"But the blood for one of the women is really different than the others."

Kade frowned. "How?"

"I suppose the easiest way to describe the inconsistency is that it doesn't have the power to fight off a few of the viruses the other samples can. The immunity isn't quite as…complete."

He cocked his head. "Why are you sitting behind a microscope, love?"

"What do you mean?" she asked.

"The way you simplify everything. You'd be an incredible comfort to a parent who can't understand the medical verbiage."

"I have a hard enough time talking to people, let alone a parent whose child is sick. No thank you."

"You talk to me without a problem," he pointed out.

She wrinkled her nose. "Yeah, still trying to figure out how that works."

"Because you knew me the moment you met me."

"Yeah, yeah."

"Still, you have a gift."

"Because I sound simple?"

"Yes, that's exactly what I was trying to say," he droned.

Sam grinned. "I can't take any credit for it. You can thank Dr. Bean. She was this hippie dippy professor who forced us to take every medical finding and break it down in layman's terms. I always thought it was a waste of time, since I knew my destiny was for the lab, but she insisted, and now I have a tough time using the proper terminology."

"Well, I like it."

Sam rolled her eyes. "That's because we're in the honeymoon stage of our relationship. I can't do anything wrong just yet."

"That *is* true." She narrowed her eyes and Kade laughed as he reached out and pulled her close. "What I meant to say is that even when we've been together for fifty years, you still won't ever do anything wrong."

"Good save, honey."

He leaned down and kissed her. "I love you."

"I love you too. Can we go to work now?"

"One more kiss."

She obliged.

CHAPTER THIRTEEN

Sᴀᴍ ʟᴇᴛ ʜᴇʀsᴇʟꜰ into her office and gasped. The room felt like a sauna. The thermostat on the wall had been set to the highest setting, thirty degrees Celsius. She adjusted it to a more comfortable temperature and quickly hung up her coat.

A knock and then, "Sam?" had her turning to find Fiona in her doorway.

"Hi, Fiona."

Fiona stepped back with a hiss. "Why is it so bloody hot in there?"

Sam shrugged. "I don't know. The heat was turned way up, but I don't know why."

"Hmm. We should probably tell Kade."

"No, don't bug him. He's slammed right now. It was probably the cleaning crew. I'll just leave a note for them." Sam stepped into the hallway to cool down. "Did you need me for something?"

Fiona smiled. "Yes. Kade closes the lab whenever there's a fifth Friday in a month, which means tomorrow you have the day off."

"I do?"

"Yep, and since Kade and Angus are going to be busy prepping for the shareholders' meeting, I was wondering if you'd like to go shopping."

Sam rubbed her hands together. "Ooh, a day without men…and shopping to boot. Yes, please."

Fiona frowned. "We'll still have a man with us."

"Alasdair doesn't count."

"I won't tell him you said that."

"Probably a good idea."

Fiona waved and headed to the elevator. "I'll pick you up around ten."

"Perfect." Sam stepped back into her office, still uncomfortably hot.

* * *

Sam had been in the lab, bent over her microscope for close to an hour, when she heard the swish of the lab doors and turned to find Kade walking toward her.

She grinned. "Hi, honey."

"Hi yourself. I thought I'd come and tell you I have lunch ready in my office."

"Okay. Do you want to see what I was talking about this morning?"

He nodded. "Please."

She put her sample away and then removed her protective clothing. Leading him to the computer, she pulled up her findings. "See, here's the one from the sample you gave me at the beginning." She pulled up the pictures that provided a side-by-side comparison. "And this is one of the refrigerated samples."

"What's the number on the refrigerated sample?"

"Three-two-nine-six," Sam said.

"And the other?"

"That's the one with the compromised immunity. Four-eight-seven-two," she read.

"Shite," Kade hissed as he stared at the screen.

She laid her hand on his chest and frowned up at him. "What's wrong?"

"The sample with the weakened immunity is Fiona's," he whispered.

"Really?" She focused back on her findings. "Could it be a mistake? Maybe the blood was taken wrong."

"Angus drew it, so we can be sure he made sure it's right."

"We'll figure this out, honey. I promise." She shut off her computer and faced Kade again. "I'm going to need more information though, okay? Particularly symptoms."

"Aye. We can talk about it on our way home tomorrow."

"I feel your fear, Kade. What's going on?"

"Not here."

"Okay. Let's go to your office. I'm starved." Sam hung up her lab coat and then made her way with him to the elevator.

Once inside the elevator, Sam linked her fingers with his and waited for his emotions to calm. He took a deep breath and lifted her hand to his lips. "Thank you."

She smiled.

The elevator arrived at his floor and although Kade dropped Sam's hand, he kept his connection with her by placing his hand on her back. She led him past Anna's desk and into his office and then turned to face him. "Tell me."

"I don't know what to tell you, Sam, other than we've had several women die suddenly and the only thing we know is that it has something to do with temperature. We are all affected by heat, however, our women have a lower threshold. Fiona's the worst hit. If the heat rises to just below seventeen degrees, she'll pass out, among other things. Normally, we're able to handle twenty degrees, but she's not."

114

Sam did a quick calculation in her head. "Sixty-eight degrees Fahrenheit. That's not particularly warm."

"Aye."

"So, if Fiona's blood is the immune-deficient one, who do the other samples belong to?" He raised an eyebrow and Sam crossed her arms. "You don't have to tell me, you know. I could find out by just touching you."

"That might be easier."

"Just tell me."

Kade slipped his hands into his pockets and faced the window. "Payton and Shannon."

"Shannon *Fraser*? She's Cauld Ane?" Samantha groaned. "Of course she is. No wonder she felt like she was made for you! She literally was."

Kade shook his head. "Don't do that, sweetheart. Even if I hadn't found you, it would have never been her. And she's gone. Forever."

"There's comfort in that, I suppose," she retorted.

He held his hand out to her. "Come here."

She closed the distance between them. "Sorry. I'm just tired."

"I know you are." He kissed her forehead. "I can also feel your headache. You're grumpy when you're in pain."

"Okay, don't think you know me that well. *Everyone's* grumpy when they're in pain."

"Point taken."

Sam smiled. "Are you going to tell me what you said this morning?"

"I said a lot of things this morning."

She stepped back and crossed her arms. "Start talkin'."

He studied her for several seconds and then shook his head. "I simply reminded you that you should be thinking of me when you're out tonight."

Samantha snorted. "You are a ridiculous man."

He advanced on her. "Do you need another reminder?"

She grinned. "I certainly wouldn't turn one down."

He pulled her close and kissed her until she could barely breathe. She broke the kiss and dropped her head onto his shoulder. "Wow."

"So?"

She stared up at him. "Of course I'll be thinking of you, honey. I would have been even if you hadn't played the slide show in my head." She tapped his face gently. "Now I'll just be wanting a little something more."

"You could always cancel."

"Nah, I'll just make Cole kiss me if it gets too bad." A low growl sounded in Kade's throat and Samantha laughed. "Serves you right."

"If he touches you, Samantha, I'll know about it."

"Of course you will, because I'll tell you." Samantha slid her hands around his waist. "Cole's a friend, sweetheart. Nothing more."

"Just make sure it stays that way."

"It will. Besides, your sister wants to go shopping tomorrow, so it won't be a late night."

"Good. Let's eat." He pulled her to the table. "Chef's prepared something glorious, I'm sure."

* * *

Samantha checked her appearance in the bedroom mirror and felt satisfied with her choice of apparel. She wore jeans and a black long-sleeved tee under her 49ers football jersey. She finished off the ensemble with her favorite Nikes and pulled her hair into a ponytail high on her head. She and Cole would be watching a game between the 'Niners and the Lions, so the competition was on.

Despite her arguments, Kade had insisted, and she'd reluctantly agreed, to allow Alasdair to drive her to the bar rather than have Cole pick her up. She saw the logic to a certain degree, Kade not wanting his enemies to know exactly where she lived, but even though she tried to point out that Cole wasn't an enemy, Kade wouldn't hear it.

She'd promised to see Kade before she left, so she locked up her apartment and made her way to his door. He opened it before she had a chance to knock.

"Hi," she said.

"Hi." He leaned down and kissed her and then pulled her inside. "You're not wearing that, are you?"

Sam frowned. "Yes. Why? What's wrong with it?"

"You're too bloody adorable is what's wrong with it. You need to go home and change into some kind of a sack."

Samantha laughed. "I could always wear what I wore for our first dinner."

"Absolutely not." Kade sighed. "I should come with you."

"You're funny." Samantha stroked his cheek. "Stop worrying. I'm going out with a friend. It's no big deal."

"And if I said I was going out with Shannon? Would you have an issue with that?"

Samantha couldn't stop the quiet hiss that escaped.

He frowned. "I'm sorry, love. That was unkind."

"If you're really this upset about it, I'll cancel."

"Really?" he asked, hopefully.

"No."

"Shite," he said. "I don't need you to cancel. But I do need you to be careful."

"I will be." Sam checked her watch. "I need to go. Where's Alasdair?"

"He's on his way up."

She nodded. "Okay. I'll see you tomorrow, right?"

"No. You'll see me tonight."

She raised an eyebrow. "Oh, really?"

"Yes, stop by when you get home."

"It might be late."

Kade groaned. "You're trying to kill me, aren't you?"

Samantha smiled and looped her arms around his neck. "What aren't you telling me?"

"What do you mean?"

"You know how I feel about you...you know my commitment, so I don't understand where your reservation is coming from. I can only assume it's based on information I don't have. If it were simple jealousy, I'd feel it."

Kade settled his hands on her hips and sighed. "The issue is that I don't know enough about this Cole fellow."

"What did you find when you investigated him?"

"Not much. Nothing more than what you know, actually."

She ran her fingers through his hair absently. "So then what's the problem? He's obviously not a liar, so that should give you some comfort, right?"

"The fact that we can't find out anything more than that *is* the problem. It's as though his dossier has been scripted. Put there for those looking, but no other information, and that's a red flag."

"Honey, you're trying to find something bad where there isn't anything. I think I'm a pretty good judge of character, and I don't get a weird vibe from the guy. He's a friend, and everything's going to go great tonight."

"It will if he keeps his hands to himself."

"Don't you trust me?"

"It's him I don't trust, love."

"Kade, he doesn't think of me as anything other than a friend. Seriously. How about we invite him over for dinner before he has to go home? He's here for a few more weeks, and I'd love it if you two became friends."

The doorbell pealed and Kade kissed her quickly before heading toward the door. "All right, love. We'll host a dinner party for your friend."

"Thanks for being so supportive," she droned sarcastically.

"Any time," he said and pulled open the door.

Connall stood with Alasdair on the other side.

Kade frowned. "Con?"

"Sorry to barge in," Connall said.

Something silent passed between the men and Kade stepped back. "Come in."

What's wrong? Samantha wondered.

Kade glanced at her and shook his head.

She stared at him. *Can you hear my words? Actual words?*

He nodded. Sam's mouth dropped open. *I thought we could only do that when we're touching.*

So did I.

Connall interrupted their exchange by greeting Sam, giving her a warm hug. "Is my brother letting you off the leash tonight?"

Sam chuckled. "More like I gnawed my way through."

"Well done."

"Are you ready, Dr. Moore?" Alasdair asked.

"Ah. Yeah." She shrugged on her jacket and turned to Kade. "I'll see you later, okay?"

"Aye. If you need me, call me."

He kissed her quickly and Sam followed Alasdair to the car. She slid into the backseat and secured her seatbelt. As Alasdair started the car and pulled out onto the street, Sam decided to do a little experiment.

Hey, I love you, silly man.

She waited for several seconds and just when she was about to give up, she heard him.

I love you too.

Sam sighed.

"Dr. Moore? Are you all right?"

"Yes, I'm fine." She caught his eye in the rearview mirror. "You don't have to stay when you drop me off. You can come back later."

"I'm not dropping you off. I'm joining you."

"Wh-what?" she stammered.

"Don't worry, Dr. Moore, you won't even know I'm there."

She pulled out her cell phone and punched in Kade's number.

"Yes, love, he's going to stay," Kade said as he answered the phone.

"No, he's not. Tell him he doesn't have to."

"He bloody well does have to stay, and we'll not discuss this any further."

"Kade, I'm a grown woman. Are you seriously telling me I'm required to have a babysitter everywhere I go?"

"Only when you go somewhere without me."

"I didn't sign up for this," she snapped.

"Sweetheart, I'm in the middle of something with Connall, can we talk about this when you get home? I promise, I'll explain."

"Fine," she huffed. "'Bye."

She hung up and tried not to squeal in frustration. She pushed the button for the privacy window and dialed Pepper.

"Sam?" Pepper sounded tired.

"Oh, sorry, it's early, huh?"

"Yeah, but that's okay. What's up?"

Samantha groaned. "I now have a babysitter."

"What do you mean?"

"Kade has assigned me someone to go with me on my night out with Cole."

"Like a bodyguard?"

"More like a freakin' wet nurse!" Sam snapped.

Pepper chuckled. "You're a bit old for breastfeeding, aren't you?"

"Pepper!"

"Sorry." Rustling sounded in the background and then she heard Pepper yawn. "Let's break this down logically, okay? Did you or did you not get attacked just a few days ago?"

"So?" she grumbled.

"So, do you think maybe Kade's just being a good boyfriend and making sure you're safe? He's got a lot of money, so he has resources most people don't."

"That doesn't give him the right to watch me every second of every day."

"I personally think it's really romantic," Pepper said.

"Coming from the eternal bleeding heart," Samantha complained.

"Look, I get that you need your down time and that you haven't had any in a few weeks, and I get that you're an emotional wreck, but you're the one who said you trust him implicitly, so what's this really about?"

Sam felt tears threaten to fall. "I can't tell you."

"Aw, honey, you can tell me anything. I don't understand what's so bad you can't tell me."

"I know," Sam said. "I'm sorry, but I can't, and I think that's what's driving me crazy. I can't share the biggest part of my life with my best friend."

"You know this just makes me more curious?"

"I know. It would do the same to me."

"Will you be able to tell me when I get there?" Pepper asked.

"I hope so."

"Okay. Well for now, I have to trust your judgment about this Kade guy. If you love him as much as you say you do, then he must be pretty incredible, right?"

"Yeah, he is."

"Then trust him. I'm sure you're blowing the whole bodyguard thing a little out of proportion."

"Whose side are you on?"

Pepper chuckled. "I'm on the side that keeps you safe."

"I swear I feel like I've been dropped into some James Bond movie. Coming from our little town, I would have never guessed that I'd move to Scotland, fall in love with a billionaire, and run the risk of being kidnapped. It's all very overwhelming."

"He's a billionaire?"

Sam snorted. "That's what you took away from that?"

Pepper laughed. "It's not like you didn't grow up with money, Sam."

"No, I know. But Daddy never had security or drivers at his beck and call."

"Listen, this is all temporary. You're going to have an amazing time with this Cole guy...I'm jealous, by the way. Two hot men in less than a month...not fair."

Sam stared at her hands. "I wouldn't call Cole hot, necessarily."

"Kade sure as hell is. I haven't seen Cole yet. How about you take a picture tonight and send it to me?"

"Yeah, yeah."

"Are you off the ledge?"

Sam sighed. "Yes, I'm away from the window."

"Good. Cut your man some slack. If he had some weird agenda, you'd know about it. You always do."

"You're right. I guess it just irritates me that he's making these judgment calls without talking to me."

"You never were good at being taken care of. Even as a kid you hated being treated like a child."

"When was I ever a kid?" Sam challenged.

"You're kind of acting like one now."

"I'm ignoring you now."

"Okay, so long as I got my point across." Pepper laughed. "Talk to Kade. You'll figure it out."

"I can't wait for you to get here."

"Me neither." Pepper yawned. "For now, though, it's two hours before I'm supposed to get up for work, so I'm going to say good-bye."

"Sorry, friend."

"No worries. You'll make it up to me when I fall in love."

Sam laughed. "Damn straight."

"Have fun tonight. Remember to take that picture."

"I will. 'Bye."

CHAPTER FOURTEEN

SAMANTHA HUNG UP, shoved her phone back in her purse, and lowered the privacy glass. Alasdair smiled at her from the rearview mirror. She felt decidedly better, which meant she felt a little less like yelling.

Who do you want to yell at, love?

She jumped, startled by his voice so strong in her mind. She pulled her phone out again and dialed Kade's number.

He picked up on the first ring. "As strange as that is for me, I quite like the surprise it causes you," he said.

"I bet."

Kade chuckled. "You have to admit, it will come in handy when we want to talk about people behind their backs."

Samantha couldn't stop the laugh. "I didn't take you for a gossip."

"With this new ability, I might just start."

The car slowed and Alasdair informed her they'd arrived.

"I've got to go, Kade. We're here."

"I love you. You know that right?"

Samantha sighed. "Yes, I know."

She hung up without saying it back, more to make a point, but then felt so guilty, she closed her eyes and whispered it to him anyway.

Hafa gaman, elskan.

Which means?

I'll tell you when you get home.

Brat.

Alasdair opened Sam's door and she asked him what Kade's words meant, surprised to see the large man blush. "It means, 'have fun, baby.'"

Sam smiled. "Oh. Thanks."

"I won't be far, Dr. Moore," Alasdair said. "But I'll try to stay out of your way."

"Thanks. I appreciate it."

Cole waited by the front door and grinned as he made his way to her. "Hey there, beautiful."

"Hi," Sam said. "How are you?"

He kissed her cheek and gave her a hug. "I'm good now that I'm seeing you. You look great."

"Thanks. Are you ready to lose?"

"Never going to happen." Cole held the door for her and followed her inside the bar. "How do you feel?"

Sam smiled. "Ready for some football."

"Excellent."

Sam followed him to a secluded booth in the back corner of the bar and took her seat.

* * *

Kade slapped the file onto his dining room table and rose to his feet. "Do you think he's working for Ármann?"

Connall shook his head. "It's much, much worse. He's FBI and working with Interpol and MI-6."

"Why?"

"Someone flagged our financial interests, and with the closing of the intern program so soon after it was started, someone's put a wee word in their ears that something fishy's going on."

"What does the intern program have to do with money? There wasn't much allocated."

Connall opened the file and slid it toward Kade, his finger resting on a highlighted line. "According to this, a million was transferred into the intern program and then right back out, but not back into the main account."

"Where did it go?"

"We don't know. Duncan's looking into it."

"Shite, Con. You, Brodie, and I are the only ones in this bloody company with the authority to move money around. You didn't notice?"

"Did you?"

"No, damn it. I would have had to sign off on this."

Connall shook his head. "Not necessarily. You have to be informed of anything being paid over one hundred thousand, but moving money from account to account is fine for anything under one point five million."

"I understand that, however, I see everything anyway." Connall stared at him and Kade sighed. "Spit it out."

Connall shook his head. "You've been a wee bit distracted over the past few weeks. Is it possible you may have missed something?"

"Damn it." Kade slapped his hands on the table. Connall had a point. "Fyrirgefðu."

"Apologies aren't going to make this right," Kade snapped. "I want a full audit of every account, even petty bloody cash, and I want it on my desk before end of day tomorrow."

"Aye." Connall stood. "I'll get Rònan on it."

Rònan was Hamish and Shannon's father.

"No. I don't want a Fraser anywhere near the accounts. It needs to be someone we trust."

"All right. What do you want me to do?"

"Talk to Duncan."

Connall nodded. "Okay. Do you want me to hang around?"

"No. I'm going to call Ali and have him bring Samantha home."

"Is that wise?" Connall asked.

Kade frowned. "Probably not."

Kade ushered Connall from the flat and pulled out his phone. He dialed Alasdair, issued instructions, and then made the call he knew may cause bodily harm.

* * *

Samantha was forced to sit next to Cole in the booth they shared in order to see the television screen. Since her conversation with Kade earlier, she admitted she was a little on alert, but Cole had been nothing but a perfect gentleman, and she'd finally allowed herself to relax. Until her phone rang…again. Kade was beginning to irritate her. "I'm sorry, Cole."

"The guy's a little possessive, huh?"

She sighed. "Not typically. He's just under a bit more stress these days."

"Oh?" Cole sipped his beer. "What kind of stress?"

Sam smiled. "Nice try."

"Sorry, you can take the cop out of the force…" Cole raised an eyebrow. "What's with your protective detail?"

She nodded toward Alasdair. "He's my driver for the night."

Cole shook his head. "There are four others on Samantha watch."

"What?" she squeaked and glanced around the room.

"The guy in the corner with the suspiciously butch-looking woman. No way in hell they're on a date. And the two guys playing darts."

"How do you know?" she asked.

"It's what I do." He leaned back against the wall. "Is everything okay with you?"

"I don't know what you mean." Her phone buzzed again. "Really?"

Cole smiled. "Just answer it."

She shook her head. "No. I'm having dinner with my friend and Kade has to get over it."

Cole frowned.

"What did I say?" she asked.

"I hate being referred to as the friend."

Sam wasn't quite sure what to think of that statement. "Cole."

He waved his hand. "Don't worry about it, Sam. I guess I just hoped that since I met you first, I might have a snowball's chance in hell."

"It's complicated," she said.

"How much do you know about this guy?"

Sam traced the pattern in the tablecloth. "I know enough."

"From what I understand, the Gunnachs own Edinburgh."

"A little bit of an overstatement, don't you think?"

He shrugged. "People with that much power and money usually have something to hide."

Sam narrowed her eyes. "Are you trying to tell me something without actually telling me *anything*, Cole?"

"I just want you to be careful. They aren't to be trusted."

"You don't even know them." Sam frowned. "Where's all this coming from? I thought we were having dinner, not discussing the company I work for." Cole raised an eyebrow but didn't respond, which made Sam more and more uncomfortable. "What?"

"Have you given any thought to the fact that Kade Gunnach might not be a good fit for you?"

Sam rolled her eyes. "Excuse me?"

"I'm just saying that he owns most of Scotland and you're a small-town girl. Can't you see the disconnect?"

Sam clenched her fists in an effort not to throw her beer at him. "Enlighten me."

"He's been paired with several high-profile women from entertainment to heiresses, but hasn't settled down with any of them. Do you think you might be a little starry-eyed when it comes to him?"

"Are you saying I'm not *good* enough for him?"

"No!"

"You know nothing about him, Cole."

"Maybe you don't either. Have you thought about that? I think you might want to reevaluate what you're doing with this guy."

Sam scowled. "Where do you get off telling me what I should and shouldn't do?"

"Sam, I just want you to be careful."

"That implies you think I'm not."

He sighed. "No, not at all. I just wonder if…"

"What?"

Before she could register what he was doing, he'd slid his hand into her hair and laid his lips on hers. She shoved him away with a surprised squeak and slid from the booth.

"Aw, come on, Sam. Don't be mad. I'm just looking out for you."

"By kissing me?" she snapped. "You have no right to tell me the man I'm in love with is not the one for me." She rummaged in her purse for some money and dropped it on the table. "You're not my brother or my father, Cole. It's none of your business."

He slid the money back to her. "This was my treat, Sam."

"Dr. Moore?"

She turned to find Alasdair standing behind her. "I'd like to go home."

He nodded. "Yes, m'lady."

"Sam, come on." Cole stood and reached for her. "Don't go. You haven't finished your dinner."

Alasdair stepped between them, effectively cutting off Cole's attempt to grasp her arm. Sam started toward the door, watching the "detail" Cole had pointed out. He was right. They seemed awfully interested in her.

Sweetheart? Kade's voice swam in her mind. *What's wrong?*

Just leave me alone, she snapped.

Alasdair led Sam to the car and opened the back door for her. She slid inside and laid her head back on the headrest. So much for a fun night out. Now she was tired, irritated, *and* starving.

* * *

Cole closed his hotel door with a click and pulled out his "other" cell phone. The one that if anyone were to find it, would prove to be both revealing and dangerous. "Hey, it's Cole."

"What the hell is going on?" came the voice on the other end.

"She won't give me anything."

"Yeah, well my sister could never be accused of being an idiot," Dalton said.

"Look, do you think it's possible the Gunnach family's on the up-and-up?"

"No. At least, not all of them."

"Your sister really likes this guy, Dalton. I don't know that you'll be able to convince her that he's a scumbag."

"Damn it, Cole. You were supposed to charm her! Why the hell do you think we picked you? You've had over a month to woo her! I hadn't banked on her falling for some guy in a skirt. She's a football-loving southern belle. *You* were supposed to be her ideal."

"I apologize for not being her type," Cole snapped.

"On paper you are," Dalton informed him.

"Apparently, the universe had other ideas. She's gaga for this guy, Dalton." Cole rolled his eyes. "I even kissed her."

Dalton swore. "You kissed her? Damn it, Cole, you're an idiot!"

Cole forced himself not to release a litany of curses. "I'm not typically turned down."

"Yeah, but Sam's different. I need to find out about this guy. My parents seem to like him too, which could pose another issue."

Cole laughed. "Are you saying you can't control your family?"

"Keep laughing, buddy," Dalton warned. "The bigger issue is, that if Sam likes this Kade guy, he's more than likely some kind of a saint. She has a higher bullshit meter than anyone I know, which poses a problem."

"Only one?"

"It means that even if he isn't a criminal, he might be being duped by someone, and Samantha might get caught in the crossfire."

"What do you want me to do?"

Dalton sighed. "Let me think about it. I may need to visit."

"How are you going to explain that?"

"Pepper's moving there in a few weeks. I'm thinking perhaps I should escort her."

"I thought she hated you," Cole observed.

"Nah." Dalton chuckled. "She just thinks she does."

* * *

Samantha felt the familiar bump of the entrance to the parking garage and opened her eyes as Alasdair drove into the darkness of their private floor. She slipped her phone back in her purse, and when she looked up again, Kade stood near the elevator bay.

"If it's all right, I'll drop you here, Dr. Moore," Alasdair said.

"Do I have a choice?" She caught his eye in the rearview and frowned. "Fine."

Alasdair pulled the car to a stop. Kade opened the door and held his hand out to her. She ignored him and climbed out of the car. He dropped his hand and leaned in the window to speak to Alasdair. Sam took advantage of his distraction and rushed to the elevator. Pushing the button, she was irked to find the elevator didn't come at her whim. It came at Kade's, arriving just as he caught up to her. The doors opened and Sam stepped inside. Kade followed.

Halfway to their floor, he pulled her into his arms and kissed the crown of her head. "Are you going to ignore me all night?"

She felt the prick of tears as she sagged against him. "Yes," she sniffed.

"I made you some pasta. You can ignore me while you eat."

"I'd rather go home and sleep."

"And you will. After *you* eat and *I* talk."

"I am a little hungry," she admitted.

The elevator stopped at their floor and he ushered her into his apartment. He headed to the kitchen while Samantha set her purse and coat on the sofa and then dropped into what used to be Kade's favorite chair.

She noticed the vase that had been on the table was missing and frowned. "Kade, where's the vase?"

"It broke," he called from the kitchen.

"How?"

"It fell off the table."

She frowned as she slid her shoes off and tucked her feet under her bottom.

Kade returned with a plate and glass of wine. He handed her the food and set the wine on the table next to her. "I'm never getting my chair back, am I?"

"Probably not. What happened to the vase, Kade?"

"Eat, love."

Sam took a bite and sighed. "I'm going to gain fifty pounds a year dating you."

"I plan to make you a fat and happy wife." He smiled and sat on the ottoman in front of her. "What happened with Cole?"

"What happened to the vase?"

"*Samantha.*"

She took another bite and swallowed. "I don't really want to talk about it."

"It's important, Sam."

She set her fork on the plate. "He warned me away from you."

"Did he now?" He squeezed her leg. "What else?"

"Nothing."

"Sam."

"He admitted he liked me."

"*And.*"

"He kissed me." She felt the tension build in the room and made the mistake of looking at him. His eyes were burning and she shivered as she shifted in her seat, laying her hand on his leg to calm him. "But you knew that already, didn't you? Where's the vase?"

"In the bloody rubbish." Kade pulled away from her touch and stood. "Damn it, Samantha. I want to kill the bastard."

"Get in line," she grumbled. "I just don't know what to do now."

"You'll stay away from him."

"Why?"

"Because he's not who he says he is," Kade said.

"He said something similar about you." Samantha set her plate aside and stood. "Why is it so important to you men that I follow your absolute orders and forgo my own judgment? I'm perfectly capable of making up my own mind about people." She took her plate into the kitchen.

Kade followed. "You haven't finished, love."

She dumped the plate in the sink. "I'm not hungry anymore."

Kade crossed his arms and leaned against the counter. "I'm not asking you to forgo your judgment, Sam. I'm simply asking that you keep your distance."

"Is that why you called forty-two times during dinner?"

He smiled. "Three times…it was three."

"So you called me three times to tell me to keep my distance."

"No. I called you to tell you Cole's working for Interpol."

"Interpol? Why?"

Kade shrugged. "There's apparently an investigation into our family."

"*That's* why he kept asking all those questions," she hissed.

"What did you tell him?"

"Nothing!" She slapped her hand on the counter. "Damn it! Why do you assume I'm going to spill my guts to everyone?"

"I don't. I just need to determine what you said, so I can figure out what he might infer from it. Whether it's no information or vague."

"Well, it was neither. I told him that I would not discuss you or the company with him and it didn't matter what he said, my relationship with you was off limits. Nothing vague about that." Sam crossed her arms. "Why is there an investigation, anyway?"

"Not sure. Connall's looking into it at the moment. It's probably nothing, but I'll know more in the next couple of days."

Samantha rubbed her forehead.

Kade closed the distance between them and pulled her close. "I'm sorry, sweetheart. I didn't want to be right about Cole."

She let out a snort. "Yes you did."

"Okay, maybe I did."

She wrapped her arms around his waist and settled her cheek against his chest. "I wish I knew what his agenda was."

"Can I ask you to keep your distance?"

She shook her head. "Nope, but I will. Because *I* want to."

"Thank you."

She pulled away from him and started to do the dishes. "Can you answer something for me?"

"Of course."

"Why did you have a protective detail on me tonight?"

"How did you know?"

"I didn't. Cole figured it out."

"Maybe I should give him a job," Kade retorted.

Sam turned from the sink and leaned a hip against the counter. "Right."

"I was trying to keep you safe without making you feel like you were being watched." He pulled the plate from her hand and set it in the dishwasher before closing it and handing her a towel. "Leave those, love. I'll take care of them."

She dried her hands and dropped the towel on the counter. "I should probably go. It's late."

"Or you could stay for a while," he suggested.

"Honey, it's almost midnight. And even if you've closed the lab tomorrow, your sister wants to spend the day with me. I don't want to be yawning all day."

"Perhaps I should go with you."

"Outside of the fact you have a big dinner to prepare for, I get the feeling your sister wants to find out if I'm good enough for her big brother, and I'd personally like some girl time."

"Are you sick of me already?"

"Yep, pretty much." She looped her arms around his neck.

He chuckled and kissed her. "Tomorrow's going to be horrid."

"For you, maybe. I'm going to have a blast." She grinned. "I won't be thinking of you stuck in meetings with Angus and your brothers while your sister and I buy up Edinburgh."

"Since you're going to have such an amazing day, will you stay for another hour and give me something to think about tomorrow other than stocks?"

Sam laughed. "Oh, you are good."

He pulled away and executed a very formal bow. "Thank you, m'lady. Years of practice."

"Yes, I'll stay for one more hour." She took the open bottle of wine on the counter and headed back to the living room. "I'm thirsty anyway."

Kade followed and pulled her down beside him in his chair. "This is one way of getting my chair back, I suppose."

She shifted so she sat on his lap. "Now that I've done you a favor, I'm wondering if I can ask one of you."

"Of course."

"Pepper arrives in a little over a month. Do you mind if she stays in my apartment until we find something together?"

He cocked his head. "I don't mind in the least, but you're not going to look for something together."

"Oh, really? Why not?"

"Because she can just stay with you until we're married."

Sam groaned. "You slid that in so seamlessly."

Kade chuckled. "In all seriousness, you don't have to look for anything else. Your friend is welcome to stay as long as you'd like her to. Of course, when we're *married*, you won't be able to live with her anymore."

Sam wrinkled her nose. "*If* we get married, it won't be for a while, which will give her plenty of time to find something else."

"She's welcome to stay even *when* we get married. You'll move in here, after all."

"What happens *if* we get married and I like my place better?"

"Well, *when* we get married, if you decide you'd rather live there, then Pepper is welcome to move in here," he kissed her nose, "and I'll move in there."

She kissed him. "*If* we get married, I'd probably move in here. I quite like this place."

"I noticed…especially considering you're here every night." He kissed her neck. "This will mean, of course, that *when* we get married, you'll have an easier time adjusting to your new home."

As he kissed the sensitive spot behind her ear, Sam bit the inside of her cheek to keep from moaning. "That is a good point. *If* we get married."

Kade covered her mouth with his and all talk of roommates and marriage were quickly forgotten as he gave her just a taste of what she could look forward to…as soon as they were married.

CHAPTER FIFTEEN

SAMANTHA YAWNED AS she pulled on her black, knee-high boots. "Curse you, Kade Gunnach," she said to the floor. She'd stayed far past the one-hour promise, falling asleep in Kade's lap and waking up in his guest room at almost four. She'd attempted to slide out from under the covers, but found herself pulled up against him instead.

"Where are *you* going?" he'd grumbled.

"Kade, I'm still fully clothed and under a pile of blankets," she'd complained. "I was thinking I'd go home and sleep there where I can be comfortable."

He nuzzled her neck and hummed his disagreement. "I like you just where you are. Stay."

"I'm in jeans and a long-sleeved shirt, babe. I really need to get into something else."

He sat up and rubbed his hands down his face. "If I get you a pair of my pajamas, will you stay?"

Sam yawned. "Do I really have a choice?"

"Of course," he retorted. "Head *all* the way home, climb into a cold bed, and find yourself miserable without me."

Sam giggled. "Well, when you put it that way…"

He gathered up a pair of cotton pajamas that she had a feeling he'd never worn and once she'd changed into them, she met him back in the guestroom. He was now in a T-shirt and flannel pants, which showcased his physique nicely. He took her hand and led her to the master bedroom.

"What are you doing?" Sam asked.

"I hate that bed. I want to sleep with you in my bed."

"Why did you sleep in there to begin with?"

"I didn't want you to wake up and get scared." He held the covers back on his large king-sized bed and waited for her to climb in.

"You are entirely too good to be true." She'd kissed him and then was suddenly jarred awake by his alarm.

Now she sat in her apartment, working on her second cup of coffee and wishing she could sleep for another six hours. Kade was already at work, and she was waiting for Fiona to pick her up for their day of fun.

Don't fall asleep, love.

She started and wrinkled her nose. *I wasn't falling asleep, I was checking for holes in my eyelids.*

Laughter sounded in her mind. *I do love your southern expressions.*

Good to know.

I'll make it up to you tonight.

She sighed. *I just end up more like the walking dead when you "make it up to me." Besides, you'll be at your dinner tonight.*

After *the meeting.*

She let out a quiet snort. *I will be sleeping.*

Fiona's at your door. Have fun. I love you.

"How did you know that?" she wondered aloud, and then her doorbell rang.

She pulled open the door and grinned. Fiona stood with Payton in the hallway.

"I hope you don't mind that I brought Payton," Fiona said. "She doesn't like to be without me."

Samantha laughed. "Hi. Come in."

The ladies breezed inside and Samantha closed the door. She hugged them and then gathered up her purse and jacket.

"How did you get the day off?" she asked Payton.

Payton smiled. "Fiona finagled it. Anna's taking notes for the meetings. It pays to have your future sister-in-law related to the owners of the company."

Sam laughed again as they left the apartment and headed to the elevator. "No doubt. This is going to be fun. Where are you taking me?"

Fiona pressed the button to the private garage. "Much to Payton's disappointment, I thought we'd take you to the Royal Mile. It's really touristy, but the shops are adorable, and you can get a bit of Scottish flavor in each store."

"Let me guess," Sam mused. "Lots of walking?"

Payton groaned. "Up and down a bloody long hill."

Sam clapped her hands. "I *cannot* wait!"

The elevator doors opened and they made their way to the car. Alasdair held the door open and waited for them to slide inside. He drove them to Fiona's favorite jewelry store and dropped them off with the promise to return in an hour to pick up any packages they may have.

"I'm just picking up the watch I bought Angus for his birthday. They were engraving it for me," Fiona explained.

"When's his birthday?" Sam asked as he followed her inside.

"On the fourth." Fiona grinned. "We usually have dinner together with the family…obviously, you're invited."

Sam smiled. "Thanks."

The bell jingled over the door as Fiona let the door close.

"Ah, Miss Gunnach, perfect timing," an elderly gentleman said as he came toward them. "I just finished polishing the watch."

"Thank you, Mr. Ferguson. I can't wait to see it."

While Fiona and Payton waited at the counter, Sam made her way around the small shop. Unique jewelry, along with pewter tankards and fun Scottish souvenirs, filled the cases and shelves. She was drawn to a glass case that had necklaces inside. One in particular caught her eye and she had a pang of homesickness. A large ruby surrounded by pomegranates and the pomegranate flower, all interwoven with Celtic knots in white gold hung from a white gold chain. To say it was stunning was an understatement. She'd have to bring Pepper here.

"May I help you with anything?"

Sam glanced at the young man behind the counter and grinned. "No, thank you. Just admiring."

Payton waved her over to the other side of the store. "Look at these, Sam."

Sam joined her and felt her eyes widen. Trays of one-of-a-kind engagement rings took up an entire case and the sparkle from the diamonds was impressive.

"Try one on," Payton said.

"No, that's okay."

"*Sam*, dream a little. If you could pick anything, what would you pick?"

"Oh, stop," Sam said with a nervous laugh.

"Come on," she pressed. "Fiona's going to be a while, so just try a couple. I'm going to."

The young man who had offered to help with the necklaces stood waiting for them again.

Payton pointed to a ring with a diamond the size of her head. "May I try that one, please?"

"Of course." He pulled it out and settled it gently on a blue and green tartan cloth.

Payton slipped it on and held it up. "Gorgeous."

"It's a little much, don't you think?" Sam said as she studied the jewelry.

"But look how it sparkles."

The sales clerk smiled. "Yes ma'am. It's one of a kind."

Sam grimaced. "I don't even want to know what it costs."

"Four-hundred thousand," he said.

"*Dollars?*" she squeaked.

"Pounds," he corrected.

"Payton, take that off right now," Sam ordered. "It costs more than a house."

Payton giggled. "I know, but it's gorgeous, don't you think? And certainly within Kade's budget."

"So that's your plan!" Sam exclaimed. "Sneaky."

"Admit it…this one's stunning, right?"

Sam shook her head. "You need to quit. Even if we were heading in that direction and even if he had the budget, I would never choose something like that."

"Killjoy." Payton handed the ring back. "Show me what you'd choose, then."

"No, it's fine, Payton."

"*Please*, Sam. Dream with me," she insisted.

Sam raised an eyebrow and hesitated, but the lure of the beautiful jewelry was too hard to resist. Besides, it was just pretend, right?

Payton pointed to a ring and grinned. "What about that one?"

"No. Too much."

Sam continued to walk the length of the counter and then, as though it was written in the stars, a ring caught her eye. Celtic knots were woven around the band, coming together to cradle a princess-cut diamond in white gold. "May I see that one, please?" she asked.

"Lovely choice. The center diamond is three-point-nine-five-carats and is as close to perfect as they get. No inclusions, brilliant color, and cut for maximum sparkle." The clerk pulled it out and after giving it a quick polish, handed it to her. Sam slipped it on her finger and her heart began to slam against her chest.

Sweetheart? What are *you doing?*

Kade sounded curious and somewhat amused.

Sam took a deep breath and smiled. *Nothing, honey.*

Why do you sound like the cat that swallowed the canary?

I have no idea. Go back to your meeting.

"It's beautiful, Sam," Payton said.

She nodded and studied it for a few seconds before sliding it off and handing it back to the salesman. "Thank you."

He put it back in the case. "Is there anything else you'd like to look at?"

Sam shook her head.

"Are you sure?" Payton asked. "What about a wedding ring for Kade?"

"You are too much, Payton McFadden."

She grinned. "Come on, there's more to see."

Sam perused the men's rings and groaned when she found one that was similar to the one she'd tried on. A thick platinum band with Celtic knots wrapping around the ring.

"Oh, Sam. It's like it was meant to be."

"*Payton*. Enough with the finagling." Sam chuckled. "We should get Fiona."

The attendant gave her a nod and moved to assist another customer while Sam and Payton made their way back to Fiona. She showed them the watch and then let the owner of the shop wrap it before setting it safely in her purse. "Ready?"

Sam nodded. "Yes."

Just as they stepped out of the store, her phone rang. Kade's name came up on the screen.

"Hi."

"Hi yourself. You're not having too much fun without me, are you?" he asked.

Sam giggled. "Absolutely."

"Hmm. Maybe I should meet you. I miss you terribly."

"Me too, but I have to go. You have work to do and I have shopping to get back to."

"I love you."

Sam smiled. "Same here, honey."

Sam hung up and was led into store after store as they made their way up The Mile to Edinburgh Castle. Lunchtime approached, so Fiona suggested they stop at a restaurant before continuing their trek.

As they waited for their table, Sam let out a quiet squeal when strong arms wrapped around her waist and warm lips connected with her cheek. "Góðan dag, fallegur."

"Hi." She grinned up at Kade. "What are you doing here?"

"We decided we couldn't survive the rest of the day without you," he said.

"We?"

He nodded toward the front door. Angus and Brodie were greeting Fiona and Payton.

Samantha squeezed Kade's hand. "Are Payton and Brodie...you know?"

"It's complicated."

"Well, you can explain it to me later, then."

He chuckled. "Can't wait."

"You don't need to worry about me, you know." Sam slid a hand around his waist. "But I am glad you're here."

He kissed her temple. "Are you sure you're having a good time?"

"I am. Your sister's a blast and Payton is beyond sweet."

He smiled. "Are you still tired?"

"Yes, evil one. I am. I could use another dose of coffee."

"Good thing we're in a restaurant, then."

"You're on fire today, honey."

Kade chuckled. "Are you sure you won't come with me tonight?"

"I have a date with a feather bed and comforter. You're on your own," she said. "But if you want to call me when you get home, I might let you say goodnight."

"How generous."

Sam giggled. "I know. You're a very lucky man."

He swept her hair away from her face and ran his fingers through it. "I loved waking up with you."

She gave him a gentle squeeze. "Mmm. Me too."

"Our table's ready, lovebirds," Fiona said. "If you could stop making googly eyes at each other for five minutes, we can actually sit down."

The host led the group to the table and Sam smiled when the men seated the women. Sam took her seat, wishing Kade wasn't at the head of the table. She would have liked to have been sitting next to him, close enough to lean against him and sleep. She stifled a yawn and ordered a triple espresso before staring down at the menu.

Conversation swirled around the table as they waited for their food. Sam leaned forward and reached for Kade's hand under the table. He gave hers a gentle squeeze. "What?"

She smiled. "I'm just hoping this connection we have works to wake me up."

* * *

Samantha sat in Kade's living room and surfed through the limited choices of television stations. The shopping excursion wrapped up after the ladies had dinner and she'd been delivered back home to sleep. She managed almost four hours before being awakened by Kade when his dinner was over.

Now she sat in her favorite chair and waited for him to open a bottle of wine. She changed the channel and landed on the local news. What she wasn't expecting was to see Kade's face flash across the screen.

"Are you kidding me?" Sam sat stunned, her mouth gaping open.

"Well, ladies, it appears Scotland's richest bachelor may be off the market soon," the news reporter reported. *"Dr. Kade Gunnach was seen leaving the Royal McGregor, his arm wrapped around a mysterious brunette, along with his brother Brodie and sister Fiona."*

A photo of Samantha walking next to Kade came up on the screen. She hit the pause button. "Kade?" she called.

"Yes, love?"

"Um, we're on TV."

He emerged from the kitchen, a wine bottle and two glasses in his hands. "What do you mean?"

She pointed to the screen with the remote and pressed play again. "Look."

Kade set the bottle and glasses on the coffee table and sat on the sofa.

"An anonymous source tells us the lady is a new researcher working for Gunnach Pharmaceutical. We haven't learned her name yet, but we will. She was also seen earlier in the morning leaving our favorite wee jewelry store with Fiona Gunnach and Payton McFadden. Will there be a wedding soon? It's the question of the hour, and you'll hear it here first."

Video of the group emerging from the restaurant played and then a close-up of Kade leaning down to kiss Samantha.

Kade swore and pulled his phone from his pocket. "Hi, Con. Yeah, I'm watching it now. Find out how the hell these vultures know anything about Samantha."

Sam laid her hand on Kade's leg. His irritation ebbed a bit, but his voice stayed forceful as he spoke with Connall about the current predicament. When he hung up, Samantha took his phone from him and laid it on the table.

He tried to grab for it. "I need to call Ali."

She shook her head. "No. You're freaking out about nothing. Did we or did we not go to a public restaurant and kiss on a public street?"

"Not the point."

She laughed. "Uhhh...kind of is the point."

"We have privacy laws in this country, and the damn press is stepping over the line."

"I didn't realize you were famous."

He snorted. "We're wealthy. We can't escape it, I'm afraid."

Rising from the chair, Sam straddled his lap and balanced her hands on his shoulders. "Well, I'll just make sure I'm wearing something fabulous next time I go out in public. My hair was a mess!"

"You could shave your head and go out in a burlap sack, and you'd still be the prettiest lass in Scotland."

She kissed him. "I wonder if all the other women in Scotland know what a charmer you are. I don't relish the competition for your affecttion."

He flipped her so she was under him on the couch. "You have no competition, love. There will never be anyone else for me." He kissed her deeply and Sam smiled in vindication. Kade was effectively distracted from his vendetta.

CHAPTER SIXTEEN

SATURDAY MORNING ARRIVED and Sam felt like she was ten and heading to Disneyworld. She practically ripped the door off the hinges when Kade knocked. He gave her a quick kiss and then stepped inside. "I can feel your excitement."

"Shoot." Sam wrinkled her nose. "I was hoping to appear bored. Make you work hard at entertaining me."

Kade laughed. "I'll still work hard to entertain you, love. Have no fear. Where's your bag?"

"By the sofa."

Kade wheeled her large suitcase to the door. "Do you have bricks in here?"

Sam shrugged. "Shoes."

"Of course you have shoes."

"Now you sound like Pepper. Her philosophy is one pair tennies, one pair dressy, and riding boots."

"Riding boots? Really?"

"Yep. Even in the middle of the city...any city. If there's a horse in the vicinity, she'll figure out a way to ride it." Sam followed Kade into the hallway, locking her apartment before they headed to the elevators. "No luggage?" she asked.

He smiled. "It's already in the car."

Sam pulled on her coat and gloves. "Ah, so I'm not the only one excited for our vacation, hmm?"

He laughed. "I've been on pins and needles for days."

He led her to the garage and settled her bag in the trunk. Sam waited for him to let her in the front seat.

"Are you planning on driving?" he asked.

"Oh, right." She laughed. "I don't know if I'll ever get used to the steering wheel being on the *wrong* side of the car."

She went around the car and he grinned, opening the passenger door for her.

"Where's my faithful watchdog today?" she asked as she slipped inside. "I'm surprised Alasdair's not driving."

"Both of those responsibilities fall to me while we're on holiday."

"Aren't you lucky?"

"I think so. For so many reasons." He closed her door and made his way to the driver's side. "Ready?"

"Absolutely."

* * *

Kade glanced at Samantha, who'd fallen asleep an hour into their trip. He lowered the music and focused back on the road. He'd driven this road for years, but it still wasn't lost on him the ease of traveling by car rather than horse.

As he entered Gunnach land, his heart grew peaceful. Even when he felt all was right with the world, when he came home, he was always glad to be there. He didn't come home nearly enough, but now that he'd found his mate, he felt it would be a good idea to change that.

He laid his hand on Sam's thigh and focused back on the road. Her small hand covered his and he turned his head.

She smiled sleepily. "How long have I been asleep?"

"Not long."

"Are we close?"

He nodded. "We're on Gunnach land now, so about thirty minutes or so."

"It's so beautiful here." Sam turned and took in the scenery. "The gray with the misting rain makes me feel like I'm in a romantic movie."

"Or a horror film."

She laughed. "Nah, I've got my guy next to me. Definitely romantic."

"Isn't the couple in love usually the first ones to die?"

"Only if they're naked."

Kade laughed as he linked his fingers with hers. "I wouldn't be opposed to that idea."

Sam sighed. "Don't tempt me. I'm already ignoring my upbringing."

"Oh? How so?"

"No staying overnight with a man and no going on trips with him until you're engaged," she said mimicking the voice of an old woman.

"Based on Thursday night alone, you really *have* ignored your up-bringing."

"Damn skippy." She grinned and focused on the landscape again. White fencing came into view and horses grazed in the open fields. "Pepper will love this."

"That's the road leading to Connall's place. Those are a few of his mares."

"They're beautiful."

"I'm sure he'd love to give you a tour." He lifted her hand to his lips and kissed her palm. "As we drive over this hill, you'll be able to see my house."

Sam shifted in her seat and watched as Kade guided the car over the ridge and the magnificence of his home came into view.

"Kade!" Sam exclaimed, and smacked his leg. "You didn't tell me it's a freaking castle!"

Kade chuckled. "I wanted to surprise you."

The car phone rang and Kade pressed the button to answer.

"Welcome home, my lord," came the male voice.

"My *lord*?" Sam whispered.

Kade smiled. "Thank you, Eymundur. Please lower the gate."

"Já, herra minn."

Kade hung up and wished he wasn't driving. He wanted to see Sam's face as the drawbridge lowered.

"You have a drawbridge?" She smacked his leg again as she leaned forward. "Don't tell me you have a moat as well."

Kade chuckled. "It's not a full one. Just enough for the ducks to swim in."

"Shut up!"

* * *

Samantha couldn't believe Kade had grown up in a bona fide castle. The drawbridge lowered and Kade drove them across it and into a large courtyard where a small crowd had assembled.

"Who are all these people? Do they live here?" she asked.

"Yes. Some in the house, some on the land."

"Really? Wow."

He brought the car to a stop. "There's something you should know."

Sam shifted to face him. "What?"

"All of this is mine."

She grinned. "I know that."

He shook his head. "I mean, it's my home and these are my people. I'm their chieftain…laird…so you're going to see some things that might seem strange."

"Chieftain?"

"Aye."

"Like their leader?"

"Something like that, yes," he said.

She swallowed. "So, you really are some kind of royalty, aren't you?"

"Amongst humans, aristocracy would be more accurate." He paused briefly and then took her hand. "I'm the Duke of Avoch."

"Shut up."

He smiled. "It's a very old title…no one really pays any attention to it anymore. I'm also the Laird of Gunnach."

"Ooh, you *so* avoided my question a few weeks ago, didn't you?"

"I promised I'd explain more when we got to know each other better. I've been trying to ease you in."

"You said amongst humans. Are there others like me who know about you?"

He shook his head. "The Crown recognizes me as the Duke of Avoch and Laird of Gunnach."

"But the Cauld Ane recognize you as something else?"

"Yes." He kissed her fingertips and smiled.

Sam groaned. "Spit it out already."

"I'm their king."

"*King*? How am I supposed to act, Kade?" She groaned. "Oh, crap, was I supposed to curtsy when I met you?"

Kade laughed. "Sweetheart, just be yourself…and yes, you were supposed to curtsy, but I forgave you because you were so bloody cute."

She gave him a playful shove. "You're a beast."

"Come on, the kids want to say hi."

Kade slid from the car and a group of children rushed him. He laughed and spoke to each of them briefly as Sam sat in the car and tried to calm her racing heart.

"All right, wee ones, I have to help Samantha from the car. She's dying to meet all of you."

I am, am I?

Kade smiled as he made his way to her side of the car and pulled open the door. "Ready, love?"

"Not in the slightest." She slipped her hand in his and climbed out of the car.

He led her to a group of people waiting by the large front doors and settled her in front of him. "Everyone, this is Samantha. Please make her feel welcome."

The group either bowed or curtsied in unison and Samantha found herself surrounded by children, several of them handing her bouquets of flowers, which she thought was beyond adorable.

A petite woman who looked quite a bit like Fiona folded her into an awkward hug. "It's nice to meet you."

"This is my mother, Alice," Kade supplied.

"It's nice to meet you too," Samantha said.

She was a little taken aback to find that the woman who looked no older than her mid to late forties could be Kade's mother.

"Why don't you come in and I'll show you to your room," Alice said.

"I'll get the bags," Kade said.

Samantha grabbed for his hand. "I'm sure the bags can wait for a bit, huh?"

Kade gave her hand a gentle squeeze and smiled. "I'll be in shortly, love."

Sam followed Kade's mother through the double doors and into the house. She entered a roomy foyer and then was led into what Alice called the great hall. Sam turned in several circles in an attempt to take in the room that was bigger than her house at home. Three stories high, with balconies peering down from the top floors, the ceiling came to a large arch with a wooden beam running the length of the room, holding six chandeliers.

The fireplace was as tall as Kade and wide enough to fit a small army. It was lit, but it barely made a dent in the warmth of the room. Sam pulled her coat tighter and crossed her arms to keep from shivering. The room was set up in sections. A large table was off to the left, with tall chairs surrounding it. She counted twenty-four, and wondered when they'd have an opportunity to have that many seated for a meal.

To the right was a sitting area in front of the fire. Three sofas and two overstuffed chairs surrounded a coffee table that looked rather modern in the historical home. The third section housed a piano, with folding chairs propped against the wall.

"There is a garderobe just around the corner, Samantha," Alice said.

"Okay."

What's a garderobe?

Kade chuckled. *Bathroom.*

Oh.

Sam forced a smile and followed her from the room.

"The kitchen is at the back of the house, but you shouldn't have any reason to go there. Just ask one of the staff if you require food or drink."

Sam nodded. "Thank you."

Alice waved her hand toward the foyer. "I'll show you to your room."

Sam forced a smile and followed her from the room.

You are coming back, right?

I'm speaking with one of my men. I'll be in shortly. Is Mother show-ing you to your room?

Yes.

Good. I'll meet you up there.

Sam pressed her lips together as she followed Alice up the staircase to the left of the foyer. They continued up the second staircase to the third floor and then to a large door fourth from the landing. Alice pushed open the door and Sam stepped inside.

A large bed was the centerpiece of the room. Ornately carved posts held a canopy draped in dark green velvet. She knew that when the fabric was pulled around the bed, it would create a pitch black cocoon. Other than the bed, the room housed a dresser and two high-backed chairs that faced a small fireplace.

"It's beautiful," Sam said appreciatively.

Alice pointed to the door in the right-hand corner. "That's your private washroom, and that door," she nodded toward the door on the left of the room, "is your closet."

"Thank you."

"I'll leave you to rest now," Alice said.

"Oh. Okay. Thank you."

Alice scurried from the room and pulled the door closed without another word, and Sam made her way to the window between the "doors."

I'm outside your door, love.

Come in.

Kade walked in and set Sam's suitcase next to the dresser. "Is the room to your liking?"

"It's beautiful."

He grinned and took her hand. "Good. It's next to mine."

"It is?"

"I'll show you."

He pushed the closet door open and Sam couldn't stop a quiet gasp. "This is not a closet! It's the size of my bedroom at home."

The room housed several full-length mirrors, a vanity, and racks for shoes and accessories.

"It's our dressing room." He nodded to another door and smiled. "That door leads to my bedroom."

"*Our* dressing room?"

"Aye. This floor is ours. No one will bother us."

Sam licked her lips. "Hmm. The whole floor, you say?"

Kade grinned and wrapped his arms around her, leaning down to nuzzle her neck. "The *whole* floor."

"You are a terrible temptation, honey."

"Look who's talking," he said.

"What's the plan for the rest of the day?"

"I'd hoped to show you the grounds, but the weather's not cooperating. Let's unpack and then tonight we'll have a quiet dinner with my mother. Tomorrow we'll head out on our adventure."

She smiled. "Sounds perfect."

* * *

After breakfast the next morning, Sam headed to her bedroom to change for Kade's promised tour of the grounds. Just as she arrived at her door, she overheard a couple of the maids talking.

"I don't know why she's in a separate room," the older maid said.

"It's strange, Hilda. Shouldn't they have been bound by now?"

"Elsie," Hilda admonished. "It's none of our business. She's American. Maybe they have different traditions."

"But he's the *king*! He could force her."

"Elsie!"

Sam bit her lip and walked back down the hall to Kade's room.

"Come," he called after her knock. She pushed the door open just as he pulled on a T-shirt. "I thought you were going to change?"

Sam closed the door and leaned against it. "I was, but a couple of the maids were in my room and I didn't want to interrupt them."

"What's the matter?"

"Is it a problem that we're not sleeping together?"

He ran his fingers through his hair to smooth it. "Of course not. Why?"

She shrugged. "The maids were just saying that it was weird."

Kade sighed. "I'll deal with them."

"No, don't! I don't want to get anyone in trouble. They're confused that we're not bound, that's all."

"Which is none of their business."

"Maybe," she said. "But the bigger question is, what am I missing?"

Kade slid his watch onto his wrist. "Nothing."

"Honey, that's not true. I know you're easing me into all of this information, but I think you need to tell me what typically happens with the binding process. You know, when both people are Cauld Ane."

Kade leaned against the bed. "When we find our mate, binding happens almost immediately."

"What do you mean, immediately?"

"Twenty-five is the *Ár mökun*, the mating year. It's when our hearts turn to whoever our mates are, if they're close. If they're not, then we wait."

"Close, meaning proximity?"

"Aye."

"Do you think that's why I ended up here just months after I turned twenty-five?"

"It wouldn't surprise me. And the moment I opened my office door, I knew exactly who you were. It's not something we have to guess."

"Okay, so if mates are close, then what happens?"

"If they're both of age, it happens within a day or so. We are bound, and the legal...human ceremony happens once the binding is done."

Sam bit her lip. "So you have sex first and then celebrate?"

"Something like that."

"How very Old Testament of you," she observed.

"Aye." He smiled. "It's very personal and not something you'd want an audience for."

"Why do I have visions of a large bed with a bunch of people standing around waiting for a bloody sheet?"

He chuckled. "That practice was phased out."

"So are Angus and Fiona bound then?"

He shook his head.

"Why not?"

"Because I'm not."

"What?" she squeaked. "Seriously?"

He nodded. "Yes. If the head of the family is unbound, the rest aren't free to complete the ceremony. For her it's worse, because I'm laird. In rare situations, a laird can bless a couple's union with the head of family being unbound, but she doesn't have that option open to her."

"Why don't you bless it?"

"It's a bit like a doctor treating a family member," he explained. "It's frowned upon and not generally a good idea."

"How long has Fiona been waiting?"

Kade frowned. "You don't really want to know that, love."

Her heart dropped. "I'm so sorry, Kade. I didn't realize my indecision was making this so hard on everyone."

He stood and made his way to her. "Sweetheart, it's not. All of this is an adjustment. I've been past the age of mating for several hundred years and thought I'd never find you. I can wait as long as you need."

"But can Fiona?"

He pulled her in his arms and held her close. "She can. At the very least, I want to have the chance to meet your family in person. My intention has always been to talk to your father before I do anything. Fiona understands that. Angus had to ask me."

Sam frowned. "How did that go?"

"I made him squirm. It was fun."

She rolled her eyes. "What's the deal with Brodie and Payton?"

"Payton is only twenty-four."

"How old is Brodie?"

"Six years younger than me."

"Oh," she said with a gasp. "So, he's also been waiting a long time."

Kade nodded.

"Is she his mate?"

"Like I said, it's complicated."

"So make it less complicated."

He sat in the chair next to the fireplace and indicated the other one next to it. "This might take a minute."

Sam clapped her hands and sat down. "I love stories."

"Angus's mother died almost seventy years ago I believe, and his father seemed to lose his mind for a time. The McFadden clan has been a part of ours for several hundred years, so we all rallied around Stuart and did our best to help with his grief. What none of us expected was that he would fall in love with another woman, Phyllis Mann. She had been part of the Gunn clan for many years and met Stuart when we hosted the Highland games thirty years ago or so."

"So, are they bound?"

Kade shook his head. "No. Mating only happens once in a lifetime. Phyllis was a widow; her mate had been killed three years before. But I believe they love each other deeply. They have six children together, which, with the four from Stuart's bonded mate, Angus's mother, makes for a large brood."

"The Cauld Ane Brady Bunch."

Kade chuckled. "You could say that."

"So, Cauld Ane's can and do marry without being bound?"

"Aye. It's always better to wait for one's mate, but sometimes, the wait can be unbearable. And there are often consequences to marrying the wrong person."

"That's a universal problem, really."

He smiled. "Aye."

"So, what's the problem with Payton and Brodie's mating?"

"From what I gather from Angus, Phyllis is deeply religious and I think she's filled Payton's head with some things that may not be entirely accurate."

"About?"

"God and men, to name a few."

"Catholic guilt type stuff?"

Kade nodded. "Probably."

"Angus seems normal…well, sort of," she added with grin.

"He was grown by the time Stuart married Phyllis. He's also male."

"Right. Because little boys don't deal with God or guilt," she retorted.

"I wouldn't know." Kade chuckled. "I don't get that deep with Angus."

"He's going to be your brother-in-law, maybe you should."

"I'm perfectly happy with our relationship right where it is."

Sam grinned. "Fine. I'll take on the task of going deeper with Angus."

"Like hell you will," he countered.

"That didn't sound quite so bad in my mind." Sam giggled. "Continue with the story."

"With his boys raised, Stuart decided to get to know Phyllis's family, so he joined her clan for a time. They returned here when Payton was fifteen. She is the second-oldest of their children and the moment she arrived, Brodie went a little off the deep-end."

"Why?"

"He'd waited several hundred years for his mate, but the wait was easier when he didn't know who he was waiting for. Payton isn't available to him until she's twenty-five. At least, she can't be bound until then."

"How does she feel about him? I mean, does she even like him?" Sam asked.

"Payton has always been sheltered and shy, so I don't know if she would ever say. Certainly not to me. And Brodie knew that, at fifteen, she was too young, so he joined the Royal Air Force. He was gone for almost five years."

"Wow. What happened when he got back?"

"He's been trying to let her get to know him; however, he's a bit like a bull in a china shop most of the time, so she's leery of him."

"Doesn't she trust that he's her mate? She must know in her heart, right?"

"She won't know for sure until she's twenty-five, and she's been taught from an early age that there are predatory men out there just waiting to get their hands on a bonny girl like her."

Sam rolled her eyes. "She doesn't seem the type to be so easily fooled by these so-called predatory men."

"I don't think she is, but she's also not going to rush into anything. Her mother's put just enough fear in her to be cautious, I think."

"When's her birthday?"

He settled an ankle over his knee. "In five months."

"Poor Brodie."

"Aye."

Samantha slid forward in her chair. "What about Connall?"

"He has yet to meet his mate. We don't even know if she's been born yet."

Sam whistled. "That's such a weird thought!"

"Luckily, he's the patient one." He rose to his feet and held his hand out to her. "Now, go change so we can go for our hike. I'd like to kiss you in my garden."

"Twist my arm," she retorted, and headed to her room, this time through the connecting door.

CHAPTER SEVENTEEN

Sᴀᴍ ʀᴇᴛᴜʀɴᴇᴅ ᴡᴇᴀʀɪɴɢ a comfortable pair of jeans and a white T-shirt covered by her hoodie. "I'm ready."

"Let's head out to the stables. You can determine whether or not Pepper will be satisfied with our horses."

Sam laughed. "If it's a horse, she'll love it."

The sun was having a hard time peeking through the dark grey clouds overhead, but the morning was still warmer than the previous few days. Kade took her hand and they strolled through the gardens at the back of the castle, stopping for several kisses, then heading toward the stables.

"I'm amazed at how everything is right here within the walls," Sam mused.

"If you like, we can go for a ride this week outside the castle. Gunnach land is the best in the Highlands."

Sam grinned. "From the lips of someone so totally unbiased."

"Of course."

"I'd love to go for a ride. It's been a long time." Sam pulled her hoodie off and tied it around her waist. "It's turning into a beautiful day. I thought it rains all the time in Scotland."

Kade grinned and took her hand again. "Give it a few minutes and it will."

"It's a good thing you're here then. I forgot my new umbrella."

Before Kade could comment, the rain started. Slow at first, but quickly turning into a downpour. "Come on, love, the stables aren't far."

Sam paced him as they made a run for the large building in the distance. By the time they made it inside, she was laughing hysterically and soaked to the bone. "You weren't kidding."

Kade wiped water from his face and hummed in appreciation. "Och, love. We need to do this more often."

"How come?"

"You've become my wet T-shirt fantasy."

Sam glanced down and groaned. Her lacy pink bra was stuck to the wet shirt that left nothing to the imagination. She crossed her arms over her chest. "I didn't plan that very well, did I?"

"I'd say it was planned perfectly." Kade pulled her arms away and leaned down to kiss her.

"You really are making me want to forget my manners, Kade Gunnach."

"I have no problem with that," he retorted. "Come on, we have towels in the tack room, and I'll have someone come get us. Mum wants to meet with us before lunch. Then, I can show you everything I have on the history of my people."

Sam followed him to the back of the barn and succumbed to another manner-forgetting moment.

* * *

Kade ushered Samantha into the library and smiled at his mother, who sat by the window drinking a cup of tea. He kissed her cheek and then held a chair for Samantha. His mother appeared unsettled; her hand shook as she lifted the teacup to her lips.

Samantha frowned. "I think maybe you two should talk privately."

"No, dear," Alice said. "Even if I say it to Kade alone, you would know immediately anyway."

Kade sat in the seat next to Samantha and looped his arm around the back of her chair. "I suppose now's as good a time as any, Mum."

"I had an affair," she said.

Kade's eyes narrowed. "Excuse me?"

Wow, way to ease you in.

Kade nodded.

"I think I should go," Sam said, but Kade laid his hand on her shoulder.

"You had an affair?" he said quietly.

"Yes. I'm not proud of it. But there it is. I slept with someone other than your father, and Fiona was the result of that union."

Sam gasped. "Really. This is private, Kade. I should give you two some space."

"Stay," he said as he rose to his feet and made his way to the middle of the room. "Explain, Mother."

Samantha wanted to be sick. Kade had told her that his mother had a big secret she was going to reveal, but neither of them would have guessed it was something so shocking.

"You're old enough now to know that love isn't always black and white," she said. "Your father and I were having difficulties…"

"You cheated on him because you were having "difficulties?" You didn't raise us to be dishonest, so why would it be okay for you?" he snapped.

"Don't think your father didn't do the same thing, Kade."

"We aren't talking about his indiscretions, Mother, we're talking about yours." He crossed his arms. "Who was the other man?"

His mother shifted in her seat and cleared her throat. "That's not really important."

"It bloody well is!"

"I don't know if you'd remember him."

"It's someone I *knew*?" he bellowed. "When did all this happen?"

"Just before we left Iceland."

"How long before we left?"

"Just over a year."

Kade clenched his fists at his sides. "Fiona was three months old when we left Iceland."

"*Já.*" (Yes.)

"Who was he?"

His mother pressed her lips into a thin line. "Einar."

"The blacksmith?"

"*Já.*"

Kade crossed his arms. "He wasn't Cauld Ane."

"I know." She lowered her head. "He was human."

"You gave up everything just so you could have it off with a human?"

Sam sat in stunned silence. Did she really just hear him say that?

His mother tsked. "Kadie, it's not that simple."

"How is it complicated?" he asked. "You were bound to my father and you had sex with a *human*. Sounds pretty simple to me."

"I wasn't," Alice said.

"Excuse me?"

"I wasn't bound to your father, Kade. He wasn't my true mate."

"Bloody hell!" Kade picked up a vase sitting on an end table and threw it against the wall.

Sam stood, but his mother held out her hand. "Don't. He's too angry, Samantha. Look at his eyes. He's too strong now."

Sam looked at Kade. His eyes burned red. Her heart raced as she gripped the back of a chair.

Kade? Honey. I need you to calm down.

He turned his head slowly toward her, his expression one of rage mixed with confusion.

Am I safe?

He stared straight through her, but managed a curt nod.

"He won't hurt me." She rushed to him and laid her shaking hands on his chest.

The flame receded and his eyes returned to their familiar blue. His body shuddered and then he wrapped his arms around her and took a deep breath. "Thank you."

"Better?"

"I think so." He linked his fingers with hers then turned to his mother. "Explain to me why you joined with someone who wasn't your mate."

"Our marriage had been arranged since we were born, combining the Haarde and Vilhjálmsson clans. It was a different time. My father didn't have much regard for mating. He was only interested in what he could get out of a union between our two families. They wanted peace between the clans. They got it. For a time. It's why we sailed here."

"We sailed here because we didn't want to be under Danish rule," Kade pointed out.

"Not really. Your uncle had close ties to the Danish crown. We sailed here because of my indiscretion."

"Were you bound with Einar?" Sam asked.

She shook her head. "I would not have had that power. Only men can bind their mates."

Really?

I'll explain later, Kade promised

He focused back on his mother. "Did you know of any human women bound to Cauld Ane?"

His mother nodded. "Yes. Not many, but there were a few. Since Samantha is human, your…" She cleared her throat and spoke to Sam. "Well, you will become Cauld Ane. You will be as we are, and you and Kade will age at the same rate. You will die together because your bodies are one, unless one of you is taken before their time."

Sam sagged against Kade. This was a lot to take in. He squeezed her hand.

"Did you ever meet your true mate?" Kade asked his mother.

"No. But it doesn't matter." She sighed. "Your father may not have been my mate, but he was a jealous husband. He didn't take kindly to his wife um…*svindla á honum*…and meant to put distance between me and Einar."

"Cheating on him," Kade explained to Sam.

"Ah."

"I can't imagine why he'd be upset, mother," Kade droned.

"Kade," Sam whispered.

"It's all right, Samantha," Mrs. Gunnach said. "He's right. What I did was wrong and I've paid for it my whole life."

"Why tell me now?" Kade asked.

"Because I believe Fiona's issues may be a direct result of my sins."

"What do you mean?"

"She's not fully Cauld Ane. She's of mixed race, which might contribute to the danger to her health."

"Shite," Kade said as he dropped Samantha's hand.

Sam laid her hand on his back, attempting to keep him calm, but she felt the anger pouring off him and didn't know if she had any sway over him in this state.

"All this over a bloody human," he snapped.

Kade's mother lowered her head.

"I need some air," he said, and ripped open the library door and stalked out.

Sam stood, stunned.

"Are you going to go after him?" Alice asked.

Sam glanced at her and then shook her head. "No, I don't think I will. Will you excuse me, please?" She didn't wait for a response. She headed out of the library and to her room.

After pacing the floor for several minutes, she pulled out her suitcase and threw it on the bed. She wasn't going to stay where she wasn't wanted. She threw a few clothes into her bag but quickly realized she didn't have anywhere to go. She didn't know where she was, and without Alasdair to call on, she had no way out. *Cole.*

She pulled out her cell phone and dialed his number.

"Hey, Sam. Everything okay?" he asked when he answered.

"Hi, Cole. Um, I kind of need a favor."

"I'm forgiven, then?"

Sam bit her lip. "Yes…if you promise not to try anything again."

"What do you need?"

"Do you know where the Gunnach Castle is?"

"The what?"

Sam groaned. "Don't play dumb, okay?"

Pause.

"Yeah. I know where it is," he said.

"Could you come get me?"

"Sam? What's going on?"

"I can't tell you. I just need to get back to the city."

"What about your boyfriend?"

Sam squeezed her eyes shut. "Forget it. I knew this was a bad idea."

"Wait. I'm sorry. Yes, I can come and get you. Give me thirty minutes."

"Thirty minutes? Where are you?" she asked.

"Let's just say I'm not far."

Sam sighed. "I should have guessed."

"I'll be right there."

"Thanks," she said and hung up.

She took a deep breath and continued with her packing. She felt quite philosophical about the whole thing, really. She didn't want to be with someone who didn't want her…it didn't really matter why. Right?

Right.

"Sam?"

* * *

Sam turned to find Kade standing in the doorway. He looked tired, but still, oh so gorgeous.

"What are you doing?" he asked.

"I'm going back to the city, then I think I should go home." She tugged open a drawer and pulled out a stack of shirts.

"You're not going anywhere."

She clenched her jaw and set her shirts in the suitcase.

"Didn't you hear me?"

"Oh, I heard you. I'm just not impressed."

"Sweetheart, I'm sorry if I scared you. But you must know I'd never hurt you."

She snorted. "Of course I know that, despite the fact that I'm a lowly human."

"Samantha."

"What, Kade? You have an aversion to Cauld Ane and human inter-action, so I'm going to make the difficulty easy for you. I'm going home."

"That's not what I meant, and you know it."

"Do I? Your mother slept with a human and you're disgusted by it. You shouldn't be with someone so much less worthy than a Cauld Ane woman, and I won't be with someone who doesn't love me completely."

"I'm disgusted with the fact she *cheated* on my father!" he snapped. "It wouldn't have mattered if the man was human or Cauld Ane."

"But that's not what you said!" Sam jabbed a finger at him. "You were so frustrated and angry, you said what you really feel in your heart and I can't compete with that."

He squeezed his eyes shut. "Sweetheart, I'm sorry if I said anything in there that led you to believe I think you're anything less than perfect. I obviously let my anger get the best of me."

"I appreciate your apology." She opened another drawer and pulled out a stack of clothes.

Kade took her T-shirts from her suitcase and set them back into the bureau. "Stop it, Kade. I'm still leaving."

"No, you're not. I'm not taking you anywhere until we work this out."

She shrugged. "I don't need you to take me anywhere."

"You're going to walk?"

"No."

He frowned. "What did you do?"

She shrugged and dropped more clothes into the suitcase.

"Samantha?" he pressed.

"Cole's picking me up in twenty minutes."

He dropped her clothes in the open drawer. "Like hell he is."

"This is never going to work, Kade. I have accepted that. I think you should too."

He grasped her hand and pulled the clothes from her grip. "I'm not bloody well accepting anything that has you leaving. Now, stop this nonsense so we can talk."

She shook her head and stared at her feet. "No."

He lifted her chin and frowned. "Sweetheart, tell me what's really going on."

"I just think we have everything against us and it's better to cut it off now. If we keep going, it'll hurt more." Kade stared at her and it took her a minute to realize what he was doing. She stepped away from him. "Stop reading my mind."

"Our children are going to be fine, Samantha."

"Stop it." Her resolve crumbled and she felt the prick of tears. "Besides, we're not having children, so it's a moot point."

He held his hand out to her. "Come here."

"No."

He took a deep breath and closed the distance between them. "When we decide to have children, and we will, they will be perfectly healthy."

"But Fiona's not. She's dying."

He wrapped his arms around her. "She's not dying, love. She just has to be careful. Much like a diabetic has to take their insulin or someone with a bee allergy has to make sure they carry an EpiPen."

She tried to pull away from his touch. "Stop making me feel better."

"Call Cole and tell him not to come."

"I think it might be too late. He left almost half an hour ago."

Kade's cell phone rang. "Eymundur? Aye. Hmm, should we let him in?"

"Kade," Sam droned. "Don't be difficult."

"Yes, lower the gate. Thank you, Eymundur." He hung up and slipped his phone in his pocket. "Time to meet your other boyfriend."

Sam shook her head. "Oh, you're funny."

"You and I have a lot to talk about, eh?"

She shrugged. "I guess."

"No leaving until everything's resolved, okay? I have a few things planned for us this weekend, and I don't want my foot-in-mouth disease to ruin anything."

She couldn't help but smile. "How could I refuse?"

He stroked her cheek and kissed her quickly. "I love you, Samantha, you must know that."

She nodded. "I do. You just scare me sometimes."

"I'll try to be less scary. Just don't run. Please."

"I won't run." She smiled. "But you have to stop hating us humans."

"Och, Samantha, I don't. I'm sorry. I was angry and lashed out."

"Forgiven."

He kissed her again, then linked his fingers with hers and led her from the room. They arrived in the main hall, where Cole stood speaking with one of the maids. She was obviously taken with him and Cole seemed to like the attention. Sam felt Kade's hold tighten, and she glanced up at him with a raised eyebrow.

You failed to mention his charm.

She grinned. *Did I? How remiss of me.*

Kade released her hand and wrapped an arm firmly around her shoulders.

Sam raised an eyebrow. *You saw him at the park the day I was attacked, don't you remember?*

Honestly, I was more concerned about you. I didn't remember him being competition.

Kade. He's not. He's a friend. She pulled away and headed toward Cole. "Hi, Cole."

He grinned. "Hey, Sam."

The maid glanced at Kade and then lowered her head and scurried out of sight.

Cole hugged Sam and as soon as she broke the hug, she found herself pulled back against Kade. "It's good to see you again, Agent Drake," Kade said.

A flicker of surprise crossed his face, but he didn't attempt pretense. "So you know who I am."

"We do," Kade said.

Cole shifted from one foot to the other and then nodded. "Are you ready to go, Sam?"

Kade patted Samantha's hip. "She's not going anywhere. However, I'd love it if you'd stay so we can chat."

Cole frowned. "Sam called me."

Sam groaned. "I'm sorry. I shouldn't have."

He crossed his arms and glanced at Kade and then back at her. "If you don't feel safe, I'll take you out of here right now."

She realized what Cole must be thinking. Firmly settled against Kade, who looked like a warrior of old, she must appear to be some kind of hostage.

Kade, seriously? If you keep doing that, he's going to get the impression you're holding me against my will.

Doing what?

She disengaged herself from Kade and pushed him gently away. "Sorry, Cole. Kade and I had a disagreement, and I kind of made a snap judgment. It was unfair of me to call you, but you really are welcome to stay if you'd like."

He stepped closer to her. "Are you sure?"

She nodded. "Definitely. Whatever you might think about him, Cole, Kade would never hurt me, and I'm not one who'd stick around if he did."

"Okay. I can stay for a bit. I have a little time."

Sam glanced at Kade. *Are you going to be nice?*

Kade rolled his eyes. *I'm always nice, love.*

"It's almost time for lunch, Cole. Join us?" Sam asked.

He shrugged. "Sure."

Kade tapped his ear. "That has to be somewhere else."

Sam frowned. "What are you talking about?"

Cole pulled out a small ear bud and held it in his palm.

Sam turned to Kade. "How did you know?"

Kade put his finger to his lips.

Sam scowled at Cole and stepped back to Kade, a firm indication as to whose side she was on. He wrapped an arm around her waist and waited for Cole to make a decision.

Cole dropped the ear bud in the vase of flowers on the table.

"Anything else?" Kade asked.

"Nope, that was it," Cole said.

Two men Sam didn't recognize appeared out of nowhere and flanked her and Kade. Kade waved them toward Cole. "You won't mind if we check, will you?"

Sam waved her hands in the air. "This all too James Bond for me. You two have your pissing contest and I'll meet you in the sunroom." She left them and headed toward her new favorite place to be.

CHAPTER EIGHTEEN

COLE STAYED THROUGH dinner and Sam saw the reluctant mutual respect growing between him and Kade. Cole lowered his guard; so far in fact, that he shared what the FBI was doing looking into the Gunnach affairs. He also told them of his suspicions that there was someone on the inside at Gunnach Pharmaceuticals attempting to sabotage the family business and name.

"What exactly are "they" trying to do?" Sam asked.

"There have been rumblings that some kind of bio-warfare attack is being planned, on home soil—your home, Kade, not ours," Cole explained. "At first we thought you personally were behind the plans. But then we discovered that, although it appears Gunnach Pharmaceutical is supplying the money and resources for the attack, it is, in fact, Haarde Pharmaceuticals that is backing it. Víkingasveitin has been working with MI-6 and now the CIA to shut it down."

"Víkingasveitin?" Sam asked.

"Iceland's counter-terrorism unit," Kade provided.

"Oh."

"Do you have any idea who at Haarde is trying to make us look responsible?" Kade asked Cole.

Cole shook his head. "Not yet. They've covered their tracks well and did a damn good job setting you up. Including the purchase of several black market chemicals that have been made around Edinburgh. It looks as though someone within Gunnach Pharmaceuticals paid for them."

"How did you get involved?" Sam asked.

Cole cocked his head. "You mean the FBI?"

She nodded.

"I can't tell you that."

"Why not?"

Sam," Kade admonished gently and reached for her hand.She took his hand and tried to stamp down her irritation. "How did you figure out it wasn't Kade behind all this?"

"The trail to him was too obvious. I'm always suspicious of things that come easy."

"I'd like the suspicion to stay on me at this point," Kade said.

Sam's jaw dropped open. "What? Why?"

"If we take it off him, the real culprit might get nervous and bolt...or cover up more," Cole explained. "If we keep it on Kade, the hope is they'll get sloppy."

Sam frowned. "I don't know how I feel about this."

"Sweetheart, someone is threatening to kill people in *my* name," Kade said. "We have to make sure the intended targets are safe."

"What about your safety? What about Connall and Brodie?"

Kade squeezed her hand. "It's fine. Cole and I will work out a strategy with Con and Brodie. Don't worry."

I can't help it.

I know, love. But we are not so easy to kill.

Dinner wrapped up and they ushered Cole to the front door, following him outside. The rain was coming down in sheets, so Sam stayed under the protective covering, her back against Kade's chest. She hugged Cole and he climbed into his car and pulled away from the house. Sam waved then followed Kade back inside.

"I have a surprise for you," Kade said.

"You do?"

Taking her hand, he led her down the hall to one of the rooms she'd yet to see.

"Close your eyes," he instructed. "Don't peek. Don't read my mind either."

She gave a mock huff, but did as he asked, gripping his hand as he guided her forward. A quiet click indicated they were through the door and she sighed when she felt his lips on the back of her neck. "Open your eyes."

She did and couldn't stop an appreciative hum. The room had shelves of books covering two of the walls, along with a sofa in front of a large fireplace. A small desk was nestled in the corner and on the opposite side of the room, a bottle of champagne sat chilling in a silver ice bucket next to two ornate flutes. Candles were the only source of light. Sam smiled as she turned to face Kade. "It's beautiful. What's the occasion?"

"That depends on you."

"Oh?"

"I love you," he said, and then kissed her.

Sam felt the depth of his emotion and smiled against his lips. "Aw, honey, I love you too."

"Good to know." He dug in his pocket, pulling out a small box, and knelt in front of her. "Samantha Christene Moore, will you do me the honor of being my wife?"

She gasped as tears filled her eyes. She wasn't completely certain she wasn't in a dream. Could she believe that this beautiful man loved her as much as she loved him? Could she trust this was all real?

"Sam, my leg is cramping, love."

"Oh, sorry!" She giggled. "Yes. Yes, I would love to marry you." He popped the lid on the box and Sam thought she might pass out. Inside was the ring she'd tried on in the store. "Kade! You didn't! That's the ring...how did you know?"

"Why do you think Payton got the day off?" He grinned and rose to his feet. "She was my spy."

"Do you really close the lab when there's a fifth Friday?"

"No."

Sam let out a quiet squeal. "You're terrible!"

He slid the ring on her finger with a chuckle. It fit perfectly.

"It's stunning," she said.

"When your heart was racing in the store, was that when you tried it on?"

She nodded. "How did you guess?"

"Because you weren't afraid. I had a feeling something was up."

"How did you keep this from me?" she asked.

"It hasn't been easy," he complained. "Although, today you were distracted enough I could block you out."

She stared at the ring, the feeling so much more intense than what she felt in the store. She pressed her palm against her chest.

"Are you okay?" he asked.

Sam nodded. "Yes, I just feel...so...I don't know...everything."

"I know."

She gave him a challenging smile. "Weren't you supposed to ask my dad?"

"I did."

"What?" she exclaimed. "When?"

"Yesterday. While you were napping, I called and spoke with both your parents." He grinned. "I also called Pepper. She gave me more of a grilling than your parents did."

"I'll bet." Sam sighed. "You're full of surprises, honey. I don't know if I can keep up."

"You're doing just fine." He kissed her palm. "Are you certain you like the ring?"

"Yes! I absolutely love it." She raised an eyebrow. "What would you have done if I didn't like it?"

"I'd buy you something else."

"You would not."

"I would," he insisted.

"Well, you'll have to pry this off my cold, dead body."

"Good." Kade chuckled. "Payton was disappointed you didn't pick the one she tried on."

"Did she tell you how much it cost?"

"No." He shrugged. "But it wouldn't matter. If that was the one you liked, you could have had it."

"Kade, it was four hundred thousand pounds."

He raised an eyebrow. "Did you like it?"

"Not really. I didn't feel anything when I put it on. This one, though…" She ran her hand down his chest, the diamond sparkling in the candlelight. "It makes me feel like you make me feel."

"How's that?"

She stroked his cheek. "Safe. Home."

He kissed her and she slid her arms around his neck and ran her fingers through his hair.

Ég elska þig. Þakka þér fyrir að samþykkja að vera kona mín.

"Which means?" Sam said.

"I love you. Thank you for agreeing to be my wife." He kissed her nose.

"Will you please explain to me the rest of the binding process?"

"Only if you promise not to run."

Sam groaned. "Honey, I'm not going anywhere. At this point, even if you said you had to bite my neck, I think I'd stick around."

"Oh?"

She gave him a look of suspicion. "You don't have to bite my neck, do you?"

Kade chuckled. "No."

"Phew. Good."

"I brought several of our family records." He nodded to the table in the corner.

Six large tomes were stacked taller than she was, and Sam sighed. "Um. What are the odds of a story instead?"

"You preferred your lecture classes, didn't you?"

"You got me. But I promise, I'll look those over at some point before I die." She pulled him to one of the chairs. "Sit."

He lowered himself into the chair and Sam settled herself on his lap.

"Where do you want to start?" he asked.

"Let's start with the fact that only men can bind their mate. Why is that? And how will I become immortal?"

"It has to do with our…uh…*Sæði*…"

Sam cocked her head in question.

Kade smiled. "Semen."

Sam blushed beet red, she knew she did, her face was on fire. "Seriously?"

"We have an additional protein that human men don't have. I can only assume that that's how a human woman would be transformed into a Cauld Ane."

160

"But how do you stop the binding if you sleep with a woman who isn't your mate?"

"Binding is primarily spiritual rather than physical, so it's more involved than just the joining of bodies. I don't know what the ramifications would be if a Cauld Ane slept with a human woman who wasn't his mate, however. Perhaps Fiona can find something in our archives."

Sam let out a quiet gasp. "Fiona! If a human is made immortal, doesn't that mean her issues will be solved when Angus binds her?"

Kade smiled. "My beautiful genius. You may be onto something there."

"How does the aging thing work? Why don't you look six-hundred-something years old?"

"We age normally, or I should say, at the same rate as humans, until mating year. After that, we age at about one year per one hundred human years. It's not exact, but that's about the average. Once we are mated, the aging process slows, so it's more like one year per two hundred human years. If you lose your mate unnaturally, you age faster…much faster."

"So that's why your mother doesn't look old enough to be your mother."

"Aye. But had my father been her true mate, she'd look more like my grandmother. She would have aged faster after he died."

Sam cocked her head. "And that didn't tip you off that your mom and dad weren't mates?"

Kade kissed her nose. "Apparently, I'm not as observant as you are, smarty-pants."

"Apparently." She giggled. "Are there more of you?"

"You mean, outside of Iceland and Scotland?"

She nodded.

"We have several clans in Russia and Canada."

"What about at home?"

"We have a few families in the States, but only in Oregon, Washington and Alaska. However, the Eastern states are great vacation places for us during the winter."

"Right, Hawaii wouldn't work, would it?"

He grinned. "Not so much, no."

"Anything else I should know?"

"The Cauld Ane have a few things they need to avoid."

"Like?"

He gave her a patient smile. "Almonds, particularly anything that contains the concentrated extract—"

"Oh." Her eyes filled with tears. "My favorite cookies are my mama's chocolate almond surprise."

"I'm sorry, love."

She took a deep breath. "Nope, it's okay. I can live without cookies." She narrowed her eyes. "Wine's okay, though right?" He chuckled and nodded toward the bottle of champagne on the table. "Oh, right. Of course. I panicked a little. Life without wine would be too much to take."

"There's a native flower in Iceland that's extremely dangerous to the Cauld Ane. I highly doubt you'll come across it, unless I take you there for a visit, so I wouldn't concern yourself with it."

"What's it called?"

"In English, it's called the Red Fang. Its Latin name is *Decipio Décor*, in Icelandic, *Villandi Fegurð*."

She raised an eyebrow. "Something decorate?"

He chuckled. "Deceptive beauty."

"What does it do?"

"It has a thorn that paralyzes us. Either by pricking the skin, or it can be ground into a powder and used in food and drink. The effects aren't permanent, but they are enough to incapacitate us."

"Why would anyone want to do that?"

"They probably wouldn't." He smiled. "If someone managed to slip it into our food or drink, it wouldn't do any major damage. The only way to kill us is heat."

"What if you're stabbed or shot?"

"We'll heal."

"Seriously?"

"Seriously," he said. "Anything above sixty-eight degrees Fahrenheit will kill us within a few hours or days, depending on how high."

"How high?"

"We are sluggish in the seventies, lethargic in the eighties, and dead in the nineties."

"What do you do in the summer?"

"Our office building and all of our houses and apartments are air-conditioned. It's not a problem."

"But Pepper loves the sun! What if she wants me to go to the beach with her?"

Kade squeezed her hand. "Sweetheart, we're not vampires. The sun won't harm us. You just have to avoid the heat...and the beach with Pepper if it's over sixty-eight."

"You said we're sluggish in the seventies. I can do sluggish."

"No. You. Can't."

She pursed her lips. "So serious, my lord."

He sighed. "Perhaps not serious enough when it comes to you. I really should lock you away in the tower. That would at least ensure you're safe."

"You have a tower?" she asked hopefully.

He shook his head. "Sam."

She clambered from his lap. "You need to bind me."

"I will."

"Now. You need to do it now."

"Sam." Kade stood and narrowed his eyes. "You've just found out your whole world is going to change. Don't you want to sleep on it?"

"Why? I want to spend the rest of my life with you. It doesn't really matter what that process entails at this point. I'm kind of in."

"Kind of in?"

She grinned. "Yes, I just want one promise."

"What?"

"I want to get married in America, with my family. I feel like if we have a ceremony here after the binding I'll be cheating them out of something."

"Are you sure you're ready?"

"Absolutely. Honey, your sister has waited long enough."

Kade frowned. "If this is about my sister—"

"It's not," she interrupted. She placed his palm against her chest. "Listen."

Kade closed his eyes and took a deep breath. It didn't take long for him to open them again and smile down at Sam. "Now?"

She nodded. "Yes, please."

Kade pulled her from the room and upstairs to his bedroom.

* * *

Kade closed the door to his room and locked it. Sam rubbed her hands together and grinned. "Okay, what now?"

"Once again, my love, that depends on you."

"Oh." She frowned. "What am I supposed to do?"

Kade stroked her cheek. "It's our wedding night. Have you ever dreamt about how you'd like it to go?"

She shrugged. "Sort of. I guess."

"I don't want to rush this. I want you to have nothing but wonderful memories. So, you tell me what you want to do."

Sam worried her lower lip. "I guess I always thought I'd have a sexy nightgown and champagne and stuff. But I don't need any of that." She smiled. "Just you."

Kade kissed her. "Why don't you head into the dressing room and open the door to the left of the vanity. I'll get the champagne and meet you back here in fifteen minutes."

Sam tried not to look disappointed…or nervous. She took a deep breath and forced a smile. "Okay."

He kissed her again and then left the room. Sam made her way into the dressing room and opened the door Kade mentioned, her eyes widening in surprise. It was a closet, and it was filled with clothes. She ran her hands over the silks, satins, and chiffons. An envelope taped to the wall had her name scrawled on it with Kade's bold handwriting. She opened it and pulled out the card inside.

If you're reading this, then one of two things has happened: either you've been snooping or you've agreed to marry me. I do hope it's the latter. I love you, Samantha, and I will endeavor to make our life together as perfect as possible. Consider the gowns and lingerie just as much a gift for me as they are for you. After all, I will get to see you in them. Yours forever, K.

Sam flattened the note to her chest and closed her eyes.

You are too good to be true, Kade Gunnach.

His chuckle sounded in her mind. *Wear the white.*

Sam scanned the racks, found the white lingerie, and hummed in appreciation.

It's beautiful.

I know. I too have been dreaming of our wedding night.

Sam narrowed her eyes. *Did Payton pick this out?*

Absolutely not. I picked everything in that closet. I didn't even use Fiona's personal shopper at Jenners.

Oh. Thank you.

Believe me, it was my pleasure. I'll see you in ten minutes.

Sam took the nightgown and made her way to her bathroom. After a quick shower, she brushed her teeth and combed out her hair so it fell in soft waves down her back. She stared at herself in the mirror and frowned. She looked a little pale, so she pinched her cheeks in an effort to look more alive.

She smoothed lotion onto her skin and took a closer look at the lingerie. Her heart raced in anticipation. Sliding on the lacy boy shorts, she was surprised at how well they fit. She turned in the mirror and grinned. They enhanced her rear end quite nicely.

Next came the chiffon top. The bra was fitted, enhancing her cleavage, and the sheer fabric attached to it fell to just below her bottom. She checked her appearance and her heart swelled. The design was almost identical to the blue top she'd worn on their first date. Kade seemed to remember everything when it came to her.

A dab of her favorite perfume was the finishing touch, then she turned the light off in the bathroom and pulled on the matching robe as she made her way back to Kade's room. She paused outside the door and licked her lips. Knocking quietly, she entered.

Sam gasped. The room was lit with candles and the fire had been stoked to create a perfect romantic scene. Kade turned from the table and Sam's stomach dropped. Shirtless and wearing black pj bottoms, he was beyond gorgeous.

He set the champagne bottle back in the ice bucket and held his hand out to her. "You are stunning, love."

Sam made her way to him. "You're not so bad yourself."

He slid her robe open and pushed it from her shoulders. "Och, Samantha, I couldn't have imagined this more beautiful on you."

"It looks like…"

He stroked her cheek. "What you wore to our first dinner."

"You *did* remember."

He ran his finger across her collarbone. "Do you know how hard it was for me not to bind you then? I thought I'd die on the spot."

"You should have told me how you felt," she joked.

"How remiss of me." He leaned down and kissed her, wrapping an arm around her waist and pulling her close. Sam sank into him, her hands gripping his arms in an effort to stay upright. He broke the kiss and wove his fingers with hers. "Are you sure you're ready? We can wait as long as you need to."

"I'm beyond ready."

"You may feel a bit weak."

Sam raised an eyebrow. "I always feel weak in your presence."

"Oh, I'm aware." He grinned. "Repeat after me. *Ég gef þér allt sem ég er, allt sem ég vil vera og allt sem ég get verið.*"

"I can't remember all of that."

"Read my mind," he suggested. "Try again. *Ég gef þér allt sem ég er, allt sem ég vil vera og allt sem ég get verið.*"

"Ég gef þér allt sem ég er, allt sem ég vil vera og allt sem ég get verið," Sam said, and she felt her knees weaken. She let out a frightened squeak. "I didn't think you meant literally."

"I've got you, sweetheart. Just hold onto me."

"Okay."

"*Ég er þinn að eilífu. Eining okkar mun aldrei bresta.*"

"Ég er þín að eilífu Eining okkar mun aldrei bresta." Sam gripped Kade's arms. "I'm going to fall."

"You're not going to fall. I have you. It's part of the bonding. Just relax and trust me. Ready?" At her nod, he continued, "*Ást mín er alger.*"

"Ást mín er alger."

"Are you okay?" he asked.

She smiled. "Definitely."

"Can you say it again in full?"

She drew her eyebrows together. "Um. I think so."

"I'm going to hold you tighter. Ready?"

"Yes."

"Together," he instructed.

"Ég gef þér allt ég, allt sem ég vil vera og allt sem ég get verið. Ég er þín að eilífu. Skuldabréf okkar mun aldrei vera brotinn. Ást mín er alger."

As they said the last syllable of the last word, Kade swept her into his arms and kissed her. She looped her arms around his neck and held on for dear life. If he hadn't picked her up, she knew she'd be in a puddle on the floor. He carried her to the bed and settled her gently on top of the down comforter.

"Kade?"

"Hmm?"

"I know what that meant."

He raised an eyebrow. "What?"

"I give you everything I am, all I want to be and all I can be. I'm yours forever. Our bond will never be broken. My love is absolute. Right?"

"Yes, exactly."

She grinned and sat up on her knees. "Say something else."

He gave her a Cheshire smile and said, "*Ég er ástfanginn af brjálaðri manneskju.*" (I'm in love with a crazy person.)

Sam gasped and then giggled. "I'm no crazier than you!" She clapped her hands. "More."

"*Ég ætla að kyssa þig núna þar til þú öskrar.*" (I'm going to kiss you now and then I'm going to make you scream.)

Sam's heart stuttered. "Oh, my."

CHAPTER NINETEEN

KADE TOOK HIS time making love to her. His emotion was overwhelming and when he felt hers as well, it nearly sent him over the edge. As the fire started to die in the room, he pulled the covers around them and settled her firmly on his chest.

"I love you," he said, and kissed her hair.

Sam sighed. "Not nearly as much as I love you." She kissed his chest then grinned up at him. "Are we done?"

"With the binding process, yes. With making love, only if you want to be. Tomorrow would typically be the day we meet with the parson and sign the paperwork, but we'll do that after we have our human wedding with your family and friends."

"Thank you." She laid her hand on his chest and settled her chin on top. "I thought I might have ruined it."

"Ruined what, love?" he asked.

"The binding. All my talking. I was afraid I talked us out of being connected. But it was so fun to know I could understand you."

Kade chuckled. "The only things required are the ceremonial words and the physical consummation. Outside of that, it can be as fun as we make it."

"Are you happy?"

"Och, love. *Ég hef aldrei verið hamingjusamari.*" (I've never been happier.) He kissed her again and ran his hands along her back. Suddenly, she broke the kiss with a whimper. "Sweetheart? What's wrong?"

"My stomach hurts a bit." She took a deep breath and smiled. "It passed. I'm okay."

He pulled her closer.

"But I *am* really hot. Will you please douse the fire?"

He glanced at the hearth. "It's dead, love."

"Really?" She whimpered again. "Ow."

"Your stomach?"

"No." She took several deep breaths and started to pant. "My legs."

"You're burning up." He pulled the covers from her body.

She slid across the sheet. "I feel like I'm on fire."

He turned the lamp on and let out a curse. Her skin was a blotchy, unhealthy red, looking much like a sunburn.

"Kade!" she screamed. "It hurts! I'm burning."

"Hold on, sweetheart." He scrambled from the bed and rushed into his bathroom. He turned the cold water on and put the plug in the bath. He grabbed his medical bag and ran back to Sam, setting it next to her. Looping his stethoscope around his neck, he leaned over her. "I'm going to listen to your heart."

"No. Don't touch…" She grasped the stethoscope and yanked it from his neck. "Make it stop. Kade! Please!" she screamed.

"Shite." He lifted her from the bed, grabbing the stethoscope and trying not to react to another agonizing yelp of pain. He carried her to the bathroom and settled her into the cold water. She squealed in shock, but then she took a deep breath and relaxed against the cool porcelain of the tub. "Better?"

She licked her lips and nodded. "Hmm-mmm."

"Can I check your heart now?"

"Hmm-mmm."

He laid the stethoscope diaphragm over her chest and frowned. Her heart was racing. He checked her pulse and sighed. "Sweetheart, your pulse is dangerously high. I need to find out what's going on. I'm going to call my mother. Are you all right with that?"

"Huh?" She closed her eyes and shook her head. "You don't need to call your mom. I'm okay now."

Kade warred with her desire for privacy and his need for answers.

Within minutes, though, her eyes flew open and she whimpered. "Maybe not. I'm hot," she rasped.

Kade felt the water and frowned. "I think your body may actually be heating the water." He pulled the plug and turned the cold water back on. Switching it to the shower setting, he adjusted the nozzle directly over her.

She licked her lips and sighed. "Thirsty."

Kade grabbed a glass from the counter and filled it with cold water. Holding her head gently, he tipped the water into her mouth. She drank greedily and then slumped against the back of the tub.

"I'll be right back, love." He stepped into the bedroom, pulled on pj bottoms and a T-shirt, and unplugged his phone from the charger. He scrolled down to his mother's number as he rushed back into the bathroom.

"You're bound," his mother said.

"Aye."

"I'll contact the parson."

"Sam's sick, mum. We should wait. Do you know what's going on?"

"Oh, aye. It's the change. It's going to get worse before it gets better. I'll get the book and come to you."

"The book? What book?" he asked as he knelt beside Sam and felt her forehead. Still too warm.

"Our family history. It's filled with information, including ways to ease the suffering for humans when they make the change."

"I don't recall seeing anything in the books I have."

"I have the book I refer to in my private apartments."

Kade took a deep breath. If his mother had been standing in front of him, he might have been tempted to commit matricide. "You don't think this knowledge would have been good to have before I put her through this?"

"If you'd known she'd go through this, Kade, would you have still bound her?"

He glanced at Sam, her body red and her face pinched in agony. "Absolutely not."

"I'll be right there," his mother said, and hung up.

"Sam?" Kade felt Sam's pulse. It was racing. "Sweetheart?"

"Can't talk. Pain." She licked her lips again and grimaced. He grasped her hand, but she pulled it away. "Don't touch."

"If I touch you, love, I can ease the pain. You're going through the change—let me help you through it."

She blinked and turned glassy eyes on him. "It hurts."

"*Ég veit, elskan. vilt þú að leyfa mér að reyna?*" (I know, baby. Will you let me try?)

She pressed her lips together and nodded. He took her hand again and laid it against his, palm to palm. She took a deep breath and squeezed her eyes shut. Her face relaxed, and he realized his body had been on alert as he felt the air fill his lungs again. His phone rang and he would have ignored it, had it not been Connall.

"Bad time, Con."

"I can feel it. What's wrong with Sam?" he asked.

"She's sick," Kade snapped.

"I'm hanging up now," Connall said.

Kade set the phone on the floor and focused back on Sam. She was smiling at him. "Better?" he asked.

"A little. Connall's worried about you, honey."

"I know," he said. "But I don't have time for his worry right now. I have my own to deal with." He felt her pulse again. It was beginning to slow down. "I'm so sorry, Sam. If I'd known this was going to happen, I would have never put you through it."

Sam's eyes widened. "Yes, you would have. I would have made you."

He shook his head.

"I love you, Kade. I'll take this if it means being with you. It's just a little pain. If women couldn't handle pain, there'd never be children."

He stroked her cheek. "Och, Sam, I don't deserve you."

"Kade?" his mother's voice floated through the door. "May I come in?"

"No," Sam squeaked. "I'm naked."

"I wasn't going to let her in, love." He smiled gently. "Mum, you're going to need to wait a bit."

"You need to check for something," she called through the door.

"What?"

"The birthmark below your right buttock, has it appeared on Samantha's body?"

Kade frowned. "Where should I look?"

"Why is your mother talking about your butt?" Sam rasped.

"She did give birth to me," Kade whispered.

"It will more than likely mirror yours, so check her left side," his mother said.

"I'm going to shift you, love, okay?"

Sam nodded.

"Don't let go of my hand," he directed and lifted her hip. "Aye, mum, it's the direct opposite of mine, but it's faint."

"All right. It will darken and then turn blood red. When that happens, be prepared. Samantha is going to be in excruciating pain and some physical changes are going to happen that may be frightening to her."

"What's going to happen?" Sam rasped and gripped his hand. "Kade, don't leave me."

"I'm not going anywhere, love. I promise."

"I have the ice sheets in here, Kade," his mother said. "Sam is going to need to be out of that tub before the next phase."

Kade let out a frustrated breath. He glanced at Sam and his heart broke. She stared at him with a mixture of fear and trust. He shut off the water and reached for the towel closest to him. "I'm going to lift you out of here, Sam. I need you to keep contact with me. Slide your hand up to my neck." She shook her head. "I know it's hard, love. Just try."

She did as he asked, but her weakness alarmed him as she slid a shaky hand to his neck. He wrapped the towel around her, ignoring her protests, and carried her from the bathroom into the bedroom. Either his mother or one of the maids had brought the king-sized ice sheets and prepared his bed.

"Lay her here, Kade." His mother pointed to the bed.

Kade nodded and settled Sam in the middle of the mattress. She sighed as her body connected with the cold.

"You'll need to remove the towel so that the top sheet cools her," his mother instructed.

Kade nodded, grateful his mother turned her back for the sake of Sam's dignity. He pulled the towel away and slid the top ice sheet over Sam.

She sighed again and smiled. "This is heavenly."

He gave her a wary smile. "I'd have to agree."

"I feel like…like when you're freezing and you take a really hot bath, only in reverse." Sam turned her head toward him. "Now, if I could just stay awake enough to enjoy it."

"Don't fight it. Sleep, sweetheart." Kade sat next to her and stroked her cheek. "Mum's here and we're going to do a little research, okay?"

Sam nodded. Kade joined his mother at the fireplace.

* * *

His mother handed Kade the large antique book and he started reading. A sigh from Sam brought him back to his surroundings.

"You need to check her mark, Kade," his mother said.

Glancing at the clock on the mantel, he realized he'd been reading for almost two hours. He handed the book back to his mother and made his way to the bed. Sam still slept, her face looking much more relaxed, easing his worry immensely. He pulled the sheet back and lifted her hip gently. "It's dark brown," he whispered.

His mother nodded. "Good. She's strong, Kade. It usually happens much faster than this."

"What do I do now?" he asked.

"We have to wait, love. The staff has the tea and other herbal remedies ready. They will help ease the discomfort, and we have plenty of ice sheets. You should try to get some sleep. This is a long process, and you'll need all your strength."

Kade touched Sam's hair gently. "I can't sleep, Mum."

He sat in the chair next to the bed and took Sam's hand. The clock moved painstakingly slowly, but he still wasn't ready for the next phase that occurred almost an hour later.

Sam whimpered and her eyes flew open, horror covering her face. Her scream was like a dagger to Kade's heart, and his body froze.

"Check her mark, Kade," his mother said. She had to repeat herself.

Kade went into motion. "It's red."

"I'll get the staff." Alice rose to her feet, setting the book on the chair. "Don't panic. I'll be back as soon as I can, but you need to not panic. She won't die, even if it looks like she might."

"Aye," Kade said.

Sam screamed again, then her body began to thrash violently. He understood now why his mother said she needed to be out of the tub. He wrapped his fingers around her wrist and waited for her to calm, but it took several minutes.

"I'm going to be sick."

He grabbed a bowl and held it under her chin. Once her retching calmed, he laid a cool cloth over her forehead.

"Help me, please." Her eyes searched for him.

Kade laid his palm on hers. "I'm going to do everything I can, love. I'm here. Shhh."

"It hurts, baby."

"Are you still hot?"

"No. Just pain." Sam shifted and squeezed his hand. "My skin feels too tight. And I feel like I'm being crushed. Tell me what's happening. Please."

Kade moved the sheet aside and bit back a curse as he studied her stomach. Her skin was red again. The book said that once the mark turned red, the human would experience horrific pain. "You're changing, becoming Cauld Ane."

"Kade Úlfur Gunnach," she ground out. "Tell me something I haven't already figured out."

Kade covered her again. "I don't know much more. I haven't read the entire book."

"Can you please find me someone who does know? Preferably a female?"

"My mother will be back shortly." A knock sounded and Kade pulled the sheet back up to cover her. "Come in."

Fiona peeked inside.

"Fi? What are you doing here?"

"Con called. I'm here to help," she said, and stepped inside. "Everyone's downstairs, and I've been speaking with a few of the elders about the change."

"Fiona," Sam rasped. "Do you know what's happening?"

"In layman's terms, yes." She made her way to the bed. "The best analogy is that your body's acting a bit like a self-cleaning oven. It's burning up the human parts of your body that don't work with the Cauld Ane parts. It's really clinical and complicated. I'm sorry I don't have the correct medical terminology."

Sam groaned and fisted her hands in the sheets. "No, that's perfect."

"Fi, I'll come down when this is done," Kade said.

"No problem. Call us if you need us."

Fiona left the room and Sam screamed again. Kade held her wrist again, but this time he wasn't able to calm her. His mother arrived with two of the housemaids. Bearnas and Iona were mother and daughter and had been with his family since their arrival from Iceland. The women had been caught in the middle of a bloody clan war at the time and both of their husbands had been killed. Kade's father offered them refuge and they'd stayed with the family, assisting with their acclimation to the Highlands.

"As soon as she calms we'll give her the herbs," Bearnas said.

"How long will that take?" Kade asked.

"Your mother says she's strong, my lord," Iona said. "It won't take long."

Kade sat on the edge of the bed and held Sam's hand.

Several hours later, Sam's fever broke and her skin returned to normal, although he noticed it was softer and younger looking than before. Her steady breathing was a relief, and Bearnas declared she was over the worst. "Let's sit her up so she can take some tea. It will boost her strength."

Kade stroked Sam's cheek. "Sweetheart, I need to sit you up. You need to drink some tea." She nodded, but kept her eyes closed. Kade lifted her and settled her against the pillows, making sure the sheet still covered her chest. "Can you open your eyes, love?"

She shook her head.

"I'm going to put the cup to your lips. I want you to drink, okay?"

She nodded. Kade fed her the tea, grateful that she drank almost the entire cup.

"My lord, we need to change the sheets," Iona said. "She's past the change now. She'll be very tired for the next day or two, but she's going to be fine."

Kade nodded and wrapped a robe around Sam before lifting her from the bed and settling her on his lap in one of the large chairs by the fireplace. He kissed her neck, breathing in her familiar vanilla scent. She sighed and snuggled closer to him. Once the bed was changed, the women left him and his mother reached to take the book with her.

He laid his hand on hers. "No, Mum. That stays with me."

She frowned, but nodded and then left as well. Kade took Sam back to bed and climbed in beside her. He hadn't realized how exhausted he was until he had her safely in his arms again. He pulled her close and closed his eyes.

* * *

Samantha woke to the sound of quiet crying. She forced her eyes open, still heavy with exhaustion, although the pain of the night before was gone. Kade wasn't in their bed, and at some point, someone had dressed her in a light nightgown.

She turned her head to the sound of sadness and frowned. Fiona sat in the chair in the corner with a handkerchief pressed to her nose.

"Fiona?"

"Oh, Sam. Did I wake you? I'm so sorry," she said as she stood and made her way to the bed.

"What's wrong? Where's Kade? Is he okay?" Sam's heart started to race.

Sweetheart? Are you all right? he asked.

"Kade's fine." Fiona rushed to assure her. "Sorry if I scared you. He's meeting with my brothers and the Council. Are you all right?"

I'm fine, honey, Sam thought. She took a deep breath. "A little tired, but feeling much better."

"Can I get you anything?" Fiona asked.

"No. I'm fine. How long have I been asleep?"

Fiona checked her watch. "About twenty-six hours."

"Really?"

"Aye."

Sam stretched and then patted the mattress. "Tell me why you're so upset."

Fiona sat on the edge of the bed and sighed. "It's nothing. Really. I'm just glad you're okay."

"Fiona," Sam admonished. "Tell me."

"I'll not burden you with my insignificant disappointments when you went through all of that pain for me."

"Aw, honey, who told you your disappointments were insignificant?"

Fiona shook her head and pressed her lips into a thin line.

Sam laid her hand over Fiona's. "Let's forget for the moment that I'm your chieftain's mate."

"You mean, my queen?"

"Yeah, that too." She smiled. "He's also your big brother, and I'm pretty sure he can be a pain in the butt, right? Mine sure as heck can. I'm sure Kade gave you a myriad of well-intentioned instructions on everything you're *not* supposed to say or do, just in case you might upset me, but I'm a big girl and you and I have a relationship outside of your brother that's quite frankly none of his business."

Fiona let out a quiet gasp and then giggled.

Sam smiled. "Tell me."

"I'm not a Gunnach."

"Oh, Fi. Of course you are."

"Not technically. I'm the result of my mother's infidelity." She squeezed her eyes shut. "My father *hated* me. I never understood why. Now I do. I always thought it was because I was a girl. But it's because I wasn't legitimate. I thought my life was…I don't know…set, I guess."

"It's hard to change tack when you think your life's going one way but it's really going another. It doesn't always mean the change is a bad thing. And if you look at the situation for what it is, nothing's really changing. Your family's still your family and Angus is still your mate."

Fiona stood and paced the floor. "But I'm not the woman he thought he was getting."

Sam frowned. "What's that supposed to mean?"

"You wouldn't understand, Sam. You're American."

"Try me," she ground out, her irritation with Fiona's condescension rising.

You're supposed to be resting, Kade reprimanded.

I'm fine, honey. Go back to your meeting.

"Kade is king and my brothers are nobility. I always believed I was as well, but with my mother's confession, I'm now not only half-human, I'm also a nobody. Angus was to bind Lady Fiona Gunnach, but now he's stuck with the bastard daughter of Einar Jónsson."

Sam pushed herself to a more upright position and stifled a snort. "Fiona, Angus loves you, and you're still Lady Fiona Gunnach. Nothing has changed."

Samantha, love, you need to sleep.

I will when I'm tired, Kade. I'm fine. Just go back to your meeting.

"*I've* changed. Everything my mother told me is a lie. How can I trust that everything else isn't as well?" Fiona's cell phone pealed and she made her way to her phone. "Just a second, Sam." Fiona answered the call. "Hi. Fyrirgefðu. (I'm sorry)." She sighed. "Yes. Yes. I'll tell her. Okay. 'Bye." She hung up and dropped her phone on the chair. "You're supposed to rest."

Sam rolled her eyes. "He's not the boss of me."

Fiona chuckled. "Well, he's the boss of me, so I should probably quit whining."

Sam smiled. "We can talk whenever you need to. But keep in mind that unless I have this all wrong, we only have one mate and we mate for life, right?"

Fiona nodded.

"Well, then it wouldn't matter if you were Fiona, the Queen of England, or Fiona the janitor, Angus would still be your mate, right?"

She raised an eyebrow. "Yes, but—"

Sam held up her hand. "No buts. He loves you. Don't start putting words in his mouth about what he might be thinking or feeling. I'm pretty sure you'd be wrong."

Sam's door flew open, causing her to jump.

CHAPTER TWENTY

KADE FILLED THE doorway and Sam rolled her eyes at the dramatics.

"Leave us," Kade snapped at his sister.

Fiona kissed Sam's cheek. "Sorry."

"Think about what I said, okay?"

Fiona nodded and then headed toward the door.

"I'll talk to you later," Kade threatened.

"Já, herra minn," Fiona said, and left the room.

Kade closed and locked the door before making his way to the bed. He slipped off his shoes, stretched out beside Sam, and pulled her into his arms. "You're supposed to be asleep."

"And you're supposed to be in a meeting," she said, and snuggled against him.

"We're finished."

"Really finished, or you called it to a close early because I wasn't doing what you wanted me to do?"

Kade lifted her chin and gave her a quick kiss. "Finished is finished."

"Hmm-mm. Fiona said you were meeting with your brothers and the Council. What does that mean? Who's on the Council?"

He kissed the top of her head. "Nothing you need to worry about, love. Right now, I need you to worry about resting."

"Is that code for I'm on a need-to-know basis and I don't need to know?"

Kade chuckled. "No, it's code for you need to sleep."

Sam tried to stifle a yawn, but she failed. "Okay, maybe I'm a little tired."

"I know, love."

His cell phone rang and he stared at the screen. "It's yer mum, love."

"Why's she calling you?"

"Mrs. Moore?" he said without answering Sam's question. "I'm sorry about that. Sam's had a bit of tummy bug, so I turned off her phone so she could rest. She's right here, would you like to speak to her?"

He handed Sam the phone.

"Hi, Mom."

"I have been worried sick! What's going on with you?" she asked.

"I think it might have been something I ate. Not sure."

"Oh, honey, are you okay?"

"I'm fine. Just really tired. Sorry about my phone." Sam scowled at her mate. "I'm sure Kade was just trying to help, but I'll turn it on right now so you can get me if you need to."

"I'm just glad you're okay…I began to imagine all sorts of horrible things."

Sam grimaced. "Sorry."

"How did everything go?"

"Y'all held the secret very well," Sam said. "I was sufficiently surprised."

"Did you say yes?"

Sam giggled. "Absolutely."

"Good. I won't keep you. Get some rest."

"I will, Mom. Love you." She hung up and settled herself back in Kade's embrace. "No more phone tampering."

He set his phone back on the side table. "No promises."

"Brat." She closed her eyes and kissed his chest. "Don't be hard on your sister, okay? Her world's been turned upside down."

He sighed. "I know."

"Promise me you'll give her heaps of grace."

"Heaps?" he asked. "Do I have to promise *heaps*?"

Sam giggled, her eyes growing heavier by the second. "Heaps," she mumbled.

* * *

The room was dark the next time Sam opened her eyes. She felt for Kade, but he wasn't in their bed. She rubbed her eyes and yawned.

This is becoming a habit, honey. Where are you?

"I'm here, love," he said from the chair by the fireplace. He rose to his feet and made his way to the bed.

She sat up and sighed. "I don't like waking without you."

He sat on the edge of the mattress. "I'm sorry. How do you feel?"

"Better. I'm a little groggy and my muscles feel like I've run a marathon, but otherwise I'm good." She dropped her head onto his shoulder. "Are you okay?"

"Aye."

She frowned up at him. "Why don't I believe you?"

He smiled. "Are you hungry?"

"A little. But first, I'd really love a shower." She slid her legs off the bed and pushed herself up, grasping Kade's arm when she felt unsteady.

"Careful," he said as he wrapped an arm around her waist. "Let's start with food."

"Seriously?"

He smiled. "Fruit and cheese are perfect in the middle of the night."

Sam grimaced. "I heard cheese gives you nightmares."

"So will your mate if you refuse to eat."

Sam giggled. "Fine."

She ate as much as her stomach could take at three in the morning and then insisted on a shower. She rose to her feet but still felt dizzy.

"I've got you." Kade took the brunt of her weight as he guided her into the bathroom and set her on the toilet lid. "I think a bath might be safer."

Sam smiled. "Maybe you're right."

He filled the tub and then helped her with her nightgown before lifting her into the cool water.

Sam sighed. "This is heaven. Thank you."

He knelt beside her. "Would you like me to wash your hair?"

Sam reached out and stroked his cheek. "Nothing sounds better, but first, I'd like you to tell me why you're worried."

He grimaced. "I need to learn how to control my emotions."

"No you don't. Baby, tell me what's going on."

"I don't want to add stress to your recovery."

Sam snorted. "It's far more stressful knowing you're dealing with something heavy and not talking to me about it. I'm here to take part of the burden away, or did you miss that part in mate training?"

He sighed.

"Now, tell me who's on the Council and what it is to begin with. Then you can fill me in on the rest."

He pinched the bridge of his nose.

"Kade," she admonished. "You're either going to tell me or I'm going to "listen" to you. I think you'll feel better if you tell me."

"You're a wee stubborn wench, aren't you?"

She cocked her head. "Aye."

He chuckled. "Well done."

"Thank you. Now tell me." She handed him the shampoo. "You can wash while you talk."

He chuckled and squeezed the soap into his palm. "The Council is made up of elders of the Cauld Ane within not only our clan, but a few others in Scotland. Con, Brodie, and I are on it, along with Max and Niall MacMillan, who you'll meet soon, I'm sure. Also, Angus and his father, Stuart, and ten others from five of the larger clans in the country. Individually, we deal with our personal clan business, however, when it comes to Cauld Ane issues, the Council comes together and I make the ultimate decisions."

"So, you've had a Cauld Ane issue, then?"

"A few."

"Like?"

"The Fraser family for one, my mother for another."

Sam frowned. "Your mom's a Cauld Ane issue? How does that work?"

"She kept vital information from her laird and king, committed adultery that produced an illegitimate child, and lied to our people, among other minor infractions; however, the list goes on."

Sam sat up, the water sloshing around her. "How is that anyone's business outside of her family?"

"It's complicated."

"Then un-complicate it."

"Rinse," he directed, and she slid under the water quickly.

"All rinsed...keep talkin'," she ordered as she wiped water from her face, but quickly pressed on her stomach. "After you get me some more cheese, please. Wow, I'm starving."

He left her briefly and returned with the food platter. "This is why you need to eat every two hours."

He set a cracker in her mouth and she hummed in appreciation as she chewed. "This is so good. Everything feels...I don't know...so intense. Like this is the best cheese I've *ever* had in my life and this water is the most amazing temperature, ever." She lifted her hand, the soapy water sliding down her arm. "And my skin. It's flawless. The scar I got from Home Ec is gone and my nails actually look healthy." She looked at Kade. "Do I look different?"

He shook his head. "You're as beautiful as you were. Just in stereo."

She giggled and opened her mouth for another treat. She swallowed and sat up in the tub. "Thank you. Now, tell me about your mom."

He stood and leaned against the counter. "My mother was joined to the Laird of Gunnach, which is a job within itself. But not only was my father laird of our clan, he was also king of the Cauld Ane, and that meant she had obligations to fulfill, including giving birth to an heir and being the perfect spouse."

"Why do I have visions of Henry the VIII and his propensity to kill women who didn't do what he wanted them to do?"

Kade sighed. "You've hit the nail on the head, love. My father may not have killed my mother for her indiscretion when he found out about it, but he more than likely tried to drive her mad. According to the elders of the Council, there were rumors that his true mate was murdered by one of his rivals, and I suppose it's possible that he might have gone a bit mad as well."

"But no one thought that would be good information for you to have?"

"Hence my dilemma." He crossed his arms. "So many people were attempting to either shelter us or deceive us; I'm having a difficult time sorting out who had good intentions and who didn't. On top of trying to work out why my mother did what she did."

179

"I guess her actions are somewhat understandable, right?"

"I don't know." He frowned again. "Her adultery alone is a beheading offense—"

"What?" Sam gasped. "You can't be serious! *Beheading*?"

He raised his hands. "Don't worry, I have no intention of beheading my mother, but had she been discovered by the Council while my father was alive, she would have been. Now it's up to me to decide what to do, and it's a thin line between showing mercy and showing weakness."

Sam added more water to the tub. "What are you going to do?"

"If you'd asked me yesterday, beheading would have been too good for her. I'm a little calmer today."

Sam bit her lip. "Your poor mother."

"Don't let your heart bleed for my mother, Samantha."

"Only if you promise not to let yours harden."

"Samantha."

"No, Kade. I get that she did some pretty awful things, and I'm not saying you have to be her best friend. I'm not even saying you have to have a relationship with her, but if you hate her, it's like drinking poison and hoping the other person dies."

He stared at her for several seconds. "I don't know what I feel about her, but I don't think I love her enough to hate her. She wasn't the most nurturing."

"Oh, honey, I'm sorry."

He shook his head. "Don't be."

"So what's the next step?"

"We have made the decision to exile our mother."

"What?" Sam sat up again. "To where?"

"We're working on that."

"Where do you typically exile your dissidents?"

"Pohnpei."

She frowned. "Italy?"

"No, Micronesia."

"Micronesia?" she exclaimed. "You can't be serious. Isn't it tropical and really warm there? You send your people to a place where they're sure to die?"

He shrugged. "They have air-conditioning there, and I have it on good authority there are some wonderful missionaries who will help them mend their ways."

"Kade!" she admonished. "You can't do that to your mother…I'm not sure you should do it to anyone, but definitely not your mother."

"I know. This is why the dilemma is even more confusing."

"What does the rest of the Council say? What do your *brothers* say?"

"Brodie wants her beheaded, Con wants her to stay here and for us to deal with it privately, Max agrees with Con, but he usually does. Niall will do what I decide. Angus is concerned about Fiona, so he's not objective. The older men want her exiled to the surface of the sun."

"Wow." Sam sighed. "Why does Brodie want her beheaded?"

Kade grimaced. "My father was abusive to say the least, and my mother wasn't much better. With me and Con, she'd try to calm my father's rages, although many times it just added fuel to the fire, but at least she tried. However, Brodie, for whatever reason, got the brunt of *her* anger. Con and I did our best to protect him, but it's difficult to do when you're a child. Brodie was often bruised or worse, emotionally raw. Now his go-to emotion is anger."

Sam held her hand out to him. "Come here."

Kade pushed away from the counter and knelt beside the tub.

Sam cupped his cheek. "I'm so sorry your parents were less than what you deserved."

He smiled. "Thank you, love. Honestly, I haven't given it much thought in a long, long time."

"But it's coming to the surface now, isn't it?"

"Aye." He sighed. "For all of us."

Sam pulled the plug on the bath and then stared up at him. "If I cheat on you, will I be exiled to Micronesia?"

"That will never happen." He scowled. "You cheating, I mean."

"*Very* true. And just so you know, if you cheat on me, no one will find your body."

He slid his hand behind her neck and covered her lips with his. The kiss quickly turned heated as she slipped her hands into his hair. Kade broke the kiss and Sam tried to catch her breath.

He lifted her out of the tub and wrapped a towel around her. "I will never cheat on you, Sam. It would be a physical and emotional impossibility."

She slid the towel from her body and let it drop to the floor. "Prove it."

"You should rest."

"I will. After you take me to bed."

He frowned. "I don't want to overtax you."

Sam smiled and slipped her hands under his T-shirt. "I need less of the talky-talky, baby."

Kade grinned and lifted her off the ground. Sam wrapped her legs around his waist and kissed him while he carried her to the bed.

CHAPTER TWENTY-ONE

"INTERESTING," FIONA MUSED as she read out loud from the ancestral book that Kade had confiscated from their mother.

"What?" Kade asked. He sat in the great room of his ancestral home with Sam on his lap. It had been two days since her full conversion and was the first day she felt "normal." They still had much to talk about with regards to the Council and other decisions weighing heavy on his mind, but Sam had insisted they take some time to process all the information before revisiting the discussion.

For now, his mother was securely settled in a small home in Edinburgh to await her appeal to the Council. The rest of the family was gathered around the large fireplace and they had already put a dent in several bottles of his finest from the wine cellar.

"If one mate is an empath," she read, "they can communicate telepathically even without touching."

"Aye," Kade confirmed. "We found that out by accident."

Sam grinned. "You weren't quite prepared to have someone read your thoughts, were you?"

He chuckled. "Not in the least."

"What I don't understand is how I was able to do it as a human," Sam mused.

Fiona stared at the book. "It says here that some of the natural gifts humans have are similar to what we experience as Cauld Ane's. For instance, the gifts of discernment and prophecy fall into the empath category." She glanced at Connall. "That means you'll be able to speak thoughts with your mate when you find her." She wrinkled her nose. "I'm so jealous."

"How come?" Sam asked.

"Angus and I can speak if we're touching and we know if one or the other is upset, but I can't talk to him across the room, let alone across an ocean."

"Would you rather your mate be an empath or a healer?" Brodie asked.

Angus raised an eyebrow. "Yes, which one, Fi?"

Fiona sighed. "I love that you're a healer, sweetheart. Don't get me wrong...I just wish *I* had sexier abilities."

"Like?" Connall prodded.

"I'd love to be able to make things fly around the room like Brodie."

"No you wouldn't," Brodie said quietly.

"What are your abilities now?" Sam asked.

"I haven't really thought about it. According to the book, my abilities are closer to human than Cauld Ane, so until I have gone through the conversion, mine won't fully manifest."

"It'll be interesting to see what happens, eh, Fi," Connall said.

She snorted. "I just hope it's not psychometry...it's so boring. I want something sexy. Like being able to start a fire with my mind."

"Payton has psychometry," Brodie said. "And there's nothing boring about her."

Kade stiffened. Brodie tended to be a little defensive when it came to Payton.

"What's psychometry?" Sam asked.

"The ability to know something about someone by touching an object they own," Fiona explained. "Pay says she doesn't really get much when she does it."

"*Or*, it could be she just doesn't gossip," Brodie pointed out.

Fiona rolled her eyes. "Calm down, big brother. I'm not saying Payton's not perfect."

Brodie stared at her, a mixture of irritation and amusement on his face.

"Now, if I could just figure mine out," she continued.

"Keep reading," Kade directed. "You might find out something more. And I personally think your ability to learn and retain information's pretty amazing."

Fiona grinned. "Thanks, Kade."

Sam kissed his cheek. *I hope we can excuse ourselves soon. I want to see what else my new body can do...preferably naked.*

Kade glanced at Sam, whose face was passive.

Minx.

She grinned.

"You two really should get a room," Fiona complained.

Sam blushed and Kade turned a warning glance on his sister.

"Sorry," she said, and leaned against Angus.

"Now that I'm settled, Fi, you and Angus are free," Kade said.

"I know," she said.

"What's the matter?" Connall asked.

Fiona shuddered. "I just don't know exactly what's going to happen to me."

Angus kissed her temple. "There's no rush."

Fiona snorted. "We've been waiting a long time. I don't want my fear to stop us from finally bonding."

"It's not really that bad," Samantha said. "In the moment, it's painful, but I have a feeling the change will go easier on you. You're already halfway there."

Fiona's face lit up. "Oh, Sam! Yes. I hadn't thought of that."

Kade smiled at Sam. She was simply perfect.

I am not.

He kissed her fingertips and focused on his sister. "So, the question is, when and where do you want the party to be?"

Fiona leaned forward and raised an eyebrow. "After the bonding, I want an actual ceremony. Not just the parson writing in the book. I want to be married at Old High and I want you to pay for it."

"Fi!" Angus admonished. "I am quite capable of paying for our wedding."

She squeezed his knee. "That's not the point. My brother is the reason we've had to wait so long, and I'd like him to make it up to me."

Kade chuckled. "It's the least I can do."

Fiona smiled. "Good. I'll find out when the church is free and we'll go from there."

Sam yawned and laid her head on Kade's shoulder.

"Tired, love?"

She nodded. "Absolutely pooped."

"I think I should get Sam upstairs," Kade said.

"Oh, yes." Fiona sighed. "I'm sorry, Sam. I've monopolized Kade's time, and you must be exhausted."

"Nonsense," Sam said. "This was an important conversation."

"And now it's done." Kade stood with Sam in his arms and gently set her on the ground. "Good night, all."

Sam hugged Fiona and then Kade led her upstairs. Once inside their bedroom, he closed and locked the door. Sam giggled and clapped her hands. "I seriously thought we were going to be stuck down there all night."

"I thought you were tired," he said.

Sam snorted. "Not in the slightest. I just wanted you all to myself. Now, let's talk about your shirt."

He glanced down at his fitted T-shirt. "What about it?"

"Why is it still on?" she asked as she slipped the buttons on her own, revealing a piece of lingerie he'd purchased for her weeks ago.

He yanked his shirt off and rushed her. She was so shocked, she let out a squeal and started giggling uncontrollably as he dropped her on the bed and began to tickle her.

Her face, free from pain and full of joy, was more of a turn-on than her removing her clothing. He leaned down and kissed her, quickly divesting her of the rest of her clothes.

* * *

A strange buzzing interrupted Samantha's dream. By the time she realized it was her cell phone, the buzzing stopped. Snuggling closer to Kade, she thought to ignore it and find out who called in the morning, but then it began again. She rubbed her eyes and focused on the screen. It was her father.

"Daddy? What's wrong?"

"I'm sorry to call so early, button. Can you come home?"

"Yes." She sat up, her blood running cold. "What's happened?"

Kade stirred next to her.

"There's been an incident and your brother's been shot," her father said.

"Shot? What kind of incident?"

"We think it was a robbery attempt at the Abercorn store. He managed to get to his panic room and call the cops."

Kade sat up and wrapped an arm around her waist, pulling her back to his chest.

Her pulse started to slow. "Is he okay?"

"He's in a private room now," her father said. "The surgeon was able to repair the damage and he says he'll make a full recovery. The injury wasn't life-threatening."

"In a private room? Already? When did this happen?"

"Yesterday.

"Daddy, why didn't you call me earlier?"

"I'm sorry, honey. He made me promise not to."

Sam let out an uncharacteristic curse. "And you *listened* to him? Who the hell does he think he is?"

Kade gave her a gentle squeeze and kissed her shoulder.

"I know." Her father sighed. "I'm sorry."

Sam squeezed her eyes shut. "Is Mom okay?"

"She's better now that he's fine, but she'd really like you to come home for a week or so if at all possible."

"Of course I'll come. But if Dalton really is perfectly fine when I get there, I'm going to kill him."

Her father chuckled. "I'll let you."

"I'll get the first flight I can."

"Good. Call me when you're set and I'll pick you up."

"Thanks. 'Bye, Daddy." She hung up.

"What happened?" Kade asked.

"My stupid idiot moron of a brother went and got himself shot and made my parents promise not to call me," she snapped.

Kade stayed quiet as she pulled out of his arms and stomped around the bedroom, opening drawers and pulling out random clothing.

"Knowing him, he probably tried to be the big macho hero and stop the robbery at his store." She let out an anguished groan. "He could have been killed. Over his damn, precious, piece-of-crap cars!"

Kade slid from the bed and stopped her from pulling on a pair of sweatpants. "Those are mine, love."

Sam burst into angry tears. "He could have been killed, Kade."

"Come here." He pulled her close. "I've got you."

"He doesn't think! He's the most selfish, arrogant, egotistical…" Her sob stopped her tirade. "He could have died."

"I know, sweetheart." Kade stroked her back.

They stood in the middle of the room, Kade rubbing her back and Sam waffling between tears and lobbing unflattering adjectives toward her brother. Her emotions were so strong, it took several minutes for Kade to calm her.

"Sorry, baby." Pulling away from him, she grimaced. "I've gotten you all wet."

"I don't mind in the least." Kade chuckled and wiped her cheeks with his thumbs. "How's your mum?"

"Daddy said she's doing better now, but wants me to come home." She found a pair of her sweatpants and pulled them on. "Can you help me book a flight?"

"Of course." He retrieved his cell phone from the side table and dialed a number. "Hi, Russell. Sorry to wake you. Can you organize a flight to Hilton Head, Savannah, please? Aye, the States. Thanks."

"We could have waited until morning, honey," she said.

"You need to get home." He made his way to the closet, returning with two suitcases.

"What are you doing?" Sam asked. "I don't need two."

"I'm going with you," he said as he laid the bags on the bed.

Samantha couldn't stop another quiet sob.

Kade rushed to comfort her. "Don't you want me to come?"

"No. I mean, yes. I just didn't want to ask. You're so busy."

"Och, love. I'm never too busy for you."

"But there's all the Council stuff and your mom."

He lifted her chin. "*No one* is more important than you."

His phone rang and he answered it while keeping an arm firmly around her. "Hi, Russell. Excellent. Aye, we'll be ready." He hung up and kissed Sam's head. "Wheels up at nine. How about we get a few more hours of sleep, hmm?"

"It'll never happen."

"Let's try," he suggested and climbed back into the bed.

Samantha gratefully slid into his safe embrace and kissed his neck. "I can't get close enough."

"I know, sweetheart. Quiet your heart. I've got you."

She took a deep breath and closed her eyes.

* * *

Kade heard his phone buzz, but turned it off before it could wake Samantha. She didn't need to wake up for another hour. Easing out of the bed, he stepped into the dressing room and dialed Connall.

"I hear you're taking a trip," Connall said without greeting Kade.

"Aye. Her brother's been shot. I'm taking her home."

"What happened?"

"Something about a robbery, but it's not sitting well with me, Con. Find out what really happened, hmm?"

"Aye," Connall said. "I also think we're going to need to sort out Ármann sooner than later. I know we have Mum to deal with, but I think he takes precedence."

Kade pinched the bridge of his nose. "I agree. Just give me a few days."

"Okay. Don't worry about anything here or at the office. I'll call you as soon as we find anything on Sam's brother, and I'll also sort out the Iceland details."

"What about your horses?"

"Max is taking care of those interests for the time being."

"Thanks."

"Tell Sam we're praying for her brother."

Samantha's scream filtered into the room.

"I will. Gotta go." He rushed into the bedroom, set his phone on the side table, and climbed into bed with her. "Bad dream?"

She nodded. Her breathing was heavy and her face was in her hands. "Waking up without you doesn't help."

"Sorry, sweetheart. Come here."

She settled herself onto his chest. "I don't think he got shot because of a robbery."

Kade raised an eyebrow. "What makes you think that?"

"Just a weird feeling. I could be wrong."

"We'll know more soon." Kade stroked her cheek. "Why don't you go take a shower and I'll finish packing?"

Samantha reluctantly left him, grabbing an apple on the way to the bathroom. She was hungry again and this time she couldn't ignore it.

Once showered, she dressed in a soft T-shirt, comfortable sweats, and shoes. Forgoing makeup, she pulled her damp hair into a ponytail. At this point, she didn't care who she met on the plane, she just wanted to get home. She glanced at Kade pulling on a clean shirt. "What time's the flight again?"

187

"Nine." He looked at his watch. "The car will be here soon."

Sam glanced at her watch and frowned. It was just after eight. "Cutting it a bit close, don't you think? Aren't we supposed to be there like two hours ahead or something like that?"

He shook his head. "We've got plenty of time."

"Well, I'm ready."

"Good. Would you like to eat more now or on the plane?"

Sam raised an eyebrow. "I get a choice, huh?"

"You make me sound like an ogre."

"When it comes to forcing food in my mouth, you are a bit Shrek-like."

"Your metabolism has tripled, love. You have to eat twice as much as you used to or you could get sick."

"I know, honey. And I appreciate you looking out for me." She looped her hands around his neck. "But the apple helped, so I'd rather wait."

"You're lucky you're cute."

"Oh, really?"

He patted her bottom. "Yes, I cannot seem to resist you."

"Kiss me, then."

He obliged.

Kade's phone buzzed and Sam reluctantly broke the kiss and followed him downstairs. He set her bag next to his in the foyer just as a large man dressed in a suit and tie walked through the door.

"Sam, this is Tavish," Kade said.

The man bowed.

Sam gave him a nervous smile. "It's nice to meet you."

"Thank you, m'lady." Tavish reached for Kade's bag. "Are you ready?"

Kade nodded and waited for Sam to precede him out the door. He held the car door open for her and she slid inside, leaning heavily against him when he sat next to her. He wrapped an arm around her and pulled her as close as the seatbelt would allow. "I talked to the attending."

She glanced up at him. "Dr. Selliken?"

"Yes. You know her?"

"I do. I attended one of her guest lectures. She's notoriously tight-lipped. How did you manage a conversation?"

"I have my ways."

"I know you do." Sam smiled. "What did she say?"

"That your brother sustained a flesh wound to his bicep and bruised his shoulder in his attempt to avoid the bullet. He has to wear a sling for a couple of weeks, but otherwise, he'll make a full recovery."

"Did she say when he'll be released?"

"Tomorrow."

"He really is the luckiest man alive." She kissed his cheek. "Thank you."

As Tavish drove them to the airport, Sam let the comfort Kade offered seep into her. She was relieved that her brother was going to be fine, but she couldn't shake the feeling that something wasn't quite right.

Within minutes, Kade broke contact and squeezed her hand. "We're here."

Sam glanced outside. "This doesn't look like an airport…well, not a big one anyway."

Kade grinned and climbed from the car. He leaned in and reached for her. "I have a bit of a surprise, love."

She took his hand and slid from the car. "What did you do?"

"We're not flying commercial."

She bit back a groan. "You have your own freaking plane, don't you?"

"Aye." He nodded at the jet in front of them. "That's one of ours."

"*One* of yours?"

"We have the family jet and the company jet."

She shook her head. "Kade. I can't fly in a small plane. They *crash*."

"They do not." He laid his hands on her shoulders. "I will make sure you're calm without pills. Do you trust me?"

"It's not you I have an issue with."

"Let's board, and then you can see how you feel, okay? One step at a time, love."

"I don't know if I can."

"Yes, you can. Come on." He took her hand and pulled her toward the plane.

Sam swallowed and shuffled behind him in an effort to delay the inevitable.

Lynyrd Skynyrd, Buddy Holly, Ritchie Valens, um…

"Samantha," Kade admonished with a chuckle. "You are not going to die…at least not in a plane crash."

"Get out of my brain."

"Lynyrd Skynyrd, really?" he asked.

"You can blame my brother for that one." Sam bit her lip. "He used to sing "Sweet Home Savannah" instead of Alabama whenever I was having a bad day."

"Good brother."

Sam snorted. "You haven't heard him sing."

He laughed, and before she knew what was happening, she was climbing the stairs and entering the cabin of his private jet. As her gaze swept the space, she couldn't stop an appreciative hum.

Large leather chairs that looked more like recliners filled the interior and a young woman dressed in something out of a fifties flight attendant magazine stood holding a tray with assorted pastries.

"Welcome m'lady," she said.

"Thank you."

Sam felt Kade's gentle push on her lower back. "There's a nice bathroom in the back and a couple of beds as well. You won't even know you're in the air."

She frowned at him over her shoulder. "Yes I will."

He chuckled again. "Well, you won't care."

She turned to face him and laid her hands on his chest. "I don't know about this."

"I know you're scared, love. But I've flown all over the world in this plane. Nothing has ever gone wrong."

"There's always a first time."

"Do you want to meet my pilot?"

"Now?"

"Yes."

"No."

He chuckled. "I think it would be a good idea."

"Are you saying I should meet him now because there's a chance I won't be able to meet him later, because we'll be dead?"

Kade laughed. "Och, love, you are adorable."

She wrinkled her nose. "I'll be happy to meet him…after we arrive safely."

He raised an eyebrow. "So that's a yes, then?"

"What kind of a woman would I be if I turned down the chance to fly home in a private Learjet?"

"A crazy one." He grinned. "I'll speak with Russell quickly. Have some breakfast."

"I'll wait for you."

He nodded and disappeared into the cockpit.

CHAPTER TWENTY-TWO

"Dr. MOORE?"

Sam turned to face the flight attendant.

The woman indicated the chairs and smiled. "Please make yourself comfortable. Would you like some coffee?"

"I'd love some. Thank you," Sam said, and settled into the chair *not* near the window.

Kade returned and sat next to Sam. The flight attendant set a cup of coffee in front of Sam, handed her sugar and cream, and turned to Kade. "Would you like some coffee, my lord?"

"Yes, Maureen. Thank you." Once he secured his seatbelt, he laid his hand on Sam's thigh and gave it a gentle squeeze. "Russell's doing his final checks. We'll be taking off in just a few minutes."

Sam grimaced. "Yippee."

Kade grinned. "Maybe you should have scotch added to your coffee."

"Maybe I should."

Sam managed to finish her coffee before Maureen collected their cups in preparation for takeoff. As the engines whirred and the doors were secured, Kade linked his fingers with hers and Sam grasped his bicep with her other hand, leaning against him. The plane began its taxi and she laid her head on his shoulder. When the nose lifted into the air, she squeezed her eyes shut and took several deep breaths.

"Let me in, love."

She shook her head.

"If you block me, I can't calm you."

"I can't."

Kade pulled out of her death grip. He covered her lips with his and kissed her until she couldn't think straight. Within seconds her panic was gone.

He linked his fingers with hers again and smiled. "Better?"

"Much." She sighed. "Thank you."

"My pleasure."

"Um…" She settled against him again. "How are we going to eat with just one hand?"

Kade chuckled. "As long as we stay connected, you'll be fine. We don't have to hold hands."

"Good to know."

* * *

Samantha had one more panic attack when Kade left her to check in with the pilot. But he didn't stay away long and gave her another heart-melting kiss to distract her. After lunch, he insisted she rest and led her to a room with a surprisingly large bed.

She crossed her arms. "Just how many women have joined your mile-high club, Kade?"

"Subtle," Kade mused.

She raised an eyebrow. "Was it?"

He wrapped his arms around her waist. "You're the only woman I've ever brought on this plane outside of my sister and mother."

"What about the actresses and heiresses you dated?"

He frowned. "Who have you been talking to?"

She shrugged, feeling very vulnerable at his fixed gaze. "Cole mentioned them, and the little news story kind of confirmed it."

"Bloody bastards."

"Forget it, Kade. It's none of my business." She slipped off her shoes and sat on the bed. "What you did before me isn't relevant."

"Of course it is. You're my mate." He sat next to her. "I will tell you anything you want to know and maybe some things you don't."

"*Great.*"

He smiled. "I have dated a few powerful women, it's true, but much to my sister's irritation, I knew none of them were my mate, and the relationships never lasted very long."

"What did they think about that?"

"I'm sure some of them didn't like it. They told me as much."

"What about sex?"

"I had a very nice experience last night, if you recall."

Sam rolled her eyes.

"Before you, it had been a very long time."

She cocked her head. "How long?"

"Years."

"How *many* years?"

"Eons." He chuckled. "I'll give you a little back story, shall I?"

"I love stories."

"I know you do."

"Especially when they get to the point quickly," she clarified.

"Duly noted." He stretched out on the bed and pulled her up against him. "After my father died, I went off the deep end a bit and drank a little more than I should. I didn't want the lairdship or the crown or the responsibility that came with it. I did everything I could to convince everyone I was the wrong person for the job. Finally, Connall got involved and I came to my senses."

"When did your father die?"

"1847."

"Seriously? How did you handle that?"

"I thought I was relieved at the time, but regardless of what kind of father you have, it's still going to affect you when he dies. Connall helped me see that I could be different than the legacy my father had left me. That I could be better than what he said I was. That I *was* better than what he said I was."

"He was right. You're kind of amazing."

Kade grinned. "Thank you."

"How did your father die?"

"He was murdered."

She gasped. "How?"

"I won't give you the details, love, because they aren't things you can un-hear. His enemies managed to slip Red Fang into his ale and he was assassinated."

"Was he alone? I mean, with the amount of security you have, I'm surprised someone could get close enough to hurt him."

"They turned on him. He wasn't a kind man, so there weren't people rushing to his defense."

"Are you telling me your own people let your father get killed? What about you and your brothers?"

He rolled onto his back and ran his hands through his hair. "We were duped by someone we thought we trusted, and found out after the fact. I don't want to give you the details, can you please let it rest?"

Sam laid her hand on his chest. "But what if you're in trouble? How will I know what to do? If you're slipped Red Fang, what do I do? Are you sure everyone working for you has your back?"

He grasped her hand. "Take a breath."

Sam blinked back the tears threatening to fall. "Sorry."

"Nothing is going to happen to me…or you. I made changes when I became king and have done as much as possible to create peace amongst the clans. My brothers have my back, as do my closest friends. I'm not worried."

"Who do you consider friends? I only ever see you with your brothers."

He faced her and ran his hand through her hair. "I don't trust easily, but Duncan is certainly someone I consider a friend. I also trust the MacMillans, Max and Niall, although they're closer to Connall."

"There's also Angus," she pointed out.

He shrugged. "Angus is more of an annoyance, but I trust him."

Sam grinned. "I like Angus."

Kade grunted, but didn't respond.

"So if I can't get hold of you or your brothers, I can call them, right?"

"Of course. But you won't need them, sweetheart. Nothing's going to happen. If you feel something's off, let me know, and I'll deal with it."

"Like?"

"It could be anything from someone offering you something suspect to drink or…"

"A warm office?"

"Excuse me?"

Sam groaned. "My office thermostat was tampered with."

"What?" he snapped. "When!"

"The *first* time—"

"The *first* time?" he interrupted. "Exactly how many times has this happened?"

She bit her lip. "Three. I thought it was the cleaning crew. I left notes, but it happened again."

He sat up. "Damn it, Samantha! Why didn't you tell me?"

"At the time, I didn't realize the importance of temperature control! I couldn't figure out why Fiona wouldn't come into my office, but now I know why."

"*Fiona* knew?"

"The first time. She was there. I told her not to tell you, because I didn't think it was a big deal."

"I'll deal with her."

She grasped his arm. "No! Don't, honey. It was the day before our shopping excursion and we were all distracted. It's my fault. I should have told you. Please don't blame your sister."

"She knows better," he snapped.

"Maybe. But she was also letting me make the call. I'm your mate and asked that she let me deal with it. She was being loyal. Not to mention the fact, I was human! It's not like they could hurt me."

"But they could have hurt me," he pointed out.

"I didn't think of that." She sat up on her knees. "They were trying to get to you…I'm so sorry!"

He shook his head and sighed.

"I promise I'll tell you if it happens again."

"It *won't* happen again," he said.

"Okay." She smiled and stroked his cheek. "So…are you telling me you haven't slept with anyone in over a hundred and sixty years?"

Kade smirked. "Your ability to get back to your original point is quite impressive."

"Thanks…I think."

"I haven't slept with anyone in almost a hundred years."

Her mouth dropped open. "Really? Who was she?" She held her hand up. "Wait, if it was Shannon, I don't want to know."

His lip curled up in a sneer. "I have never had any kind of romantic relationship with her."

"I'm surprised."

"Why?"

"She's beautiful."

"If you think vipers are beautiful," he said.

Sam couldn't stop a smile. "I love that the most about you."

"That I don't like snakes?"

"That you can see through the façade."

He stretched out on the bed again and held his hand out to her. "Come here, love."

She snuggled against him and wrapped an arm around his waist.

"The woman was someone I thought I could marry. She was a great friend and she would have been a good partner. It would have been more of an arrangement, somewhat like my parents, I suppose, although without the mutual hatred. I had no intention of sleeping with her. She pursued the physical part of our relationship and at the time, I didn't see any reason why it would be a bad idea."

"Outside of your faith, you mean?" she challenged.

"Admittedly, at the time, I wasn't particularly living the way I should have been, so sex meant a lot less to me."

"Why didn't you marry her?"

"She found her mate." He ran his hand down Samantha's back. "He'd come from Iceland to Scotland to visit family. The moment his ship came into port, she changed. She became distant and irritable. I realized that even if she "got over" whatever was ailing her that we wouldn't work. This mating process really is similar to magnets. As soon as you're close to your mate, you can't help but gravitate toward them. They had both been invited to a party by two different people in Edinburgh and as soon as they touched we were done."

"Like us."

"Sort of."

"What was different?" she asked.

"He had to deal with the fact that she didn't save herself for him."

"Did he save *himself*?"

"No. But in our world there's still a double standard. He bound her and moved her back to Iceland. Away from me, even though I was no longer a threat."

"It's a good thing you don't care about that," she said with a cheeky grin.

He chuckled. "I wish I was that evolved. I knew before I bound you that you'd be mine only."

"I'm never going to have any secrets in this relationship, am I?"

He lifted her chin. "Do you really want any?"

"Not really. I think I just want the option."

"I'll pretend I know less, then."

She kissed him. "That's all I ask."

"You should try to sleep. We have several hours before dinner."

"I have something else in mind."

"Oh, really?"

She sat up and straddled him. "I'd like to check out the membership requirements for the Mile-High Club."

"Would you now?" He settled his hands on her hips. "It starts with you passing a particularly *stiff* test."

Sam licked her lips. "I can see you're already in the full and upright position."

"I'm sorry. I wasn't paying attention during the safety demonstration; can you please show me your flotation devices?"

"I'd be happy to, so long as you don't experience a sudden loss of cabin pressure."

"Very well, then, you might want to brace yourself for turbulence."

* * *

Kade woke Samantha an hour before they were set to land. They had time to eat and freshen up before they were forced to buckle up. Sam gripped Kade's hand as the plane began to descend and didn't let go until the plane came to a complete stop.

"You made it, love," Kade said. "I'm very proud of you."

"I couldn't have done it without you." She pulled her cell phone out of her purse. "I completely forgot to call my dad."

"You don't need to. There's a car waiting for us."

"Of course there is."

"The driver will take us straight to the hospital and then drop the bags at the hotel."

She shook her head. "Honey, I *cannot* stay at a hotel. My mother would be really hurt. I have a feeling she won't want you to stay at one either."

"We have to remember our limits, love."

"Our limits?" Sam asked, and then it dawned on her. "Oh! Right. Luckily, my parents are cheap. Thermostat is set to sixty-five or below during the winter. They always told us that if we were cold we could put on more clothes."

"Dr. Gunnach?" Maureen inquired as she stepped from the cockpit. "Your bags have been transferred to the car, my lord. You may disembark anytime."

"Thank you," Kade said, and squeezed Sam's arm. "Ready?"

"Absolutely."

Kade guided her out of the plane and to the awaiting Towncar. Once settled inside, Sam dialed her father, but it went straight to voice mail. She left a quick message and then called her mother.

"Hi, sweetie."

Sam smiled. "Hi, Mom."

"Have you got your flights?"

"Actually, we're here. We just landed."

"Wonderful. Do you need Daddy to come and get you?"

"No, we have a car."

"We'll be picking Dalton up from the hospital some time before dinner, so you can come with us if you like or hang out at home."

"Is that too much? Kade's happy to get a hotel room."

"Absolutely not. We want to get to know your man. I want to hear all about the proposal as well. We even raised the temperature so he'll be more comfortable."

"You know, mom, could you maybe keep it below sixty-seven? Scotland's much colder than Savannah, and he prefers the cold."

"Not a problem. Are you sure?"

Sam grinned. "Very."

"Okay then. I've asked Pepper to stay for a few days. Her mom's not doing well, so she'll be in the guest room."

"Good." Sam sighed. "We'll be there in about half an hour. Do you need us to stop anywhere?"

"No, honey, we're good. Just looking forward to seeing you."

"Me too. We'll see you soon." She hung up and dropped her phone back in her purse. "I'm guessing you'll be staying in Dalt's room."

Kade raised an eyebrow. "What about when he's out of the hospital?"

She snorted. "He'll insist on going back to his place, especially since Pepper's staying for a few days."

"Don't they get along?"

"They do. Sort of. They seemed really close for a while, but a few years ago, something happened, I think an argument or something. Neither of them would tell me. They both said it was no big deal, but they've been cool to each other ever since. I didn't want to pry." Sam rolled her eyes. "Anyway, sorry about the separate rooms."

"I can survive a few nights without you in my bed, love."

"Yeah, well I don't know if I can."

Kade chuckled. "We'll figure something out."

Sam settled further into the seat and watched the terrain fly by as they made their way to her parents' house. She couldn't stop thinking about how much her life had changed in such a short amount of time.

The driver pulled into the driveway and Sam smiled when the front door opened and her parents rushed outside. Kade slid from the car and held the door for her. She climbed out and ran straight into her mother's arms.

"Aw, honey, I've been wantin' to hug your neck for weeks!"

"Me too, Mom." Sam sniffed, trying to force the tears away.

Her father hugged her quickly and then went to help Kade with the bags. They shook hands and her father gave her a wink.

"How are you feeling?" her mom asked.

"Much better," Sam said. "It didn't last long. What about Dalton? How is he…really?"

Her mom frowned. "He's perfectly fine. I don't know what that boy was thinkin'! He said the robber came up behind him and he got out of the way just in time. He shot the man before he could get away, but the officers haven't said whether or not they've found him. I don't imagine they'll tell us anything, but still. I'm just glad your daddy taught you both to shoot."

Sam grimaced. "Yes. I suppose that's a good thing."

"Let's talk about better things, hmm? I had no idea Kade was so tall." She studied Sam's fiancé. "I suppose you were sitting down over Skype, huh? He's taller than Dalton."

Sam smiled as Kade and her father finished grabbing the bags from the trunk. "He's better looking too."

"I won't touch that one." Her mother chuckled. "Now, do you have something to show me?"

"Oh, yes," Sam said, and held her hand out.

Her mother studied the ring and then hugged her. "Oh, honey, it's stunning."

Kade and her father made their way to them and set the bags on the ground. Kade held his hand out to Sam's mother.

"We'll have none of that," she said as she pulled him into a motherly hug.

Kade grinned and hugged her back.

"You made it here in record time," her father said.

Sam chuckled. "We did. Your future son-in-law has connections."

"We're happy you said yes."

"Like I could resist him, Daddy." She leaned closer, lowering her voice. "He's almost perfect."

I'll remember that when you argue with me.

Sam grinned. *No arguing. No point. I'm always right.*

Her mother ushered them toward the house. "Why don't we get you two settled and we'll talk after you've rested."

Wait, love. Let me check the temperature.

Sam distracted her parents long enough for Kade to peek inside. When he was satisfied, Kade picked up the bags and waited for the ladies to precede him.

Sam's father followed. "You kids rest up," he said. "I'll see you at dinner."

"Okay," Sam said.

"We have you in Dalton's old room, Kade, and Sam, you're back in yours," her mother explained as she led them upstairs.

Sam glanced over her shoulder and gave him a wink. Kade smiled and shook his head. Sam stopped at her room long enough to drop her bag inside, and then followed Kade into Dalton's. Sam and Dalton's rooms were separated by a Jack-and-Jill bathroom, which had been updated with new fixtures and accessories. "Mom, the bathroom looks really good. I can't believe Daddy finally got around to doing it."

Her mother snorted. "He didn't. I broke down and hired someone. He's still stewin' about it, so let's not talk about it in front of him, okay?"

Sam giggled. "No problem."

"I'll leave you two for now. We'll get Dalton and then eat around six, okay?"

"Thanks, Mom." Sam hugged her again. "Love you."

Her mom stroked her cheek. "Love you too, honey."

CHAPTER TWENTY-THREE

Her mother left them alone and Sam flopped onto Dalton's bed, crossing her legs and settling her chin in her hand.

"What's going on in that fascinating mind of yours?" Kade asked as he set his bag on the bed behind her.

"If my mother knew how old you actually were, I wonder if she'd still force us to sleep in separate rooms."

"I'm going to venture a guess and say yes." Kade laughed. "I think it has more to do with the fact she doesn't know we're boun...uh, married."

Sam blew out a sigh. "I know. Still, it's annoying. We can't even lock the doors—they removed the locks when we were kids."

Kade chuckled.

"What's so funny?"

"It's just interesting to see such a confident young woman turn into an irritated teenager in the presence of her mother."

Sam sighed. "I don't know about confident, but I'll agree with feeling like a teenager again."

Kade pulled the desk chair to the end of the bed and sat facing her. "Every mum and dad will always see their daughter as a little girl."

She wrinkled her nose. "Maybe we *should* get a hotel."

He grinned. "I have no intention of giving up the room I already booked. We'll sleep here at night and "sightsee" during the day."

Sam straightened. "I knew there was a reason I love you."

"Just one?" He leaned over to kiss her, but his phone rang, interrupting the moment. "Hold that thought." He answered the call. "Hi, Con."

"Hi, Kade. How's Sam's brother?"

"Fine. He's being released tonight." Kade smiled as Sam stood and started to unpack his bag. "What's up?"

"I've run into a wee bit of a snag."

"With which issue?" Kade asked.

"Ármann. He's making moves. We need to be at Haarde sooner than later."

Kade swore. "Okay. Set it up and I can meet you there."

Sam raised an eyebrow, but Kade forced a smile and she went back to her task.

"Good," Connall said. "There's one other thing."

"What?" he asked as he focused on Connall.

Why are you blocking me? she complained. *Why do you have to go to Iceland sooner?*

"Can you hold a sec, Con? Sorry." He lowered the phone and looked at Sam. "I don't want you to worry, so will you trust me, love?"

"Why would I worry?" she challenged.

"Sam."

"Fine." She waved her hand. "Go back to your super-secret conversation."

I love you.

She stuck her tongue out at him and he chuckled. "Sorry, Con. What else?"

"Cole's working with someone, and you're not going to like who it is."

"Who is it?"

"It's Dalton Moore."

Kade turned away from Sam. "What?"

"Samantha's brother is not who he says he is. He's FBI."

"What?" Sam snapped.

"Damn it!" Kade exclaimed. "How did you do that?"

"Me?" Connall asked.

"No," Kade said. "Hold on." He is stared at his mate. "Sam?"

Sam shrugged and made a show of refolding one of his T-shirts. "I guess you could say you're not a very good multi-tasker."

Kade sighed in frustration. "Con, do you mind if I put you on speaker? Sam should hear this as well."

"Not at all," Con said.

Sam sat on the bed, a triumphant expression on her face.

Kade switched to speaker and said, "I thought Dalton owned car dealerships."

"He does. But it's also a good cover, wouldn't you agree?"

"Are you sure?" Sam asked.

"Aye."

"How did you find this out?" Kade asked.

"It wasn't easy, but there's more. I think Dalton might have been the one who sent your résumé to Duncan, Sam."

"You can't be serious," Sam said. "Is there proof?"

"More of hunch at this point," Connall admitted. "But I'm looking into it."

"Thanks, Con. Let us know what you come up with. I'll call you later," Kade said, and hung up.

Sam frowned. "Connall could be wrong, couldn't he?"

"I'll know more in a few days, but I intend to talk with your brother while I'm here," Kade warned.

She stood and started to pace. "Why would Dalton do this?"

"Connall will ask Cole, I'm sure, and I'll ask Dalton."

"I want to be there when you talk to my idiot brother."

He chuckled. "I'm not sure that's a good idea and not just because you may cause him bodily harm."

Samantha crossed her arms. "He'll be more forthcoming if I'm there. My brother has never been able to lie to me."

"Never?"

"Never. He has a tell."

"Does he now?"

She grinned. "Yep. If he's lying, his left ear turns red."

"You can't be serious."

"You'll be able to see for yourself...if he's lying." She wagged a finger at him. "But like Pepper's real name, that tidbit of information stays between you and me. Got it?"

"I'd never share your secrets." He settled his hands on her hips. "Especially considering that they're so entertaining."

"Why does that matter?"

"If I spill the beans, you might stop telling me those secrets."

Sam giggled. "Are you forgetting you can read my mind?"

"There is that." He leaned down and kissed her. "But I prefer it when you tell me."

"Good thing I like to tell you everything." She looped her hands around his neck. "What was the other thing?"

He sighed. "I have to go to Iceland."

"Right. Iceland."

"My cousin's making trouble. The bottom line is that he needs to be replaced. I should have gotten rid of him a while ago, but I've been trying to give him the benefit of the doubt."

"Can I come?"

"Not this time."

She bit her lip. "Will it be dangerous?"

He slid a lock of her hair behind her ear. "Potentially."

"Don't go then."

"My brothers will be there, love. There's nothing to worry about."

"Famous last words." A horn sounded outside and Sam sighed. "My brother's home. Yay," she droned.

Kade grinned. "I'm looking forward to meeting him."

Sam rolled her eyes and dragged him downstairs just as her mother opened the front door and stepped outside. Sam followed and couldn't stop her smile. Pepper was in the front seat. Sam's father obviously convinced her to let him pick her up…something often difficult to do.

Sam's smile faded as her best friend climbed from the car. Pepper didn't look well. She'd lost even more weight and had dark rings under her eyes. She looked exhausted. When she caught sight of Sam, she managed to paste a smile on her gorgeous face and hold her arms out, but it looked forced.

Her brother climbed out of the back seat and Sam hugged him carefully. Niceties continued as the group made their way inside and spent the next thirty minutes introducing everyone and then lobbing question after question to Dalton. He answered them vaguely, which made Samantha more and more frustrated.

* * *

Kade sat with the family and observed the small group. Samantha's mother was just as she had appeared during their Skype chats. Strong southern matriarch to the core. Pepper was certainly treated like another daughter. Dalton was not what Kade had expected, on any level. Sam had described him as a rich playboy, and although he may give that impression, Kade noticed something he doubted many people did. Dalton Moore missed nothing. He was on constant alert.

A familiar hand on his cheek had him glancing at Sam.

"Where did you go?" she asked.

"Just thinking." He kissed her palm. "How are you?"

"Hungry," she said. "We're all feeling like burgers, so I'm dragging Pepper down to Louie's to pick up food to go. What would you like?"

"Everything on the biggest burger they have."

Sam giggled. "Got it. Fries?"

"Of course. What else goes well with a bona fide American burger?"

"Split a milkshake with me?" she asked hopefully.

"No way. I want my own. Vanilla, please."

She kissed him. "If you insist."

* * *

Sam grabbed her purse and her father's keys and led Pepper outside. She loved driving her dad's BMW. She just wished she had somewhere farther away to go. She pulled out of the driveway and glanced at Pepper. "You're quiet."

Pepper sighed. "Sorry. Just tired."

"I'm glad we get a little time alone."

Pepper nodded. "Me too. I'm so glad you could get a flight."

"You could say that." Sam couldn't stop a chuckle.

"What?" Pepper asked.

"Let's just say he owns his own plane."

"Shut the front door! And you got on it?"

Sam nodded. "He has amazing powers of persuasion."

Pepper laughed. "I noticed that the moment you walked into the room."

"Really?"

Pepper nodded. "He adores you."

Sam grinned. "The feeling's mutual."

"Your brother looks good, huh?"

"Yeah. Typical Dalton…he gets shot and manages to come out with a flesh wound, minor bruise, and his hair still perfectly coiffed."

Pepper rolled her eyes. "Totally."

They arrived at the restaurant and Sam parked the car. The girls headed inside, ordered the food, and then sat in a booth at the bar to wait for it.

"I think we have time for a beer," Pepper said.

"You're reading my mind."

"How's Scotland?"

"It's amazing. I can't wait for you to see everything."

"Me too."

A server stopped by their table and they each ordered their favorite beer.

"What about you? Hmm? What's going on with you?" Sam asked.

Pepper grimaced. "Nothing. Just counting the days until I leave."

Sam frowned. "Pepper, what's really going on? You don't look like you're sleeping…or eating enough."

"I'm fine, really. Normal stress, you know? Trying to finish up a few classes so I don't have to retake them. And then, working full time just happens to be tiring." Pepper played with the napkin in front of her. "Then, your brother."

Sam reached over and squeezed her hand. "Thank you for being here, Pepper. Sometimes I really feel like you're the glue, you know?"

Pepper smiled. "Crazy Glue, maybe."

Sam laughed. "I have missed you! I can't wait until you see the apartment. It's gorgeous."

"I can't wait to be there in person. The tour with your laptop made me feel a bit motion sick."

"Well, Kade says you don't have to find a different place. You're welcome to stay as long as you want. And we'll be right down the hall, so your fear of living alone won't apply."

"This guy really sounds too good to be true sometimes."

Sam nodded. "I know. If I didn't know him, know him, I think I'd wonder."

"Hmm-mmm."

"Have you been riding much?"

Pepper shook her head. "Ah. No. Not really."

"Were you able to get someone to look after Jonesy while you're gone?"

Pepper bit her lip and stared at the table.

"Pepper?"

"I sold him."

"What?" Sam gasped. "When? Why?"

"Three weeks ago. He needs someone who can really take care of him."

"Who did you sell him to?"

"Britney."

Sam frowned. "Rich bitch Brit?"

Pepper nodded.

"You can't stand her. She's vapid and spoiled and only has horses because her parents buy her whatever the heck she wants."

"I know that, Sam," she snapped. "Just drop it."

The server returned with their beers and Sam smiled her thanks. Focusing back on Pepper, she asked, "Honey, what's going on?"

"Nothing. I'm sorry." Pepper sat back. "How do you know someone, Sam?"

"What do you mean?"

"How do you know if someone's telling you the truth?"

Sam shrugged. "I guess it's a gut feeling. I know when people are lying to me because I never lie to myself. I don't try to explain away the flags…be they green, yellow, or red."

Pepper sipped her beer. "I know. I just wish I knew how to do that."

"Pepper, *what* is going on?"

"Nothing, Sam. It's nothing."

Sam grasped Pepper's arm. "You're lying to me. Now, tell me what the hell is wrong."

"You have enough on your plate right now."

"Samantha, your order's ready," a voice crackled over the loudspeaker.

"This isn't done, Pep," Sam warned. "You and I are going to sit down and have a serious conversation tonight. Got it?"

"I have to work."

"Then *after* work."

Pepper shrugged. "Let's get dinner back to the masses. I'm sure they're hungry."

Sam let the matter drop, but when they arrived home, she pulled her brother aside, grateful Kade helped her mother with serving everyone.

"Do you know what's going on with Pepper?"

Dalton glanced at her and then back at Sam. "What do you mean?"

"Seriously? Sometimes I wonder how many times you were dropped on your head as a baby."

Dalton gave her a moronic chuckle. "You're so funny, sis."

"Something's wrong with her, Dalt. She's exhausted, she's jumpy, and she's not eating. She sold her horse—"

"She sold Jonesy?" he asked in shock.

"Yes," Sam said. "Remember when I asked you to look out for her?"

"I checked on her at home. She seemed fine."

"Kids?" her mother called. "We're ready."

"Thanks, Mom." Sam scowled at her brother in frustration. "We'll talk later."

"Can't wait," he droned.

* * *

Dinner wrapped up and the group seemed to scatter. Pepper had to go to work and Dalton insisted he head home.

"Wait, Dalt. Kade and I need to talk to you about something before you go," Sam said. "Dad, can we borrow your office, please?"

"Sure, honey."

"Everything okay?" her mom asked.

"Car advice, mom. No biggie." Sam led Kade and Dalton to the back of the house and pushed open the door. Stepping inside, she closed and locked the door.

"Are you planning on torturing me?" Dalton quipped.

"He won't let me," Sam grumbled.

Kade smiled. "We have much to discuss, Agent Dalton."

Dalton groaned. "Figured. Damn it!"

Kade gestured to the chair facing the desk. "Have a seat."

Dalton sat down and settled his ankle over his knee. "When did you find out?"

Kade sat in the chair facing him. "Not long ago. Your partner confirmed it."

"Did you *really* send my résumé to the company?" Sam asked.

Dalton at least had the sense to grimace. "Yeah, I did."

"*Why?*"

"Because we needed to get inside. You had the skill set they were looking for and you needed to get out of this dead end town anyway."

"That wasn't your decision to make," Sam snapped.

"You put your sister into a potentially dangerous situation, without thought to her safety," Kade said quietly.

Sam knew he was holding back, keeping himself from beating her brother to near death.

"Not really," Dalton argued. "We knew where she was at all times, we had her cell phone tracked, and Cole was keeping an eye on her."

"So he was a plant on the plane, too?" she asked.

"Yes," Dalton confirmed. "The fact you were flying first class was a hiccup, though. We had to fight with our superiors to get Cole next to you, but we pointed out that if Cole was going to earn your trust, he had to be with you on the plane."

"So you used my fear to get what you wanted."

Dalton lowered his head. "Sorry."

"No you're not!" Sam bellowed. "You haven't changed. It's always "all about Dalton." You barrel over people without any thought to their feelings. Just so long as you get what you want out of the deal, you don't care who you leave lying in the dust behind you."

Kade grasped her hand and gave it a gentle squeeze.

"I had a job to do, Sam. Someone is gaining access to Gunnach Pharmaceutical and we believe it's in order to put together a terrorist attack. I'm trying to save Scotland from a potentially deadly threat."

"You know what, Dalton? I no longer give a rat's ass what you're trying to do. You should've talked to me."

"Wow, you're mad." He smiled at Kade and then chuckled. "She only swears when she's pissed."

Sam saw red. She curled up her fist and clocked her brother just under his right eye.

"Whoa, Sam! What the hell?"

"I hate you!" Screeching like a banshee, she jumped on him, unsettling the chair as she tried to get another hit in. Dalton was quicker.

"Sam. He's got an injury and it'd be a good idea not to kill him," Kade said as he wrapped his arms around her waist and pulled her off her brother.

She fought against Kade, but failed miserably and was forced to jab her finger at her brother. "Everything to you is a joke. You don't care about anyone but yourself. You didn't even do what I asked you to do with Pepper."

He shrugged. "She didn't want my help."

"So? She's family and she's in trouble!" Sam squeezed her eyes shut and took a deep breath. "I'm done, Dalton. Done! You're dead to me."

"Okay, love." Kade continued to hold her firmly. "Maybe you should take a minute, eh?"

Dalton stood and righted the chair, laying a hand over his bruised eye. "Sam, come on. I had a job to do."

She sneered at him as she raised her hand in dismissal.

"Oh, great. The silent treatment," Dalton said. "Fine, Sam, have it your way!"

Sam pushed away from Kade and stormed out of the room, slamming the door behind her.

* * *

Kade sat back in his chair and indicated Dalton should do the same. Dalton sat down and slumped against the back of his seat.

"That was quite the performance," Kade said.

Dalton stared at him.

"You already know that Cole's filled us in on what the FBI's looking for."

"I do," Dalton said.

"What about Pepper?" Kade asked. "What have you found out?"

"I told you, she didn't want my help."

"And I know that this"—Kade waved his hand toward Dalton—"is simply a façade. You care entirely too much for your family, including Pepper, to be put off. Whether or not you want to share that with your sister is up to you, but it won't work with me."

Dalton sighed and sat up. "I haven't been able to find out much at this point. I'm pretty sure Pepper's dealing with threats, but I can't determine if it's a stalker issue or an ex-boyfriend. She's not one to have enemies."

"Your injuries? Not because of a robbery?"

Dalton shook his head. "No, it was the guy after Pepper. Still don't know who he is, though."

"But you're going to find out."

"Of course I'm going to find out." Dalton ran his good hand through his hair. "I have a tail on her when I can't watch her myself."

"Good. Any updates on my situation?"

Dalton hesitated, but Kade didn't back down. "Only what Cole's told you, but we're close to finding them."

"And if you do?"

"We'll deal with it."

Kade shook his head. "No. I'd like to take care of it."

Dalton snorted. "That's not gonna happen."

"It will if we find the person first."

"Don't get in our way, Kade. It's not a good idea."

Kade raised an eyebrow. "You may want to heed your own advice. We are not people who back down."

"Yeah, I've seen Braveheart."

Before Kade could respond, Dalton's cell phone pealed. "I have to get this, Kade. Moore here. Okay, I'll be right there." Dalton stood and hung up. "Something's up with Pepper," he said, and left the room.

CHAPTER TWENTY-FOUR

KADE WENT LOOKING for Sam. He found her pulling on her running shoes, her face red with irritation. "Samantha?"

"I need to run."

"Do you want me to come with you?"

She shrugged. "Whatever. I just need to do something or I'll kill him."

"Give me a minute."

Kade changed quickly and met her at the front door. She was outside and down the street before he'd even passed the mailbox at the end of the driveway. He followed her for a little over a mile before pacing her.

"You know, I know my brother's a narcissistic jackass most of the time, and we have to work within the limitations of his dumbassery—"

"Dumbassery?" he asked.

"Don't interrupt."

Kade chuckled. "Sorry."

"But this…this just goes beyond selfishness. If he's this big time FBI agent, he has resources available to him to at least find out if Pepper's in trouble. He's not even willing to do that." Sam stopped running and paced in a circle. "Seriously, Kade. I want to tear him limb from limb right now!"

Kade grasped her arms and smiled. "Your brother *is* looking into Pepper's trouble."

"What?"

"He's watching her. He has been since you asked him to, which is why he got shot."

"So it *wasn't* a robbery?"

"No."

"Then why didn't he just tell me that?" Sam snapped.

"Because no one's supposed to know he's working for the FBI."

"But I'm his sister!"

"I know, love," Kade said. "You also failed to notice his ear was red."

"I was too mad to notice much of anything, to be honest." Sam sighed and dropped her head onto his chest. Kade pulled her close and held her until her emotions calmed. She looked up at him and grimaced. "I told him I hated him."

"He knows you don't."

Sam groaned. "Now I have to apologize. I *hate* apologizing to my idiot brother."

Kade took her hand and started back toward the house. "I have a feeling he knows that."

"Which means he's going to make my life *miserable*."

"If you were Fiona, I'd do the same thing."

Sam smacked his arm. "You know, you should really be more protective of your mate."

He lifted her hand to his lips. "I'll work on that."

She frowned.

"What's wrong?"

"I'm not hot. Or sweating."

Kade nodded. "We don't unless the temperature's high."

She widened her eyes. "Ever?"

"Never."

"But we're supposed to get a good sweat going…you know, for heart health and all that mumbo jumbo. Are you telling me we don't have to exercise anymore?"

Kade chuckled. "No, it's still good to exercise. Our bodies just don't react the way humans do."

"So we only have an issue if it's hot outside? Our bodies won't overheat?"

"No. Our bodies self-regulate, unless they're compromised by the external temperature."

She grinned. "That's so cool."

He laughed. "I guess it is."

* * *

Two days later, Kade had managed a quick shower before a knock at his door brought Sam with extra towels. "Good morning, beautiful." He leaned down to kiss her. "Och, I've missed you."

"Me too. I feel like I haven't seen you for days," she complained as she set the towels on his bed.

He grinned and wrapped his arms around her. "That's because you were asleep when I finished my call with Con."

"You were supposed to wake me."

"You needed to sleep. I made a judgment call."

She ran her hands up his chest. "Next time, make a different call."

"And have your mother catch me sneaking into your room?"

She wrinkled her nose. "You could just go through the bathroom."

"You sound like you've done that before."

"What? *No.* I don't know what you're talking about," she retorted.

"We could tell her the cat's already out of the bag, so to speak."

"She'd still make us sleep in separate beds because we are not "legally" wed and then she'd look at me differently." Sam sighed. "I hate lying to her, but it's not like I can tell her you and I are joined forever because you're an immortal Viking and we did this ceremony and stuff. Besides, she'd be devastated to know we got married without her. I'd rather keep her in the dark." She wrinkled her nose. "You know what I mean?"

Kade laughed. "I think I need to record these conversations for our kids."

"I'm glad I'm entertaining." She smirked. "I'm doing a load of laundry. Where's your stuff?"

He pointed to the hamper in the corner of the room.

"Thanks."

"Hey," he said and took her arm. "We *will* have a wedding, love. We could even have it here...now. Or at the very least, soon."

"It's something to think about, I guess." She smiled. "I don't need anything big."

"I know. Whatever you want."

She looped her arms around his neck. "Thank you."

"My pleasure." He kissed her nose and grinned. "Now, about my delicates."

She patted his chest. "I'll be sure to put them on the heaviest wash cycle for you."

"I'm enjoying your service, love."

"Oh, don't get used to it. I'm doing this to kill some time. Mom and Dad are going out for lunch, so we'll have the house to ourselves for a few hours before my night out with Pepper." She slipped her hands inside his shirt and ran her fingers over his chest. "I plan to take full advantage."

Kade settled his mouth over hers, his already crumbling composure slipping further into the abyss that was his desire for his mate. The shrillness of his cell phone shattered the moment and he broke the kiss with a groan. "Sorry, love."

He sat at the small desk in Dalton's old bedroom while Samantha gathered his laundry and left the room. She returned just as he hung up with Connall. Her face fell. "You have to leave."

"Aye." He sighed. "Tomorrow."

"When will you come back?"

"My plan is no more than a week. I don't think I could live without you for very long."

She bit her lip. "Me neither. If Pepper wasn't acting so out of character, I'd be tempted to blow off our girls' night. But this really hot guy managed to get us front row tickets to The Citizens..."

"What's the appeal with that band, hmm?"

"Oh, it's the lead guitarist. Anthony Powell. He's gorgeous and has an angelic voice…" She sighed. "I plan to get dolled up, just in case he notices me. Maybe he'll pull me up on stage."

Kade shook his head. "Isn't he engaged? I believe I saw the notice in all the magazines."

"*Engaged.* Which means, not married. Still hope for me."

Kade growled as he threw her on the bed and tickled her. Sam squealed in surprise.

"I think I should lock you in a gilded cage until we're married."

"Hey! You promised it would be a tower." She giggled. "And, we're already married, aren't we?"

Kade paused. "There is that, yes."

"But I suppose, not legally, right? So, there's still that small chance."

He tickled her again.

"Kade," she squealed.

"What was that about this Anthony character?"

"Um…he's talented. I understand he plays multiple instruments."

Kade's hands hovered over her stomach. "Anything else?"

"Nope, nothing else." She raised an eyebrow. "Did I mention he was cute?"

He tickled her again, then kissed her into submission. He broke the kiss and grinned. "How cute?"

"Nowhere near as gorgeous as you."

"Good answer," he said.

She stroked his cheek. "I wish you were coming tonight."

"You need to spend time with Pepper."

"I know."

He gave her his secret smile. "Let's have lunch at the hotel."

"In bed?"

"Of course in bed. What kind of a mate do you think I am?"

She jumped off the bed and clapped her hands. "I'm in."

* * *

The next morning, Sam woke with a heavy heart. She sighed as she felt Kade tighten his hold, and turned to face him. "Hi."

"Good morning, love. How was last night?"

"Amazing. The band was better than ever." She rolled to face him. "I just wish it wasn't morning."

"Don't be sad," he said as he slipped her hair away from her face. "My business isn't going to take long. I'll be back before you know it."

"I just feel like everything's so jumbled right now."

"You don't do well when things aren't resolved, do you?"

She wrinkled her nose. "Not so much, no."

He kissed her and pulled her close. "This too shall pass, Sam. I'll get everything settled in Iceland and then we can go home and make babies."

"I know. I'm just worried about Pepper."

"Why doesn't she come home with us?"

"She hadn't planned on coming for another month. I don't know if she has more stuff to do before she leaves."

He linked his fingers with hers. "She doesn't have anything holding her here now that she sold her horse, right? She could give notice, pack her bags, and save the cost of a flight by joining us. You could do some sightseeing before she starts school and help take her mind off whatever's bothering her."

"I can ask her." Sam smiled. "You really are the most amazing man on earth."

"You just make me look that way."

"Sam? Honey, where are you?" her mother called.

Sam sat up. "Crap! If she finds me in here..."

Kade chuckled. "You're not a teenager hiding your boyfriend."

"I know that, Kade," she whispered as she pulled on her sweats. "But this is still her house, and she'll think I'm breaking the house rules. Get some clothes on."

He nodded toward the bathroom. "Why don't you just sneak back in the way you came?"

"That's where I'm headed." Sam slipped into the bathroom and pulled the door closed.

"Sam?"

"In here, Mom," she called.

Kade took the distraction to get dressed as Sam and her mother talked in the next room. Sam returned a few minutes later.

"Everything okay?" he asked.

"Yep. My parents will be back sometime before you leave. Not that I needed to know that." Sam wrinkled her nose. "I'm pretty sure she just wanted to see if I was in my room. I mean, *really*."

"Sweetheart, your mother is not an idiot."

Sam settled her hands on her hips. "How do you know?"

"Because I've had more than a five-minute conversation with her. Why don't you just tell her?"

"No. It's not the southern way. We deny, deny, deny, and then we sweep it all under the rug."

Kade laughed. "I'll keep that in mind."

They spent the next few hours finalizing Kade's trip, and Sam grew more and more pensive as the minutes ticked by. She couldn't even focus on the game of pool she'd challenged him to almost an hour ago. To make matters worse, her father came looking for Kade not long before he was scheduled to leave.

"Kade? I have a rather personal question. May I borrow you for a few minutes?"

Kade set the pool cue down. "Of course."

"Sam, honey, would you excuse us?" her father asked.

"Huh?" she said. "Oh, sure."

Kade gave her a quick kiss and she made her way to the kitchen, where she found her mother baking...again. Sam guessed she'd already gained ten pounds with the amount of sweets her mother had already made. Between her mother and Kade force-feeding her, Sam was sure she'd end up being rolled back to Scotland.

Her mother glanced up from the cookie sheet. "Is Kade with your dad?"

"Yep. Super-secret guy talk, apparently. Need some help?"

"The cookies have to cool, so nothing at the moment."

"I'll do the dishes," Sam offered.

"Thanks." Her mother removed her apron. "Honey, are you okay? You're wound up like a top."

"I know. Sorry. I just wish Kade wasn't leaving."

"You can go with him, you know. We're fine here."

Sam turned away from the sink. "I can't, mom. He's got to tie something up with work, so I'd be alone in Scotland, too. I'd rather be here without him than there without any of you."

"I'm glad we rate," she joked.

"Just below highest." Sam smiled as she slipped a baking sheet into the dishwasher. "Something's going on with Pepper. Do you have any idea what?"

"No. I noticed the same. She's jumpy and ridiculously skinny. She won't talk to me about it, but I've tried."

"I have, too. It's not like her. I never have to guess what she's thinking or feeling," Sam said.

Her mother laid a hand on her back. "You're in a bit of emotional upheaval right now. Give yourself a break. When your heart is calm, you'll see things more clearly."

"Better advice has never been given," Kade said from the doorway.

Sam faced him. "Are you leaving now?"

"Soon. The car's on the way."

Her mother left the kitchen and Sam turned back to the sink. "Let me make you something to eat." She kept her back to him as she made her way to the fridge. "We have some ham left over from last night. Would you like me to slice some for you?"

"That sounds lovely."

She nodded and pulled the food out. As she began to prepare everything, Kade wrapped his arms around her waist and kissed the nape of her neck. "This is not going to take long."

Sam sighed. "All of it's too long."

"I know."

"I'm refraining from asking exactly what you're doing. And I'm not trying to get through your block…flimsy as it is. Have you picked up on that?"

"I did pick up on that," Kade said. "And I appreciate it. You know that, right?"

"Yes." She squeezed her eyes shut briefly, regretting it instantly as she sliced open her finger. She let out a shout of pain. Kade grasped her hand and held it over the sink. He rinsed the cut and Sam let out a whimper as it stung. She wasn't prepared for what he did next. He wrapped his lips around her finger and gave a gentle suck. "What are you doing?"

I'm healing you. Just relax.

Sam felt instant relief and she let out a deep breath. Kade released her finger and Sam washed her hands. She studied where the cut should be and let out a quiet whistle. "It's as if nothing happened. How did you do that?"

"Remember the discussion about gifts?"

She nodded.

"Angus and I both have the gift of healing."

"Is that why you're doctors?"

"Probably."

"Is the healing property in your saliva?"

He grinned. "No."

She narrowed her eyes. "Then how—?"

He tapped his temple. "It's all in the mind."

"So you didn't have to suck on my finger?"

"No." He laughed when she thumped his arm. "Technically, I can heal you with touch. I just enjoy the process of suck—"

She laid her fingers over his mouth. "Shhh," she hissed. "No naughty talk in the vicinity of my parents."

He disengaged from her hand and wrapped his arms around her. "I'll be sure to keep that in mind."

She rolled her eyes. "You are impossible."

Think of the possibilities with our ability to communicate so privately.

"Kade," she admonished.

I'll start every conversation with "What are you wearing?"

Samantha groaned. "Stop or I'm going to lock you up and make you stay."

"Hmm, that sounds fun." He chuckled and leaned down to kiss her.

She broke the kiss and frowned up at him. "Hold that thought, buddy. Could you have healed my concussion right away?"

He had the good sense to drop his head and look somewhat remorseful. "Aye."

"Then why didn't you?"

He smiled. "Because you would have gone back to your flat and I wouldn't have had an excuse to keep you close."

"Brat," she said as she ran her fingers through his hair. "Is that why you're not easy to kill?"

He nodded.

"So, if someone shoots you…" she trailed off.

"No one's going to shoot me."

"But if they did?" she whispered.

"If they did, I'd be able to heal myself."

"What if you're unconscious?"

He frowned. "Sweetheart. *No* one's going to shoot me!"

She fisted her hands in his shirt. "What if you're unconscious, Kade?"

"Well, I would imagine Angus or Connall would heal me."

"What if they're not there?"

"Samantha! Stop it. One, no one will get close enough to shoot me and, two, someone is always around. *Nothing's* going to happen to me."

She bit her lip and stared up at him for a few seconds. "What if someone stabs you?"

"Samantha." Kade laughed. "No one's going to stab me…or shoot me."

She sighed. "You promise not to be alone?"

He kissed her. "I promise not to be alone."

"Fine." She smoothed his shirt. "What did my dad want?"

Kade shook his head. "Doctor-patient confidentiality."

"You're not technically his doctor, Kade. He doesn't really have one, since he refuses to go to one."

He grinned. "He wanted some advice."

"Oh? Is he okay?"

"Yes, love. He's fine."

"Well, tell me," she pressed.

"You don't really want to know."

"I do so want to know."

"This falls under the category of something you can't un-hear."

"*Kade.* Tell me."

He leaned in and whispered, "He asked about the little blue pill."

"WHAT? *Eww*! Kade!" Sam squealed. "Ew, ew, ew. Why didn't you ignore me?"

"Because you would have hounded me until I told you."

"Gross!"

He grinned. "I'm personally comforted that your parents are still having fun."

"He's almost seventy. He's had plenty of fun!"

"But your mother's much younger, love."

Sam laid her fingers over his lips again. "No more. I will not hear anymore of this. Total HIPAA violation. Ew."

He kissed her hand and pulled her away from the sink. "Come with me. I have something for you."

He led her upstairs to Dalton's room and handed her an envelope. She opened it to find cash and a credit card. "What's this?"

"I have added you to my accounts at home, so if you want or need anything, buy it. The credit card's unlimited, so go crazy if you want."

"Kade, I have my own money."

"I know you do."

Sam smiled. "But you need to make sure I'm taken care of, right?"

"I'm well aware that you can take care of yourself, sweetheart, but I kind of hoped you'd plan our wedding while I'm away and I wanted you to have all the resources available to you."

Sam laid the envelope on the bureau. "First, well done with the acknowledgment that I can take care of myself. I appreciate the words, even if you feel the need to have security follow me constantly. Second, planning a wedding would certainly help distract me from the hopelessness I feel about you being gone. So, again, you are the most amazing man alive, and even though I'm not happy you're going, I love you, love you, love you for making it as easy as it can be." She pulled his head down for a heart-stopping kiss, and she groaned when he broke it.

"If you continue with this type of gratitude, you will be naked and I will be late," he warned.

"Darn. Evil plan thwarted."

Kade grinned. "I'm going to bring Con and Brodie back with me, so we can have the ceremony and then go home, if that works for you. I should be back here in five days, but I'll let you know if that changes." His phone buzzed and he checked the screen. "The car's here. I need to go."

"Okay." Sam made a ridiculous attempt to hold back tears that were already streaming down her cheeks.

"Kade, honey," Sam's mother called up the stairs. "There's someone here to take you to the airport."

He peeked out of the room. "Thank you, Mrs. Moore. I'll be right down." He handed Sam a handkerchief then slipped his wallet into his inside pocket. He tapped his temple. "I'm only a call away."

She dried her tears and nodded. "Will it work that far away?"

"We'll know in a few hours."

She nodded, squeezing her eyes shut.

"Please don't cry, love. You're breaking my heart."

"Now you know *my* pain."

He kissed her quickly and smiled. "Be a good mate and come and kiss me at the door. You can use the hanky to wave me off."

Sam snorted, unable to stop the giggle. "Don't make me laugh or I won't let you leave."

They made their way to the car and Kade kissed her longer than might have been wise, considering the longer he lingered, the harder it was for Sam to let him go. "I love you."

"I love you too," Sam said. "Please be careful."

"Always."

Sam waited in the driveway, waving Kade's handkerchief until the car was out of sight, then made her way back inside and closed the door. "Mom! We have a wedding to plan."

* * *

Kade waited until the car was well underway before he dialed Connall.

"Hey there," Connall said. "How did Sam do?"

"She's planning our wedding, so I'm hoping that will distract her. Is everything set?"

"Yep. The Gunnach plane is ready to go. Brodie, Alasdair, and I'll be arriving within minutes of you."

Kade checked his watch. "Good. I want this done, Con. No more mercy."

"I'm with you."

"Are you sure?"

Connall sighed. "Just because I'm nice doesn't mean I'm willing to show these bastards my throat. Ármann's become a problem. We're gonna take care of the problem. Simple."

"Okay. I don't want you do to anything you don't want to do."

Connall laughed. "Like that's ever happened. Just help me reel Brodie in."

"Why?"

"Payton's been getting pressure from Annis."

Payton's sister, Annis, was bound to Baldvin Daðason and currently living in Iceland with his family. Baldvin worked for Ármann, however, and Kade hadn't determined where his loyalties lay.

"What kind of pressure?" Kade asked.

"She won't give specifics. Not even to Angus. Brodie's convinced Ármann's pulling the strings, but for Payton's sake, none of us want to jump to conclusions."

"Aye. I'll find something for Payton to do. She should probably get out of Scotland for a while." Kade sighed. "Who's watching Sam and her family here?"

Connall paused.

"Con?"

"Cole organized protection for her. It made the most sense and with her brother close, he'll be able to double down on security," Connall rushed to add.

"Aye," Kade reluctantly agreed. "I don't like it, but I see the logic."

"I knew you would."

"I'll see you at the airport."

CHAPTER TWENTY-FIVE

KADE HUNG UP and tapped his cell phone against his palm. He'd have to find a way to hold Brodie back or there could be an international incident. On the other hand, his brother could kill a man in less than five seconds, and that might come in handy.

What might come in handy?

He grimaced. *Nothing, love. Are you planning?*

You've been gone for all of five minutes.

And your point is?

Sam giggled. *Mom's on the phone with our pastor.*

Ah, so the apple doesn't fall far from the tree, then.

Oh, you are soooo funny.

He grinned. *I have a very important question for you.*

Oh, really? Ask away, my love.

What kind of wedding band did you have in mind?

Surprise me.

He couldn't stop a grin. *That would require some privacy.*

Hello, pot. I'm kettle...

Kade laughed. *Point taken. Just pulled up to the plane.*

Please be safe.

Always. Ég elska þig, elskan.

I love you too.

Kade climbed out of the car and boarded the plane, taking one of the seats next to the window. His heart was heavy without Samantha and if he could finish his business in a day, he would. He doubted his cousin would make it that easy for him, however.

"We're ready to take off, my lord," Russell announced over the loudspeaker. "Please buckle up."

Kade adjusted his seatbelt and smiled at Maureen as she finished buckling herself into the jump seat. An hour into the flight, Kade felt a little pent up and restless. Unusual for him during flights. He relished his time alone more often than not.

Samantha?

When he didn't hear a response, he felt bereft. Maybe their connection was broken so far from each other.

Honey, I'm here. Sorry. I was on the phone and the woman wouldn't let me get a word in edgewise. I couldn't pause the conversation.

He sighed in relief.

It looks like we're still connected, huh? Are you okay?

Missing you, he said.

Me too, baby. How was take-off?

It was fine.

Why do you sound so blue?

I just wasn't expecting to miss you so much.

Her laugh sounded in his mind. *I'm not sure if I should be offended by that.*

Kade grinned. *Why don't you meet me?*

Pause.

Don't tempt me, Kade, because if I had my choice, I'd get on the next plane out of Savannah.

I'm sorry, love.

Pepper's here, so I should go. I love you.

I love you too.

Kade felt much better knowing he could "talk" to Sam anytime he wanted. He pulled out his laptop and went about finishing some of the work he'd neglected over the past few days.

* * *

Samantha hugged Pepper and pulled her farther into the house. "How are you?"

Pepper smiled. "You mean, since last night?"

"Yes, missie, since last night." Sam frowned. "Are you ever going to tell me what the heck is going on?"

Pepper grimaced. "I can't, Sam."

Sam let out a deep breath. "That's the first honest thing you've said since I got back."

"I know. I'm sorry. Things are just really complicated at the moment."

"Will you tell me soon?"

"I hope so."

"Okay. Come into the kitchen. Mom's been baking and you need some calories."

"Did she make chocolate chip cookies?" Pepper asked hopefully.

"Enough to feed an army."

Pepper clapped her hands. "Yay. Let's go."

Sam poured milk while Pepper put together a plate full of cookies, and they sat down at the table to go over options for dresses. Sam's phone buzzed mid-chew. She grinned and answered the phone. "Well, hello, Payton."

"Hullo yourself. I understand there's to be a wedding."

Sam grinned. "Yes. Are you going to come?"

"I haven't officially been invited."

"Oh, stop!" Sam admonished. "Get your butt on a plane. I'd like you to be one of my bridesmaids, if you're open to that."

"I'd love to, Sam. Thank you."

"Oh! Can you do me a favor, please?"

Payton chuckled. "Pick up the ring?"

"Seriously, how do you *do* that?"

"It's a gift. And yes, I'll pick it up."

"Thank you. Please don't say anything to Fiona. I haven't asked her yet, but I'd like her to be in the wedding as well."

"I'm sure she'll be honored."

"Thanks. When can you get here?" Samantha asked.

"Well, the boys have both planes, so we either wait or fly commercial. I'll talk to Fi once you've talked to her. Kade has asked that I book one of the local hotels. What do you think of the Gastonian?"

"Oh, it's lovely, Payton," Sam said. "It's a popular place, though. It might be booked."

Payton laughed. "A minor inconvenience. I'll work on that and you call Fiona."

"I'll call her now," Sam promised. "It would be amazing if you could get here within the week. We'll need to fit you for dresses. Will Duncan let you come?"

"He'll do whatever Kade tells him to."

Sam smiled. "Well, Kade will do what *I* tell him to, so let Duncan know it's decided."

"I will. Let me know when you've spoken to Fi, and I'll let you know what we're doing about flights."

"Perfect, thanks. See you soon."

While Samantha called Fiona, Pepper grabbed more cookies and milk. Samantha smiled, relieved to see her friend was eating something. Once the details were given to Fiona, she hung up and lifted a cookie to her lips.

No!

Sam dropped the sweet with a squeak.

"You okay?" Pepper asked.

Almonds, love. You can't have anything *with almonds in them*, Kade warned.

Right. I forgot.

"Yeah, I'm fine. Sorry. I can't eat that." Sam frowned and pushed the cookie away from her.

"But they're your favorite," Pepper pointed out.

"I know." Sam grimaced. "I just found out that I've developed an allergy to almonds."

"Seriously? That sucks."

"I know." Sam stood and washed her hands before returning to the table. "Such is life, I suppose."

She took a deep breath. *Honey, your heart's racing. I'm okay. I didn't eat it.*

Yes, but you touched it. If you start to feel faint, please lie down and let me know.

Sam rolled her eyes. *I feel fine.*

Samantha, don't minimize this. It could be serious. Tell me if you feel faint.

I will. But I really am fine. Sam smiled. *You're scowling, aren't you? Don't scowl, baby, it makes you look old.*

Kade chuckled. *I'll keep that in mind.*

Good. I have to get back to spending your money. I've asked Payton and Fi to be in the wedding. Is that okay?

Of course. I'll let Duncan know.

Thanks. I love you.

I love you too.

Sam glanced up at Pepper, who was regarding her with confusion. "What?"

"You have a really weird look on your face," Pepper said.

"Really? Sorry. It just sunk in that I'll never get to eat my favorite cookie again."

Pepper smiled sympathetically. "At least it's not a wine allergy."

Sam gasped. "Can you imagine?"

"No!"

Several minutes of giggling followed before the girls composed themselves and went back to the wedding planning.

* * *

Kade stepped off the plane, his concern for Samantha still heavy on his mind. He hated not being there to protect her.

"Kade!"

Kade looked up to see Connall walking toward him, Brodie not far behind.

"Did you set everything up?" Kade asked.

Connall nodded. "Aye."

Kade nodded and followed his brothers to the car waiting on the tarmac. They climbed in and the driver set off toward their destination.

"What's wrong?" Connall asked.

Kade sighed. "Sam nearly ate something she shouldn't have."

"But you stopped her," Brodie stated.

"Aye."

"Then why are you wound so tight?" Connall asked. "You know we've got this covered, right?"

223

"Aye." Kade pinched the bridge of his nose. "I just don't like leaving Sam alone."

Brodie nodded. "I know."

Kade smiled sympathetically. He didn't know how his brother managed to stay sane. Ten years *was* a long time to wait for someone, especially if that someone was constantly dangled in front of you like a carrot to a horse.

Um…honey? I feel a little dizzy.

Lie down! Kade snapped.

I am.

Connall frowned. "Kade?"

"Sam's dizzy," Kade said.

"Is she lying down?"

He nodded. *Do not move, Sam. You stay there until the dizziness passes. If you notice anything strange on your skin…*

He couldn't finish the sentence. If it got that far, without Cauld Ane medicine she'd be in real trouble. "I need to go back."

No, you don't, she countered. *I'm fine. My skin looks fine. Better than it ever has, actually, and other than some mild dizziness, I'm fine. I shouldn't have told you.*

Sam.

I promise that if anything else happens, I'll let you know. I touched the cookie for all of ten seconds and washed my hands right after. It's nothing.

He dragged his hands down his face.

"Do we need to turn around?" Connall asked. "Because we will."

"She doesn't want me to."

Kade, please. Do what you need to do. I'm fine.

"Damn it," he snapped.

Kade, if you come back, I will not marry you.

He couldn't stop his smile. *Stubborn wench.*

You're just figuring that out?

All right, love, but you tell me if you notice any changes.

Of course.

And we're already married, so that threat doesn't work. But if you don't keep me apprised, I will *tell your mother we eloped.*

Brat. Okay, go away, honey. Pepper went to work, so I'm going to take a nap.

Kade sat back and shook his head.

"Everything okay?" Connall asked.

"For now."

Kade made a quick call as they drove to the center of town. The driver pulled up to Haarde Pharmaceutical, located in downtown Reykjavík. Kade wasn't surprised that two of Ármann's henchman stood sentry in front of the revolving doors. The driver opened Kade's door and he slid out of the car and strode into the building, confident his brothers followed, along with the "muscle."

Technically, Kade owned the building and the company housed inside, but had agreed to allow Ármann to run it, provided he followed the rules. Unfortunately for Ármann, he didn't, and now Kade had to deal with his disloyalty.

Arriving at the top floor, he stepped into the lobby of the executive offices to find Angus standing with Max.

"Max?" Connall frowned. "What are you doing here?"

"Backup," he said with a grin. "Don't worry, Niall can deal with the horses for a few days."

Kade shook the men's hands. "I take it this was your doing, Angus?"

"Aye," Angus said. "I wasn't letting the three of you come in here alone."

"I appreciate it…even if it's unnecessary." Kade turned to the receptionist, who stood with her head bowed.

"*Velkomin, herra minn,*" she said as she curtsied. (Welcome, my lord)

Kade nodded. "*Við munum fylgja þér.*" (We will follow you.)

Ice blue eyes met his and she nodded. "*Já herra minn.*"

The men followed her to a large door at the end of the hallway. She knocked, and pushed the door open.

"Cousin!" Ármann crooned as he moved from behind his large desk. "Come in, come in. Velkomin."

Kade studied the man standing before him. Ármann Haarde was five years older than him, the son of his father's brother. Tall and blond like the Gunnachs, he had deep blue eyes that many women had swooned over, particularly when they were younger. That was where the similarities ended, however. Ármann could only be described as slimy, which is why Kade kept him close in order to watch him.

"I will make this short, hmm?" Kade said and glanced behind him.

Max had already "suggested" the receptionist leave them alone and Brodie flicked his wrist, closing and locking the door. It wouldn't keep Ármann's goons out for long, but Kade didn't need much time.

"No need for all of this," Ármann said. "It's been so long since we all visited. Let's be cordial."

"You attacked my mate, Ármann. We're done with cordial."

"I did nothing of the sort."

Connall handed Kade the file that had the proof and he handed it to his cousin. "I will not banter with you, Ármann. You are stripped of your position here, and will be dealt with in our courts."

Ármann hissed in disgust. "You no longer have power here, Kade."

Before Kade could respond, the door flew open and two men pushed their way in, guns raised. Connall and Max got them under control just as

Brodie "removed" the gun from Ármann's hand...pointed at Kade's heart. Kade sniggered and wrapped his hand around his cousin's neck. "We are done here. If you come anywhere near my woman again, I will find you. You and your family are no longer welcome. You have forfeited your right to trial by Council. Do you understand?"

Ármann nodded, his face red from the effort to breathe.

Kade released him and stepped aside. Cauld Ane authorities were waiting in the foyer to take Ármann away, and they informed Kade that Ármann's sister and mother had also been picked up. Once Ármann was shipped off to Pohnpei, his family would suffer the same punishment.

"Well, that went well," Angus observed.

"Aye," Kade said. "A little too well."

* * *

The next day, Samantha was drinking her coffee and trying not to miss Kade when her cell phone buzzed. "Hi, Payton."

"Hi. Are you interested in some company?"

Sam grinned. "Are you here?"

"Just pulling up to your driveway now...Fiona's with me."

Sam let out an excited squeal and headed to the front door. The limo pulled up and the driver helped the women out of the car. Sam rushed them and they hugged like long-lost friends. "I thought you weren't going to make it until the end of the week?"

Payton laughed. "Kade organized everything."

"Of course he did."

Fiona smiled. "He's worried about you."

Sam nodded toward the two large Saxon-looking men who emerged from the car after the women. "Hence the muscle?"

"Ignore them." Payton linked her arm with Sam's. "How are you feeling?"

"I'm fine," Sam assured her.

"Are you sure?" Fiona took her hand, using it as a chance to study Sam's skin.

"Yep. Nothing on my arms, see?" Sam felt an unusual sensation as Fiona held her hand. A vibration of sorts. "Fi?"

"Hmm?"

"You're bound!" Sam gasped. "How did I know that?"

"Family bond," Payton said. "It's in our DNA."

"Congratulations!" Sam hugged Fiona.

"Thanks." Fiona giggled. "I never thought it would happen."

"Are you still going to have your big wedding?" Sam asked.

Fiona shook her head. "No."

"Are you okay with that?"

Fiona sighed. "I am now."

"Come inside and we can talk about it. My parents are out, so we have an hour or so before they get back."

Payton gave instructions to the driver and the security to park on the street.

"Wait," Sam instructed and made her way to one of the men. "Can I get you boys something to drink?"

The taller one glanced at the other and then back at her. "No, m'lady."

"Are you sure?"

"Aye, m'lady."

"If you need anything, just ring the doorbell, okay?"

They nodded and then headed back to the car.

"You didn't need to do that, Sam," Fiona said.

"Of course I did. This is the South. We have a reputation to maintain. Now, who wants coffee?" she asked as she led the women inside.

"Me, please," Payton said.

"Do you have tea?" Fiona asked.

"We do, but it's probably not as good as Whittard's."

Fiona shrugged. "I don't mind."

Payton and Fiona sat at the kitchen island and Sam boiled some water. As she went about preparing everything, she smiled. *Checking up on me?*

I take it my sister and Payton arrived safely?

No. They had a weird accident and are both irrevocably deformed.

Okay, you got me. I wanted to make sure you didn't have any ill effects from the almonds.

Sam sighed. *I would have told you.*

By then it would have been too late. Fiona has the necessary counter-actions to a few things with her.

And the security?

"Sam? Do you need some help?" Payton asked.

"No, I'm good," Sam said.

The security's not just for you, sweetheart.

Sam pulled down mugs. *Okay, I'll let that one slide.*

I miss you, love.

I miss you way more. Believe me. I'm glad the girls are here. It'll be a nice distraction. Sam tried to squelch the tears pricking her eyes. *How much longer?*

A few more days. Please stay close to the men. Something's up with Ármann's people and you need to be careful.

I will be.

Kade cut off any further communication and Sam swept aside her sadness. A gentle squeeze on her arm had her turning to face Payton.

"He'll be fine, Sam."

"I know that..." Sam grimaced. "...logically."

"Brodie's with him. No one gets past Brodie." Payton suddenly found one of the magnets on the fridge fascinating. "And Connall, of course."

Sam raised an eyebrow. "Do I hear a little softening towards Brodie?"

Payton shrugged. "No."

Fiona snorted from her place at the table.

"It's not like I hate him, Fi," Payton insisted. "He's just intimidating, and I don't trust him."

"In five months, you'll think differently."

Payton bit her lip. "Unless he's wrong."

"He's not wrong, Payton," Fiona insisted.

"Why don't you trust him?" Sam asked.

Payton shrugged.

"It's because of Heather," Fiona offered.

"Fi!" Payton snapped.

"What? We're all going to be related. If you can't talk to us, who can you talk to?"

"Who's Heather?" Sam asked.

"She's a woman Brodie has been seeing for the past couple of years." Fiona sipped her tea. "No one knows anything about her. Just her name."

"He can see whoever he wants to see," Payton said. "I'm not his keeper."

Sam raised an eyebrow. "Why do I get the feeling that bothers you a lot more than you're letting on?"

"Did Kade tell you about the American security Connall set up?"

"Payton!" This time it was Fiona's turn to admonish.

Sam smiled. "Security's security, Payton. It doesn't matter where it came from. Now, quit changing the subject."

Payton flopped into one of the kitchen chairs and groaned. "Brodie says he's my mate, but he spends all his time with another woman. In five months, I'll know in my heart if what he's telling me is true. I don't think I can believe him, though."

"Why?" Sam asked.

"Because siblings don't mate with siblings," Fiona said.

Sam wrinkled her nose. "That sounds very wrong."

"Not like that!" Fiona chuckled. "Because I'm bound to Angus, it would be unusual for Payton to mate with Brodie. I mean, there aren't any references to it in our books, and those records go back over a thousand years."

"That doesn't mean it *doesn't* happen, right?" Sam pointed out.

"I guess not," Payton admitted. "But until I know for sure, it's better that I keep my distance."

Sam gave her a sympathetic smile. "We all assumed Brodie's been going through hell all by himself. We've been wrong, huh?"

She shrugged. "I didn't realize he'd been 'going through hell.'"

Fiona snorted. "Then you're blind. He's been a blitherin' idiot since the day you arrived."

"He says two words a year," Payton snapped. "Neither of which sound blitherin' to me."

Sam shook her head. "Okay, okay. I don't think a contest on how incapacitated Brodie Gunnach has become is necessary."

"I don't think any of *this* is necessary," Payton said. "Let's just drop it, okay? If I'm to be bound to Brodie, I'll know soon enough. I'd rather not think about it for now." She stood and placed her mug in the sink. "I have too much on my plate as it is."

Fiona's phone rang and she grimaced. "Hi, Brodie."

CHAPTER TWENTY-SIX

PAYTON LET OUT a frustrated squeak and rushed out of the room. Sam followed her and guided her into the family room. Payton paced the room.

Sam sat on the sofa and watched her. "Do you want to talk about it?"

Payton shook her head.

"It might help," Sam pressed.

"Sam, I can't talk to you about this."

"Why not?"

"Things have changed."

Sam frowned. "What things?"

Payton gave her an exasperated look.

"What?" Sam asked.

"This is not something you should be dealing with."

"Why not?"

"Because you're…well…you're Kade's mate."

"So?"

"He's our *king*, Sam."

Sam laughed. "So?"

"*So*, that makes you our queen."

Sam swallowed. "Oh, crap. Right. I keep forgetting about that."

Payton sighed. "Sorry."

"Whatever. It doesn't change anything. I'm still your friend, Payton. You can talk to me about anything."

Payton sat next to her and frowned. "I appreciate that, but I can't bring matters of the heart to my queen."

"Who made that stupid rule?"

"I don't know. We just don't do that. Fiona didn't discuss things with her mother, and I'm not going to start burdening you with my problems just because we were friends first."

Samantha's mouth fell open and then she started to laugh. She had a difficult time stopping.

"What's so funny?"

Sam squeezed Payton's hand. "It just hit me that I'm this small-town girl who moved to Scotland for a job and ended up being bound to a virtually immortal king. A *king*, Payton! If I wasn't living it, I'd think it was ludicrous."

Payton giggled. "I suppose that would seem strange."

"Very. But the bottom line is that we're friends, and if what I understand to be true *is* true, in less than six months you and I will be sisters. So, will you please put aside tradition and *talk* to me? If I have to make a new law or rule or whatever, I'll speak to my king and make it so." She started laughing again. "King. Sorry, he's just so not kingly to me."

"He's not?"

"No. He's...well, he's Kade. Gorgeous and wonderful and normal all rolled into one."

Payton smiled.

"Spill."

Payton sank further into the couch. "Between us."

"Of course."

"I'm in love with the idiot."

"Oh, honey, that's great."

Payton shook her head. "No, it's not. If he really is my mate, then why is he seeing another woman? He loses his mind if I even talk to another man, but it's okay for him to spend all this time with this mystery woman? He'll not bind me and think that's going to continue."

Sam nodded. "I can see the dilemma."

"He also left me," she whispered.

"When?"

"When we first met. Our family arrived in the village and he and I spoke for several hours. I really liked him. Even then. But he left within the week. For *five* years. Mates don't do that."

"That must have been hard," Sam commiserated.

"The bottom line is that we're expected to go willingly into our mate's arms, let them bind us, and then be the dutiful Stepford wife at all times. Well, I can't do it." She shuddered. "The thought of sex is difficult enough, but him sleeping with someone else is worse."

Sam frowned. "Why is the thought of sex difficult?"

"Because it's for procreation, Sam, and my thoughts when it comes to him are wicked."

"Wicked? How?"

Payton squeezed her eyes shut. "When I'm close to Brodie, I feel fluttery. I can't think straight. I saw him once with his shirt off and... well...never mind."

"Payton," Sam said gently. "All of those feelings are normal. Especially when you're in love with someone. And for the record, sex is for a lot more than procreation. If it weren't, God wouldn't have made it so fun."

231

"There you are," Fiona said as she sailed into the room, cutting off their conversation. She held her phone out. "Brodie would like to talk to you, Payton. You're not picking up your phone."

Payton rolled her eyes and took the phone. "Hi, Brodie. Yes, I'm fine. No, I'm not ignoring you. We're trying to plan the wedding. Is something wrong? Okay, good. Yep." She paused. "Aye, my liege. Whatever you say." Her sarcasm was rising.

Sam glanced at Fiona, who shrugged.

"Don't you dare. No. Fine. Yes. *Okay*. I'm hanging up now," she said and handed the phone back to Fiona. "I am *not* bonding with that man!"

"Uh-oh, what happened?" Fiona asked.

"He said if I didn't carry my phone with me at all times, he was going to get on a plane and come and get me."

"He felt your stress," Fiona said. "When he couldn't get you on the phone, he thought the worst."

"He told me." Payton took a deep breath. "But I don't have the brain capacity to deal with him right now."

"You calling him 'my liege' only irks him, you know."

"Him being bossy irks me." Payton pressed her lips into a thin line. "Kade doesn't even lord over me the way Brodie does and *Kade's* my king!" She raised her hands in surrender. "I'd like to be done talking about Brodie Gunnach. Aren't there some bridesmaids' dresses we need to look at?"

Sam smiled. "Tomorrow. I have an appointment for a wedding dress fitting and I think we could combine the visit."

"Perfect," Fiona said.

"You need to fill me in on what happened with your big fancy wedding Kade was going to pay for, Fi."

"Ha!" Payton exclaimed. "Angus was *not* happy."

Fiona sighed. "I know."

"How come?" Sam asked.

"Because I demanded Kade pay," Fiona explained. "I overstepped."

Sam waved her hand in dismissal. "Oh, Fi. Kade didn't care."

"But Angus did." Fiona smiled. "It all worked out in the end. We were bound, and although the conversion was uncomfortable, you were right about it being easier on me than you."

"Good. I have to admit, I downplayed the pain a bit. Kade was entirely freaked out by the whole ordeal, so I didn't want to be too honest."

"I think he figured it out, Sam. He was more on edge than normal," Fiona said.

Sam grimaced. "I know. What did you find out about your gifts?"

"I have taken on Angus's healing, which is amazing, and apparently, something that happens with all mates."

Sam raised an eyebrow. "Really? So, I'll be able to heal, too?"

Fiona nodded. "You should be able to. According to the book, the longer you're bound, the more gifts you share. My personal gift seems to be telekinesis, but Angus hasn't taken it on, yet. I'm assuming more will show up as time goes by."

"Very cool," Sam said. "With that good news, I think we should have some fun tonight."

"What do you suggest?" Payton asked.

"I say we pick Pepper up from work and head on over to the Tin Ear Saloon for drinks."

"What's the Tin Ear Saloon?" Fiona asked.

"The best karaoke in town."

"I can't sing!" Fiona exclaimed.

Sam laughed. "But Pepper can, and we can drink while she entertains us."

Payton clapped her hands. "Love it."

Sam pulled out her phone. "Now I just have to talk Pepper into it."

* * *

The night at the Tin Ear wrapped up just before midnight, when Pepper insisted she needed to get up early the next morning. Samantha hugged her friend, reluctant to let her leave.

"I'm fine, Sam," Pepper insisted.

"Are you sure?"

"Yes. I'll text you when I get home, okay?"

"Fine." Sam raised an eyebrow. "But I want to know you're all tucked in and comfy."

Pepper laughed. "Okay, Mom." She turned to Fiona and Payton. "It was really nice to meet you both."

"You too," they chimed in simultaneously.

Pepper climbed into her VW Rabbit, affectionately called "Thumper," and peeled out of the parking lot.

Fiona squeezed Sam's arm with a hiss. "Something's off."

"What do you mean?" she whispered.

Samantha, where are you, love?

I'm at a club.

Specifically, Kade pressed.

The Tin Ear Saloon on Lincoln.

I need you to go back inside. Right now.

Are you here?

Aye. Go back into the building.

"Kade wants us to go back inside."

"So does Angus," Fiona said.

Before they could move an inch, an eerily familiar voice sounded in the dark.

"Well, well, well."

233

Sam found herself looking at Shannon Fraser, followed by Alexander Baird and another man she didn't recognize. The men had guns aimed at Payton and Fiona.

Payton gasped. "Baldvin."

"Who?" Sam asked.

"My brother-in-law."

"Alex?" Sam said, surprised the young IT expert would be involved in this.

"I'm truly sorry, Sam," he said. "I liked you. But Kade has to learn."

"Enough!" Shannon snapped. "You're difficult to corner, Samantha."

Sam stood a little taller. "What do you want, Shannon?"

"I thought that would be obvious."

You may see things that frighten you. I need you to stay behind Payton and Fiona.

Sam took a deep breath. *I am* not *hiding behind anyone, Kade.*

"Enlighten me, Shannon, because even you aren't stupid enough to think you had a snowball's chance in hell with Kade."

She sneered. "I thought you and I might be friends, Samantha. I'm disappointed."

"And I'm disappointed you haven't bowed before your queen."

A quiet gasp sounded behind her. Sam forced herself not to look at Payton as she tried to keep her bravado intact. She was completely out of her element here, but something within her began to awaken and she was determined to see where it led her.

"Consider us revolutionaries taking a stand against a dictatorship," Shannon said.

"And what were your plans for the chemicals, Shannon? A lot of innocent people could have been killed."

"Are humans really ever innocent?" Shannon let out a sigh of irritation. "Besides, only a few would have ultimately died. We had an iron-clad plan until you arrived. You were an unforeseen problem."

Sam snorted. "I think the real problem here is that my mate has been entirely too nice to you."

She noticed Baldvin move out of the corner of her eye and before she could react, Payton slumped to the ground. Alex headed toward Fiona and Sam shouted, "Don't!"

Alex froze. Sam blinked and focused on Shannon, whose eyes expressed fear.

You have the gift of suggestion, love. Use it.

What do you mean, "suggestion?"

You can make them do what you ask them to do. You are their queen, they must listen to you.

Sam bit her lip. *Kade, I don't know how I feel about this.*

Sweetheart, I need you not *to feel right now. I just need you to keep them from hurting you. We can discuss your feelings later. We're almost there.*

Payton's hurt.

I know. Just stay calm.

Sam forced herself not to swear. *Stay calm. Thanks, honey. Great advice.*

She stayed locked onto the three adversaries while Fiona saw to Payton.

Fiona let out a curse. "You're a real bitch, Shannon."

"What is it, Fi?" Sam asked.

"Red Fang."

Shannon's hand twitched, but when Sam snapped, "Don't move," she froze again.

The plodding sound of feet distracted Sam and she found herself slammed to the ground, staring up at the sneering face of Shannon. A shot rang out, but before Sam could react, Shannon was hauled off her and Sam was lifted into Kade's arms.

She wrapped her arms around his neck and sighed. "Hi."

He gave her a gentle squeeze. "Are you hurt?"

"No. Who got shot?"

"No one. They missed."

She tried to push out of his arms. "Let me check on Payton."

He shook his head. "Brodie has her and Angus is administering the antidote."

"Will she be okay?"

"Aye," he rasped. "Be still, love. I need to make sure you're all right."

Sam took the time to finally look at him. The worry in his eyes made her heart stutter. She stroked his cheek. "I'm fine, honey. I promise."

He closed his eyes and took a deep breath. Sam stayed quiet, offering her whole heart to him. He relaxed after a few seconds and opened his eyes again. "I was terrified."

She smiled. "I know."

"I didn't think we'd make it in time."

"I know, honey. But you did and I'm fine," she said. "Put me down, hmm?"

He gently lowered her to the ground, but kept an arm firmly around her waist. She felt his emotion, the heaviness of it, and laid her palm against his chest, willing him to calm. "I really need to check on Payton. Okay?"

He took another deep breath and gave her a curt nod. She stepped away from him, not surprised that he followed.

Brodie was on the ground, cradling Payton in his arms. Her eyes were wide and she appeared frightened, but the rest of her body was limp. Tears slid down her cheeks and Brodie wiped them away gently as Angus stuck a needle into her arm and pressed the plunger in.

Connall and a man Samantha didn't recognize were in a deep discussion, while the security detail secured the three "revolutionaries."

A deep, frightened groan from Payton had Sam's heart racing, but Brodie pulled her closer and Sam smiled when Payton wrapped her arms around his neck and sobbed into his chest. She would be fine. Brodie would make sure of it.

Kade grasped her hand, and Sam sighed as he pulled her back into the safety of his arms. "Everything's secure now. Connall and Max are going to remove Shannon and the others, and we'll head back to the hotel."

"So, that's Max?" Sam nodded toward the handsome, athletic man with dark hair and ice-blue eyes.

He nodded. "Aye."

"He's on the Council, right?"

"Why?"

She smiled up at him. "Just putting a face to the name."

"You'll meet him later. Right now, I want you all to myself."

She linked her fingers with his and gave his hand a gentle squeeze. He forced a smile, but she could feel his stress. "Hey. I'm okay."

He nodded.

"Did you get everything done in Iceland?"

He scowled.

Baby, tell me.

He closed his eyes and gripped her hand tighter. *Iceland was a decoy.*

In order to get to me here?

He nodded again.

Why?

They knew that if they could kill you, they could move forward with their plan, and I wouldn't have been able to stop them.

Sam frowned. *Yes you would.*

No. I. Wouldn't. "If you were to die, Sam, I would follow."

"Don't say that, Kade. Lots of people survive the loss of a spouse and you're needed here."

Kade's sudden rage was so strong, Sam jumped away from him just before he slammed his fist into the car next to them, forcing it sideways with a screech of its tires.

A collective gasp sounded from the group as Connall rushed to Samantha, pushing her behind his back, and holding a palm out to Kade. "My lord."

Sam stepped out from behind Connall and approached her mate. "Kade. Honey, I'm so sorry."

Kade's eyes burned red as he stood drawing deep breaths into his lungs.

"Sam, careful," Connall warned.

Kade turned toward Connall and his eyes narrowed. Sam swallowed, but continued toward Kade. *Baby, I'm here. I'm safe. The danger's over.*

He didn't seem to understand her, so she tried again.

Kade. Honey. Despite her fear, she reached out and laid a hand on his arm. He stared down at her hand and Sam gave his arm a gentle squeeze. *Shhh. Everything's okay.*

Kade blinked several times and Sam relaxed when she saw the flame recede and his eyes return to normal. He pulled her against him and buried his face in her hair. Sam wrapped her arms around his waist and held him tightly.

Fyrirgefðu ef ég hræddur þig, elska. (I'm sorry if I scared you, love.)

What? That little display? Pishaw.

He chuckled and Sam felt the rest of the group relax. Her familial bond with Kade's siblings was made more remarkable by the fact that she could feel their stress.

I need you. Now.

Sam nodded and let him lead her to the car. Another large Saxon-looking man held the back door open for her. She didn't recognize him, but that didn't surprise her. Kade probably had hundreds of large, fierce, wrestler-types at his disposal. She slid into the seat and secured her seatbelt. Kade did the same and quickly grasped her hand.

You okay?

He nodded. *I should have known this was going to happen.*

How could you have possibly known?

Because my mother set it up.

Sam gasped. "Really?"

He nodded. *She betrayed us all.*

Before she could respond, the car pulled up to the hotel and Kade ushered her out of the car, into the hotel, and up to their room. He closed and locked the door, then rushed her. She was lifted off her feet and had to wrap her arms around his neck in order not to fall backward. His lips covered hers and she responded without thought.

* * *

Samantha licked her lips and tried to catch her breath. She pushed her hair away from her face and turned towards Kade. "My word, honey. I think you need to go away more often."

Kade growled. "Never again, Samantha."

"Sorry." Sam giggled. "Too soon?"

He pulled her close and kissed her. "I thought I was going to lose you."

"I know." She stroked his chest. "But whatever this gift is came at just the right time."

He nodded. "You'll find more abilities manifest as time goes on."

"That's what Fiona said. Kind of cool, because I thought this might be the only one I get. Not that I'm complaining. It's really kind of cool, but I'm not sure the ability to make people do what I want them to do is a good thing. I would never want to abuse it."

"The fact that you're concerned about that is probably why you got the gift in the first place. And according to the book, as my mate, you'll be gifted with more."

She settled her chin on her hand and raised an eyebrow. "So you're good value, then?" He chuckled and Sam grinned. "There it is."

"What?" he asked.

"Your laugh." She kissed his chest. "I have missed that most of all."

He raised an eyebrow. "You've missed my laugh most of all?"

She grinned. "If you'd like to repeat what you did earlier, I could amend that statement."

"Is that a challenge?"

"More like an invitation," she retorted.

"I accept."

He flipped her onto her back, laid a fingertip gently on her forehead and whispered, "*Ég ætla að kyssa þig hér ...*," and then ran his fin-ger down to her hip and then her ankle. "*...og hér og alls staðar þar á milli.*" (I am going to kiss you here...and here and everywhere in be-tween.)

Sam sighed and raised her chin to receive his kiss.

* * *

Two days later, Samantha stood in front of the mirror and tried to bring her wayward hair to heel. Pepper sat in her desk chair while Fiona and Payton sat on the bed and read a gossip rag. Kade had reluctantly left her to pick up his brothers and Angus, who had flown to Scotland with the "dissidents" and delivered them to the Council for decision of their fate. They were due to arrive at the Gastonian in an hour, where the ladies were scheduled to meet them.

"Kade just left you ten minutes ago," Pepper said.

Sam scowled at her in the mirror. "Your point?"

Pepper crossed her arms and rolled her eyes. "My point, strange one, is that you can't look any better than you already do and your fiancé wouldn't care if you shaved your head. He'd still look at you like you're the only woman on the planet."

"I agree," Payton piped in.

"Are you suggesting I shave my head?" Samantha retorted.

Pepper giggled. "Oh, I'm not suggesting, Sammi...I'm *saying*."

Sam smiled and opened her mouth to say something just as Pepper's cell phone rang. She ignored it.

"Your mom?" Sam asked.

Pepper nodded. The phone pealed again and Pepper let out a frustrated groan.

Sam laid the brush on the bureau. "Just answer it, Pep. She'll keep calling, especially if she's drunk."

Pepper nodded and answered the call. "Hi, Mom."

She listened for a few minutes and cringed. "I don't know where your cat is, Mom. He's probably roaming."

Sam raised an eyebrow in question. Pepper's mom was probably drunk and the cat was probably sitting on her lap.

Pepper's face went ashen. "What do you mean?" she asked as she stepped out of the room. She returned within a few minutes. "Hey. I need to take care of something. Can you do without me for a bit?"

Sam nodded. "Sure. Everything okay?"

"Yeah. Mom's melting down. I'll be back by dinner."

"Can we do anything?" Fiona asked.

"No. She does this a lot," Pepper said.

Sam hugged her. "Are you sure you're okay?"

"Yes." Pepper forced a smile. "Now, enjoy your man. I'll see you later."

Sweetheart? What's wrong?

Pepper. Sam sighed. *Something's going with her mom. Are they here?*

Landing in about twenty minutes.

Are you coming here or to the hotel first?

I'm surprised you have to ask. You are always first.

Sam smiled. *What about your brothers?*

Kade chuckled. *They aren't nearly as beautiful as you.*

Ah, so I'm first because you think I'm cuter than them?

Aye.

Sam stopped herself from laughing out loud. *I don't know, honey, Connall's really pretty for a man.*

I'll tell him you said that. I'll see in you in a little bit.

Hurry.

Of course.

CHAPTER TWENTY-SEVEN

LESS THAN THIRTY minutes later, the doorbell pealed and Sam rushed to open the front door. She was gathered up into Kade's embrace and kissed until neither of them could form a coherent sentence. She looped her arms around his neck. "Hi."

"Hi." He kissed her again. "Och, love, I missed ye."

"I've missed you more."

He grinned. "Not possible."

"You've been apart for less than an hour," Connall retorted as he pushed Kade aside and hugged Sam. "You two really should get a room."

"If Kade didn't have to pick you up from the airport, we would have," Sam challenged.

Connall laughed. "Touché. How are you?"

"I'm great." Sam grinned as Kade pulled her back against him.

Brodie and Angus had managed to slip inside and were speaking with their mates. Payton seemed a little warmer to Brodie since her scare, but Sam could tell she was still a little leery.

"Are your parents home?" Kade asked.

Sam shook her head. "No, they left a while ago. I'll set the alarm and we can go."

The group made their way outside so that Samantha could lock up and then she followed Kade to the car. They'd planned ahead and rented the stretch limo for the week, knowing they'd more than likely travel often as a group.

"I'm glad he's back with you, Sam," Connall said. "He's been a pain in the arse."

Sam laughed. "How is that even possible?"

"You have her fooled, it would appear," Brodie complained.

Kade took Sam's hand and smiled. "Absolutely. Like taking candy from a baby."

Sam snorted. "Have you ever *tried* to take candy from a baby?"

"Admittedly, no." He kissed her fingers. "But I'd imagine it's about as easy as convincing you I'm perfect."

The banter continued as the group climbed back into the limo. Sam noticed a darkness cover Connall's face and she frowned. Within seconds, her phone rang and Dalton's name came up. "Hey, Dalt."

"Hey. Pepper's mom was attacked."

"What? What happened?"

Kade squeezed her hand and she gratefully took the comfort.

"We're not sure," Dalton said. "I've got a team going through the house now, but Pepper's gotta be somewhere else."

Sam sighed. "Bring her to the Gastonian. Kade booked the whole place and there's plenty of room for her. Don't take no for an answer."

"I won't."

"Meet us at the hotel and we'll all head to the restaurant together, okay?"

"Okay, great. Thanks."

Sam hung up and sagged against Kade. "Pepper's mom was attacked."

"What did Dalton say happened?" Kade asked.

"He's not sure. He's got a team at the house now."

Kade kissed her fingers. "We'll protect Pepper, you know that, right?"

Sam nodded. "I know. The big issue is whether or not she'll let you."

"She won't have much of a choice, Sam," Connall said as the car pulled up at the hotel.

Kade slid from the back seat and then assisted Sam. She was pleasantly surprised that the rest of the group scattered, with the promise to meet up in an hour for dinner.

Kade gave her a lascivious grin and whisked her up to the penthouse suite, where she found herself kissed and undressed in record time. She didn't come back to earth until they were forced to acknowledge the time.

Sam glanced up at the bed from her place on the floor, sprawled over Kade's chest. "I remember that bed being quite comfy."

He chuckled. "I do too. I'm looking forward to actually sleeping there tonight."

Samantha giggled. "Me too."

Kade's phone buzzed. "Where are my pants?"

"Here," Sam said and handed them to him.

He pulled his phone from the pocket and sighed. "Everyone's waiting for us in the parlor."

She kissed his chest. "Thank you for the quickie."

He grinned. "There'll be much more to look forward to after dinner."

"Can't wait."

Kade and Samantha headed downstairs and met everyone in the foyer. They arrived just as Dalton walked in the front door with Pepper.

Samantha planned to hug her friend, but hesitated when she saw Pepper catch sight of Connall.

Like magnets drawn together, Connall approached Pepper and smiled as he held his hand out to her. "Pepper, lass."

"Yes," Pepper said.

"I'm Connall," he said.

"I'll be damned," Kade whispered.

Sam glanced up at him. "Are they?"

"They're mates."

Sam laid her fingers over her lips. "Kade, really?"

He kissed her temple. "Aye."

"Well, that worked out just about perfectly, didn't it?"

"Did it?" he asked.

"She has been my sister-in-heart since we were seven. Now, she'll be my sister-in-law for real." He grinned and Sam sagged against him. "I didn't really need to say that out loud, did I?"

"Remember when I said I loved hearing your thoughts and secrets?"

She smiled up at him. "I love you. You know that right?"

"Intimately." He leaned down and whispered, "I love you too."

Sam leaned closer to Kade, reveling in his strong arms wrapped around her, and watched as her best friend started her own magical journey.

"*Galdrastafir virðist ófullnægjandi á einhvern hátt* (Magical seems inadequate in some way)," he whispered.

She glanced up at him. "It does, doesn't it?"

"*Tilvera högg með boltanum af eldingum vafinn í regnbogans.*"

She giggled. "Exactly! Lightning wrapped in a rainbow."

As he kissed her, Sam said a silent prayer of thanks. She'd found the man of her dreams and she couldn't have been happier.

Look for Pepper's story in 2013

I was born and raised in New Zealand. With an American father, Scottish grandmother, and Kiwi mother, it's no doubt I have a unique personality.

After pursuing my American roots and disappearing into my time travel series, The Civil War Brides, I thought I'd explore the Scottish side of my family. I have loved delving into the Cauld Ane's and all their abilities…I hope you do too.

I've been happily married and gooey in love with my husband for eighteen years. We live in the Pacific Northwest with our two sons.

I hope you've enjoyed **Bound by Blood**
For other titles in the Cauld Ane Series,
or to learn about The Civil War Brides Series, please visit:
www.traceyjanejackson.com

Find me on Facebook, too!
www.facebook.com/traceyjanejackson

If you'd like to listen to The Citizens, feel free to visit:
www.jacksonjacksonandthecitizens.com

Made in the USA
San Bernardino, CA
15 September 2014